I0771388

THE EVOLVER

Copyright © 2024 Jessica Grace Vargas

All rights reserved. No part of this book may be reproduced, distributed, or transmitted in any form or by any means, including photocopying, recording, or other electronic or mechanical methods, without the prior written permission of the publisher, except in the case of brief quotations embodied in critical reviews and certain other noncommercial uses permitted by copyright law. For permission requests, write to the publisher at the address below.

Published by Hover House Publishing
www.hoverhousepublishing.com

This is a work of fiction. Names, characters, places, and incidents either are products of the author's imagination or are used fictitiously. Any resemblance to actual persons, living or dead, or actual events is purely coincidental.

ISBN 979-8-9911390-0-7 (hardcover)
ISBN 979-8-9911390-1-4 (paperback)

Printed in the United States

First Edition: September 2024
For more information, visit www.jessicagracevargas.com

THE EVOLVER

JESSICA GRACE VARGAS

HOVER HOUSE PUBLISHING

For Rich—
The best thing that has ever happened in my universe.
I love you.

ONE

Kennedy Neff stared at a motivational poster of the cosmos, which read: *Shoot for the moon. Even if you miss, you'll land among the stars.* Four gold push pins secured it to a corkboard at the front of the classroom. Kennedy focused on the top right pushpin. She smiled as it wiggled free from the corkboard and hit the dusty tile floor with the tiniest of clanks. The poster folded down behind Mrs. Barnes, who was currently inhaling a sleeve of mini powdered donuts. Kennedy looked around detention to see if anyone else had seen what she'd done, but no one ever paid any attention to what Kennedy Neff did.

Kennedy closed her eyes and tried to sense the energy of the other three pushpins, hoping she could get them to pop out in unison.

Mrs. Barnes clapped, and a cloud of powdered sugar flew into the air. "There will be no sleeping, Ms. Neff!"

"Sorry," Kennedy said, even though she was more startled than sorry.

Mrs. Barnes waddled to a nearby trashcan and threw away the empty donut sleeve. She reached for her Arizona Wildcats coffee mug and peered around the classroom, searching for someone to pick on. Kennedy tried her best to look busy. She opened her spiral notebook and doodled a large X with four other x's springing from the tips of it. After high school, she was going to get this symbol tattooed on the inside of her wrist, just like her father.

"What is that?" Mrs. Barnes grabbed Kennedy's notebook and held it close to her thick-framed glasses.

Kennedy grabbed it back. "It's nothing."

Mrs. Barnes, who still had powdered sugar caked into the corners of her mouth, took a loud slurp of coffee. "If I were you, I'd use this time wisely."

"I already finished my homework."

"Ever tried reading a book?"

Kennedy gave her the fakest smile she could muster. "No, but I've heard great things."

"Don't get snippy with me, young lady. If you ask me, Principal Vasquez went too easy on you; I would have suspended you." Earlier that day, Principal Vasquez sentenced Kennedy to three days' worth of detention for refusing to participate in an active-shooter drill. "You know these drills were created for your own safety."

"Turn out the lights and lock the door. Got it. That's a foolproof plan. I feel *so* much safer already."

Mrs. Barnes sneered at Kennedy. "You think you know everything, don't you?"

"I know what happens when you bring a desk to a gunfight."

The grinding of the air conditioner filled the silence between Kennedy and Mrs. Barnes, who did not like the active-shooter drills either. It was obvious she had enough on her plate, trying to manage her oversized classroom with her limited budget and meager salary. Fortunately, at that moment, Mrs. Barnes caught a sophomore on his phone. "No phones!" she yelled. Everyone in detention jumped, except for Kennedy, who breathed a sigh of relief when Mrs. Barnes finally waddled away from her.

Principal Vasquez practically had Kennedy's mother, Roberta, on speed dial. He was single—for obvious reasons—and often asked Roberta if she would like to grab a drink and discuss Kennedy's academic future. Roberta begged Kennedy to stay out of trouble just so she would not have to deal with his unwanted advances. But this proved to be an impossible request for Kennedy. Teachers would catch her under the bleachers eating her lunch or hiding in the deserted baseball dugout. She was too humiliated to sit in the cafeteria by herself and too proud to admit that her classmates' rejection hurt her. Kennedy did not have a friend in the world, other than some sympathetic cousins and her cat, Phantom.

The last social event Kennedy attended was Ellie Goldman's slumber party in the seventh grade, where she made Ellie float eight feet off the ground during a harmless game of Light as a Feather, Stiff as a Board. Well, it would have been harmless had Ellie's screams not ruined Kennedy's concentration, which in turn sent Ellie crashing to the floor. That was the night Kennedy's nickname was born: Freak. It was unoriginal yet effective because it summarized what she really was: a freak of nature.

When the bell rang, Kennedy seized her backpack and nearly sprinted from the room. She walked out into the September heat and removed the red hoodie she'd worn to brave the arctic temperatures of detention. She shoved it inside her backpack and cut across the west parking lot, where a group of seniors loitered around a black, electric Audi SUV with New York plates.

Why would anyone ever want to move to Tucson? thought Kennedy, who had never been further east than Texas. Tucson's only redeeming quality, in Kennedy's mind, was that it had once been mentioned in a Beatles song. Which reminded her... Kennedy reached into the front zipper of her backpack, put in her earbuds, and pressed play on the cracked screen of her dated smartphone. 'Penny Lane' was now in her ears, while the minimum-security prison called Desert Hills High School was in her eyes. Its sprawling, 1960s-style campus was overcrowded and underfunded. Portable trailers parked at the edge of campus served as temporary classrooms. This was the best third-rate education tax dollars could buy.

The varsity cheerleading squad clapped their hands, stomped their feet, and spelled out the word C-O-Y-O-T-E-S from the red running track. Audrey Lambert, Kennedy's older sister, paused to double-check the rolled-up waistband of her revealing cheer shorts. Audrey was the envy of the entire student body; she was captain of the cheerleading squad and homecoming queen. She had never gone through an ugly duckling phase; she was born a swan. Kennedy was a pretty girl, too, although she would be the last one to ever tell you so. She possessed a kind of beauty only her mother and old ladies seemed to notice. Her features were sharp, and her large hazel eyes had a depth to them that no high school boy would ever appreciate. Audrey, on the other hand, was a walking dress code violation, which every high school boy could appreciate. Kennedy felt invisible standing next to her.

Audrey jogged towards Kennedy and popped out her earbud.

Before it fell, Kennedy caught it. "Do you *mind*?"

Audrey combed her fingers through her silky brown hair. "Mom picked up a shift tonight, so if you could find somewhere else to be, that would be great."

Kennedy tightened the rubber band of her unruly, chestnut-colored ponytail. She was about to respond to her sister when the black Audi chirped. Kennedy watched its owner, Reddick Vincent, load his gym bag into the back. Reddick was timelessly gorgeous; his blue eyes and tan skin made his symmetrical face look like it was in technicolor. The seniors loitering around his car immediately slapped hands with him, and some of the girls hugged him.

Audrey snapped her fingers. "Hello? Earth to Kennedy. Did you hear me?"

"Huh?"

"I need the apartment."

"Where do you want me to go?" Kennedy asked.

"I don't know; take an Uber somewhere or whatever."

"I don't have any money." Kennedy's funds had dried up considerably since her summer job busing tables at the golf course ended.

"Look, I don't care what you do. I need the apartment."

Kennedy pointed to the monsoon clouds rolling in over the mountains. "But it's going to storm." Her phone vibrated inside her pocket, and she knew immediately who it was because only one person called her. She answered it. "Hi, Mom."

Audrey held a threatening finger to her lips. "Don't say a word."

Kennedy walked away from Audrey as though she might, but they both knew she never would, because deep down Kennedy still longed for her older sister's approval.

"Detention again, Kennedy?" Roberta asked. "Why do you always insist on making things harder for yourself?" Kennedy could hear opera music playing in the background. A few nights a week, Roberta served tables at an upscale Italian restaurant to help supplement her inconsistent real estate income. "Gary says you're skating on thin ice."

Kennedy grimaced. "Gary?"

"Yes, *Gary*. Principal Vasquez wants me to call him Gary now; he asked if I wanted to get drinks again. He said his door is always open."

"Yeah, his bedroom door."

"Gross, Kennedy."

"He's the gross one!"

"Nedy..." Roberta called Kennedy by her nickname, which was a tribute to Roberta's grandpa, Ned. "I think we should probably sit down and have a talk." This was a normal occurrence in their household. Roberta would applaud Kennedy's issues with authority while simultaneously telling her that her life would be easier if she just let them *think* they were in charge.

Roberta was a single mother of two who was constantly behind on bills and sleep. She didn't try to make any of it look easy because it wasn't. She had been married once, briefly to Audrey's father, Brian, but that lasted less than a year. Brian's unfaithfulness provided Roberta with a valid excuse to leave a man she never truly loved. After her marriage ended, Roberta traveled to San Diego to visit her girlfriend, and that is where she met Kennedy's father.

Kennedy's parents shared a romantic weekend together and never saw each other again.

"Maybe we haven't considered all our options," Roberta said.

"We have options? Since when?"

Roberta's voice sounded muffled as she spoke to someone in the restaurant. She came back on the line. "I have to go, Nedy. I just got a table. We'll continue this conversation when I get home. I love you."

"Love you, too." Kennedy let the phone fall to her side in a daze. Her mind ran wild with the "options" that might be available to her. Boarding school? They couldn't afford it. Military school? Still couldn't afford it. Mental institution? Their health insurance was too crappy.

Kennedy changed direction and headed back towards the E building, which provided the quickest route to the desert. Stale air and putrid green lockers greeted her as she opened the hollow metal door. She walked inside the empty hall, still listening to the Beatles, when the door opened behind her once more. Fresh air traveled through the hallway. The sight of him startled her. She dropped her phone, adding more cracks to its damaged screen. Kennedy removed her earbuds while he kneeled and picked up her phone from the vinyl composition tiles.

Reddick Vincent ran a hand through his thick brown hair,

grasping the front part up and away from his forehead. He looked down at the *Magical Mystery Tour* album cover shining from her phone. "*And* you have good taste in music," he said, as though they were already in the middle of a conversation.

Kennedy tried not to gawk, but it was the closest she'd ever been to him. At five foot ten inches, Kennedy was one of the tallest girls in her class, but Reddick Vincent still towered over her. His athletic build and broad shoulders prevented her from seeing anything beyond him.

"It's Kennedy, right?"

Kennedy had to think about it for a minute. "Yeah," she managed. Reddick knowing her name validated her entire existence.

Reddick Vincent was a senior who had transferred to Desert Hills High from New York last spring. Kennedy had heard all kinds of rumors about him: that he had once been a model, that he had once dated an influencer, and that he already had a full football scholarship to a Division One university. People followed his every move, but Kennedy had reasons to keep her distance.

It happened the first week of school. Kennedy had been walking down a different hallway when she overheard a loudmouth named Cassie accosting two girls for speaking Spanish. Cassie told them to go back to Mexico, where they belonged. Kennedy, whose Nana Silvia was from Chihuahua, took extreme offense to this. Kennedy wanted to remind Cassie that the very spot they were standing in had once *been* Mexico, but people like Cassie did not care about history or facts.

Kennedy focused on the slightly ajar door of Cassie's locker and tried not to laugh when it flew open and popped Cassie in her big, ignorant mouth. She was very satisfied with herself until she saw the blood gushing from Cassie's broken nose. Kennedy felt awful. She looked across the hallway and caught eyes with Reddick, who had apparently seen the whole thing unfold. Reddick did not say a word to her; he only nodded. Since then, whenever he saw her, he would nod at her—no hello, no introduction, just a knowing nod.

Until now.

Reddick opened a locker behind her and retrieved a notebook. "You know, I'm actually heading over to your house. Your sister invited a few of us over."

It's not a house.

Kennedy thought of her run-down apartment. She pictured the dated appliances and Reddick sitting on the hand-me-down couch that Phantom had clawed to death. She imagined Reddick counting the bedroom doors and realizing there were only two, one of which she had to share with her mother. Kennedy had shared a room with Audrey for a while, but their frequent fights had pushed them all to the brink of eviction. Then Kennedy thought of her mother, and a wave of guilt flooded her. Roberta was at her second job, ensuring they could keep that apartment, and here Kennedy was embarrassed about it.

Reddick freed her from her shame spiral when he said, "Do you want a ride?"

"Where?"

"To your place?"

"Um, no, I'm fine; thank you; I have plans," she lied.

He gave her a wide, bashful smile—a smile capable of leveling lesser girls. But Kennedy refused to be lesser, so she tried to make him look away first. Reddick's hair was still damp from showering after football practice. His clean scent clouded her thoughts; she couldn't tell if it was cologne or soap, but she was willing to make it her life's work to find out.

"Well, I guess I'll see you later then."

"Um, yeah maybe." She gave him an awkward wave and continued down the hallway, actively reminding herself how to walk as she felt his eyes on her. She stopped at the end of the hallway to give him another awkward wave—because one was clearly not enough—but when Kennedy turned around, he was gone.

Kennedy walked alone through the stretch of desert behind the baseball field, dissecting every word of the conversation she'd just had with Reddick. *"And you have good taste in music..."*

Kennedy was experiencing wordnesia, or semantic satiation, because the word "And" suddenly made zero sense to her.

And? she thought. *What a word! What a life-affirming conjunction! What does AND mean? Does it have something to do with the nodding? And... And... And?*

And remained an enigma as Kennedy hiked nearly two miles to her sanctuary—a small clearing at the base of the Santa Catalinas. It wasn't much of a sanctuary, but she had read in one of her mother's new-age books that one could create her own sanctuary anywhere, and this was Kennedy's. Five giant saguaro cactuses encircled the small clearing. Kennedy had always believed they were her protectors, the knights of her round table, with their long arms outstretched at the ready. This was the only place on Earth where she could completely be herself. Here, she was not weird or different; she just was.

And.

Kennedy used to be scared of traveling into the desert alone, but not anymore. She knew to watch where she stepped and to heed her intuition, which sometimes told her to stay away. There were long stretches of the year where Kennedy could not come out here at all due to Tucson's extreme heat. From May until September, she felt she was in hibernation. This was only the second time since summer break that she had made it out here.

Kennedy dropped her backpack, and the sound of it landing echoed throughout the mountains. Thunder rolled in the distance, but Kennedy was too busy thinking about Reddick to worry about rain. She smiled up at her majestic saguaros. "Boy, I've had a day," she told them. A lizard observed her through the side of its face. She beamed at it, as though it were a dear friend of hers. "Good evening," she said before it scurried off.

Kennedy felt a reverence for just about everything in nature. It was so much easier to revere these living things than the living things that overpopulated her school. It wasn't that Kennedy didn't *like* humans, it was that she could not be herself around them, and she could not help but resent them for it. Society was traveling at a snail's pace towards tolerance, but Kennedy knew it would never be able to tolerate her. Mostly because her condition could not be explained, not even by her.

When Kennedy was a baby, she would stare at a desired object for hours. She would not throw a tantrum the way other children did; she would just stare. At first, her mother thought there might be something developmentally wrong with her. She did not know her daughter could actually *see* energy and was trying to match the vibrational frequency of the desired object. She was also unaware that her daughter had the ability to feel her emotions, which was by far the worst of Kennedy's abilities. Feeling someone's emotions was far more taxing than reading someone's mind. People's minds were full of thoughts that did not belong to them, yet their emotions were uniquely their own. Kennedy had already experienced both the heights and depths of human emotion second-hand. She would turn seventeen in December, but at times, this ability made her feel twice that age.

Kennedy did not view her abilities as superpowers, because superpowers were just that—super. These were nothing of the kind. These were a burden—a burden that no cape or slow-motion walk away from an explosion could glamorize. Although she *had* saved a few lives... Well, she had saved two. The first was a senile woman in her grandparents' neighborhood who forgot to turn off her stove and caught her house on fire. The woman, who was unconscious due to smoke inhalation, swore she remembered a graceful, angelic woman swaddling her in a blanket and carrying her down the stairs to safety. In reality, it had been a sweaty, coughing Kennedy, dragging her in a blanket like an old sack of potatoes. Kennedy managed to flee before the fire department arrived. The police did, however, find female-sized footprints at the scene, which Kennedy took as a compliment, considering she wore a size eleven.

The second life she saved belonged to a little boy named Jacob Gorski. Jacob's family had been having a barbeque at the pool in Kennedy's apartment complex and had failed to notice the toddler fall into the deep end by himself. Luckily, Kennedy had been passing by on her way to steal cookies set out by the office for future residents. She jumped the fence, retrieved Jacob's small body from the water, and performed CPR on him. Channel Nine labeled Kennedy a teenage hero in their coverage of the incident, but they still could not change the hearts and minds of her peers, who continued to call her a freak.

The sun broke through the thick clouds and illuminated the silver-speckled rocks on the desert floor. When the clouds covered the sun again, the rocks turned a flat color, but not to Kennedy, who connected with their tiny, abundant pings of vibration. Kennedy focused intensely on them until the world of form began to fade away. Her vision became carbonated and filled with tiny bubbles moving at different speeds. Kennedy adjusted her vibration until it matched the frequency of the rocks. The rocks responded by rising off the desert floor and orbiting her like an asteroid belt. Kennedy listened in to make sure she was still alone. She could hear the distant traffic on Oracle Road, hawks screeching in flight, and a Gila woodpecker hammering a new home into the side of a saguaro with a dull thump. Kennedy always kept an ear out for rattling tails and human footsteps. Both sent an equal amount of dread through her, but at least rattlesnakes were courteous enough to warn they were going to attack. She was always on the lookout for wildlife, and she had encountered just about all of it out here—javelinas, coyotes, even a mountain lion once who had been generous enough not to maul

Kennedy to death.

Then her thoughts returned to Reddick, and the rocks fell. The world turned solid again. Kennedy imagined him in her apartment. She wondered what he was doing, what he was thinking, and where he was sitting.

Kennedy decided she needed to find out. So, she sat down on a boulder and willed herself into a deep, meditative state. Then she allowed her consciousness to travel home while her physical body remained in the desert—another of the many unexplainable things she could do.

Kennedy's consciousness arrived in the bedroom she shared with her mother. Her cat, Phantom, was curled up into a ball on Kennedy's side of the bed. A cushion sat in a corner of the walk-in closet, surrounded by postcards from San Diego and magazine cutouts of the Beatles. The closet was where Kennedy did most of her reading and daydreaming.

Kennedy's consciousness floated down the hallway towards the living room, where eight of Audrey's friends made themselves at home. Audrey had her legs draped over her boyfriend, Cody Ramirez's, lap while she distantly scrolled her cell phone.

Cody's major ticks were flattening the front of his Caesar haircut with his hand and practicing his pitching windup. Currently his eyes were glued to the TV screen, where Miles Pierce—a handsome movie star with mocha skin and a perfectly toned body—ran for his life. He was bloody, sweaty, and shirtless. Miles's character jumped off a cliff to avoid the bullets of the bad guys chasing him. Cody tapped Audrey's leg. "Did you know Miles Pierce does all his own stunts?" This was a nice change of conversation for them, because all Cody usually wanted to talk about was baseball.

Reddick sat on the loveseat next to Olivia Thomas, a senior cheerleader with a tanning addiction. He observed a framed photo on the side table and then picked it up. The photo was of Roberta, Audrey, and Kennedy from last Christmas. Olivia took the opportunity to scoot closer to him. "It's crazy that they're related, isn't it? I mean, Audrey is so normal, and Kennedy is just like... off," she said.

Audrey noticed them whispering in the corner. "What are you two lovebirds talking about?"

Olivia blushed a deeper shade of orange, but Reddick was not embarrassed by Audrey's insinuation; he did not even acknowledge it; instead, he held up the frame. "You and your sister look nothing alike."

Kennedy immediately took it as an insult because *who wouldn't want to look like Audrey Lambert?*

"We have different dads," Audrey said.

"Audrey's dad is a lawyer up in Phoenix," Cody said, with his eyes still glued to the screen. "And Kennedy's dad was just some random their mom hooked up with in San Diego."

Audrey backhanded Cody.

"Ah," he cried. "That's what you told me."

"Yeah, well, I'm allowed to talk shit about my family. You're not."

Reddick finally set down the frame. "So, she's never met her father?"

"All my mom remembers is that his name was Aaron. I think Kennedy has Googled every Aaron in the country. She's obsessed with finding him."

"That must be tough."

"It's annoying. Anyway, she's better off. In my experience, fathers are a huge letdown."

"Yeah." Reddick sighed as though he were in complete agreement. His response intrigued Kennedy, who wanted to learn everything there was to know about him.

Then Phantom began to meow. He looked up at Kennedy's consciousness and licked his lips, begging for food. His fluffy tail whipped back and forth as he waited for her to feed him. All of Audrey's friends turned to look at Phantom, meowing at nothing.

Kennedy had no idea what to do.

"Dude, what's up with your cat? I think he sees a ghost," Cody said. "They can see spirits, you know?"

Audrey laughed at Cody and said, "You sound insane."

"What? They can! They can see into higher dimensions and shit." Cody flattened the front of his haircut.

"Yeah, okay." Audrey continued laughing, and all her friends joined her.

Luckily for Kennedy, they quickly lost interest and returned to their screens. Kennedy thought she was in the clear until she refocused her attention on Reddick, who stared directly at her, as if he could see her as plain as day.

TWO

Kennedy's consciousness returned to her physical body, where it belonged. *Did he see me? How? There was nothing to see. Was there?* Reddick looked at Kennedy like he knew more about her than she knew about herself. His intense stares should have made Kennedy feel seen, but instead they made her feel caught.

She paced around her sanctuary, her thoughts spiraling the entire time. Reddick probably only stared at her because Kennedy always stared at him. Also, now that she thought about it, there *were* picture frames behind her in the hallway; maybe that was what he had been staring at. She was panicking for no reason. There was no way he saw her. It was all in her imagination—a coincidence. It had to have been.

Still, Kennedy hated that her sister had just told everyone about her all-consuming obsession with finding her father. She had no idea how pathetic it sounded until she heard it out loud—not that any part of it had been untrue. Kennedy *did* spend an absurd amount of time trying to find him. She believed she had inherited her abilities from him, and she was convinced he was the only one who would ever be able to understand her. She knew she would meet him one day; she just had no idea how. Kennedy attached so much of her self-worth to this meeting. All she needed was for him to accept her, and then she could finally accept herself. Most people have this going on subconsciously with one or both of their parents, but it wasn't subconscious for Kennedy; it was the engine of her life.

Kennedy tried her best to be industrious because her mother always told her that if she was going to get anything done in this life, she had to do it herself. She had spent countless hours online searching for San Diego Aaron's around her mother's age. Eventually, Roberta grew so tired of Kennedy asking, *"Is this him, is this him?"* that she threatened to cancel the wi-fi.

Sometimes Kennedy would be grinning about something funny, and Roberta would yank her out of the moment by saying, *"You have his smile."* Kennedy didn't daydream about her father being rich or famous; she just hoped he was nice. She also hoped he was looking for her, which was pretty impossible considering he did not know she existed. Still, Kennedy truly believed she could *Parent Trap* them all into being a big, happy family. Happiness swelled up inside her every time she considered it. But then she reminded herself that things rarely worked out for her. She had wanted this for years—her whole life really—why would it all of a sudden happen now? The small, incessant voice inside of her—which sometimes not even Kennedy could detect—played the same old, familiar recording: *He doesn't want you. Why would anyone want you? You are unnatural. You are a freak.*

Then the voice of Kennedy's higher angels broke through, reminding her to breathe. She closed her eyes and focused solely on her breath: in and out, in and out, in and out. The voice faded as Kennedy eased into a meditative state. In that moment, she let it all go, even the "*and...*"

Thunder rumbled throughout the desert. Fat raindrops fell on Kennedy's forehead, then the sky opened up, and it began to pour. Kennedy could already feel her wavy hair planning its revenge. She put her red hoodie back on, picked up her backpack, and ran home. She needed to hustle to make it home before dark. Usually, she walked through the wash to get home, but the risk of a flash flood made her take an alternate route. She headed west through the desert, towards a plot of land where an expensive home was currently under construction. Kennedy ignored the private property sign and tiptoed around some jumping cholla cactus, making sure to keep a wide breadth. A bolt of lightning lit up her surroundings while she ran for shelter inside the half-built home.

Sawdust filled Kennedy's nostrils as she waited out the storm against the foundation of what would soon be a kitchen island. Then she heard a car arrive outside and prepared to run. She peeked out of an empty window frame and found a parked truck.

Kennedy eavesdropped on an argument drifting from the truck's cracked open back window and made a nauseated face when she noticed a pair of truck nuts hanging from the rear hitch. "Come on, don't be like that," a boy said.

"No," came the voice of a girl, who was clearly upset. "I want to go home now."

But the boy would not stop doing what he was doing.

"I'm serious. I want to go home," the girl said again.

"You wouldn't have come out here with me if this wasn't what you wanted."

"I didn't know we were coming out here."

He still wouldn't listen.

"I said no!"

There was a slap, followed by a sudden silence. Then Kennedy heard the boy deliver a fierce blow to whoever the girl was, and the truck began to rock as he continued hitting her.

Kennedy ran towards the truck and threw down her backpack. The rain still fell on her, but the lightning was now a comfortable distance away. Kennedy attempted to open the locked driver's side door. Through the glass, she met the eyes of a terrified redhead named Molly, who had been in Kennedy's Language Arts class freshman year.

The boy rolled down his window and yelled at Kennedy. "If you ever touch my truck again, I'll kill you!"

"Easy there, Truck Nuts," Kennedy replied.

The distraction was enough to allow Molly to manually unlock the passenger side door and flee for safety.

"Hey!" he yelled after her. "Get back here!" He opened his door, and Kennedy leapt out of the way.

"Are you okay?" Kennedy looked past him to Molly, whose cheek was welted and bloody. "Do you want me to call the cops?"

Truck Nuts puffed out his chest. "You're not calling anyone."

"Was I talking to you?" Kennedy asked him. "Did you hear me say, 'Hey, dipshit?'"

He turned his camouflage baseball cap backwards. "What did you call me?"

"You heard me." Kennedy pulled out her phone, and Truck Nuts slapped it from her hands.

He grabbed a handful of her red hoodie. "Why don't you mind your own business?"

"Get your meat hooks off me," Kennedy warned him.

"Or what? What are you going to do about it?" He pulled her so close that she could smell the energy drink on his breath. "You know it's dangerous for a girl to be out here all by herself. Something could happen to you, and no one would even know about it—not until the vultures started circling."

Kennedy struggled for her phone again, but he stopped her. "I told you no."

Kennedy peered at him. "Funny, I didn't think you knew what that word meant."

He grabbed Kennedy by the throat. His red knuckles turned white as they attempted to squeeze the life out of her. She could feel an untethered rage coursing through him as he gripped her neck, his bitter inner life on full display—Kennedy had underestimated him.

Molly ran towards them and tried to pry his fingers from Kennedy's throat. "Let her go! Stop it!"

But Truck Nuts just squeezed tighter. Kennedy's face was turning purple.

"You're killing her!" Molly screamed.

Kennedy did her best to focus on a pile of gravel behind him. The gravel levitated off the ground until it looked like a swarm of locusts hanging in the sky. A piece hit Truck Nuts in the head, and another piece struck him on the cheek. He dropped Kennedy and shielded himself.

The plague of gravel still hung in the air, awaiting her next command.

Truck Nuts could not believe his eyes.

Kennedy braced herself on a stack of cinderblocks and shakily rose to her feet, struggling to breathe. She refocused on the rocks until they felt like an extension of her. On her command, the rocks assaulted his truck like tiny pieces of hail, nicking cellulite into his shiny paint job and cracking his windshield in a hundred different places.

"My truck!" he screamed as though it were his firstborn child.

Kennedy coughed out a laugh, and he lunged for her, but Kennedy would not underestimate him again. She sensed his movements before he made them. The tiniest jerk of his shoulder let her know he was about to strike; his frustration grew as she repeatedly dodged him.

Kennedy lured him away from Molly, back towards the private property sign.

Truck Nuts stalked her, still arrogantly believing he had the upper hand. Once Kennedy cleared the jumping cholla cactus, she stopped, but he did not. She closed her eyes, and the cactus began to shake ever-so-slightly. He smirked at her, like she was an idiot weirdo—an idiot weirdo he was about to kill. Then Kennedy opened her eyes, and the cactus stems shot into the air, burying themselves deep inside his exposed skin. His face curled up in pain, and he gasped like a toddler who had just taken a frightful fall. He finally figured out it was her—the rocks, the cactus—all her.

"No! Please, no! I'm sorry!" He scrambled back to his truck. Tears, snot, and cactus now covered his face. The stems gouged deeper into his skin each time he moved. "Please, please. I'm sorry. I'll never hit her again. Just please don't kill me!"

Kennedy glowered at him. "You know it's dangerous for a boy to be out here all by himself. Something could happen to you, and no one would even know about it—not until the vultures started circling."

Kennedy heard Molly screaming hysterically into her cell phone. "Come quick! We're at the construction site at the end of Sharp Ridge Road. Please hurry! They're going to kill each other!"

Kennedy panicked, wondering how she would explain this situation to the cops. Her first instinct was to run.

Truck Nuts sobbed while plucking the cactus from his face. "Wait until the cops find out about this, you crazy bitch!"

The epithet set Kennedy off again. She charged at him, but then someone appeared in front of her. A formidable woman in her forties held Kennedy back. She wore a beige jumpsuit and had the type of body that late-night infomercials promised you could have too. Kennedy had seen her around before, once at her summer job and twice at her apartment complex, but she had never seen her—or anyone else for that matter—appear out of thin air like that.

"That's enough," the woman told Kennedy.

The woman whispered something into her palm, then removed two small, triangular keys from a triangular pack around her waist. The gold keys floated into the air, aiming lasers of blue light into the temples of Truck Nuts and Molly. Projections of their recent memories appeared next to their silent, dazed faces. The woman reviewed the rewinding footage of their memories and then modified it, deleting the segment of time they had spent at the construction site.

The woman removed a small blue weed from her pack and rubbed it on Molly's welted cheek, healing it instantly. She then whispered something into Molly's ear.

The 911 operator yelled from Molly's phone. *"Ma'am? Hello? Are you there? Ma'am?"*

Kennedy knew she should run, but her wretched curiosity glued her to the spot.

The woman looked at the truck. "Well, there's not much we can do about that." Then she turned around and beamed at Kennedy as though she were the brightest star in the universe. "It is an honor to encounter your energy, young creator. I am Zuele Zuniz."

"What are those?" Kennedy pointed to the triangular keys.

"Those are Roterin Keys. I'm modifying their memories."

"What did you just whisper to her?"

"I shifted her paradigm. I fed her subconscious mind a more empowering story—a story that will keep her far away from beings like him."

Then a pair of headlights cut through the gathering darkness. Kennedy assumed it was the cops but instead found a black Audi with New York plates.

"Your ride is here," Zuele said.

Reddick Vincent got out of his car and walked directly to

Kennedy. "Let's go."

Kennedy furrowed her brow in extreme confusion as sirens wailed in the distance. "What are you doing here?"

"Go with him, Kennedy."

Kennedy looked back at Zuele. "How do you know my name?"

"There's no time for that."

Reddick grabbed Kennedy's backpack and threw it in the back of his SUV.

"Who are you people?" Kennedy asked.

Zuele smiled again. "We are Evolvers."

"And what do you want with me?"

"To see if you'd like to become one, too," Zuele said, as though it were obvious.

Reddick opened his passenger door and motioned for Kennedy to get in.

Kennedy made a run for it instead.

Reddick Materialized in front of her, blocking her path. The white ring he wore on his right hand now glowed a blinding white. With wide eyes, Kennedy turned and tried to run in the opposite direction, but he just Materialized in front of her again. "Stop doing that!" she screamed at him. She tried to run once more, but he grabbed her by the forearms. "Let me go!"

"We are on your side, Kennedy."

Kennedy still struggled.

"You have to trust us." Reddick pleaded with her.

"Why should I?"

"Because we are your best shot at finding your father."

Zuele gave Reddick a disapproving look, as though he had

deviated from the script.

Kennedy stopped struggling and gazed up at him.

He finally let her go.

The sirens were close now. Zuele held a hand in front of Truck Nuts, who was beginning to drool, and the cactus stems wiggled out of his flesh. Then Zuele smoothed her hands back and forth in the air, and with each movement she made, the mud shifted, erasing Kennedy's footprints from the area. She pointed a hand at the scattered gravel and summoned it neatly back into a single pile. Reddick motioned to his open passenger door. Kennedy looked around the construction site and weighed her options, then she got into his car.

THREE

Reddick reversed speedily out of the long driveway and then drove casually down Sharp Ridge Road. Two cop cars raced past them in the opposite direction.

Kennedy massaged her tender throat.

Reddick pulled his car to the side of the road, put it in park, and reached for something in his glove compartment. "Let me see." He examined her neck, then applied some blue weed to Kennedy's skin. She jerked away from him. "It's okay, Kennedy." He applied the weed once more, now only inches from her face. "Better?" he asked.

Kennedy gazed into his piercing blue eyes, which looked like the bottom of a swimming pool on a sunny day. She was convinced he was the most beautiful person she had ever seen up close. "What is that stuff?"

"Firest Weed; it's a healing herb." Reddick handed it to her and got back on the road. Kennedy held the firest weed to her throat like an ice pack, amazed by the instant relief it brought her. She didn't say anything more to him until he was passing her apartment building. "That was my street," she said.

"I know, I'm not taking you home yet."

"Where are you taking me?"

He did not respond.

Why did you get in his car? He's a stranger! Kennedy inwardly screamed at herself. *Is it because he's gorgeous? Gosh, you're pathetic! And now you're going to be dead, too! He and that lady are going to murder you and chop you up into bits and scatter you across the desert, and you deserve it, you practically begged for it—*

Reddick interrupted her hysterical thoughts when he noticed she was shivering. "Are you cold?"

"Are you going to kill me?" she asked, point-blank.

He laughed. "You're funny."

"*So...?*"

"No, Kennedy, I am not going to kill you."

"Then can you please tell me what the hell is going on?"

Reddick ran a hand over his face and then looked at her. Instead of easing her confusion, he added to it. "It is my honor to inform you of your acceptance into the Evolver Institute."

"What are you talking about?"

"The Evolver Institute is for beings like you—beings who are sensitive, beings who can manipulate energy—some of the most advanced minds in the universe have gone through the Evolver program."

Kennedy gulped. "The *universe*?"

"Surely, you know by now that you are not from here."

"By *here,* you mean?"

"Earth."

She laughed. "What is this, some kind of joke?"

"Your mother is undoubtedly from this planet, and you obviously have some very human traits, especially your seeming inability to avoid trouble." He tapped his thumbs on the steering wheel. "Do you understand what I am trying to tell you, Kennedy?"

"That I... am... an alien?"

Reddick gave her a slight nod.

"But how?" She covered her mouth as the realization hit her: "My dad." Kennedy was half-waiting for the hidden camera crew to pop out and say this was all some sort of elaborate prank, but she knew from the look on Reddick's face it was not.

"I am sorry to tell you this way, but we won't always be here to clean up after you."

"You saw what I did to Cassie that day in the hallway, didn't you?"

"It *was* pretty hard to miss."

Kennedy wiped her hands on her muddy shorts and nodded, finally understanding what it meant to be in shock. "Does my mom know?"

Reddick grew visibly uncomfortable. "I think it is best to let the two of you discuss it."

"She doesn't know anything about my dad," Kennedy assured him.

Reddick's expression was a sympathetic one. "We've been in contact with your mother for several months. I do not know how much she knows about your father, but she knows now—at least because of us—that you are not fully human."

Kennedy removed the top strap of her seatbelt and turned her body towards him. "What else does she know? What else do *you* know? Do you know why I am the way I am? Do you know who my dad is?

Reddick sighed. "Zuele will be able to answer all of your questions."

"I don't want *Zuele* to answer them. I want you to. Tell me about my father. Who is he?"

"I don't know..." Reddick stopped at a red light.

"But you do know that he is, for sure, an alien?"

"Alien means "other," and since we are all made of the same energy, there is technically no such thing. But yes, your father is a sentient being from another planet."

Kennedy went back to tangling her fingers, surprised by the relief washing over her. She finally had an explanation for why she was the way she was. She wasn't a freak of nature or a giant birth defect; she was just... an alien.

The sound of the rain falling, and the rhythm of the windshield wipers provided them with a steady soundtrack. Lightning bolts cracked through the night sky as the storm headed east ahead of them.

"I'm sorry, Kennedy. I know this is a lot to process."

"Are you an alien, too—I mean, where are you from?"

"I am from a small planet called Symetra, which is where the Evolvers originated and where the Institute is located."

"Is Zuele from there, too?"

"No, Zuele is from the planet Millintica."

Kennedy nodded as though she had heard of it before, and then she openly stared at his gorgeous face. "Is that really what you look like?"

He shook his head weakly and peeled the flesh near his collarbone. He convulsed and groaned violently. Kennedy covered her mouth, preemptively stifling the horrified scream threatening to erupt from her. Reddick started laughing. "I so had you! Not all *"aliens"* are green and slimy. I can't believe you thought this was a mask."

"I think it'd be easier to believe that was a mask," she said under her breath.

"What?" he asked as self-consciously as someone who looked like him could.

"Nothing. How old are you?"

"I am three hundred and eighty-nine years old."

Kennedy wheezed.

He slapped the steering wheel. "You have to stop being so gullible. You're making it too easy for me... By human calculations, I am around eighteen."

"Is Reddick your real name?"

"Yes, but my last name isn't Vincent, it's Brandth. I was supposed to change my first name too, but do I look like a Dylan or a Jayden to you?" Reddick messed with the radio. "Do you want to put some music on?"

Kennedy shook her head.

Reddick turned it down and tapped his fingers against the steering wheel again.

Kennedy's thoughts returned to her mother. "I can't believe

she's been lying to me."

"I think she has been protecting you from something she can't even process yet."

"Yeah, the truth." Kennedy didn't feel like talking after that. She stewed in anger as she thought about her mother keeping this life-altering information from her.

Reddick began asking her inane questions as though he were willfully trying to distract her from her anger. He finally succeeded when he told her about Symetra. "Some people call it a paradise planet. My greatest grandmother settled there so she could learn from the indigenous Triphens—they are these super powerful beings who spend their days in service and meditation. They vibrate at a frequency you wouldn't even believe, and their energy is palpable; it literally hits you when you meet them. Their teachings are the foundation of the Institute—you're going to love it."

"But what's the whole point? What does an Evolver do after the Institute?"

"We help evolve primitive planets."

Reddick turned up a private road near Sabino Canyon. Kennedy gripped her door handle as he sped up the mountain and into the darkness. 'Secrets' by One Republic played faintly on the radio. Then Kennedy watched helplessly as a deer ran out in front of the car, hitting it seemed unavoidable. She gasped from the bottom of her feet. Reddick raised his hand, flicked it to the right, and the deer quickly disappeared into the desert. It was as though some invisible hook had just yanked the deer to safety. It all happened in a matter of seconds. Reddick had never even taken his foot off the gas.

Kennedy gazed at him in reverential silence. He ignored her stare and leaned back in the driver's seat, completely unfazed. A half-mile later, they drove up to a gate. Reddick pulled down his sun visor and held his hand to a small sensor hidden inside the mirror. The gate rolled open, revealing a multi-level estate built into the side of a canyon. The house was modern and lit from the bottom up, which made it appear twice its already enormous size. Reddick pulled into a large garage filled with an array of high-end electric vehicles. The cars had license plates from Nevada, California, Texas and Sonora, Mexico.

Reddick opened Kennedy's door for her, but she just sat there, unready to face whatever lay inside the house. "Be at ease, Kennedy. This is not a decision you have to make immediately. We don't leave until next month."

But Kennedy was not at ease.

"You want to see the pool?" he asked in an attempt to delay the inevitable.

Weak flashes of lightning flickered through the purple clouds above as he led her out of the garage and up a set of stone steps. "Watch out for scorpions. I found a huge one the other day."

"The little ones are the ones you have to worry about," Kennedy said.

Reddick stopped at the top of the steps. "I love the smell of Tucson's rain. It doesn't smell this good anywhere else in the universe."

Kennedy walked to a bush a few feet away and plucked a tiny yellow flower from it; she placed it inside Reddick's palm. "It's the creosote bushes."

Kennedy then caught sight of the pool. A neon light turned the water purple, then pink, then blue, then green. Half of the pool was indoors, and the other half was outdoors. The pool's outdoor portion spilled down onto the boulders below, and glass enclosed the indoor portion, which boasted cathedral ceilings. Kennedy discovered a family splashing around inside. A dad took turns launching his two young daughters across the water, eliciting squeals of delight as they soared through the air.

"Who are they?" Kennedy asked.

"They're no one." Reddick knocked against the glass. "It's Trick Tint; we can see out, but nobody can see in. I'll show you." He grabbed her hand, which tensed at the intimate gesture. Reddick let go, and Kennedy immediately scolded herself for blowing her chance to touch the most beautiful boy she had ever seen. Reddick opened the glass door for her. The indoor pool was empty and still.

Kennedy ran across the pool deck to the other side of the glass, and the family was there again. "Wow," she said.

"This stock footage plays all day throughout the house's windows. Sometimes you'll see this family eating their meals, playing, watching TV—everything normal families do."

Kennedy watched one of the little girls wrap her chubby arms around her father's neck. "I kind of want them to adopt me."

"Me too..." he said sadly.

A small elevator near the pool delivered them to the top floor of the house. Sweeping views of Tucson's city lights sparkled beyond a modern living room filled with abstract paintings and expensive furniture. "Come on, we can wait for Zuele in here." Reddick led her into his tastefully decorated bedroom. A textured stone accent wall stood behind a king-size platform bed while an asymmetrical gold chandelier dangled from the ceiling, reflecting off the moody landscapes hanging on the walls. A chaise lounge in the corner held a vinyl-stickered laptop and his AP history textbook.

Kennedy gazed around the room. "Where did she go?"

"She went to try and get your mother's consent one last time."

Kennedy crossed her arms at the mention of her mother, furious that she was having to find out her true heritage from a good-looking stranger instead of the woman who had brought her into the world. She did not think it was right for these important conversations about her future to take place without her. "Um, do you have a bathroom I could use?" she asked him.

"Sure, right through there." He handed her a folded, blue suit from his drawer. "And while you're in there..."

"What is this?"

"All of our technology is integrated, right down to our clothes. If your mom gives her consent, this suit will make your orientation easier."

Kennedy carried the folded suit into the bathroom, tossed it on the counter, and locked the door behind her. She sat against the wall and thought of her mother's work—the white table-cloths, the dim lighting, the romantic opera music, and the fresco paintings of cherubs frolicking in the sky above the main dining room. She could smell the aromas of simmering pasta sauce and freshly baked bread. Then Kennedy's consciousness arrived there, just in time to see her mother emerge from the bar, carrying a tray of cocktails. Roberta was an attractive though exhausted-looking woman who possessed Latin eyes and long, wavy hair a few shades darker than Kennedy's.

Kennedy drifted behind her as Roberta delivered drinks to a couple of young working professionals who were clearly on a first date. Roberta took their order, then made her way to the table of an older couple who ate their dinner in silence. "I am sorry to interrupt, but I wanted to tell you about our chocolate souffle," Roberta told them.

The old man dropped his fork. "We aren't even done with our dinner yet, and you are already trying to sell us dessert?" He was gruffer than necessary—Kennedy wished she had her body with her so she could dump his spaghetti into his old, crochety lap.

"It's just that it takes twenty minutes."

He held up a liver-spotted hand. "We are not interested."

"*Prick*," Roberta muttered under her breath as she walked away.

A hostess, who couldn't have been much older than Kennedy, gave Roberta a chit and took the tray from her. "I just sat you on forty-four. She requested you."

Zuele sat like a statue at table forty-four. Her French twist hairdo gave her added elegance, though she did not need any.

Roberta stormed towards her. "Now you're bothering me

at work?"

"Kennedy knows," Zuele said.

"She *what*? You said that you couldn't approach her without my consent."

"Yeah, well, that was before she nearly killed a boy in the desert."

Roberta began to panic.

"Don't worry, she's fine; they both are. No one will ever know she was even there." Zuele placed both of her hands on the table. "I am begging you to reconsider my offer, Roberta."

"You are crazy if you think I am letting you take my daughter with you."

"What other option do you have? School has been in session for three weeks. How many of those days has she already spent in detention?"

"She has issues with authority."

"One of her many admirable qualities." A server assistant stopped at the table to fill Zuele's water glass. Zuele thanked him, took a sip of the water, and waited for him to walk away. "I know you think this is going to get better, but it won't. She'll end up in jail or some government laboratory. You can't expect her to hide her true nature forever."

Roberta shifted uncomfortably. "I keep trying to tell her—I was going to tell her tonight—but every time I try—" Roberta's bottom lip quivered. "She's my baby."

"Roberta, you have raised an amazing daughter, but we both know she cannot stay here any longer. She does not know how to fit in here. Let me train her. Let me protect her."

"Are you a mother?"

A pained expression crossed Zuele's face. "No."

"Then you don't realize how much you are asking of me."

"All I am asking is that you let *her* make this decision."

Roberta covered her tired eyes with her hands. "Fine."

"Yes?"

"I said fine... She can make the decision. I've got to go. I have other tables." Roberta walked away.

Kennedy's consciousness remained next to Zuele, while Roberta cleared dirty plates from the gruff man's table. Then Zuele's hand began to vibrate; she quickly got up from the table and walked to the bathroom.

Kennedy's consciousness followed her inside.

Zuele checked the stalls to make sure she was alone, then opened her vibrating hand. A miniature hologram of a pale man with graying, slick hair emerged from Zuele's palm.

"It is a pleasure to encounter your energy, Guardian Zuniz," he said. "You are looking well as always."

The technology fascinated Kennedy.

"What do you want, Tusk? I am busy."

"I hate to be the one to tell you this; perhaps I shouldn't."

Zuele seemed to lose what little patience she already had for him. "Out with it."

"Janekis Opris was caught breaking into the Deepest Layer of Millintica. King Malant tortured her for information, but she wouldn't give him any and—" He struggled for the right words. "She's dead, Zuele."

Zuele was speechless. She leaned back onto the bathroom counter.

Tusk cleared his throat and clasped his hands firmly behind his back. "This has not gone public yet, but I thought you should know. I remember how close the two of you were when we were recruits. I'm sorry, Zue."

Zuele turned her face away, so Tusk couldn't see the distress splayed across it.

"Do you have any idea why she would do something so reckless?" he asked. "Do you think the Alliance was behind this? They have not been operational for years. Was Janekis deliberately trying to start a war?"

Zuele collected herself when she heard the clicking of high heels approaching the bathroom door. "I have to go. Someone's coming."

"I understand, Zue, but if you ever need to talk—"

Zuele closed her hand into a fist, and the hologram of Tusk disappeared inside it. A young woman walked into the bathroom and checked herself out in the mirror while Zuele washed her hands. When the young woman clicked her heels into a stall, Zuele formed a triangle with her fingers and brought it up in a line from her chest to her lips to her forehead, and then she sent it up as far as her arms would stretch. She exhaled heavily and then walked out of the bathroom.

Kennedy's consciousness followed her closely, but Zuele stopped just outside the door and looked over her shoulder. "Kennedy," she said, her voice thick with smothered emotion.

It jolted Kennedy, who was unable to respond.

"Your mother has given her consent, but you already knew that. I will notify Reddick so he can begin your orientation." Zuele kept walking, but this time Kennedy did not follow her.

FOUR

Kennedy brought her consciousness back into Reddick's bathroom, feeling guilty that she had eavesdropped on Zuele during such a sad moment. She quickly changed into the blue suit Reddick had proffered. The material was otherworldly. It was softer than cotton but felt somehow alive, like it was fusing with her skin. At first, it had been too big, but the suit quickly adapted and tailored itself to her body type. When she exited the bathroom, Reddick was standing there with an amused smirk stretched across his face. "Bilocating, huh?"

Kennedy packed her school clothes into her backpack. "What?"

"How did you learn how to do it?"

She moved past him, leaving her shoes in the bathroom. "I don't know what you're talking about."

"At your apartment this afternoon, I sensed you, and so did your cat."

"I knew it! You looked right at me!"

"So?"

"So what?"

"Who taught you?"

"I did."

"How?"

Kennedy shrugged. "It was an accident... Freshman year, Principal Vasquez tried to suspend me for ditching, but I didn't ditch class; I ditched a stupid pep rally. I sat outside his office while he talked to my mom." Kennedy bit the inside of her cheek. "I needed to get in that room; I needed to explain my side of the story. I tried to meditate to calm down, but the more I tried to quiet my mind, the more I realized I needed in there. I visualized his office, and then suddenly I was inside, even though my body was still out in the hallway. It scared the crap out of me."

Reddick stared at her, but his expression was imperceptible.

She grew nervous and kept talking. "It only works on the places I have been before."

"So, you can't bilocate to Paris when you're bored?"

"Unfortunately, no."

"Wow."

"What?"

"It's just amazing you taught yourself all this. I've been study-ing it for years and am barely, finally, starting to get it."

"So, you saw me earlier?"

"No, I sensed you. Our training teaches us how to identify shifts in energy."

Learning that the Evolvers could see energy in the same way Kennedy could made her feel less lonely. Reddick lowered his chin and smiled, silently asking her if she had another question for him. Kennedy shook her head and took a turn around the room. There were images pinned to a corkboard of Reddick's earthly adventures—a photo of him at the Grand Canyon, in front of Big Ben in London, at the Statue of Liberty, scaling El Capitan, and scuba diving the Great Barrier Reef. He appeared to be adept at everything.

Roberta had made Kennedy work the concession stand at football games, believing it would somehow help her daughter make friends—it didn't—but it had given her the opportunity to witness Reddick lead the varsity football team to an unde-feated season. Reddick had an air about him—a profound sense of belonging in whichever space he occupied. He possessed an otherworldly confidence, and while he had every reason to draw that confidence from his physical appearance, Kennedy knew he drew it from somewhere much deeper. His excellence was the most alien thing about him.

"How are you so good at football? I doubt they play it where you live."

"I spent some time working with an Evolver who used to be a professional football player. Also, we have technology that can rewire your mind and body to feel like it has been doing some-thing for years."

Kennedy shifted her eyes back to his cork board. "You've seen more of the Earth than I have."

"That will change if you become an Evolver."

Kennedy kept scanning the board until she landed on an im-age of Reddick with a beautiful blonde girl standing in front of the Sydney Opera House. The girl leaned into him and laughed as though he had just said something funny. She looked like the exact kind of girl he should be with—striking, confident, feminine—perfect.

"I guess we can go ahead and start your orientation," he said.

Kennedy did not respond.

"If you're not ready—"

Kennedy turned away from the beautiful blonde's photo and walked out of the room. "I'm ready."

Reddick led Kennedy to the house's basement floor. She had left everything in his room, including her shoes. When they stepped off the elevator, they entered a nerve center filled with screens and floating holograms. Ten Evolvers, dressed in dark gray uniforms, stopped what they were doing and bowed their heads at Kennedy, who was standing before them in her kitten socks.

Kennedy bowed back and threw in an awkward half-curtsy.

Reddick laughed. "This way."

Kennedy followed him down a dark hallway, where lights lit up near their feet with each step they took. They turned left into a small interrogation room with a wall of observation glass. Reddick motioned for her to enter a door hidden inside the glass.

Kennedy walked into a dark room the size of a small movie theater. The only light available came from a pair of shining golden footprints in the center. She looked back at Reddick, standing in the doorway.

"Go ahead and step on," his voice echoed throughout the

empty room. "I'll be right here."

Kennedy stepped onto the golden footprints and was slightly embarrassed when they stretched out to accommodate her large feet. A golden light shot up from the footprints and swallowed her whole. A powerful surge of energy pierced through every pore of her skin, and every cell of her body. "It's tingly!" she yelled to Reddick.

"You'll get used to it!" she heard him yell back.

Then everything fell silent and dark again, with the exception of her skin, which now had a faint golden aura. "Reddick?" she called out, but he had vanished. The golden footprints mirrored her movements as she walked towards the outer door.

"Welcome to your orientation, young creator," said a familiar voice next to her.

"You're... you're..." Kennedy stammered when she saw him.

"I am Miles Pierce." The same golden aura enveloped him, and together they lit up the darkness. "Zuele wanted me to tell you a little about my experience as an Evolver; she thought it might be easier for you to hear from a fellow half-human."

"You're half human, too?"

"Yep, I'm a mutt just like you. My mother was from the planet Aquenal, and my dad is from Chicago." He wore a black Evolver uniform with three gold moons in various phases on the left breast pocket.

"You look so much like... you. You even sound like you. It's crazy." Kennedy gawked at him as though he were a figment of her imagination—the twinkle in his bright eyes, his unblemished mocha skin, his *follow-me-I-know-the-way* smile. Miles Pierce was known for his laid-back charm, but right now he appeared to be just as excited to meet Kennedy as she was to meet him.

"I don't get it; you're an actor. I thought Evolvers were supposed to be evolving humans, not entertaining them."

"The two are not mutually exclusive," he said.

"But why a movie star? Why not a president, or a pope, or a queen?"

"I have achieved more as an actor than I ever would have as a head of state. My films get this planet to think differently. They embrace new concepts without even realizing they are doing it; they offer no resistance. Humans have learned so much from movies. It is one of the most powerful mediums on Earth. But to be clear, there are some Evolvers currently serving as heads of state. One day, you might even be one of them."

"*Me*?" Kennedy gestured to herself.

"You won't know for sure until your Phase Three Assessments, which is a wonderful place for us to begin. There are three phases in the Evolver program. Phase One, the phase you'll be entering if you decide to go, is all about eradicating your limiting beliefs and deliberately raising your vibration."

Kennedy still gawked at him.

"We will train you on our technology in Phase Two, and during Phase Three, you get to travel the universe; it's a bit like a study abroad program."

"Is that why Reddick is here?"

Miles raised a salacious eyebrow at her, as if he were about to sing "*Kennedy and Reddick sitting in a tree.*"

"Not that I care. It's like, totally whatever. I was just wondering."

"Reddick is indeed a Phase Three." Miles smiled, as though he could see right through her.

"So why evolve primitive planets?" she asked in a desperate attempt to change the subject.

"We require their assistance in our exploration of the ever-expanding universe, or universes. I'm sure you've heard the phrase two heads are better than one."

"Of course," Kennedy answered, even though she was still trying to figure out what he meant by *universes*.

"Well, all the twenty-four intelligent life planets of the universe are better than just Symetra." Miles waved his hand, and the walls turned into a map of the cosmos. He highlighted twenty-four scattered planets, seven of which were clustered fairly close together. "Unfortunately, most planets have not evolved enough to handle our advanced technology. To share it would be like putting a live grenade in the hands of a toddler. It is our mission to prime these primitive planets for our advancements."

The stars reflected off their faces.

"Where's Earth?" Kennedy asked.

"You are here." Miles zoomed in on a planet far removed from the others. "Earth, in particular, was dangerously behind, so we've had to double our efforts here. Have you ever wondered why the majority of this planet's technological advancements have emerged in the last century or so?"

"Not really," she said. Miles laughed, but Kennedy did not. Aliens had been spoon-feeding Earth technology for a century, and she had no idea how to process it.

Miles noticed this. "I am sure you have a lot of questions."

"I have so many, I don't even know where to begin."

"Begin anywhere."

"How did you find me?"

Miles waved his hand again, and a clip of Tucson's Channel Nine news replaced the map. The clip featured Kennedy's interview from a year prior. The chyron read: Teenage Hero Saves Drowning Toddler.

"I was just walking by, and I sensed—I mean, I could feel—I saw someone was in trouble," she had said back then. Kennedy cringed at both her voice on camera and her ill-advised bangs.

Miles paused the screen with Kennedy's eyes half closed and her mouth half open.

"That's a good look," she laughed.

"You can feel what people are feeling, can't you?"

Kennedy had yet to feel what Reddick was feeling, and she certainly couldn't feel what Miles Pierce was feeling. "Most of the time."

"Strange things always seem to happen around you, Kennedy Neff, which is why it was so easy for our recruiter to find you."

Kennedy shrugged. "I call it the pull."

Miles waited eagerly for her to explain what he already seemed to know.

"Whenever someone is in trouble, I feel this pull to do something." Kennedy wasn't used to people letting her talk; she could barely get a word in edgewise at home, so she took full advantage. "The pull helps me differentiate the people I can save from the ones I can't... There's this feeling people feel when they die. It's weird. It's like they surrender. I think we're all born with it. I'm always surprised by how okay people are with letting go. When people have that going on, I stay away, but sometimes there's this kind of... I don't know... energetic distress signal they send out, and that's when I feel the pull."

Miles considered her words.

"Does that make sense?" Kennedy asked.

"Yes. The pull. That is exactly what it feels like. Similar things happened to me when I was your age. My parents wanted me to have a normal human life, but, like you, I found myself on the evening news for saving a child from a car crash. They labeled me a hero."

Kennedy wiped some imaginary dirt off her shoulder and grinned. "I have hero status too."

Miles observed her. "You remind me of someone."

"Probably one of your glamorous co-stars."

He smirked. "Yeah, that's probably it... Anyway, the Institute changed my life. On Earth, I felt like an exposed nerve who needed to hide what I was at all costs, but at the Institute, I felt like I could celebrate what made me unique and refine it."

The screen on the wall switched to a class photo featuring thirty-three recruits of all different sizes and colors; one of them had lavender-colored skin, and another had the skin of an alligator. They all appeared to be in their late teens and wore royal blue Evolver suits.

"Can you guess which one is me?"

Kennedy pointed out a scrawny teen with Mile's complexion. "Aww, you were adorable."

"I was textbook awkward."

"Well, now you're my mom's celebrity crush, if it makes you feel any better."

"Hey, at least I've got that going for me." Miles pointed out a formidable girl who stood out among the others. Kennedy immediately identified her as Zuele. "There is your guardian; *should* you accept the position. Zuele has always been a pillar of excellence. Even then, she was an Evolver among Evolvers. You should be extremely flattered that Zuele personally chose you out of thousands of hopefuls to be her recruit."

Kennedy convulsed. "Why *me*?"

"Well, your humility for one." Miles looked at the class photo with fondness, as though it were transporting him back to the best time of his life. "That is another reason why you should go, Kennedy; you will make lifelong friends at the Institute. Additionally, you will have the opportunity to consciously reinvent yourself."

Kennedy tangled her fingers. "It feels like a pretty big decision."

"Yeah, but doesn't it also feel like a "hell yes" sort of decision?"

Kennedy smiled.

"So, what do you think? Does this sound like something you'd be interested in?"

"Can I get like a brochure or something?"

Miles laughed.

Then the golden footprints beneath Kennedy's feet began to blink.

"It looks like our time is just about up." Miles bowed to her. "It was an honor to encounter your energy, young creator. I sincerely hope our paths cross again." He shook her hand, but Kennedy barely felt it. Once again, the golden light swallowed her whole.

Reddick now stood before her. "Well?" he asked.

"That was Miles *effing* Pierce." She shook with excitement. "I just met Miles Pierce!"

Reddick laughed. "So, what do you think? Are you in?"

Kennedy did not even have to think about it a minute before she said, "Hell yes."

Reddick smiled a bittersweet smile.

"What's the matter?" she asked.

"Something's happened."

FIVE

The ten Evolvers inside the nerve center now moved at a frenzied pace, hauling out machinery and packing steel crates. Reddick spoke over the commotion: "Earlier today, an Evolver died after a rogue mission. Her name was Janekis Opris."

Kennedy thought it best to pretend she was hearing this information for the first time.

Reddick drew a screen in the air and projected the image of a violet-colored woman between them. She wore a black Evolver suit and had a determined expression. Kennedy attempted to touch the floating screen, but her hand only managed to pass through to the other side. One of the Evolvers halted at the image of Janekis. He solemnly formed his index fingers and thumbs into a triangle, then raised the triangle in a straight line from his chest to his lips to his forehead and sent the triangle up over his head.

"Janekis attempted to break into the Deepest Layer of Millintica," Reddick said.

"Isn't that where Zuele is from?" Kennedy asked.

"Yes, but she hasn't been there in years. No one can enter or exit that atmosphere. It is strictly forbidden and heavily guarded. But *somehow*, Janekis discovered a way in." Reddick stared reverentially at Janekis. "Millintica is home to the universe's most lethal army. They're called the Dark Panel."

"Why are they called the Dark Panel?"

"Because they judge you before executing you. Their faces are screens that can recall your greatest shame and play it for all to see." Reddick ran a hand through the screen he had created, and the image of Janekis evaporated from the room.

At that moment, Zuele entered the nerve center and slapped on a forced smile when she saw Kennedy. "How was your orientation?"

"It was good," Kennedy told her. "And I think I want to—"

Zuele stopped her. "Before you give me your answer, there is something you should know. Out of an abundance of caution, the Evolver Council has suspended all non-essential missions, effective immediately. They are withdrawing us ahead of schedule. We leave Tucson on Saturday."

"Saturday?" Kennedy yelped. "As in two days from today?"

Zuele nodded. "We require your final decision by tomorrow morning."

Kennedy shook her head, wondering why they had to leave so soon and how this could possibly affect them on Earth. Then she thought of what that man had told Zuele in the bathroom at her mother's work. "Who is King Malant?" Kennedy blurted out.

The Evolvers in the nerve center stopped what they were doing. Reddick tilted his head in Kennedy's direction. "How do you know about Malant?"

Kennedy looked to Zuele. "That guy in your hand mentioned him. Sorry, I didn't—I shouldn't have—I didn't mean to eavesdrop."

"It's okay, Kennedy." Zuele held up her hand, and a projection of a terrifying being emerged from it. He appeared to be more of a machine than a man. His face was a blank screen, with tubes framing the edges. Red lasers emerged like claws from his titanium suit's gloves. A chill ran down Kennedy's spine as she stared into the face of evil personified. "This is Malant Tarish, the unrightful King of Millintica. He released this statement earlier today."

Malant spoke in an alien language Kennedy could not understand; his incredibly layered voice sounded like five voices shrieking in unison.

"Malant called Janekis's failed attempt an act of war," Zuele said. "He believes the Evolvers sanctioned her actions and has promised retaliation."

"*Were* her actions sanctioned by the Evolvers?" Kennedy asked.

Zuele shook her head. "We cannot override the free will of any planet or any being. It is our highest law. This law is the reason why we stay neutral in most conflicts. We cannot protect planets from themselves, no matter how badly we may want to."

Reddick glared at Malant. "I am going to go pack," he said, and then left the room.

Kennedy watched as he walked away.

Once he was gone, Zuele said, "There are not many from our side of the universe who have not been directly impacted by Malant's treachery... Come on, we better get you home. You have a big decision to make." Zuele turned to one of the Evolvers.

"Would you please retrieve Kennedy's belongings for her?" Then Zuele twisted a white band around her ring finger.

When the Evolver returned with her shoes and backpack, Kennedy was lost in thought. He placed them inside a sack that matched the material of her suit. Zuele pulled up her sleeve and revealed two thin handcuffs clasped around her right wrist. "These are called Dematerialization Cuffs." She opened one of them. "Fair warning: this will take some getting used to." Zuele clasped the open cuff around Kennedy's wrist. A powerful energy emitted from the *now-blinding* white band on Zuele's ring finger, and then everything evaporated.

Suddenly, Kennedy felt formless, like electricity traveling through a wall socket. She floated inside a white light, and her identity vanished. Her life felt like nothing more than a dream someone once had. She momentarily basked in the white light's tranquility. Then the white light faded, and Kennedy felt herself quickly return to form. When she landed on her feet, she felt wobbly and quickly noticed that the suit was still intact, but her kitten socks were missing.

Zuele stabilized Kennedy. "Easy," Zuele said. "Give yourself a moment to get acclimated."

Kennedy realized they were now standing in her apartment's living room. She looked down at her body to make sure it was still in one piece. "How the—"

Zuele's ring turned a matte white color once again. "It's called Dematerialization." She unlocked the thin handcuff on Kennedy's wrist. "I wanted to give you a little preview of one of the things we'll be working on at the Institute. Evolvers usually only use this mode of transportation when we need to make a quick getaway."

Kennedy fell back onto her couch. "How did you do that?"

"Our technology is thousands of years ahead of yours here on Earth. It revolves around consciousness and our understanding of different dimensions, whereas Earth's still relies on linear thinking and outdated forms of energy. Explaining our technology to humans would be like returning to biblical times and telling them about wi-fi—they would have you committed. Primitive humans might even call it evil, just as they called the Wright Brothers for trying to fly."

"Where was that place with the white light?"

"Everywhere. It is the Eternal Energy Field."

Zuele's answer did not make sense to Kennedy, but then again, at the moment, nothing really did.

Phantom pranced down the hallway and sniffed Zuele. Kennedy found him in the desert four years ago; he had been so tiny that he fit inside her palm. Kennedy had to bottle-feed him for the first few weeks of his life. Roberta remarked that the gray patch of fur covering his right eye made him look like the *Phantom of the Opera,* so that's what Kennedy named him.

He crawled into her lap and let her adore him. "Hi, Bubba."

"Cute cat," Zuele said.

"He's the all-time cutiest," Kennedy scratched under his chin. "Aren't you, Bubba?" He collapsed against her chest and purred. Then Kennedy realized she would have to leave him, and her heart ached. The reality of her decision had finally begun to set in. "Will I be able to come home for the holidays?"

"Unfortunately, no."

"How long will I be gone for? I mean, how long does the program last?"

"It takes as long as it takes. Everyone learns differently. Some people, like Reddick, breeze through the program, but he has been training to be an Evolver from a very young age. Others take longer. On average, the program takes between three and five years. There is no judgment or rush."

Kennedy held Phantom tighter.

Zuele looked around the apartment and focused on some water damage in the top corner of the kitchen. Audrey was home, and Kennedy could hear her music thumping behind her closed bedroom door. She had done a fantastic job cleaning up after her friends—there was zero evidence that the apartment had been brimming with seniors only hours earlier.

Zuele lingered in front of a vision board, where Roberta had pinned magazine cutouts of her dream home, dream car, dream relationship, and dream vacation. Kennedy had begged her to take it down; she felt publicly displaying your innermost desires was a lot like wearing your heart on the outside of your chest. Zuele seemed to be intrigued by it. Kennedy didn't know why, after all, you could park three of the dream homes Roberta had been envisioning inside the one Zuele had been inhabiting for the past few months.

Kennedy cleared her throat. "One day, I want to buy her a house like that. I hate that she has to work so much. I helped out a little when I had my summer job. One day I hope to make enough money to support all of us..." A thought struck Kennedy and filled her with immediate anxiety. "I guess I should have asked sooner, but how much is this going to cost? I don't know if it's a scholarship thing or—"

"It won't cost you anything. In fact, we are going to pay you for your time."

Kennedy felt immediate relief. "Is there a way for me to send any of that money home?"

Zuele nodded. "I'll take care of it. Any other questions?"

"Do you think I might be able to find my dad while I'm there?"

"This can't be about anyone but you, Kennedy. Your father cannot be the reason why you decide to go."

Her father was the reason for everything she did, but she knew Zuele would never understand.

Kennedy heard her mother's keys jingle outside the door. When the front door opened, Phantom sprang from her lap and ran down the hall. Roberta still wore her uniform—a white button-up shirt with black slacks. She threw her keys on the coffee table, rolled up her sleeves, and removed the rubber band from her hair.

Kennedy crossed her arms and refused to look at her mother.

"Kennedy Ann Neff, I told you to stay out of the desert." Roberta gripped her waist and tapped one foot in Kennedy's direction.

"Seriously, mom?" Kennedy shot to her feet. "You've been lying to me for months!"

"You watch your tone, young lady!"

Zuele tried to bring down the temperature in the room. "I know this is a stressful situation."

"Not for me," Kennedy said. "I'm going. At least there, I won't be lied to."

"I never lied to you," Roberta said.

Kennedy threw her arms in the air. "You kept life-changing information from me!"

"What was I supposed to say, Kennedy?"

"Anything!"

"Anything?"

"Yes!"

"Well, why don't you just be the parent, then? You're obviously way better at it than I am."

Audrey opened her bedroom door and yelled. "Can you psychos keep it down?"

"Mind your effing business, Audrey!" Kennedy yelled back.

"You, like, seriously need professional help, Kennedy. You're like, legit unstable." Audrey slammed her door, and the picture frames on the wall shook.

Zuele looked severely uncomfortable, then confused by the sudden pounding coming from beneath her feet.

"That's just Mrs. Matheson," Roberta whispered. "She's our downstairs neighbor; she likes to pound her broom on the ceiling when we're loud." Roberta took a deep cleansing breath, walked to the kitchen, and poured herself a healthy glass of red wine. "Would you like one?" she asked Zuele.

Zuele shook her head.

Roberta took a deep sip of her wine and said, "Kennedy, I don't want to fight with you."

Kennedy found herself growing angrier by the minute. At first, she was angry because her mother had kept crucial information from her, but now she was angry because feeling her mother's anxiety was crowding out Kennedy's ability to feel her own.

Roberta sat down next to her. "I understand why you are upset with me, but I honestly didn't know how to tell you. These people wanted to take you to the other side of the universe. At first, I thought it was a joke, but they kept coming back." Roberta trailed off. "Anyway, they said the most gifted minds in the universe have gone to this Institute, and I know you're gifted, Kennedy. I've always known. I hate that you cannot be your true self. I hate that people can't see how special you are."

"I'm not special."

"Nedy, you can *see* energy."

"Which is exactly how I know I'm not special. I know for a fact we're all made of the same stuff."

Zuele gave Kennedy a proud look.

Roberta smiled affectionately at her daughter, and then her eyes filled with tears. "It's so hard watching you struggle. All I want to do is protect you. Protect you from bullies; protect you from harm. I wanted to protect you from this too, but I can't, and it kills me. It makes me feel—" Roberta's stifled sobs kept her from continuing.

Kennedy sat paralyzed, watching and feeling her mother's inner turmoil, experiencing that special kind of helplessness reserved for seeing a parent cry.

"I was trying to protect you," Roberta said. "I was trying to protect you from my mistake. I barely even knew your father, and now look where we are. This is all my fault."

Zuele stood. "I should give you two some time to talk." She turned to Roberta. "Unfortunately, we had to move up our departure date. We are now leaving on Saturday."

"Saturday? As in two days from today?" Roberta yelped, just like Kennedy had. "Nope. Absolutely not. No way. She's not going."

Kennedy was about to yell at her mom again when Zuele stepped in. "You two have a lot to discuss." She removed a small, chrome triangle with rounded corners from her pack and placed it on the coffee table. "This should be able to answer any questions you may have."

"What is it?" Kennedy asked.

"Technically, it is called a Communicator, but you can think of it as an acceptance letter." Zuele then Dematerialized into a cloud of particles, which instantly evaporated from the room.

"I don't think I'll ever get used to that." Roberta gulped more wine. "*Saturday*?" she repeated aloud.

"I want you to tell me about my father," Kennedy said. "Tell me everything." She thought her mother would flinch the way she always did when Kennedy asked about him, but this time Roberta didn't. A wistful smile spread across her face, and it was as though she had traveled someplace else inside her mind.

"He was just what I needed—exactly when I needed it." Roberta swirled her glass of red wine. "When Brian ran off with his paralegal, I was almost relieved. He gave me Audrey, and for that, I will always love him, but really, that's the only love I had for him. I married him because everyone else told me to. Let that be a lesson to you, Kennedy: sometimes you do what everyone else expects you to do and it still doesn't work out. It's a lot easier to accept your failures when they're actually yours."

Roberta took another sip of liquid courage. "I knew a divorce wouldn't look great on my record, but I was only twenty-seven, young enough to think there were endless options still ahead for me. So, I got in my car, and I drove to San Diego by myself. I think I cried the whole way there, but once I saw the ocean, I stopped. I felt like I was returning to myself. I fell asleep on the beach, and the tide was starting to come in, so he woke me up. I thought he was a dream; he was so good-looking. He told me his name was Aaron... We went and had a drink, and I remember his tattoo, his laugh, and his smile—you have his smile, you know."

"I know."

"He seemed to be carrying the weight of the world on his shoulders; at the time, I didn't know it was a different world... I think we were both trying to escape our realities. For us, being together felt simple, easy, and uncomplicated. Well, we tried to make it that way, but as the weekend went on..."

Kennedy leaned forward, eager for her mother to continue.

"I didn't think we shared any personal details, but there's this part of me that knows it isn't true. I have these dreams where we are back in that hotel room, and I am looking at him, and I just know everything there is to know about him, and he knows everything there is to know about me—the important stuff anyway. I have subsisted off the memory of him for so long; it has weakened, but the feeling of him hasn't. The feeling of him is still there." Roberta was currently reliving a deeply magical time in her life.

Kennedy squirmed. "Geez, Mom. Gross."

"Well, don't eavesdrop on what I'm feeling!"

"You need to be hosed down."

"Anyway!" Roberta lightly shoved her. "There are long stretches of that weekend I can't remember at all. It's as though they've been removed, or maybe my mind has mercifully forgotten them. When these people told me what he was and what you are, I knew. I think I've always known. I just have no idea how."

Kennedy frowned when she realized her father had modified her mother's memory. "I'm sorry," she said.

"Don't ever be sorry. You and your sister are the two best things that have ever happened to me." Roberta wiped away tears with her uniform's sleeve, staining it with mascara and concealer. She attempted to compose herself. "Okay." She inhaled and exhaled deeply. "Okay, Kennedy, if you want to go to space and learn to be an evolutionary—"

"—An Evolver."

"An Evolver, then you have my blessing. I won't stop you."

"Even if I have to leave in two days?"

Roberta swallowed hard. "Even if you have to leave in two days." Her hand trembled as she wiped away more tears. "You deserve to be somewhere where you're free to be your entire self. What more could a mother want for her child?"

Kennedy appreciated her words but knew there was zero conviction in them. Still, putting this monumental decision in Kennedy's hands was the most selfless thing Roberta had ever done for her, and that was saying something.

"I'm going," Kennedy said mostly to herself. "I have to go."

Roberta gazed at Kennedy with bloodshot eyes. Her voice cracked as she said, "Then I guess we'd better get you packed."

That night, as Roberta completed her nightly skin care routine, Kennedy sat in the closet and ran her fingers over the chrome, rounded triangle Zuele had given her. Its surface lightly electrocuted her fingertips. She pressed her thumbprint on top of it, and the triangle shook forcefully. Kennedy dropped it and ran out of the closet.

"What is it?" Roberta asked with a face full of unblended night cream.

Kennedy kept her eyes on the triangle that seemed to suck in the room, then spit it back out. Half a second later, a life-sized hologram of a woman turned solid in front of Kennedy and Roberta. The woman was well over six feet tall and had luminous ebony skin that glowed an eggplant color. She wore an ornate gown, dense with silver and gold filigree. She had coifed white hair, even though her face looked relatively young. Kennedy watched in astonishment while the woman took in her surroundings. "Hello, I am Philena Kirat, Chancellor of the Evolver Institute. I wanted to personally congratulate you on your acceptance and answer any questions you may have. These next few years will be the most formidable of your life. I am delighted you have decided to embark on this journey." Chancellor Kirat ran her gloved fingers across the bookshelf and then rubbed them together, checking for dust. "I love when they do that in the old human movies."

Kennedy and Roberta stared at her in utter amazement.

"Mom!" Audrey called from the hallway, then opened the

door. "Mom, have you seen my cut-offs?"

Chancellor Kirat addressed Audrey. "Hello, young creator."

Audrey let out a blood-curdling scream when she finally registered the six-foot, alien woman standing in front of her. Chancellor Kirat looked curiously at the ground beneath her as Mrs. Matheson banged the end of her broom into the ceiling. It was enough to shake Roberta from her reverie. "Audrey, I think I put those shorts in the dryer. Let's go look." Roberta dragged Audrey from the room, leaving Kennedy alone with her new Chancellor.

SIX

The next day, Kennedy returned to the Evolver house and underwent a series of tests to make sure she was healthy enough for space travel. Zuele rushed the process while the Evolvers hustled to scrub all the upgrades they had made to the Tucson home. Kennedy did her best to keep up with her guardian, Zuele, as she moved from room to room.

Chancellor Kirat had done a good job of fielding Kennedy's questions the night before. The Chancellor was jovial, wise, and extremely patient in answering Kennedy's basic and sometimes redundant questions. Kennedy was relieved to learn Symetra was an Earth-like planet. She told Kennedy of all the similarities—the continents, the weather, the comparable distance from its sun—and then she told Kennedy of the ways it differed: Symetra had three moons, which meant its oceans were a "little rowdier than Earth's." Symetrans also measured time differently: they referred to days as moons, months as progressions, and hours as segments—though the conversions were far from exact.

"Our technology will simplify all of this for you, don't you worry." Chancellor Kirat told Kennedy she would encounter beings of every size, shape, color, sexual orientation, and gender identity. The Chancellor said these things "were important and irrelevant at the same time."

Kennedy did not see Reddick that day. He was too busy saying goodbye to his many fans at Desert Hills High and playing his last football game with the Coyotes. Kennedy recalled working the concession stand and hearing his name over the loudspeaker. He seemed to go out of his way to make other players look good, or maybe it was his way of staying under the radar. Kennedy liked the way Reddick talked to everyone, even those far outside his realm of popularity.

"Kennedy," Zuele said, bringing her back into the room.

"Huh?"

"Here." Zuele handed Kennedy a gold St. Jude medallion on a thin chain. Her Nana Silvia gifted it to her on the day of her first holy communion. Roberta would never let her wear it because she always feared Kennedy would lose it. "I asked your mother for something that would remind you of home, and she gave me this. I embedded it, so beings can't read you, and you can't read them. Most of the beings over forty on Symetra have learned to control their thoughts and emotions, but our adolescents still have to go through their growing pains; this prevents those pains from being public."

Kennedy clasped the gold chain around her neck and looked down at the medallion. Her favorite saint had always been St. Jude, the patron saint of desperate cases and lost causes. Nana

Silvia told Kennedy that a lot of the saints had special powers, too. Kennedy took it as a compliment, until she found out most of them were beheaded, burned at the stake, or worse.

Then a sudden panic hit Kennedy. Had Reddick been able to read her this entire time? If so, he most definitely knew about the schoolgirl crush she had been harboring for him. "Does Reddick have to wear one of these, too?"

"Yes," Zuele said. "Why?"

Kennedy tried to hide her relief. "Just wondering."

Zuele then took staged photos of Kennedy, which would go on her new, sham social media account, documenting her time at an East Coast prep school. If anyone ever asked, this was the official reason for Kennedy leaving Tucson. All Roberta had to do was stick to her given script and direct them to the feed where they would find a computer-generated Kennedy on the East Coast with her computer-generated friends.

Zuele gave Kennedy the rest of the day off to spend with her family. She had a farewell lunch with her grandparents and tried not to cry as she hugged them goodbye, praying they would live forever so she would not feel so guilty about leaving. "Remember, Mija," Nana Silvia told Kennedy with proud tears in her eyes. "In this family, we outwork everyone. It's in our blood. If you do that, you'll be fine." Then she reiterated her point in Spanish.

Grandpa Jim agreed with his wife. "That's right, Nedy. You get out of life what you put into it." He squeezed Kennedy's shoulder. "And another thing: Never pay attention to what a boy says, only what he does. Better yet, don't pay attention to them at all. You just keep focused on your studies." Then he slipped her a hundred dollars, and Kennedy accepted it, though she was pretty sure she would not be able to spend it where she was going.

That night, Kennedy pretended not to see her mother wiping tears while she made pozole in the kitchen. The soup was a Christmas tradition, but since Kennedy would not be around then, Roberta made it early. Kennedy, who was unsure of what Symetrans ate, had two bowls.

Audrey sat across from Kennedy at the dinner table with her arms crossed. She was still furious that Roberta had refused to let her go out after the football game, which the Coyotes had, of course, won. "I'm finished. Can I be excused?"

"No," Roberta said.

"But I'm done eating, and you're the one that's always telling us to listen to our bodies."

"Audrey, there's something I think you should know," Roberta began.

Kennedy gaped at her mother in disbelief. Why was Audrey privy to information Kennedy herself had only received yesterday? Audrey had enough ammunition to make fun of her little sister *without* knowing she was part alien.

"That woman you saw last night is the Chancellor of Kennedy's new school."

"You mean Kennedy's new 'prep school'?" Audrey used aggressive air quotes. "Are all the women in 'Connecticut' purple giants?"

"Audrey, you, and I both know Kennedy can do things that norm—most people can't do. Do you ever wonder why she can do those things?" Roberta asked.

"Because she's a freak."

"You're the freak!" Kennedy shouted.

"At least I don't spend all my time hiding in the desert. I swear you're like a serial killer or something."

Kennedy slammed her hand on the table.

"Girls, please!" Roberta searched for her next words: "Audrey, Kennedy's father was not from here."

Audrey swiped at her cellphone's screen. "What do you mean? Where was he from, like, another country or something?"

"No," Roberta said. "Kennedy's father was born in a different galaxy; he is from another planet."

Audrey dropped her cellphone mid-text and stared listlessly at her mother. "But he *looked* human, right?"

"I guess a lot of them do." Roberta grabbed Kennedy's hand. "Like Kennedy, she is gifted, and there are people, important people, who believe in her gifts."

Audrey glared at her little sister, and for the first time in Kennedy's life, she could feel jealousy emanating from her.

"Kennedy has gained acceptance into the Evolver Institute. It's extremely far away."

"Are you trying to tell me that Kennedy is going to a different planet tomorrow?"

"Yes."

Audrey threw her head back in scornful laughter. "Wow, that is hilarious."

"It's not funny," Kennedy said.

"It's pretty funny. I guarantee you're going to be a freak there, too."

"Don't speak to your sister like that," Roberta warned.

"She's only my half-sister, and apparently she's also an alien—I knew it, by the way." Audrey bobbled her head in contempt, but her outward behavior and her inner experience were two different things. Without her emotion blocker on, Kennedy could feel what her sister was feeling, and right now, Audrey was dealing with a terrible bout of not-enoughness. It was an experience with which Kennedy was intimately familiar.

"You're good at other things." Kennedy tried to comfort her big sister.

"Oh, shut up, Kennedy."

"Audrey!" Roberta yelled.

"What, Mother? I'm leaving. I can't handle this."

"Audrey, get back here!"

"You just told me that my sister is an alien. I'm sorry if I'm a little freaked out. And I'm sorry if I don't want to sit here and talk about my *feelings* with the two of you! Would you please just leave me alone?" Audrey stormed off, and Kennedy's heart ached for her. Audrey had always been the special one. It was her whole identity. Sure, Kennedy got better grades than Audrey, but that was obviously because Kennedy had no social life. She was not the captain of the cheerleading squad *or the* homecoming queen. No, Audrey was the special one, and there was nothing anyone could do to convince her otherwise.

"She'll come around," Roberta said, before the pounding of Mrs. Matheson's broom shook the ground beneath them.

Kennedy could not sleep that night. The excitement and fear were gnawing at her. She tossed and turned. Her dreams were scattered. She had different visions of what the next day would look like; she just hoped none of them were accurate. After a long night of little rest, Kennedy woke up and prepared for a day that would change her life forever. She was riddled with anxiety, and the thought of leaving her mother and Phantom brought tears to her eyes so instantaneously that she had to think other thoughts, faraway thoughts.

She sat on the closet floor, and Phantom collapsed in her lap, purring as she scratched under his chin. "I'm going to miss you, Bubba," she said through tears. "I'm sorry, but I have to go. I *have* to. My mom's going to take good care of you. I gave her a list of instructions. She knows to play string with you and give you whipped cream at Thanksgiving, but not too much, or you'll get all snotty."

Roberta walked into the closet. Phantom jumped out of Kennedy's lap and scurried under the bed. Roberta stared at Kennedy's red, roller suitcase as though it would be her final resting place. "There's a male model waiting for you in our living room," she said.

Kennedy smirked and wiped her eyes. "I was just saying bye to Phantom."

Roberta placed a hand on the side of her daughter's face. "I'll take care of him. He likes me—not as much as he likes you—but he'll be fine. We'll all be fine, even you." She rolled Kennedy's suitcase behind her down the hall, making sure to pound on Audrey's door as she did. "Kennedy's leaving. Get up!"

Kennedy made her way mistily down the hall, silently saying goodbye to everything she had ever known. She walked out and found Reddick standing alone in her living room. "Where's Zuele?" she asked.

"She had to tie up a few loose ends. She's going to meet us at the station."

Audrey stumbled out in her pajamas and screamed at the sight of Reddick standing in the living room. "What are *you* doing here?"

"I am here to pick up Kennedy."

Audrey fixed her hair. "But Kennedy is going away today."

"I know," he smiled. "I am the one taking her."

"So, you are a—"

"That's right." He grinned before carrying Kennedy's suitcase outside.

Audrey stood in shock. "I can't believe Reddick Vincent is an *alien*."

"He's a Symetran," Kennedy corrected her.

Audrey rolled her eyes. "Mom, can I please go back to bed now?"

"Say goodbye to your sister first."

Audrey reluctantly obeyed and wrapped a lazy arm around Kennedy. She was about to remove her arm when Kennedy pulled her in for a tighter embrace. Audrey, surprisingly, did not pull away.

Kennedy could feel her sister's smile pressing against her cheek.

"Give em' hell, Nedy." And then Audrey patted Kennedy's shoulder, signaling that the tender moment was over.

Reddick returned and called out to Audrey before she headed back to her room, "Audrey?"

"Yes?" she replied, all smiles.

"I'd appreciate it if you didn't tell everyone about this. They all think I went back to New York."

"Like anyone would believe the truth anyway." Audrey said this before disappearing around the corner.

Reddick turned to Kennedy, melting her with his gorgeous face. "Do you have everything?"

She could not read what he was feeling. Could he be anywhere near as nervous as she was? "Yes, that's about it."

"It was wonderful to meet you, Ms. Neff," Reddick said.

"You too, Reddick, take care of my baby."

"I will."

Roberta grabbed his arm. "Promise me that you will not let anything happen to her, or so help me, God, I will find a way to build my own rocket ship and beat the—"

"Mom!" yelled a mortified Kennedy.

"I promise." Reddick laughed. "I'll give you two a moment. Take as long as you need." Kennedy watched as he walked out the door. The second it closed behind him, she threw her arms around her mother and cried.

"Kennedy, you don't have to go if you don't want to."

"It's not that." Kennedy pulled away and tried to make light of the situation. "I just feel bad for leaving you here with Audrey. She's not always the most pleasant person to live with."

"She'll be fine once she gets past this stage—this monstrous, awful, demonic stage. One day, you two will be the best of friends. I guarantee it. I went through the same thing with my sisters, and now I like them—most of them." Roberta walked to the kitchen counter and grabbed a notebook and some flair pens. "Here, I got you a little something."

The notebook had a flying saucer and a little green alien on it, with one word across the top in all caps: BELIEVE.

"I thought it was kind of funny," Roberta said.

Kennedy smirked. "It is. Thanks, Ma." She zipped the notebook and flair pens inside her backpack.

Roberta grabbed her and squeezed her tight. "I am so proud of you, Kennedy." Roberta openly sobbed. "I am so, so proud. I love you."

"I love you, too, Mom."

Roberta insisted on walking Kennedy to the car. Kennedy eventually had to pry herself from Roberta's grasp to get inside. She gave her mom a sorrowful wave and then fastened her seatbelt. Kennedy kept busy in order to prevent the dramatic crying fit that was threatening to overtake her. She refused to look back at Roberta, even though she knew her mother would stand there until they were completely out of sight. In fact, she refused to look up at all for the first few miles.

"You should put on some music," Reddick said, once again trying to distract her. "Your choice."

Kennedy almost buckled under the pressure of such a request.

It was a personal thing, sharing a song with someone else. She knew that whichever song she chose was not just a song, but a representation of her. There were so many different ways she could go. She finally rose to the occasion by pulling out her phone and playing 'D'yer Mak'er' by Led Zeppelin. Reddick gave her an emphatic nod of approval and turned it up as loud as it would go. Prince's '7' was next on her shuffle, and Kennedy silently praised the shuffle gods, who seemed to be on her side for the time being.

"I love Prince," he yelled over the music.

Kennedy concluded that their shared love of Prince meant they were soulmates. "Makes sense," she yelled back. "I'm pretty sure he was from a different planet, too."

Kennedy had never before seen her hometown through the windshield of a boy's car. It felt incredibly different yet looked exactly the same. There was a memory on every corner, but none like this. This was a new memory, and it made Kennedy feel like life might still have more surprises in store for her—magical surprises rather than catastrophic ones.

"I just have to make one quick stop before we leave," Reddick said as he pulled into the Eegee's drive-thru. If it had been a weekday, Eegee's would have been packed with upperclassmen enjoying sandwiches and ranch fries during their lunchbreaks, but today was a slow day. Reddick ordered a strawberry Eegee—a frozen drink with real fruit inside. Kennedy ordered a Piña Colada Eegee and tried to pay him for it, but he refused her money.

When they were back on the road and Reddick was halfway through with his Eegee, he said, "Wanna swap?"

Reddick handed her his Eegee, and she gave him hers. Kennedy blushed when she brought his spoon to her mouth. She had never really spent much time with boys before, other than her cousins, and they didn't count. She had experienced exactly two kisses in her life: one in the seventh grade, before she was widely considered a freak, and the second with a golf caddie named Ryan last summer at her job. She did not even want to think about how many girls Reddick had kissed.

Kennedy chanced a look at his perfect profile. He was a full-frontal attack on all her senses—the way he smelled, the way he looked, the way he sounded. She wanted to reach out and touch his skin, just to see what it felt like—which made her feel like the creepiest person alive. He intimidated her. Everything about him intimidated her. A small scar on his left eyebrow was his only physical flaw. He seemed to be completely oblivious to his own perfection—Kennedy only wished that she could be, too.

They passed Roberta's real estate office, and Kennedy was back to fighting tears.

"Are you okay?" he asked, his lips and tongue stained red from his strawberry Eegee.

"I'll be fine once we get out of Tucson."

Reddick floored it. "Then let's get out of here."

Kennedy grinned. "What if you get a speeding ticket?"

"What if I don't?" He stretched out his long legs and said, "Look, I hate to be the one to tell you this, but you're using it wrong."

"Huh?"

"*What if* is a very powerful tool of creation." He opened the sunroof, and warm September air flooded inside the car. "*What if* this is the last time I ever get to drive this beautiful car down this beautiful road with this beautiful company?"

Kennedy beamed at him.

It was the exact reaction he was looking for. "*What if* today is the best day of my life? *What if* everything is constantly working out in my favor? *What if* something amazing is on the verge of happening? I could go on and on. You see my point?"

"Not really."

"Only use *what if* to get yourself into a better state; never use it to get yourself into a worse one."

Kennedy's phone shuffled to 'Golden Slumbers' by the Beatles, and Kennedy stopped it. "Nope. You have to hear the whole thing. I might not be able to show you the Taj Mahal or the Giza Pyramids, but I can show you the long medley."

He smiled at her frenzied expression. "Why do you love the Beatles so much?"

She gave him a cock-eyed look, as though he were the one acting crazy. "Um, the same reason I love air and water so much—I need them to live. The Beatles are one of the greatest things that's ever happened on this planet. If there was some alien force out there getting ready to blow up the Earth, I would play the Beatles for them, and they would give us another chance, guaranteed." She scrolled through her cell phone. "Their music is a study of the highest frequencies. They tapped into something bigger than themselves. They were soul shakers. And I don't think they even consciously knew they were doing it. They seemed to be having so much fun, and then when it stopped being fun, they broke up. Of course, Yoko was blamed for it. Women are always blamed for everything." Kennedy took a beat to explain that Yoko had been John's wife. "But that's yet another reason why I love the Beatles; Paul and John both married strong women and shared the stage with them." She took a deep breath. "Ok, I'm going to shut up now so you can listen to the long medley. I want to hear what you think."

"Am I going to be quizzed on this?" he asked.

"Absolutely."

They turned onto Tangerine Road and headed out of Oro Valley towards Interstate 10. Saguaros flashed by as Reddick sped along. Kennedy clutched her heart when 'You Never Give Me Your Money' began to play. She mouthed the words and was incredibly jealous that Reddick was getting to experience it for the first time. During 'Sun King', the sun emerged from behind a cloud. Kennedy took it as a positive omen, and then they kept getting green lights—another good sign. When 'Mean Mr. Mustard' started, Kennedy nodded her head and tapped her feet, not being able to help it. By the time 'She Came in Through the Bathroom Window' started she was dancing in her seat. Then 'Golden Slumbers' hit, and Kennedy was back to clutching her heart. Her spirit soared along with Paul's voice, as it always did. It shot out of her body and expanded to fill the entire car and the entire road ahead of and behind them. She looked in Reddick's rearview mirror at the Santa Catalina's and realized she would miss those mountains nearly as much as her family. Standing in the shadow of those mountains, she knew exactly who she was. But she had no idea where she was going or who she was about to become. This was a life moment, a life moment with the perfect soundtrack. She blinked the tears from her eyes during 'Carry That Weight' and forgot Reddick was even in the car when 'The End' started. The medley lasted for the entire length of Tangerine Road.

The car next to them had a license plate that read KAN-819—Kennedy's initials—one more positive omen. The omens somehow meant Kennedy had chosen the right path. The omens assured her, despite her fear and anxiety, that she was in the right place.

SEVEN

"Wow." Reddick exhaled when the long medley ended. "Okay, I get your obsession now," he said, merging onto the I-10. "How do you know so much about old music?

"My grandpa Jim used to manage radio stations back in the day," she said. "He educated me on all the greats... Frank Sinatra, Ella Fitzgerald, Aretha Franklin, Stevie Wonder, Johnny Cash... He has a room full of vinyl in his house; he said he left it for me in his will because I'm the only one who appreciates it." Kennedy jabbered on about how many famous people her grandfather had met and how many perks he had received in his job, and how he first saw her Nana Silvia at an Eagles concert while 'Witchy Woman' was playing under a full moon, and how he had been under her spell ever since.

She told Reddick about her Nana, who was from Chihuahua and had taught ESL for thirty years at Pima Community College. She told him her mother was the second-oldest of their five daughters. She told him how her tías would always get up and do the cumbia at family parties and make Kennedy do it, too. She told him about her cousins and how the older ones were now spread out across the country. "Having so many grandchildren in college is the greatest joy of my Nana's life. She can't even talk about it without crying... I wonder what she would think about me going to school on the other side of the universe."

Reddick watched her.

"I'm sorry," she apologized.

"For what?"

"Talking so much."

"Don't be. I like when you talk."

Kennedy blushed. "What about you? What's your family like?"

He shifted uncomfortably in his seat.

"Do you have any brothers or sisters?" she asked.

"I have an older brother, and I have twin sisters from my father's second marriage."

"What about your mom? Did she get remarried, too?"

He shook his head. "My mom died when I was little."

Kennedy did her best to remove the foot lodged in her mouth. "I'm sorry."

"It's fine," he said, as though he were trying to convince himself more than her.

She was surprised when he continued.

"After Malant killed King Rimago, he sent all of Rimago's loyalists to a lunar military base called The Crater, where he enslaved them and basically starved them. When my mother found out, she organized this elaborate rescue mission. She managed to free hundreds of them before Malant caught and killed her." Reddick white-knuckled the steering wheel. "I was five at the time."

Kennedy fought the urge to put her hand on his arm. "Sounds like she was pretty brave."

"The bravest." Then Reddick went somewhere else in his mind, and Kennedy felt it was her turn to distract him, so she decided she would ask another question, one far removed from this sad subject. Kennedy mentally sifted through questions straight from a teen compatibility quiz. She couldn't ask his astrological sign because he was from a different solar system. *Favorite color?* Lame. *Favorite food?* She wasn't sure she wanted to know. *Favorite movie? Did they even have movies on Symetra?* Yes, this was what she would ask.

But Reddick asked her a question first. "Do you ever wonder how you'd be different if you'd had a father?"

Kennedy considered his question carefully. Her Grandpa Jim was the only man she ever really had in her life. Men were a completely foreign species to Kennedy, not as exotic as women, but powerful. Their power was the reason they were considered protectors, but it was also the reason Roberta had given Kennedy pepper spray at the age of twelve.

Kennedy could feel how men responded to her mother and sister. Some of them admired Roberta and Audrey's attractiveness from afar, but others felt entitled to it. It sickened Kennedy. If she had a father, she would not feel so responsible for protecting them. If she had a father, maybe he would be the one standing guard, not her.

Kennedy recalled a time at the Tucson Mall when a creeper followed her and Audrey inside the parking garage. Kennedy could feel his disgusting energy and urged Audrey to walk faster. She thought about alerting a security guard, but as they passed one, the guard leered at Audrey the same way the creeper had. They were nearly to their car when Kennedy turned to confront him. She told Reddick the story.

"What did you say to him?" he asked.

"I told him to leave us alone, and he said he didn't mean to scare us. Then he looked at Audrey's shopping bag and asked her what she bought because his sister was about the same size and had a birthday coming up. He kept getting closer and closer, so I held up the pepper spray on my sister's keychain and told him I would spray the hell out of him if he took one more step."

"What happened then?"

Kennedy shrugged. "He called me a bitch and walked away."

Reddick wore a horrified expression.

Kennedy thought deeper. "I think if I had a father, he would have taught me how to walk around this world like I had a right to be in it. I think I would have felt *safer*." She smirked. "As much as it pains me to admit it as a feminist, I suppose there is some benefit to male energy."

He laughed. "It is gracious of you to say so."

"Still, I hate that most men are physically stronger than women."

"It's all perspective. Women are strong enough to grow and push a life out of them; men can barely survive leg day."

Kennedy locked her face into an enamored smile. "How do you think you'd be different? If your mother would have been around."

He rubbed the back of his neck. "You say your world would

have felt safer; I think mine would have felt... warmer. Does that make sense?"

Kennedy nodded. "It makes a lot of sense."

"Rantrin, my guardian, says I have this irrational fear that eventually everyone is going to leave me."

"That is irrational."

He looked at her.

"Who would ever be crazy enough to leave you?" She said this aloud, even though she had only meant to think it.

Reddick blushed.

Kennedy immediately tried to recover. "So, do you guys have movies on Symetra?"

Reddick seemed embarrassed, too. "Our movies are a little different than yours. Instead of sitting and watching the story, you can actually step into it. You can be the star or a minor character, depending on your mood. It's called Syncrocperience. You're going to love it... I'll have to take you sometime."

"Seriously, you will?" Her voice went up an octave and cracked with excitement. "I mean, um, yeah, okay, whatever, no big deal." Kennedy tangled her fingers in her lap, desperately searching for an ounce of coolness hidden within the awkward trenches of her personality. "So, is it like virtual reality?"

"No, like actual reality. You won't be able to tell the difference. Syncrocperience suits come with ripcords, just in case the story gets too intense—which, let's face it, the good ones always do."

Kennedy twitched with eager anticipation. A whole new planet, a whole new way of life, and a whole new way of thinking awaited her. And for a few blissful moments, her fear gave way to a magnificent sense of unadulterated wonder.

The airstrip was at the end of a dirt road halfway between Tucson and Phoenix. A Midwest Airlines 747, an opulent G8, and a giant plane called The Demolition Dame sat on its edge. The Demolition Dame looked like it had not seen action since World War II. A painted pin-up girl winked from the plane's nose, and several bullet holes punctured her beautiful, handcrafted face.

Airfield engineers wearing gloves, high-vis vests, and headsets exited a portable trailer on one side of the dusty airfield and took Kennedy's bags from her. "Are they Evolvers, too?" she asked Reddick.

"No, they are Nextiers. Nextiers blend us in. Before I arrived on Earth, I had to study with a Nextier for a few progressions. They make us appear human and work tirelessly to camouflage our advanced technology. For example, these planes look ordinary right?" Reddick shook his head. "The Evolvers designed these planes to fly at high altitudes and remove carbon dioxide from the atmosphere."

"How do they do that?"

"You can learn a lot from trees, Kennedy."

Kennedy liked that he said things such as, "You can learn a lot from trees." And she *especially* liked when he said her name.

Reddick stared at the planes with a gleam in his eye. "I am going to be a pilot when I graduate." Kennedy wanted to know when and why he decided to be a pilot, but before she could ask,

Reddick pointed to the Demolition Dame. "The Nextiers retro-fitted this one. Isn't it incredible?"

Kennedy's gaze shifted from the plane to him. "Yes."

Just ascending the stairs into the Demolition Dame made Kennedy woozy. Their footsteps echoed throughout the empty, cavernous, gutted interior of the plane. A single row of bolted-down chairs, hanging canvas sheets, and a large copper-colored crate occupied the back of it. The entire place reeked of mildew, which did not exactly inspire confidence in Kennedy.

Then she felt a clammy hand grab hers. A gangly man in his twenties proceeded to jerk her hand back and forth like a saw. "Hoper Morrow, pleasure to encounter your energy, Missus." There was definitely something off with this guy, and it wasn't just his clothing—a tuxedo shirt with board shorts and dress shoes. He blinked his eyes, as if he had to consciously remind himself to do so. "Weather," he told Kennedy.

"Excuse me?"

Reddick stepped in to help. "Hoper, you're supposed to talk *about* the weather, not just *say* weather. Why aren't you using your Lengualizer?"

What's a Lengualizer? thought Kennedy.

"I'm trying to learn without it." Hoper tried again. "The weather is blowing."

Reddick continued to help him. "No, that's the wind; the wind is blowing. You would say it is windy."

"What a waste of time. Anyone with basic senses can feel the weather blowing. Why state something so obvious?" Hoper directed his next question at Kennedy. "Why do you humans feel the need to talk about this?"

Kennedy shrugged. "We call it small talk."

"Small it definitely is," Hoper said. "Missus, please come; the pilot would like to meet your acquaintances." Hoper walked her to the cockpit, where a woman with an afro and a constellation of freckles adorning her honey cheeks greeted Kennedy. "Missus, this is Eka Mint."

Eka extended a hand to Kennedy. "Pleasure, Ms. Neff."

Kennedy shook her hand. "So, what's it like flying this thing?"

"We'll see," Eka said. "It's my first time." She began randomly hitting buttons. "*Oh*, that's what that does... Wait, no, I don't know. This is so confusing."

Kennedy's smile slid down to her chin.

Eka slapped her knee and fell back, laughing in her seat. "I'm joking! I've been flying the Dame for years." Eka patted the instruments.

"Eka is one of the best pilots in the Evolver Legion," Reddick said. "She's the recipient of the seven-pointed star, the highest honor a Legionnaire can receive. She shot down a Millintican ship as it approached Camaven's atmosphere and saved an entire city of civilians they were targeting."

"Oh, stop." Eka waved him off. "You're making me blush. I just did what any *superior* being would have done in the same situation." Eka turned back to the control board, and playtime was suddenly over. Kennedy watched as Eka prepared the plane for takeoff. She was so adroit and so poised. Kennedy took a mental picture of her, hoping one day to be half as exceptional as the flesh-and-blood action figure that was Eka Mint.

"Come on, let's get you suited up," Reddick said. He walked to the mock dressing rooms set up near the back of the plane and yanked open one of the dusty, green canvas sheets. Behind it, an alien metal suit stood rigidly on its own. It looked like copper, but its surface moved in intricate patterns, and an effervescent aura pulsated around it.

"Whoa!" was all Kennedy could say when she saw it.

Reddick presented her with a folded, tan Evolver suit. "Put this on underneath."

"Sorry, I'm late!" a voice called out from the plane's entrance. A beautiful blonde girl glided towards them; Kennedy immediately recognized her from Reddick's corkboard. The girl extended a perfectly manicured hand as though it were Kennedy's honor to meet her. "I'm Corijean Cabrin, Phase Three. I'm sure Reddick has told you all about me. Don't believe any of it!" She winked at him and smiled a dazzling smile. "You must be Kennedy Ness."

Kennedy corrected her: "Neff."

"Right, sorry, language barrier," Corijean replied in perfect English.

Kennedy was grateful her emotion blocker could hide her intimidation.

"What are you doing here?" Reddick asked, while Corijean straightened out one long, dangly earring on her right lobe. "I missed you," she pouted, and then hugged him for an uncomfortable amount of time.

A jealous energy seized Kennedy's chest. She grabbed the tan Evolver suit from Reddick and beelined it into her dressing room. She yanked the green canvas curtain shut and immediately sneezed at the dust that billowed from it. After putting on the tan Evolver suit, she pried open a slit on the side of the alien metal suit and was eventually able to squeeze herself inside its small opening. Little sensors inside the metal suit did a thorough appraisal of her entire being. Kennedy grabbed her clothes off the hook and inched heavily out of the dressing room.

"I'll seal you up, Missus." Hoper approached her with a drill-like device, and when he pressed its trigger, a needle-thin laser sprang from its tip. "Whatever you do, Missus, don't move." Tiny sparks flew as he welded the suit shut. Kennedy felt a small prick at the back of her skull, and that was the moment she became the suit's master. It now reacted to Kennedy's thoughts, like it was an extra appendage.

"All done, Missus." He grabbed Kennedy's pile of clothes and then noticed her distress. "You are going to do great, Missus. Hoper knows it."

His encouragement meant the world to Kennedy. "Thank you, Hoper."

"Hoper knows," he repeated.

Reddick exited his dressing room and effortlessly welded himself into his own suit.

"Do me," Corijean said, unnecessarily holding up her long, corn silk hair and exposing her neck to him. While Reddick obliged Corijean, Hoper strapped Kennedy into one of the bolted-down chairs.

Eka blared Bob Marley's 'Could You Be Loved' over the loudspeaker and danced inside the cockpit. She sang at the top of her lungs and fired up the deafening engines. Hoper danced and clapped off-beat beside her. Kennedy tapped her feet anxiously and tried to get comfortable in the unyielding suit. Reddick placed a reassuring hand on Kennedy's arm, while Corijean fought to get his attention back on her.

The Demolition Dame taxied down the chewed-up runway, then made its earsplitting ascent. Eka casually manned—rather, womanned—the relic of a plane, while Hoper kept his bug eyes on the controls. The enormous aircraft dropped several times as it caught air, taking Kennedy's stomach with it. She concentrated on Bob Marley's ethereal voice blaring over the loudspeaker, then closed her eyes and tried to get some rest. This continued for the first two hours or so of the flight. When Kennedy finally opened her eyes, she could see the Pacific Ocean stretched out on all sides of the plane. She spotted the large copper-colored crate in the corner. "What's that?" she asked Reddick.

"That's where all the luggage is," he said.

"Oh, why's it in there?"

"So, it doesn't get wet."

"Why would it get—" Kennedy looked down at her matching copper suit and felt a sudden urge to cry.

"Approaching drop zone." Eka announced over the loudspeaker.

Reddick unbuckled Kennedy's seatbelt. She tried to put it back on, but he held her hands in place. He pushed a button on her wrist, and her suit extended to cover her hands with gloves. "Trust me, Kennedy, this is fun." He pressed another button near her neck, and a thick, clear helmet emerged from her collar. She shook her head fervently inside the helmet, begging him not to make her do it.

"Approaching the drop zone in ten... nine..." Eka counted down.

Kennedy felt the floor slowly shifting beneath her. She looked to Reddick, who had an eager smile stretched across his face.

The gears churned beneath her feet.

Her heart pounded. She swore she would never make it to Symetra alive; she would die of a heart attack way before. In fact, she was almost praying to, as clouds became visible through the shifting floor. The clear helmet was supplying her with waves of oxygen, but she still could not find the air.

The glee was evident in Eka's voice. "Six... five... four..."

Hoper turned around and waved at Kennedy from the front of the plane. "Bye, Missus!"

"Three... two..."

The plane's floor was now in full downward tilt.

"One!"

The bolted-down chairs stayed.

Kennedy did not.

EIGHT

Kennedy fell backwards and caught air. When she looked up, she realized that the plane had completely vanished. Her arms flailed as she struggled to turn herself around. Once she did, she regretted it because she could see the deep blue ocean far beneath her. They had to be almost thirty thousand feet up. Her heart felt like it was in her throat. She was too scared to even cry. There was no way she would survive this fall without a parachute. She screamed inside her helmet. They were in the middle of nowhere—only the ocean for hundreds of miles on either side of them. The feeling was completely unnatural. No rush, just pure fear.

Suddenly, her alien suit made contact with something far below, and instead of falling, she found herself tearing through the air at a speed three times faster than before. She heard Corijean howling in excitement, several feet away from her. Kennedy hoped she would survive just so she could punch her in the face. She kept her eyes on the beautiful horizon and tried to make this the last image she saw before her inevitable and painful death.

As she approached the water—which, at this speed, would surely be a brick wall—Roberta came to mind. Kennedy pushed her mother's face away and cursed her sixteen-year-old heart for being strong and healthy; she wished it would just say uncle as she braced for the fatal impact.

This is going to be a terrible death, she thought.

The luggage crate hit the ocean's surface first.

Kennedy prayed that there was a heaven, and that God would grant her lackluster soul admission. She always believed there was one, but nothing tests that belief more than staring death in the face. She yearned for that moment of surrender she had felt in other people, but so far it had eluded her.

She was about twelve feet from certain death when the force pulling her began to slow, allowing her to sputter towards the water. Her alien suit magically decelerated at the very last moment and hit the surface with an uncomfortable thud.

Kennedy, Reddick and Corijean sank a few meters beneath the surface. Kennedy futilely tried to swim back up, but Reddick shook his head, and then he pointed down.

A voice inside Kennedy's suit said, "Activating Pressure Sphere," and the effervescent aura around it expanded, trapping Kennedy inside a snow globe of alien energy.

Kennedy still tried to swim up. She felt like a goldfish trapped in a plastic bag of water; she had zero control over her direction.

The force dragged them deeper, like a tractor beam pulling their suits to the ocean floor. Graphic images of sharks tearing Kennedy from limb to limb played inside her mind.

Reddick was still grinning.

Kennedy contemplated giving him the finger.

Fish, wise enough to avoid the magnet, crowded the ocean, forming a tunnel around Kennedy and the others as they sank deeper and deeper.

Even with the protective sphere, the suit throbbed as the drastic pressure change attempted to obliterate it. Kennedy could sense the power struggle and felt as though her head might explode. The suit squeezed her one minute, then expanded itself the next, providing her with only momentary relief as the struggle continued.

It was now pitch black, save for the green lights shining from their suits.

They continued into the deep, chilling darkness.

Then the tractor beam stopped, and the three of them stalled miles beneath the surface. Reddick's smile vanished. Kennedy began to shiver in the freezing water. Her suit vibrated and released little bursts of heat, but it was not enough to keep her from shivering. The suit was working overtime, and Kennedy knew if anything happened to it, she would be dead in less than a second.

It was eerily quiet; all she could hear was her own shaky breathing and the sound of her racing pulse. Reddick seemed to be upset by her apparent distress. Meanwhile, she was upset that he had the audacity to even look at her. She was going to die, and it was all his fault. She continued to quake inside the alien suit.

Kennedy could not remember ever being so uncomfortable or so scared. She took back that thing she'd said about dying from the fall; this was infinitely worse. Her mind went back to her mother, and Kennedy wondered how Roberta would react to the news of her daughter's unceremonious burial at sea.

She thought of her father—the unfinished business of her life. Sure, she was upset about all the other things she would miss out on; she didn't think much about marriage or having children, but it was something she *assumed* she would do in the future. It struck her as unfair—and even cruel—that someone could die with their dreams still inside them. She was filled with an immense sense of guilt for wasting her precious life and found herself apologizing inside her helmet. "I'm sorry," she whispered to the Eternal Energy Field she emanated from, but the apology only pushed her further away from it. Kennedy knew the quickest and easiest way to get into that energy field—that magnificent place from which everything springs—was to love. Her thoughts turned to love—love for her mother, love for her sister, love for her grandparents, love for her cat, love for her sanctuary. If Kennedy did call any of her powers "super," it would be this one: her ability to direct her thoughts. Everyone has this ability, but for Kennedy, it was a lifeline.

Reddick and Corijean began to communicate with hand signals.

And then they waited.

A few excruciating minutes later, the tractor beam resumed its pull. Kennedy was feeling dizzy as they sank. Everything was starting to get blurry. That's when she saw a cluster of lights—bright, blue spotlights aimed directly at them. The closer they got, the larger and brighter the lights became. They were so bright that Kennedy had to close her eyes, and even then, they burned. The tractor beam's power intensified; it was now pulling them through the thick layer of blue light. It wrestled with the power of the blue light until the tractor beam won. She heard a suction sound. Then the three of them fell through a dry tunnel and landed in a pool—an actual pool—the kind people had built into their backyards in Tucson.

A Japanese man—whose skunky hair suggested he might have been struck by lightning several times—retrieved Kennedy from the water. He retracted her helmet and patted her on the back. The vertigo claimed her equilibrium, and if he had not been there to catch her, she would have fallen flat on her face.

"How was the trip down?" he asked, with a big goofy grin. "I'm Toshiro. Welcome to the Submerged Station."

Kennedy realized she had to throw up but could barely move in the heavy suit. She toppled over and then propped herself up on all fours. Toshiro placed a wastebasket in front of her, and Kennedy dry-heaved over it while he checked her vitals.

"You good?" Reddick asked her.

"Are you crazy?" she screamed. Kennedy struggled to her feet while the room spun rapidly around her, then she immediately fell to her knees again and covered her eyes.

Reddick knelt beside her. "Just give it a minute. It'll pass."

Kennedy panted and kept her gaze on the ground, wanting nothing more than to rest her cheek against its cool, concrete surface. "You could've warned me."

"You wouldn't have come if I had warned you. We've learned that the hard way."

"What is this place?"

"This is where we leave Earth."

"What do you mean you *leave* Earth? How can you leave

Earth from the bottom of the ocean? It's not humanly possible."

He grinned. "You're right, it's not *humanly* possible."

"I think I'm going to be sick again."

"Here." He moved the wastebasket even closer.

She held her head over it, but she couldn't tell what her body wanted to do right now. "I thought we were dead," she said, still dry-heaving. "I thought for sure…"

Reddick turned to Toshiro. "That was the longest pause I've ever experienced."

Toshiro snickered. "I thought I'd let you squirm for a bit. See which one of you would crack first."

"*I* thought it was fun," Corijean said.

Toshiro jeered at Corijean. "Yeah right. I saw your levels; they were all red."

"I was just worried about the recruit. We're responsible for her showing up to the Institute *alive*."

Kennedy rested her forehead on the concrete. Reddick leaned down until he was face-to-face with her. "Kennedy, you're going to see and experience things that would never make sense to you on Earth. You won't be able to explain them—the marvels, the wonders of the universe. It is time for you to make yourself comfortable with that idea."

Corijean piled on: "The challenges you'll face in the coming years will be far worse than that fall."

Reddick leveled a glance at Corijean.

"What?" she asked innocently. "It's true."

Reddick placed a hand on Kennedy's shoulder. "It's been a long day, why don't I show you to your sleeping quarters?"

Kennedy nodded, and Reddick helped her to her feet.

"I'll take her," Corijean said, stepping between them.

"Suits," Toshiro said, as though he were asking them to return rented bowling shoes. He used the alien Jaws of Life to pry Kennedy and Corijean out of them, leaving them in their tan Evolver suits.

Kennedy followed Corijean down a long, cold corridor. "Is that the only way to get here?"

"No, most prefer to take the submarine."

"There's a submarine?" Kennedy cried.

"Of course, there's a submarine," Corijean said.

"Why didn't we go that way?"

"It's part of your initiation; it's a sort of baptism by fire."

After that, Kennedy had little to say to her. Corijean turned a corner and motioned to a block of rooms that resembled a storage facility. In the distance, Kennedy could hear people speaking in various alien languages. "This is where you'll be staying tonight." She pressed her handprint against a narrow door and unsealed it. Kennedy walked into a cold, windowless room with a twin bed, a large flat-screen TV, and minimal furnishings. Her suitcase was there when she arrived; she civilly thanked Corijean before the airtight door sealed shut between them. Kennedy removed her St. Jude necklace and held it in her hand, praying it would somehow endow her with special courage. She collapsed onto the bed and buried her head into the pillow.

A while later, someone delivered a tray of dinner to her, but she had no appetite. She felt exactly like the Submerged Station—dangerously out of place. The immeasurable weight of the water above felt like it was laying on her chest. In the moment, Kennedy did not give one iota about the marvels of the universe; she just wanted to be home, safe. She plotted all the ways she could get herself out of this. Kennedy had no earthly idea how many miles off the coast she currently was. She thought of her mother back in Tucson. Maybe Roberta could come and pick her up in California. It wasn't too far of a drive. Maybe they could even make a vacation out of it. Roberta would tell Kennedy she was proud of her, no matter what. It wouldn't be so bad—

There was a knock at the door.

She did not answer; she was in no state to receive guests.

"Kennedy?" Reddick called out.

"Yeah?" she said, her voice muffled by the pillow.

"Can I come in?"

"Sure."

He came in and sat at the edge of her bed. "Are you feeling better?"

She sat up, her face red and marked with pillow creases. "I guess."

Reddick looked down at her St. Jude necklace on the night-stand, and then he slowly removed the thin, charcoal band around his wrist. He put it on the bed next to Kennedy, and his emotions were finally readable. There was no fear, just a stillness and a confidence that Kennedy found unsettling. How was he not terrified?

"I want you to read me, Kennedy, and listen to me, okay?"

Kennedy took a deep breath and nodded.

"I know you are scared, and that's okay. But it will get easier for you. I need you to trust me." He patted her shoulder and made to get up.

She stopped him. "I don't know if I can do this."

"If I can do this, you can do this."

"I'm not like you," she said, with a tremendous deal of sadness.

"Yes, you are," he said definitively, and she could feel this was his belief because his emotion blocker was still on the bed. He put it back on and gave her a calming look.

"I'm really scared," she confessed.

"Fear precedes all greatness."

Kennedy tangled her fingers in her lap.

Reddick nudged her. "How about you go get ready for bed? I'll stay with you until you fall asleep."

"Okay," she said, hoping he would make her fear go away. She wanted him to keep saying inspirational things that cut through to her core, like the coach in a sports movie during the "all is lost" moment. Reddick waited in a chair by the bed while she went into the bathroom to wash her face, brush her teeth, and change into her star-printed pajamas. Under normal circumstances, she would not let him see her like this, but her overwhelming anxiety left little room for vanity or self-consciousness. For the first time, she did not care what he thought of her; she just did not want to be all alone in this cold room at the bottom of the ocean.

Kennedy stepped out of the bathroom and heard Reddick speaking in the hallway. She noticed a small screen beside the closed door, and with the press of a button, everything outside her room became visible. Corijean and Reddick were currently having a heated conversation. Kennedy could not understand a word of it, but it seemed to her as though they were speaking two different languages entirely. Reddick's language was a bit musical, while Corijean's was filled with harsh 'k' sounds. When they reached an impasse in the conversation, Corijean switched to English. "Please, just come to my room. We need to talk."

"We just did," Reddick said. "I told you I want to stay with her. You remember how terrifying your initiation was."

"I loved it." Corijean boasted. "Come on, she'll be fine."

"I'll see you tomorrow, Corijean."

Corijean scoffed. "Reddick, she's a human. She's not on your level, and she never will be."

Kennedy couldn't help but agree with Corijean there, but it stung, nonetheless.

"You have no idea which level she's on." Reddick turned around to reenter the room, and Corijean grabbed him by the arm. Kennedy went to run and jump in bed but realized she forgot to turn off the screen. She rushed back and pressed the button. Before she did, she saw Corijean wrap her arms around Reddick. Kennedy got under the covers just as Reddick opened the door.

"Sorry about that," he said.

Kennedy feigned ignorance. "Were you just talking to someone in the hallway?"

"Corijean."

Kennedy sat up and folded her legs. "Is Corijean your girlfriend?"

"No. We went out a couple of times last phase. I *think* we're friends now."

"She's really pretty."

"No one knows that more than her."

"Where is she from?"

"A planet called Madilieu." He rubbed his left temple. "She's not so bad when she's not trying to be what she wants everyone to *think* she is."

Kennedy reached over and put on her emotion blocker, fearing Reddick might be able to read her jealousy. "Go ahead and hang out with her if you want. I'll be fine."

"If I wanted to, I would."

Kennedy dodged his gaze by pretending to scratch an itch on her leg.

"How about I put on a movie—any movie in the world? What do you want to watch?" he asked.

Kennedy decided on *Toy Story* because it always made her feel better. Reddick put it on, then pulled his chair closer to her bedside. She laughed and cried at all the same parts that made her laugh and cry as a child. Still, nothing could make her forget her location or her destination.

Reddick enjoyed the movie next to her; it was the first time he had ever seen it.

Kennedy caught him watching her and immediately grew insecure. "Do you think I'm weak?" she asked.

"What would make you think that?"

"Mostly the fact that you're staying with me."

"It's not that, Kennedy." He stared into her eyes and then looked away.

"Then what is it?"

"Your TV is much better than the one in my room."

She observed him for a moment, wishing their emotion blockers were still off so she could feel what he was feeling. "The other day at school, when we first met, you said, '*And* you have good taste in music.'"

"Yeah?"

"What did *and* mean?"

"Well..." He leaned back in his chair. "I thought... this girl is brilliant, *and* she has good taste in music; that's what I meant to say."

"You think I'm brilliant?"

"You're self-taught. Yes, I think you're brilliant."

Kennedy beamed at him.

"Now get some sleep," he said. "We leave at dawn."

✦

Kennedy awoke the next morning to a piercing alarm coming from a small clock near the television. She stumbled towards it, nearly tripping over her suitcase in the process. Once she silenced the alarm, Kennedy rubbed her eyes and allowed them to adjust to the darkness. The room was much warmer than it had been the night before. She blindly felt for the light switch while she mentally prepared herself for another day of the unknown. Kennedy tried to get excited about going to space. She even tried to think of all the adventurous space movies she had seen, but for some reason, the only ones coming to mind were the terrifying ones—the ones about people who go crazy from the isolation of space and start to kill each other.

After she showered and dressed, Reddick arrived at her door

with a stress-free smile that had no place at the bottom of the ocean. "You ready?"

Not at all, she thought, even though her mouth said, "Yes."

"How'd you sleep?" he asked.

Kennedy zipped up her suitcase. "Pretty good, considering."

"Did you forget where you were?"

"I wish."

Reddick took Kennedy's suitcase from her. She did a final scan of the room to make sure she wasn't leaving anything behind, and then she followed Reddick down a long, dark corridor. Lights flickered on as they passed. A hard, transparent material, similar to glass, shaped the next corridor.

Kennedy stared out into the abyss, expecting to see some evil abomination swimming right towards her. The lights from above cast an eerie bluish glow on the ocean floor—this part of the ocean belonged to aliens. Kennedy strained her eyes, searching for creepy fish.

"Stop scaring yourself, Kennedy." Reddick grabbed her by the elbow. "Let's go." Oxygen was not free down here, and Kennedy could not seem to fill her lungs with enough of it to stay comfortable. She rubbed her throat. "It's just this part of the station," Reddick said. "This is where we keep species that aren't oxygen-dependent. We try to keep them on opposite schedules; they tend to scare the Phase Ones."

"Oh, now you care about scaring me." Kennedy peered wearily down the hallway, and Reddick laughed at her.

"Don't worry, they have already boarded the ship."

"They're coming with us?"

"Nearly everyone is being ordered home."

"Do you really think Malant would attack Earth?" Kennedy asked, suddenly fearing for her family.

"Not if we hurry up and get out of here."

A thunderous voice warning of an impending liftoff rattled the entire station. Reddick translated it for Kennedy. The beeps of alien technology grew louder as they traveled down the hallway. Then, Reddick stopped in front of an iron gate and held his hand to a keypad. The gate ticked open for them.

They walked inside a tall dome that stretched eight stories high. The top four levels served as control rooms; Kennedy could see the silhouettes of controllers milling about through the glass. A clear tunnel on the far side of the dome would transport them to the ship's entrance. Through a wall of windows, Kennedy could see a flawless, white, stingray-shaped ship docked just above the sea floor. It was the most stunning piece of technology Kennedy had ever laid eyes on, and it was bigger than she could have ever imagined.

Toshiro and Eka congregated inside the dome with a few of the Nextiers, one of whom took Kennedy's luggage. She crossed the dome with Reddick and gazed out at the ship in amazement. Kennedy tugged at her waistband like an auto mechanic. "So, what are we working with here? What's this baby run on? Hyperdrive? Warp drive?"

Reddick laughed. "We call it Zelsiat; it's a Symetran word that means something like... up until now. Zelsiat represents everything we've learned about space travel up until now. It's the reason it only takes a few moons to reach our galaxy instead of two billion years. It's kind of a kitchen sink approach."

"Zelsiat, of course." Kennedy joked, because that's what she did when she was nervous. She did not want Reddick to know she was actually thinking about treacherous asteroid belts and hostile alien pirates.

Corijean walked up behind them. "Zelsiat is really difficult for linear thinkers to grasp. It's trans-dimensional travel."

"So, like, wormholes?"

"More like portals we can create as needed." Corijean rubbed Reddick's back.

He wriggled away from her. "Morning, Corijean."

Corijean looked Kennedy up and down. "Also, Zelsiat can be a little rough for the unconditioned."

Kennedy gulped.

Reddick placed a reassuring hand on Kennedy's forearm. "Don't worry, you'll be unconscious the whole time. We will tranquilize you shortly after we leave Earth's atmosphere and put you into a state of hibernation until we reach Symetra."

"Are you going to be unconscious, too?" Kennedy questioned Reddick.

He nodded. "I have to be tranquilized, sequestered, and sealed up just like everyone else. But after Phase Three, I'll be able to remain conscious. I can't wait."

Corijean rubbed his shoulder and spoke to him in her harsh k-sounding language. Then she said to Kennedy, "I was just calling Reddick a thrill-seeker. He and I have always had that in common. How about you, Kennedy? Are you a thrill-seeker?"

Kennedy shook her head. "Nope. I'm actually a huge fan of

being alive."

Corijean combed through her long blonde hair. "I wouldn't call that being alive."

Reddick kept his eyes on Kennedy. "You are, too, a thrill-seeker. I heard you ran into a burning house to rescue a little old lady."

"Yeah, but I didn't do it because I thought it was fun." Kennedy looked back at the ship and changed the subject. "It really is something."

Reddick agreed. "This ship's creator was named Soonri Diom. Soonri spent his entire life perfecting it. Once, the invisibility shields malfunctioned, making the ship visible to humans." He laughed. "Soonri was absolutely outraged when they explained away his life's work as a weather balloon, so that's what everyone started calling it."

They walked inside the tunnel and boarded the ship. Kennedy was bewildered by the cold, artificial sunlight and the slight breeze that filled the huge atrium at its center. Exotic trees lined the walls, with numerous types of fruits hanging down from them. A sapphire piece of fruit landed on Kennedy's shoulder. It had a banana-like peel, but the inside contained ruby seeds. She examined it before they took an elevator to the fifth floor.

Corijean pointed out the restroom. "Last chance."

Kennedy turned and entered.

Corijean stayed close behind her. "So did Reddick date anyone while he was in Arizona?" she asked once they were alone.

"I don't know. Probably. Everyone liked him." Kennedy closed the door to her bathroom stall and scowled.

Corijean boasted that she had been touring Europe for the

past few months, and that a semi-famous footballer had asked her out: "Of course I told him I had a boyfriend."

Kennedy felt that jealous pressure in her chest again. "*Do* you have a boyfriend?"

"Nothing's official... yet." Corijean giggled.

Kennedy washed her hands and then gingerly followed Corijean down the hall to a large circle of high-tech, upright chambers. Most of the uprights were already facing in the opposite direction, which meant there were already aliens inside of them. A chill ran down Kennedy's spine as she considered whether they had fangs or tentacles or worse.

Corijean excused herself by telling Kennedy, "I'm going to try and snag the upright next to Reddick's." Kennedy glared at the back of her head as she skipped to the other side of the room, where Reddick was standing.

Zuele sidled up to Kennedy a few seconds later.

"When did you get here?" Kennedy asked her.

"About an hour ago. We took the submarine."

Kennedy backed into an available upright, finding its padding to be quite comfortable. "Take this," Zuele told Kennedy, holding a small, purple, triangular pill and a glass of water. "It will relax you."

Kennedy swallowed the pill as Zuele strapped her inside the upright. "How long does it take to kick in—" Kennedy's entire body suddenly went slack. Without the straps, she would have fallen to the ground. She tried to find her anxiety, but it had vanished. She attempted to panic, but the purple pill engulfed her in warmth and peace. Kennedy had never felt safer in her entire life.

Zuele administered an IV into Kennedy's hand and then double checked her straps.

Kennedy felt loopy and somewhat euphoric when the voice over the intercom warned that liftoff would be in five minutes.

"I'll see you on Symetra," Zuele said. "You are going to do great things, young creator." She was about to seal Kennedy inside her upright when Kennedy stopped her.

"Zuele?"

"Yes?"

"Thank you for choosing me."

Zuele bowed to her and then sealed the clear cover of her upright. It spun around, and Kennedy was now facing a thick, transparent wall that looked out onto the ocean, but the purple pill made it difficult for her to concentrate.

The upright released a steady stream of oxygen, and Kennedy experienced a strange spiritual moment as she listened to her breath echo inside it. She had been positive she was going to die yesterday, but this breath had stayed with her. Her heart broke wide open with gratitude for something so obvious and abundant. She again tried to find the fear that was only natural, but the purple pill eradicated it, leaving her with nothing but the most excited feeling in the world. If only she could face every situation with this absence of fear, if only they had been considerate enough to give her the pill before yesterday's little stunt, she might have enjoyed it.

The voice over the intercom announced liftoff.

Kennedy tried to clap her hands. Without the paralyzing fear, she truly understood what a miracle this was. The small, insecure voice inside her head tried to tell her she was unworthy of such an experience—the pill picked the voice up by its collar and threw it out of Kennedy's mind. Kennedy could hardly contain her excitement as the ship began to ascend from the depths of the Pacific Ocean. It was a smooth and nearly silent ride until the ship erupted from the water and raced to break free of Earth's gravity.

Kennedy could appreciate the beautiful, deep, blue ocean much more from up here. The early morning sun created glittering orange ripples across it. She watched as it grew further and further away from her, until finally she was looking down at that familiar image of Earth—the curvature she had seen on TV and in science books. No high-definition photo could do it justice. Words could not describe the feeling of insignificance and awe Kennedy was experiencing simultaneously. Everyone she loved was on that blue marble. What a glorious creation. What a beautiful planet! It was so peaceful from up here.

Her heart nearly jumped out of her chest when she realized she was in space. Then a metal wall slid over her view. The metal's surface moved left to right in liquid, silver waves. The protective wall appeared to be a living organism; it oozed towards Kennedy and slithered up her clear casing.

"Activating hibernation mode..." A cold vapor filled Kennedy's upright, and then the darkness overcame her.

NINE

Kennedy was not ready to wake up yet. She did not even want to open her eyes for fear that the loving feeling she was experiencing would dissipate. The feeling reminded her of falling asleep on her mother's lap in restaurants when she was little. Roberta would never wake her up; instead, she would carry her to the car and then put her to bed. In those moments, Kennedy knew how much her mother loved her, and now she felt that love again, but she had no idea where it was coming from.

A thin sheen of perspiration matted Kennedy's baby hair to the back of her neck and forehead. She languidly blinked her eyes open and shut. All of the other high-tech, upright chambers were now empty and facing forward. Two small women with golden auras cycled and massaged Kennedy's legs, while her top half remained buckled into the upright. Their appearance startled Kennedy into a more conscious state. They wore high-collared, marigold suits with triangular prism epaulets and were hovering several feet off the ground. The older of the two placed a hand on Kennedy's arm, filling her with even more loving energy. Their energy was the purest Kennedy had ever encountered. She felt at ease in their presence. They removed her IV, unbuckled her from her upright, and held her limp body in the air. *"Welcome to Symetra, young creator,"* they said.

What are you? Kennedy wondered.

"We are Triphens," the voices replied inside her mind. If she weren't so out of sorts, the experience would have stunned her. *"We are a great and many things,"* the voices continued. This time, Kennedy realized that there were more than just two voices speaking—a stadium full of voices. They weren't using words or moving their mouths, but Kennedy understood them instantly. *"Words are the weakest form of communication,"* they said. The experience left Kennedy feeling more disoriented than she already was. They must have sensed this because they did not flow into her mind again.

"Kennedy Neff! The pride and joy of planet Earth!" Chancellor Kirat burst into the room with her arms wide open. She squeezed Kennedy, then held her in place so she could get a proper look at her. She wore an ornate robe heavy with purple gemstones, a few shades lighter than her eggplant skin. "Welcome to Symetra! How was your trip?"

"Relaxing."

"I hope so, because now the work begins." Chancellor Kirat beamed at Kennedy as though she were a beloved grandchild. "Now, let's get you cleaned up, and then we'll get you something to eat." The Triphens carried Kennedy by the elbows to a room down the hall, filled with tiled shower stalls and lighted vanities.

Chancellor Kirat and the Triphens waited in the hallway while Kennedy took a shower, though it felt more like a car wash. Hot water sprayed her from all angles, while two mechanical hands lathered her hair with an orange shampoo oozing from their fingertips. The shampoo held a completely new scent; Kennedy did not have anything to compare it to, and for some reason, the new scent was what really opened Kennedy to the possibilities ahead for her—new scents, new sights, new faces. Two hooks clamped her mouth open, and a three-pronged toothbrush scrubbed her teeth. When it was all over, Kennedy was coughing up sweet, minty toothpaste, mixed with a little bit of blood. The mechanical hands placed a royal blue robe around her, with three moons in different phases on the left breast pocket.

The Chancellor reentered the room with even more Triphens. Kennedy sat in her robe at one of the lighted vanities, staring at them. Their facial structures set the Triphens apart from one another, yet their olive skin tone, height, aura, and marigold suits were uniform. One of them broke a pink prickly plant, combed its inner leaf juice through Kennedy's hair, and trimmed her ends. A floating, robotic blow-dry brush rolled its way through Kennedy's hair, leaving voluminous waves in its wake. One of the Triphens gave her a mani-pedi, and another groomed her eyebrows. Chancellor Kirat placed a tiny slug with a long snout like an anteater on Kennedy's face, sucking the dirt from her pores. She removed the slug and patted its snail tracks into Kennedy's skin. Kennedy politely endured all of it, imagining herself a cable TV host traveling to faraway lands and participating in the local rituals, no matter how bizarre they were. Enduring this made Kennedy feel cultured and worldly—or rather, universal. However, her open mind slammed shut when Chancellor Kirat held up an ant farm filled with hundreds of colorful bugs. "And now for your makeup."

Kennedy could see some of the alien bugs jumping like fleas through the glass. She shook her head violently at the Chancellor. "No, thank you."

"These are painting bugs. They're artists. I put some on my face every day. Trust me, you'll love it."

Kennedy tapped her toes and tangled her fingers in her lap. "Okay..."

Chancellor Kirat held the ant farm in front of Kennedy, and a light scanned her face. Then, a massive reshuffling took place inside the ant farm, as the perfect bugs for the job crawled above the others. Chancellor Kirat opened a latch at the top of the ant farm, and hundreds of colorful bugs launched themselves onto Kennedy's face. She cringed at the feel of their tiny insect legs tickling her skin. One of them sped around her eyelid's rim. Another lined her lips. Squads of bugs, with thick black paint, slid down her eyelashes like firemen down a pole. Then a juicy plump bug dragged the wet makeup on its bottom half across her lips.

"Why is it wet?" Kennedy tried to ask, but quickly realized she did not want to know. Several other bugs jumped rapidly up and down on Kennedy's cheekbones. It was one of the most unpleasant experiences of her life, but it was over in a matter of seconds. Chancellor Kirat held up the ant farm, and the bugs jumped back inside. Kennedy opened her eyes and could not believe the results.

They did her eye makeup a little darker than she was used to, but other than that, the job was completely professional.

Chancellor Kirat gave her a once-over. "You're as shiny as a Fyorisc stone!"

The Triphens nodded in agreement, while Kennedy took in this new image of herself. Her hair was soft and smooth, pinned up on one side. Perfect eyeliner outlined her large hazel eyes. A shimmering blush highlighted her cheeks. Her lips shone a glossy, spiced color. Kennedy was speechless. She looked like the best possible version of herself. She had never looked this attractive in her entire life. She had not even known it was possible; she actually liked the way she looked; she looked kinda... *pretty*. Tears of gratitude filled her eyes. She turned to thank the Triphens, but instead found them with their palms stretched in her direction. An overwhelming feeling of love hit her, causing her breath to catch in her throat. She covered her mouth, but Chancellor Kirat gently guided her hand back to the arm rest. "Don't block their blessing," she said.

The Triphens moved their triangle-shaped fingers from their chests to their mouths, then to their foreheads, sending the triangles skyward. Kennedy returned the visual prayer of alignment, and the Triphens floated from the room, leaving her reeling from the love they had just freely imparted to her.

Chancellor Kirat handed Kennedy a soft, light gray zip-up suit with the same gold monogram of three moons on the breast pocket. "Here is your Phase One uniform." She turned her back and gave Kennedy some privacy. The suit initially appeared to be too short for Kennedy, but once zipped, it adapted to fit her long legs and arms.

"What's with the makeover?" Kennedy inquired as she put on a matching pair of boots.

"We have found that when you look your best, you also feel your best, which creates a heightened state of confidence. That is what we are after. You will need all the confidence you can muster to reach the highest frequencies. Plus, cleanliness is a welcome mat for excellence."

"Oh, I thought you were just checking me for lice."

Chancellor Kirat winked. "That, too." When Kennedy rose, Chancellor Kirat appraised her. "You are now a representative of the Evolvers."

The Chancellor took Kennedy to the ship's observation deck so she could get her first proper look at Symetra. A brilliant sunset flooded through the deck's vast, unobstructed windows. Reddick had not been exaggerating when he called Symetra a paradise planet.

"*Incredible*," Kennedy whispered as she beheld the dreamlike landscape.

Three moons—one close, two distant—hung inside a sherbet sky. Rolling green hills and wildflowers sat atop extremely high cliffs, while turquoise waves crashed into them, reaching only half their height. "That is the Kathreeyan Ocean," the Chancellor said, "and that," she motioned to a small cluster of skyscrapers in the distance, "is Crystal City."

Kennedy pointed to a snowy mountain range crowned with thick purple clouds, which was out of place in the largely tropical climate. "What is that?" Kennedy, who loved mountains, asked with a smile on her face.

"Star Grave Mountain."

Kennedy kept walking in circles, taking it all in.

"We are currently docked on the Boncreel continent, located in the western hemisphere of Symetra. What do you think?" Chancellor Kirat asked her.

Her heart swelled. "I think I must've died on the way over here... It's heaven." Kennedy had her face nearly pressed against the glass when she heard Reddick's voice behind her.

"Good evening, Chancellor Kirat. It is an honor to encounter your energy," he said.

Chancellor Kirat beamed at him the same way she had beamed at Kennedy. "It is an honor to encounter yours, young creator."

Reddick wore a royal blue Phase Three uniform, which further highlighted the already piercing blue of his eyes. He did a doubletake when he saw Kennedy.

Chancellor Kirat placed a hand on each of their backs and forced them closer to one another. "Kennedy, I'll now leave you in Reddick's capable hands. He will be your official guide." Kennedy wasn't sure what she meant, so the Chancellor clarified, "Think of him as your *buddy*. Oh, how I love English!" she laughed. "I want you to reach out to him if you need anything at all."

Anything?

Chancellor Kirat left Kennedy with Reddick, who had yet to say a word to her. He looked so official in his uniform. His broad shoulders and perfect posture reminded Kennedy to stand up straight. In Tucson, he looked like he was in high school, but here, in this uniform, he looked like an Evolver, not just someone training to be one.

Kennedy nudged him with her elbow. "Hey, buddy."

He still stared at her.

Kennedy crossed her arms and became self-conscious. "Can I *help* you?" she asked with a little more attitude than intended.

He shook himself out of it. "You look different."

Kennedy posed and spun around. "Oh, yeah, it's my Triphen makeover. I can't believe you guys use bugs to put makeup on. I mean, humans are weird, but we're not that weird."

Reddick gave her a smile she had never seen before.

"You don't like it?"

He smiled wider. "I didn't say that."

Corijean stepped onto the observation deck. "Did I miss the sunset?" she whined. She wore the same Phase Three uniform as Reddick. "Well, don't you look adorable, Kennedy? I'm surprised you're conscious already. It usually takes humans the longest to wake up."

Kennedy made a face at Corijean behind her back. Reddick caught it and laughed.

"What's so funny?" Corijean asked, standing entirely too close to Reddick. "I love a good laugh. I was voted funniest in my early school back home. I've got a human joke for you, Kennedy: Why did the bike fall over?"

"I don't know. Why?"

"Because it was two-tired."

Crickets.

"Get it? Because the bike has two tires, but it's also tired?"

"The best jokes are the ones you have to explain," Kennedy said dryly.

Reddick laughed again, and Corijean pretended to laugh along with him.

"I'm going to take Kennedy to meet her guardian," he said.

"I'll come with." Corijean wedged herself between them and then spent the entire trip to the fifth floor talking about herself. In her peripheral vision, Kennedy could see Reddick staring at her. She thought it was because she was wearing so much make-up. She wanted to assure him she didn't actually think she was pretty or anything, because deliberately looking pretty meant she was deliberately willing to be seen, and she wasn't. Still, Reddick stared on. In Kennedy's insecure mind, he was viciously judging her sad attempt to look good; she was sure of it. So, what he said next took her by complete surprise. "Are your eyes green or brown, Kennedy?"

"They're hazel."

"They change, don't they?"

Kennedy grew red. "Uh, yeah, that's what my mom says anyway."

"They're..." he searched for the right word, "soulful."

Kennedy tried to take her "soulful" eyes away from his but couldn't.

"Mine are green," Corijean said, reminding the two of them she was still there.

The elevator doors pinged open. Zuele stood there in her white guardian uniform. "Kennedy, you look beautiful." She placed a finger under her chin and said, "I'm not a fan of too much makeup, but at least I can still see you in there. Shall we get something to eat?"

Kennedy gave Reddick and Corijean a wave. "I'll see you guys around."

Corijean hooked her arm through Reddick's. "Yeah, maybe."

Kennedy floated alongside Zuele, but this time it was her interaction with Reddick that carried her instead of the Triphens. Kennedy replayed Reddick's compliment about her eyes again, wishing she had said something charming in response.

The dining room faced the Kathreeyan Ocean, and the two of them took a table next to the window. A blue robot served them some sort of alien grain dish, but Kennedy was too nervous to even think about food.

Zuele drew a screen with her finger, and a consent form appeared between them. "I need you to sign this."

"What is it?" Kennedy forced herself to eat a bite of the dish, which was delicious and creamy and contained a rich, robust flavor she had never tasted before.

"I need your consent before I can embed you with learning materials."

Kennedy dropped her fork. "You want to track me?" This felt like a dealbreaker to Kennedy, who valued her freedom more than almost anything else.

"No, of course not. Remember, Evolvers cannot override the free will of any being. Tracking you would mean breaking that rule. The only Evolvers we ever track are the ones carrying out dangerous missions."

Kennedy still wasn't convinced.

Zuele raised her chin. "The Evolvers will have zero access to any of your chips unless you choose to donate them for research at the end of your life. Then future generations of Evolvers can study and learn from you, but obviously that is not something you need to decide today."

Kennedy crossed her arms and slumped her shoulders, wishing her mother were there to make this decision for her. Even though Zuele was making it sound like she had a choice, Kennedy felt she really didn't.

Zuele continued, "On Earth, your technology has outpaced the growth of humans who have not evolved alongside it. We have. Here, technology is a tool for further expansion and evolvement. True evolvement requires constant present-moment awareness. That's where our technology will be very helpful to you. We have designed these tools for your own personal development; they will track your health, monitor your thoughts, and challenge your limiting beliefs. This information is exclusively for you." Zuele navigated to a distinct page of the consent form, revealing three chips the size of rice grains. "This is a Lengualizer chip." Zuele pointed out the first one. "It allows you to speak thousands of languages effortlessly."

"That's why you guys speak such amazing English," Kennedy said.

"Yes, and that's why we can speak every other language as well. Of course, language is a living thing, so you will need to update your Lengualizer every few weeks while you sleep."

"So, you're basically turning me into a computer?"

"You've always been a computer; we are just giving you a new operating system." Zuele pointed to the second chip. "This is a Capstone chip—it syncs your body's functions with our technology and allows you to wire yourself for evolvement. It will constantly inform you of where your energy is currently vibrating, making identifying and rooting out your human limitations a lot easier."

"What does that one do?" Kennedy pointed to the last chip.

"That is a Sectnot chip." Zuele opened her palm and showed Kennedy the small screen that appeared through her flesh. "It is your textbook, communication tool, atlas, and link to all information in the discovered universe."

"Like a smartphone?"

"A smartphone, tutor, personal trainer, doctor, bodyguard..." Zuele could sense that she was losing Kennedy. "Tutor, because it will badger you to complete your assignments. Personal trainer, because it knows your physical limitations and will always push you to the brink of them. Doctor, because it will alert you when you are sick, dehydrated, or deficient in vitamins and minerals. And it's your bodyguard because it alerts you to danger."

"How?"

"There is a part of all of us that is smarter than our physical senses. Your Sectnot heeds that voice. It will never allow you to override that voice. The highest intention of your physical apparatus is survival. Humans have a lot of unfounded fears. Your Sectnot will not react to those imaginary fears, only the real threats. But you'll learn all this as you familiarize yourself with the chip. Everyone at the Institute is embedded for evolvement."

Kennedy drummed her fingers on the table and asked a question she should have asked a long time ago. "What if I don't want to do this? What if I don't want the chips? What if I decide at some point that I don't even want to be an Evolver?"

"If you don't want this, we can modify your memory—and your family's—of this experience and send you home."

Kennedy definitely didn't want to go home. Everything staying the same terrified her far more than being embedded with alien technology, so she held her breath and signed the floating consent form with her finger, hoping she would not come to regret it.

The medical suite was on the first floor of the ship. When they entered the room, a woman was waiting for them and motioned for Kennedy to lie down on a white recliner beneath surgical lights. The woman was a certain breed of fabulous; she had porcelain skin and peach-colored eyes, which dominated most of her petite face. Her bottom half was adorned with a poofy silk skirt that chimed every time she moved, while her long orange hair covered the top half of her body in a complex design. "Welcome to Symetra, young creator. My name is Doreem Gem," she said in a voice more soothing than water trickling out of a fountain. "I am the head healer at the Healing Center, and I am here to make sure your embedment is as painless as possible." Healer Gem applied a numbing agent to Kennedy's left palm, the base of her skull, and underneath her tongue. She handed Kennedy a chewable blue tablet of Firest Weed, which relaxed her, but not as much as the triangular pill had during liftoff.

Elsid Tusk walked into the room wearing heavy boots. He unlocked a silver briefcase handcuffed to his right wrist. "This is

Enforcer Tusk," Zuele said, with an edge to her voice. "He is head of security at the Institute."

Enforcer Tusk was a tall man with slicked-back hair the same color as his dark gray enforcer suit. Behind him were four patrollers—robotic, hovering, pink, diamond-shaped lights that nearly blinded Kennedy. She covered her eyes, Tusk whistled, and the patrollers dimmed their searchlights. He scrubbed his veiny, pale hands and slipped them inside a pair of surgical gloves.

"Are you ready?" he asked Kennedy, even though his ice green eyes were on Zuele.

"I think so," Kennedy said.

Tusk patted her arm. "You are going to do just fine. This will all be over before you know it." He pressed a button on the side of the recliner, which eased Kennedy into a horizontal position. Tusk grabbed Kennedy's wrists and held her palms up. She could feel the coldness of his hands seeping through his surgical gloves. Two small restraints emerged from the armrests and held her arms in place. Tusk reached inside the briefcase and placed three grain-sized chips on a surgical tray beside Kennedy.

Healer Gem handed Kennedy a breathing ball. She instructed Kennedy to sync her breath with the squishy ball's inflation and deflation.

Tusk removed a small handheld instrument from his briefcase, which resembled a staple gun. "You have a wonderful guardian, Kennedy, the best in my opinion," Tusk said.

Zuele cut him off. "Enforcer Tusk, can we please focus on the task at hand?"

"As you can see, she's not going to be easy on you, or maybe she is just like that with me," Tusk whispered to Kennedy.

Kennedy was too anxious to register anything he was saying to her.

"Please, open your mouth," he told Kennedy. Once she opened her mouth, he widened it with two of his gloved fingers. He aimed the instrument underneath her tongue and embedded the chip inside. Kennedy squeezed her eyes shut and white-knuckled the breathing ball. Doreem suctioned the blood that filled Kennedy's mouth. Tusk was already loading the staple gun with the Capstone Chip when Kennedy's tongue started to dart in and out of her mouth, seemingly possessed. Kennedy tried to speak, but her tongue was currently out of commission.

Kennedy freaked out. Aliens were experimenting on her, and she was the genius who had given them consent to do it. She jerked against her restraints, acting like Phantom every time she tried to give him medicine or a bath.

Healer Gem lifted Kennedy's head, while Tusk implanted the chip inside the base of Kennedy's skull. In response, Kennedy felt every nerve in her body and every neuron in her brain activate. The Capstone Chip gave her instant awareness of the complicated circuitry that made up the universe of her own body.

Zuele squeezed Kennedy's trembling forearm. "Almost done."

Doreem held a blue light over Kennedy's left hand until every ligament beneath her skin was visible. Tusk loaded the staple gun again and aimed the device at the fleshiest part of Kennedy's palm. This one hurt the worst, by far. It made the accumulative pain Kennedy was already experiencing unbearable. If she had been standing, the pain would have brought her to her knees. Her eyes watered and burned beneath the harsh surgical lights as she felt the technology integrate inside her body.

"All done," Tusk said.

Doreem rubbed a piece of firest weed over Kennedy's palm, providing instantaneous relief.

Tusk removed a matte, white band from the case and slipped it onto Kennedy's right ring finger. "This is your Charge Ring. It powers all your chips, enables Dematerialization, and will let you know when it is running low. Your bed will charge the ring while you sleep." He locked his briefcase. "The bylaws of the Institute are already on your Sectnot. I expect you to learn them. However, I will leave you with the two most important bylaws. One: Materialization is strictly prohibited within the Institute and Hover House. Two: Be in your *own* unit by curfew." Tusk removed his gloves. "Learn the rules, or my patrollers will discipline you, and I can guarantee they are not as gentle as I am." Tusk snapped his fingers, and long, sharp, poisonous spikes—which served the purpose of paralyzing intruders—ejected from the patrollers. Tusk doted on the floating torture devices like they were his pampered pets. "Welcome to the Evolver Institute, young creator." He snapped his fingers twice and whistled. The patrollers retracted their spikes and followed him single file into the hallway.

"Forgive the theatrics," Zuele said, referring to Tusk's little show of strength. "But these learning materials are extremely valuable, which is why we go to such great lengths to protect them."

Kennedy held two fingers to the bottom of her throbbing

tongue, but she could barely feel the small chip. "How do I know it's working?"

Zuele started speaking Bashneeth, a language spoken in the small village of Antak in the Crag Region of Millintica. Kennedy knew all of this instantly. The Lengualizer connected with the Capstone, and suddenly Kennedy was conversing comfortably in a language she had never even heard. Her mouth began to move in ways it had never moved before. Her tongue, jaw and brain seemed possessed, yet she recognized her own voice speaking the alien language. The technology was seamless; it worked so fast that her thoughts could hardly catch up to it.

Kennedy's hand began to vibrate.

"Zuele Zuniz is attempting to contact you," said a female voice inside her mind. *"Would you like to accept?"*

Yes.

A hologram of Zuele appeared over Kennedy's left hand. Kennedy minimized the hologram, and then Zuele's face appeared on a screen through the flesh of her palm. Kennedy drew a screen with her finger and projected a floating image of Zuele in front of her.

Zuele ran a hand through Kennedy's newly created screen. "This device is thought-activated. You can also activate stealth mode for confidential conversations. Try it."

Activate stealth mode, Kennedy thought. The screen on her palm disappeared, but she could still hear Zuele inside her head.

"See?" Zuele said. *"Now we can communicate wordlessly."*

Kennedy looked up, but Zuele had not moved her lips.

"Whoa," Kennedy said.

"What do you think?"

"I think I can throw my crappy cellphone away."

Questions flowed inside Kennedy's mind like a never-ending stream of consciousness, but every time one arose, so did its answer. She held up her Sectnot. "If all this information is given to me freely, what am I here to learn?"

"Information is cheap; wisdom is expensive. You are here to learn the laws of the universe, not random facts. Speaking of, I would change your Sectnot setting to 'less information', unless you want inane details about inane things constantly stealing your focus."

A small ship that looked like a smooth, white, floating sand dollar, waited for them at the east loading zone. Neon lights blinked lazily from it as a ramp ejected from its side. Kennedy's Sectnot informed her it was called a ridership. The voice of her Sectnot then described a few of this model's features.

Once they boarded, Kennedy sat in one of the six high-backed, white chairs, which encircled a control board. The ridership zipped out of the Weather Balloon, which concerned Kennedy because there was no pilot to steer it. Zuele and Kennedy's seats both rotated away from the center so they could have a better view out of the windows. Zuele aimed the small remote around her neck at the roof, and it opened. According to Kennedy's Sectnot, the remote was called a Rivil, a small instrument that allowed guardians private access to any part of the Institute.

The ridership traveled close to Star Grave Mountain, which was a winter wonderland with tall evergreens blanketed in thick snow. Kennedy shivered in the frosty night air. The ridership sensed her discomfort and formed a sphere of warmth around her.

"This is the Five Seasons Forest," Zuele said. "It goes through five seasons in a day."

"In a *day*?" Kennedy repeated it to make sure she heard her correctly.

Zuele directed the ridership to the mountaintop, where Symetra's brightest moon made the virgin snow sparkle like diamonds. "In my opinion, the Five Seasons Forest is one of our greatest achievements. We control its weather patterns. Our hope is to one day control the extreme weather patterns of uninhabitable planets. We are still a long way off from that, but the Evolvers have mastered planetary tilt technology in this forest."

"What is the fifth season?" Kennedy wondered aloud. The Sectnot seemed to understand when Kennedy was conversing with another being, so it allowed Zuele to answer.

"A star harvest, or more accurately, a meteor harvest, you will see for yourself here shortly." Zuele dimmed the lights inside the ridership. In a matter of seconds, an abundance of stars shot down from the night sky over the Five Seasons Forest. Kennedy watched in awe. "Wow," she sighed. The brightness of the stars illuminated her face and its dreamy expression.

"Hundreds of stars fall over the forest every night for about two minutes—of course, we can't take credit for that—but we declared it a season unto itself."

"It's beautiful," Kennedy said.

Zuele nodded in agreement. "It sure is."

A few miles later, the ridership descended and threaded its way through a maze of skyscrapers that appeared to be sculpted out of gigantic slabs of various colorful crystals. "Welcome to Crystal City," Zuele said. "Most of the beings who live in this city have something to do with the Evolver organization. They are Triphens, Evolvers, Nextiers, and Recruits."

According to Kennedy's Sectnot, there were two billion beings living on the small planet of Symetra. Crystal City was home to one million of those beings, which made Kennedy realize just how large the Evolver Organization really was. She saw some walking around in Evolver suits of every color and marveled at their diversity and beauty.

Symetra was not a utopian planet, but it was an evolved one. Its history did not move in cycles, only forward. Symetrans took immense pride in learning from past mistakes and evolving beyond them. The law of expansion guided the creation of every social contract on their planet. No one wasted time trying to keep things as they were because experience told them it was an impossibility. Theirs was a culture of abundance, and they even inscribed the words "more than enough" on their currency (called coyels).

Symetrans celebrated their individuality and found creative ways in which only they could serve the whole. They were extremely competitive when it came to finding solutions and improving the lives of all Symetrans. When the planet faced a challenge, they would televise experts working together to solve it; this was their most popular form of entertainment. Symetrans would gather around their screens at home and join the energy of the solution, encouraged to participate if they received guidance from the universe. Alignment was everything on Symetra. On Symetra, there were as many religions as there were beings, since everyone was encouraged to form their own personalized, moment-to-moment relationship with the Eternal Energy Field, or the Great Creator, as some preferred to call it.

A river twisted around the city's outskirts. Hundreds of Triphens lined the river, sitting in meditation poses. Zuele lowered the ridership so Kennedy could get a better look. "They are protecting the energy field of Crystal City," she said. "You will see a lot of Triphens around the Institute, though most of their days are spent in meditation. They are truly gifted beings who consider serving others to be their highest calling. They are incapable of suffering and do not identify with the self, which makes them different from nearly every other sentient species. They willingly surrender their right to be a drop of energy in order to be a collective wave."

"That's why it felt like so many of them were talking to me when there were only two," Kennedy said.

"Precisely. Do not underestimate them. They are small but mighty spirits. The Triphens reside at the peak of consciousness, which is where ultimate power lies. Centuries ago, the Triphens defeated the Millintican Guard without raising a single weapon. They dubbed it the Battle of Raining Ships, despite its lack of actual combat. Millintican ships entered Symetra's atmosphere, and the collective, energetic power of the Triphens caused them to malfunction and rain down from the sky. On the Parin Continent, there is an ancient graveyard full of them. When Cissoria Brandth discovered Symetra, she was smart enough to adopt the peaceful beliefs of the Triphens instead of imposing hers on them. Cissoria founded the Evolver Institute, teaching young Symetrans and her own children the lessons she learned from the Triphens while also teaching them about space travel and the discovery of new worlds."

"Brandth?" Kennedy asked.

"I thought you might recognize that last name."

The ridership traveled between two massive trees called Behemoths, which were as wide as a city block and taller than any tree Kennedy had ever seen on Earth. Crisscrossing streams of water pinged between them, and well-lit, cylindrical living units hung from the Behemoths' powerful branches like ornaments. A patroller streamed past the ridership, shining its pink light, looking for unusual activity.

Kennedy could see recruits studying inside the units. She saw one alien meditating on a floating mat, another blinking different colors through his window, and a girl doing flips inside her bedroom as though it contained zero gravity. Kennedy grinned as she watched them.

"Don't fall for it; it's just trick tint," Zuele said. "They want the patrollers to think they are studying instead of whatever it is they are actually doing. Zuele pointed her Rivil at the top of the right Behemoth, and the ridership entered the base of a living unit that was suspended from it. The unit's garage housed camouflaged pipes, tanks, and an unattached elevator car.

"That elevator car will take you down to the walking paths, and that is your ridership," Zuele said, motioning to a small ridership docked in the corner. Kennedy clapped in excitement. The only time she ever got to drive was when her mother had too much wine at family parties. "You will be sharing it with your roommates, of course."

Kennedy gulped. "Roommates?"

"They are lovely beings." Zuele released the ramp and motioned for Kennedy to exit the ridership. "I'll meet you here in the morning. Your Sectnot will give you all the details. Goodnight, young creator." Zuele's ridership zoomed out of the garage, leaving Kennedy in silence. She looked for a door but couldn't find one. *How do I get out of here?*

"There is a motion-activated lift in the center of the garage; please approach now," replied the voice of her Sectnot. Kennedy nearly tripped over a clear partition, which partially surrounded a circular platform. When she stepped onto the platform, the center lift ascended to the unit's second floor, the living area. The floor-to-ceiling windows offered unobstructed views of the Five Seasons Forest and the other Behemoth tree. The unit was quite cozy, with all sorts of knickknacks, potted alien plants, twinkling lights, oversized couches, and a mirage of a heat-producing fire-pit between them. A stone kitchen filled with odd gadgetry took up a third of the living area. A study nook with desks and floating screens took up another.

The center lift continued to the third floor, where Kennedy found a circular hallway covered by a glass roof. Through the glass, she could see the Behemoth's fallen foliage. Her red suitcase stood in front of one of the four doors—she deduced this must be her room. The lights turned on as she set foot inside. It was a stark white room with a view of the Five Seasons Forest. The most comfortable-looking bed she had ever seen stood in the room's center. There were two doors inside; one led to her own human bathroom and the other led to a closet filled with endless gray adaptable suits, sneakers, boots, and jackets. A built-in dresser was filled with even more Dematerialization-proof clothing—undergarments, socks, pajamas, bathing suits and athletic wear.

Kennedy heard a noise from the hallway. "Hello?" she called out.

A small white creature with a clown-like face now lurked outside her bedroom door. Its hair and eyes were orange, and its teeth were jagged and green, matching its claws and toenails. It wore the same Phase One suit as Kennedy, along with a small triangular pack around its waist. The creature clicked its teeth together. "You are trespassing."

Kennedy squirmed when she saw it. "I'm not. Um, my name is Kennedy Neff. I am your new roommate."

"There must be some mistake. I cannot have a roommate because they scare off my prey. Sometimes, I even mistake them for my prey. You see, my sight is not what it was two hundred years ago."

Two Hundred?

"Come closer," it demanded.

"No thanks. I'm all set over here."

"I need to smell you."

"*Smell* me?"

The creature's face folded down into an evil stare. "We can do this the easy way or the hard way." It clicked its teeth again.

Kennedy remained unmoving.

"So be it." The creature dropped to all fours, let out an evil growl, and scurried unnaturally towards Kennedy.

TEN

Kennedy fell inside her room and sealed the door by hitting a button next to it. She searched around the room for a make-shift weapon when she heard the raucous laughter coming from the hallway. "Kennedy!" a girl said in between laughs. "Come on out. It was a joke. Geenen, change back."

"I told you this was a terrible idea, Orien," another voice said.

"It was a joke, Pengar! Come on, Kennedy. Please come out. We're really excited to meet you. We've never had a fourth in this unit."

Kennedy reluctantly opened the door.

A girl with a cotton candy-colored pompadour cut peeked her head inside. She had dark, almond eyes and shimmering olive skin. "Greetings, my name is Orien Truin." The girl was beautiful and handsome all at once; Kennedy had never seen anyone like her before.

A petite girl with a flower-filled bun wedged herself between Kennedy and Orien. "I am Pengar Mimit. We've been waiting so long to meet you!" Pengar could have passed for Korean, but it was clear she was from someplace much further away.

Kennedy saw the creature approaching behind them and tried to close the door again.

"No, no, wait," Orien said, "that's not really what she looks like. Take the chip out, Geenen."

The terrifying creature named Geenen reached into the triangular pack around her waist and produced a small, stainless-steel kit. She opened it, sanitized her chalky hand, and plunged a scalpel into it. Kennedy had to look away.

"Don't worry, she has a high pain tolerance, and she's a very skilled surgeon," Orien assured Kennedy. "She's skilled at everything... except socializing. Geenen has that whole I-didn't-come-here-to-make-friends mentality, but we've worn her down. Isn't that right, Geenen?" Orien patted the creature on the back, and it growled at her. "She's a little ornery, but it's only because she's from a planet without a lot of sunshine."

Pengar pushed her dainty hand forward and laid it limply inside Kennedy's. "I hear humans greet one another this way. I've been learning all about humans. My uncle used to study them, interesting species. I am from the planet Camaven. Orien is from the other side of Symetra, and Geenen Reen, here, is from Crisix. So, what do you think of Symetra so far? Have you met the Triphens? They're incredible, right? Did you get the blessing? It's amazing, right?" Pengar gasped for air. "Am I talking a lot? I talk a lot when I'm nervous. I am so excited to be using the English feature on my Lengualizer. English is fun. Am I doing it right?"

Kennedy barely heard her. She was currently more interested in what was happening to Geenen, who had just plucked a small chip from her non-dominant hand. Once the chip was out, the creature disintegrated into a cloud of effervescent particles that reorganized themselves into a longer, narrower pattern and then turned solid once more. The adaptable suit stretched to fit her new, tall, skinny body. Geenen now looked like an alien in the more traditional sense, with pearlescent scales, large eyes, and a head shaped like an upside-down egg. This version of Geenen was only slightly less terrifying—still, Kennedy couldn't help but feel there was something beautiful and delicate about her otherness.

"How did you do that?" Kennedy asked.

"Crisix, my home planet, is the only planet with beings that look like me, so I'll be going undercover a lot. My guardian started me on Switchips my very first day." Geenen held up the black, blood-stained chip for Kennedy to see. "You can live with a Switchip inside you for years and no one would ever know." The chip made a small clank when Geenen dropped it inside the stainless-steel kit. "I just hope I don't get assigned a hairy spe-cies. I can't stand all that hair hanging off of me all the time." She stared at Kennedy's thick hair. "No offense."

Orien stepped in front of Geenen. "Speaking of guard-ians, I can't believe you got Zuele Zuniz. I'm *obsessed* with the Golden Phase."

"What's the Golden Phase?" Kennedy asked.

For the first time, Orien looked at Kennedy like she was from a different planet. Then she grabbed her arm and dragged her into the room next door. Orien kicked clothes and shoes out of the way, clearing a path for Kennedy, Pengar, and Geenen.

The room was filled with holograms of rebellious-looking aliens, each programmed to say:

"Wow, Orien, is it possible that you get more beautiful and brilliant with each moon?"

"Orien, the universe needs you."

"Orien, is there anything you can't do?"

An enlarged Evolver class photo was displayed against the far wall. "This is the Golden Phase," Orien said. "They were the most famous phase in history. The Golden Phase was legendary. See? There's Zuele. She was the queen of them all. Everyone lived for Zuele's approval."

"I have seen this before," Kennedy said. "Miles Pierce showed it to me during my orientation."

Orien gasped. "*You* know Miles Pierce?"

"Kind of."

"I think I'm the most like Miles, but I'm trying to be more like Zuele—you know, excellent, focused, and fierce, but Miles was a fun flirt. He dated almost everyone in the Golden Phase." Orien pointed to another being in the photo. "There's Vivith Brandth, Reddick's mom." Reddick's mother had been a lovely woman with the same striking blue eyes as her son. "Don't even get me started on the fact that Reddick Brandth is your guide." Kennedy was about to ask how she knew that, but Orien did not give her a chance. "My guide is an eight-eyed Phase Three named Ith Las, who slobbers when he talks."

Kennedy focused on a pale boy in the photo. "Hey, there's Enforcer Tusk."

"Yeah, but no one really mentions him when they talk about the Golden Phase. Can you believe Zuele used to date him?"

"She did?" Kennedy asked.

"I know, it's shocking, right? Everyone was in love with Zuele—I mean, everyone—and she chose Enforcer Tusk?"

"Maybe it's because he worships her," Kennedy said.

"How could he not? She's Zuele Zuniz." Orien pointed to another familiar face in the photo. "There is Gonzi Gretho; he's a huge singer on the planet Madilieu. There's Eka Mint and Janekis Opris—the latest to be murdered by Malant Tarish."

Geenen cleared her throat and motioned her head at Pengar, who was now looking at the floor. An uncomfortable energy filled the room. Orien formed a visual prayer of alignment, and Kennedy formed one, too, though it felt forced.

"That is Leandor Everin," Orien said, pointing to a handsome boy in the photo. "Leandor was the most famous member of the Golden Phase, mostly because he was a Veilless."

"What's a Veilless?"

"The Veilless are these super powerful beings who can infuse technology with consciousness. Rumor is Leandor and Zuele had a secret thing going for a while. Anyway, you wouldn't believe how many Syncrocperiences have been created about the Golden Phase. I wish my guardian had been in the Golden Phase. She's old and feeble, and she always forgets what she's saying halfway through saying it. You're so lucky." Orien took a strand of Kennedy's hair in her hands and searched it for split ends. "So, what's he like?"

"Who?" Kennedy asked.

"Reddick! I saw footage of him returning this evening with Corijean."

Orien drew a screen in the air and projected a gossip program called *Symetran Society* from her Sectnot. The episode analyzed a video of Reddick and Corijean from earlier that evening, as did Kennedy. "Why are they following him?"

Orien scratched her hand through the screen, and it evaporated. "You're joking, right? Reddick's family is practically royalty in this galaxy. Didn't you hear me say his mother was in the Golden Phase? His greatest grandmother, Cissoria Brandth, founded the Evolvers, and his father is the Chief Minister of the entire Evolver Organization."

Kennedy always knew there was something about Reddick that set him apart, but she had no idea that he was famous.

Orien told Kennedy all about the Brandth dynasty and briefly educated her on the scandals they had endured. "If you could confirm his and Corijean's relationship status, you could probably end up on *Symetran Society*," Orien said, "but my sources tell me Reddick's father does not want him dating anyone who is not from Symetra."

"That's not very evolved," Kennedy said.

Orien shrugged. "There's nothing evolved about tradition."

Pengar stepped between Orien and Kennedy again. "My uncle said humans are very peculiar in their mating habits. He said they take one person, put them in a mansion, and then have a bunch of people fight over that person. He also said that all the females throw drinks in each other's faces." Pengar slapped her forehead, causing one of the flowers to wilt and fall out of her high bun. "I wish I had a drink to throw in your face, Kennedy!"

"They only do that stuff on reality TV." Kennedy informed her.

Pengar was confused. "So... then it is reality?"

"No, it's entertainment."

Orien ran a finger over her emotion blocker, an ear cuff with different-colored jewels in it. "I once dated a human boy from India—technically, he was only a quarter human. His name was Raj Kapoor. Do you know him, Kennedy?"

"I've never been to India."

Geenen raised her hand, demanding immediate attention. "That's enough gossip for one night. You're going to make her think we're primitive. Kennedy has a big day tomorrow, and I'm sure she wants to get some rest."

Pengar wrapped her petite arms around Kennedy and hugged her. "If you need anything, we're not far."

Kennedy said goodnight to her new roommates and then walked inside her room. She felt anxious about the next day as she brushed her teeth and washed her face. She hopped into her large, fluffy, white bed and stared at the ceiling—hardly able to believe how far away from home she was. She wanted to contact her mother and let her know she had arrived safely, but her Sectnot informed her she would not be able to contact home until the next evening.

Kennedy tried to visualize what her first day of school on an alien planet would look like but kept coming up empty. Instead, she gazed out the floor-to-ceiling windows at the Five Seasons Forest, wondering what her father was doing at that very moment. "I'm here," she said into the darkness, hoping he could somehow sense her.

The next morning, Kennedy's Sectnot buzzed her awake; it would not stop buzzing inside her hand until she got out of bed. Once she did, her schedule became visible through the flesh of her palm.

> Segment One: Physical Conditioning/Alignment Combat
> Segment Two: Meditation
> Segment Three: Empowering Beliefs
> Segment Four: Dematerialization/Materialization
> Break
> Segment Five: Focus
> Segment Six: Planetary Studies
> Segment Seven: Elemental Allies
> Segment Eight: Gratitude/Intention

Kennedy closed her hand into a fist and the screen disappeared. The anxieties that plagued her at Desert Hills High did not exist here. There was no fear that she might slip and accidentally use her powers. There would be no hiding out at lunchtime, no rehearsed lies about why strange things were constantly happening around her. She was here *because* of her abilities, and that fact alone brought her immense comfort. Still, she needed to take the day moment-by-moment; otherwise, she would get overwhelmed, fake a stomachache, and crawl right back into bed.

Kennedy stared out her bedroom window and admired the early morning beauty of Symetra. The Five Seasons Forest was now in the middle of its daily spring. The melted snow from the previous night traveled in beautiful streams down Star Grave Mountain and irrigated the Behemoth trees before ultimately pouring into the Kathreeyan Ocean.

Her Sectnot instructed Kennedy to dress in her athletics. Once she was ready, she went down and jumped into the glass elevator car, which floated out of the garage and landed on a green path beside the Behemoth tree she now called home. Zuele stood fresh-faced in her white guardian uniform, sporting her usual French twist. In the sunlight, Kennedy could see strands of gray hair, but they were out of place beside Zuele's dewy complexion. "It is an honor to encounter your energy, young creator."

"It is an honor to encounter your energy, Guardian Zuniz," Kennedy said, but was then quickly distracted by a purple hummingbird with two sets of wings fluttering close to her face.

Zuele observed it. "That is a Himarith. I think it likes you."

Kennedy began talking to the Himarith like it was her pet. She loved nature and had always appreciated the free things in life, mostly because they were all she could afford growing up. Every time she saw a hummingbird back home, she felt it was the universe saying hello to her, and now the universe was saying hello to her in an alien language.

There was more wildlife on the winding path for Kennedy to feast her eyes upon. Large red birds with long, curved beaks flew in and out of the Behemoths, while a swarm of vibrant butterflies with circular wings fluttered north in a current of primary colors. A pack of what looked like white prairie dogs with long, flapping ears stood on their haunches and peeked their adorable faces above the tall grass.

The path ended in front of a large, glass, ivy-covered building. A fountain, ornamented with twenty-four floating planets, shone like a beacon of inclusivity out front. Half of the four-story building hovered over a body of water called Luminary Lake. Kennedy had no idea how it remained structurally sound.

"This is the Hover House," Zuele said. "This is where you will take most of your meals and do most of your studying."

Zuele and Kennedy walked past Luminary Lake until there was nothing ahead of them except the cliffs overlooking the Kathreeyan Ocean. Behind the Hover House, Kennedy could see the Institute's roof, which felt like seeing Disneyland from the freeway. She could not wait to get inside, but she would have to wait until after breakfast.

Zuele led Kennedy through a series of stretches. "Alignment Combat is how we protect ourselves. When you are trying to change the status quo, you make a lot of enemies, so it is imperative that you learn how to defend yourself."

"I thought you guys were pacifists. Isn't that why you're not fighting Malant?"

"We're not fighting Malant because Chief Minister Brandth still believes he is going to magically go away on his own. Anyway, you will receive a weapon when you graduate. Until then, you are just going to have to be resourceful."

A tall, blue robot marched towards them. "Here comes Scrawl. He is going to assist us in training." Scrawl was a full head taller than Kennedy and covered in a thin layer of silicone.

"Say hi to Kennedy Neff," Zuele told him.

Scrawl scanned Kennedy with his hand. "Your left side is weak."

"Nice to meet you, too," Kennedy muttered.

That morning, Zuele taught Kennedy how to make a proper fist, how to use momentum to land a more forceful punch, and how to read the energy of her opponent. Then she turned her loose on Scrawl, who pretended to yawn as she punched him. None of her punches landed the way she wanted them to—the way she saw them land in the movies. Her knuckles, now tender and bleeding, suffered the only damage.

Zuele mercifully brought it to an end. "Okay, that's good for today."

Scrawl laughed a robotic laugh. "I would not call that good. Let me know when you are ready to fight for real."

As he stomped away, Kennedy shook out her fist. "Boy, he's a real barrel of laughs. Can't you program him to be a little nicer?"

"No one trying to kill you will be nice." Zuele took some firest weed from her triangular pack and rubbed it on Kennedy's knuckles. "Scrawl will ensure that you are ready."

"Ready for what?"

"Anything." Zuele clapped her hands together and told Kennedy that it was time for Physical Conditioning. She pointed back towards the path that traveled around the Behemoths and up into the Five Seasons Forest. "Let's start you off easy. I want you to run three miles. Begin."

"That's easy?" Kennedy asked before jogging towards the forest. Kennedy's Sectnot was immediately dissatisfied with her speed. "*According to my calculations, you can go twenty-three percent faster,*" it said.

Kennedy sped up, but her Sectnot remained dissatisfied,

so it sent uncomfortable shocks throughout her body, making Kennedy feel like a dog in an electric collar. The only way to make them stop was to somehow find a faster speed. She was puffing smoke as she ascended another hill. Summer was rapidly approaching in the Five Seasons Forest, and the thick, humid air coated her lungs like molasses.

Kennedy had always assumed she was in decent shape. Mostly because she had to walk everywhere and was a healthy weight for her height, but she had been wrong. She was woefully underprepared for this level of physical exertion. She was not even able to enjoy the beauty of her surroundings because every time she took her focus off running, her Sectnot would shock her attention back into place. Its soothing voice encouraged her to release the human limitations she had placed on herself, which was a very ineffective pep talk. When the three miles were finally up, Kennedy fell to the grass and massaged the stitch in her side. Zuele peered down at her, looking immaculate in her white guardian uniform, while Kennedy panted. Stinging sweat spilled into Kennedy's eyes, and she squeezed them shut in discomfort.

Zuele helped her up and patted her on the back. "I will see you after meditation. Better hustle. You don't want to be late."

Kennedy braced herself on her knees and then walked back to her unit. Her roommates arrived back to their unit at the same time she did, and she was pleased to see they were just as sweaty as she was. They all took the center lift together and split off into their respective rooms to prepare for their segments. Before Geenen closed her door, she told Orien, "You better not make us late."

"You can't rush beauty," Orien yelled back at her.

Kennedy went into her bathroom and stood under her showerhead with wobbly legs. She discovered some makeup bugs on her counter, as well as a note with well wishes from Chancellor Kirat. Kennedy could not resist their convenience. The experience was just as unpleasant as it had been the night before, but once again, it was all over within thirty seconds. A blow-dry brush dried her hair, and Kennedy pulled it into a ponytail, not wanting it to be a distraction on her first day. She went inside her closet and slipped into one of her gray training suits. Then, she strapped on an empty triangular pack and walked out into the hallway, bringing nothing but herself.

Pengar waited outside Kennedy's door. Today, she adorned her high bun with purple and green leaves. She gave Kennedy a hug. "We're going to the Hover House first, and then we'll go to the Institute from there."

Geenen walked out of her room and pounded on Orien's door with her bony fists. "Come on! I don't want to miss breakfast!"

Orien opened her door. "I'm coming. I'm coming. Don't scramble your scales."

The girls hopped into their shared ridership and zipped out of their garage. Three minutes later, they pulled up to the Hover House and fell into line behind dozens of other riderships.

Orien leaned forward in her seat and invaded Kennedy's personal space while they waited for their turn to deboard. She tilted her face to one side. "Your makeup looks pretty this morning." Orien grabbed Kennedy's hand when the ramp lowered. "Come on, I am going to introduce you to everyone; if there's anyone you like, you let me know and I'll set you up." Kennedy was eternally grateful that she did not have to go through this alone. Orien waved at some Phase Two boys in forest green training suits. "This is Kennedy Neff. She's my new roommate from Earth!"

"Honor, earthling," replied one with blue skin and purple hair.

"Honor!" Kennedy yelled back at them as Orien dragged her along. When they entered a large foyer illuminated by dozens of tiny, floating, blazing suns, she smiled from ear to ear. The floor of the Hover House was transparent, so she could see into Luminary Lake. Brilliant-colored fish swam beneath Kennedy's feet. The fish were nearly as exotic as Orien, who seemed to be a close, personal friend of everyone she encountered.

When a pretty boy with acne and bad posture approached, Pengar pulled Kennedy away from Orien. "Here comes Ethwin. He is my intimate. I can't wait for you to meet him, Kennedy. I thank the Great Creator for him every day. He's a Phase Two. He's from the planet Chandwist. He doesn't talk a lot because his people have a very limited vocabulary."

"Good thing you talk enough for two." Geenen flicked Pengar's high bun.

"Thank you, Geenen," Pengar said as though it had been a compliment. Pengar introduced Kennedy to Ethwin and squealed, as if everything in her life were now perfect. Pengar hooked one arm through Ethwin's and one through Kennedy's. "What about you, Kennedy? Do you have an intimate back home?" she asked as they walked along.

"No."

"Well, I am sure a beauty like you will have an intimate in no time," Pengar assured her.

"Sounds a little too much like *inmate*," Kennedy chuckled, and so did Geenen.

Pengar didn't get the joke. "Orien doesn't want an intimate either. She likes her freedom. I wish I could be as free-spirited as she is, trying every kind of being on for size, waiting for the right fit."

"I'm not waiting for the right fit." Orien checked her flawless makeup in a small, compact mirror, which hovered on its own in front of her. "*I* am the right fit; everyone else is just fun. Besides, how am I supposed to know what I like if I don't try everything?" Orien peered around the foyer as though she were looking for something to try at that very moment. Orien did not belong to any category; she only belonged to herself. On Symetra, beings did not have to define themselves the way they did on Earth. They were not expected to stamp lifelong labels on themselves at an early age, the way humans were. Beings just liked what they liked when they liked it, and they didn't owe anyone an explanation.

The entrance hall opened into a large multi-planetary food court with different stands, one for every intelligent life planet. "I think I'll go for some earth food this morning," Orien said. "Your body can handle our food, too. Symetrans are not too different from humans. We are just more evolved, probably because we live on the same planet as Triphens." Orien grabbed Kennedy's left hand and pressed it against a scanner.

"What are you doing?" Kennedy asked.

"Your Sectnot is telling the kitchen which nutrients your body needs this morning." Then Orien pressed her own hand against the scanner.

A few minutes later, Orien reached onto a counter and

handed Kennedy a green smoothie with a sweet, edible straw protruding from it. Most of the recruits were either plant-based or pescatarian, except for the Polksequins, who possessed both the skin and eating habits of alligators.

"We always sit over here," Orien told Kennedy, leading her to a long, clear table where Geenen, Pengar, and Ethwin were already eating their breakfast. Geenen picked at an odorless ball of wax, while Pengar and Ethwin fed each other vibrant-colored fruit.

A bell chimed, and the entire dining hall stood for the Evolver pledge:

"Today, I am willing to learn.

Today, I am willing to teach.

Today, I am willing to live with an open heart and an open mind.

We are one. All is well."

Kennedy mouthed the words that appeared on her Sectnot screen, but it was hard to concentrate with so many different languages sounding throughout the room. A few of the recruits ended the pledge with a visual prayer of alignment, while Kennedy tracked a red-spotted fish swimming beneath her feet.

She sipped her surprisingly delicious smoothie and listened to the easy banter of her roommates. Several Phase Ones generously approached the table and introduced themselves to her. They appeared to be genuinely interested in Kennedy, though her emotion blocker prevented her from reading their feelings. "Why are they all speaking to me in English?" Kennedy asked Orien.

"It is customary to speak the language of the newcomer; it helps you feel welcome, and it keeps us evolving," Orien said.

Reddick walked into the dining hall, and everyone stopped to stare. Kennedy wasn't sure how she felt about this new, fancy, famous version of Reddick. She caught eyes with him, and the mutant butterflies returned with a vengeance. He nodded at her, and she nodded back. Then she watched him as he stood in line for his Symetran breakfast.

Orien followed her stare. "He's perfect, isn't he?" She stole a piece of fruit from Pengar, who was too preoccupied with Ethwin to notice. "It hasn't been easy for him, what with his mother's death and everything."

"He told me."

"Most here have a Malant story. I thank the Great Creator I don't have one, not yet anyway." Orien gazed across the table at Pengar, then back at Kennedy. "The Millintican Guard bombed Pengar's village when she was four years old," she whispered. "Malant targeted her family for sheltering refugees who had fled Millintica. Pengar lost an aunt, her cousin, and her older brother."

Kennedy looked over at Pengar, who did not seem to have a problem in the universe. "As for Reddick's mom..." Orien fanned her eyes. "I remember watching her funeral with my parents, it was one of my earliest memories. Reddick walked up to this hologram of his mother and spoke to her as though she were there. Then he stood back and said the Evolver pledge. He wasn't much older than me. He made the prayer of alignment with the wrong fingers, and in that moment, the entire planet vowed to mother him. Ever since then, he has been called Symetra's son."

Reddick now sat at his own long table, filled with other intimidating-looking aliens in their Phase Three uniforms. Orien pointed out the boy next to him: "That's Xan Ilna. We almost kissed once." He was a tall, bronzed boy with a triangle tattoo on his neck that changed colors like a mood ring. When Corijean showed up at the table and demanded that he move so she could sit next to Reddick, Xan's tattoo turned black. Thecla Atter, a purple Phase Three, scooted over for Corijean when Xan refused.

Orien watched Kennedy watch Reddick. "You like him, don't you?"

Kennedy turned a violent shade of red. "What? No. Of course not."

"It's okay if you do; everyone thinks he's gorgeous, even Geenen."

"Who?" Geenen asked.

"Reddick Brandth," Orien replied.

Geenen's alien face curled up in disgust. "No, I don't. He's weird-looking. You're all weird-looking."

ELEVEN

After breakfast, Kennedy followed her roommates behind the Hover House to a jungle-like garden, with wild, exotic flowers twisting around even larger exotic flowers. At the end of the garden was an ivy-covered tunnel, which led to the entrance of the Institute. As they traveled through the tunnel, a sweet fragrance rode the wind. Pengar told Kennedy it was the naries—blue flowers with pink centers. Ethwin had picked Pengar a whole bouquet of naries for their first progression anniversary.

Chancellor Kirat greeted them at the end of the tunnel. "Good morning, young creators. I am here to give Kennedy a tour of the Institute. How are you settling in?" the Chancellor asked.

"Good, I think," Kennedy said.

"Well, we had better move along, as there is much I want to show you before your meditation segment."

Kennedy waved at her roommates and followed the Chancellor. The end of the tunnel opened to a large lawn. To Kennedy's right were a dozen green houses and gardens; beyond them was the Kathreeyan Ocean. To her left was the Evolver

Institute. It was a large, glass, bracket-shaped building that backed into the Five Seasons Forest. It was seven stories tall and half a mile wide. Two domes capped the edges of the building, and one large one stood in its center.

The bronze doors were open, and birds flew in and out of a foyer filled with lifelike sculptures of important-looking aliens. Kennedy stopped in front of one: Cissoria Brandth, founder of the Evolvers and Reddick's greatest grandmother. She had been a stately woman, with strong features and eyes fixed permanently on the horizon.

Kennedy and Chancellor Kirat walked past a bank of elevators into a busy hallway with recruits headed in multiple directions.

"What is that?" Kennedy pointed to two crystal doors, guarded by two Triphens.

"That is the Hall of Experiences," Chancellor Kirat said. The Triphens moved aside, allowing them to enter the Institute's central dome. Sunlight streamed through the skylights, reflecting off thousands of small crystals meticulously arranged on full-height shelves. The Evolver pledge, inscribed in multiple languages, adorned the spaces between the rows of experiences. Three moons in various phases were depicted on the gleaming center tiles, while a stained-glass wall showcasing the Antastropolith Galaxy separated the Hall of Experiences from the Five Seasons Forest.

"Here, you may walk in the shoes of the Evolvers who have come before, as well as a few Evolvers who are still serving. You can see what they saw and feel what they felt. Unfortunately, you will not be able to enter this space without your guardian or guide until you are a Phase Three."

Kennedy thought of Reddick bringing her in here and smiled.

Chancellor Kirat moved Kennedy along and led her down several flights of stairs to the bowels of the Institute. They ended up in a wide, dark hallway, which was nowhere near as impressive as the Hall of Experiences had been. Kennedy felt a strange humming sensation in her chest as she entered.

"This is the Hall of Labs. Recruits may only enter this hall with their guardians consent." The Chancellor aimed her Rivil at a door, and it slid open. "That is the DNA Lab." She pointed at another door. "The Limb Regrowth Lab." She clicked her Rivil again. "That is the Proof of Life in Other Universes Lab." Kennedy tried to see inside, but it was dark. The Chancellor pointed to the double doors at the end of the hallway. "That is the Adversary Lab. We won't be opening those doors; we cannot let anything escape."

Chancellor Kirat stopped and looked around. "This is not the most beautiful part of the Institute, but it is my favorite. Sometimes at night, when everyone is gone for the day, I come down here and just marvel at it. This is where we change the universe. It gives me a thrill just thinking about it."

Then something began to pound against the Adversary Lab's doors, and the humming intensified inside Kennedy's chest.

"Let's move along," the Chancellor said. "We don't want to agitate what's behind those doors."

Chancellor Kirat then took Kennedy on a tour of the facilities, including the gym, pools, art gallery, music room, and a library brimming with ancient literature from across the universe. The hallway walls were decorated with the Institute's alumni:

Havlin Orn had discovered the Mealial Galaxy; Sabinus Aub was the first to invent invisible shields; and Rasmus Strope created Dematerialization-proof clothing. Kennedy, who did not have a scientific mind, did not believe she was capable of anything so extraordinary. She felt like an imposter standing in this hall of accomplishments.

Chancellor Kirat sensed her intimidation. "Everyone who ever traversed these hallways faced challenges, but they grew beyond them, and you will too. One day, you will have a plaque on these walls. Even though you may not see it now, I firmly believe it." Chancellor Kirat gave her a supportive shoulder squeeze. "Now, let's get you to meditation before it ends."

Chancellor Kirat delivered her to the west wing of the Institute, inside a planetarium filled with lifelike images of the cosmos. Phase Ones and Phase Twos were perched atop floating mats, already in the middle of their meditation segments. Chancellor Kirat informed Kennedy that the planetarium on the opposite side of the Institute offered zero-gravity meditation, where you could float through the silence of simulated space and quiet your mind, but that was reserved for Phase Threes.

Chancellor Kirat led Kennedy to an empty mat beside Geenen and then whispered, "Have an excellent first day, young creator."

Kennedy hopped on the floating mat and grew so relaxed that she fell asleep. She was about to slip from her mat when Geenen instinctively grabbed a handful of her suit and caught her. Kennedy had no trouble staying awake after that. When meditation ended, a bell chimed, and a line of Triphens filled the room. They outstretched their small hands towards the recruits and blessed them. Their loving energy nearly brought Kennedy to tears. They instantly raised her vibration and made her feel as though she were capable of taking on the day.

When Kennedy and her roommates walked out of the meditation planetarium, Zuele was there, waiting. Orien got to her before Kennedy could: "Guardian Zuniz, it is such an honor to encounter your energy. My name is Orien Truin, and I have been *obsessed* with the Golden Phase ever since I learned about you in early school. You've changed my life. What was it like to be such a huge part of history?"

Zuele smiled wistfully. "We did not know we were in the Golden Phase at the time."

"You are such an inspiration. I want to be just like you." Orien stared at Zuele the way Zuele had stared at the Five Seasons Forest, like she was the Evolvers' greatest achievement. "Is it true that the Emperor of Celail once proposed to you?"

"Sorry about her." Geenen dragged Orien away from Zuele. "I think her hair dye is starting to seep into her brain. We'll save you a seat at break, Kennedy."

Kennedy smiled appreciatively at Geenen and then followed Zuele to the bank of elevators. The interior was dark and filled with more lifelike images of space. "Why is everything space-themed here?" Kennedy inquired, and then observed a black hole spinning in the center of a distant galaxy.

"Our goal is to explore the ever-expanding universe; our surroundings never let us forget that."

The elevator took them up to the seventh floor. Only a handful of rooms occupied the floor. Zuele pointed her Rivil at a pair of white double doors, and they slid open to reveal a spacious white loft. A wall of windows, currently open, faced the forest. Blue birds flew in and out of a spindly tree that grew through the middle of the room. Futuristic exercise machines stood in front of a rock-climbing wall adjacent to the doors.

"Welcome to your training room," Zuele said.

"This is all for me?"

Zuele waved her hand over an interactive glass desk, and a three-dimensional mini-map of the discovered universe sprang from it. Twenty-four of the planets were highlighted. "Let's jump right in." They relaxed into matching white recliners on opposite sides of the glass desk. "This universe is constantly expanding. It is not a gentle process; there is chaos, and there are explosions. Let me dispel the idea that your expansion will be any different. I am here to remind you of your true nature. I am here to help you evolve. Our time-space reality on this planet is centuries ahead of what your time-space reality is on Earth. We have transcended linear thinking."

Kennedy was already lost.

Zuele leaned toward her. "This physical world you see is a secondary world. True power lies in the first world, the world of consciousness. It is a world of energy and frequency. A world where we can break physical laws or rewrite them entirely. The Triphens and the Dark Panel operate in that world. Unfortunately, the world of consciousness is unbiased; just like fire, it can create or destroy. Do you understand?"

"You're saying that the Triphens use consciousness for good, and the Dark Panel uses it for evil."

"Exactly, and you are going to use consciousness to become an Evolver. We have a significant amount of work ahead of us. It is not going to be easy for you to shift your paradigm and overcome your human limitations. This is normal. You will fail—often. I want you to prepare yourself for that." Zuele drummed her fingers on her armrest. "May I be blunt?"

"I thought you *were* being blunt," Kennedy said.

"You have an inferiority complex. You never feel good enough. You still think there is something wrong with you. You grew up in your sister's shadow. You have serious issues surrounding your father. You feel immense guilt over the anger you secretly harbor towards your mother... We will spend a considerable amount of time consciously replacing these subconscious patterns."

Kennedy felt the need to defend herself from Zuele's brutal diagnosis, but Zuele made it clear this was not a dialogue.

"You are creating your own reality. The mind is the most powerful tool in the entire universe. I am going to teach you how to use it properly." Zuele fished a small, curved device from the top drawer of the desk and handed it to her. "This is called a Thought Projector; it is going to help you organize your scattered thoughts. The red thoughts are those that are not beneficial to you; they typically lead to overthinking and self-doubt. Green thoughts are the ones that *serve* you, and blue ones are your beliefs, which are the hardest to change. Now, I am going to step out for a moment and leave you alone with your thoughts. Try your best to consolidate the red ones. When I come back, I want you to tell me which of your limiting beliefs you would like to eradicate first." Zuele turned off the lights and then stepped out into the hallway.

Kennedy weighed the platinum device inside her palm; multicolored lights blinked up its side. She latched it onto the curve of her ear, and a matrix of red thoughts filled the room. Beyond them, she could see her beliefs and serene thoughts splayed against the far wall, but she needed to organize the red thoughts before she could get anywhere near them.

This is not going to be easy, she thought.

Additional red thoughts began to form in her mind.

This is not going to be easy.   *This is not going to be easy.*

This is not going to be easy.

Stop, she thought.

Stop.

Stop.

Stop.

The red thoughts repeated themselves like an insolent child shouting, 'I know you are, but what am I'? Kennedy realized the thoughts moved with the movement of her hands, so she consolidated all the "stops" into one minimized pile, and they dissolved from the room. Her anxious thoughts about the program became visible:

I have no idea what I am doing.   I am already behind. This was a mistake.   This was a mistake.   Zuele already regrets choosing me.   I can't do this.   I have no idea what I am doing.   This was a mistake.

Seeing her thoughts made her feel a sense of shame—more red, shameful thoughts appeared in response. She continued to organize the thoughts into piles without thinking, because thinking only served to make the room more crowded.

Kennedy was slightly mortified by the extent to which Reddick consumed her thoughts as she continued to navigate through the swamp of her mind. The data showed that she thought about him nearly as much as the other elusive man in her life. Kennedy stayed on task, compiling all of the "I'm not pretty enough for Reddick's" into one sad pile.

Nearly half an hour later, Kennedy had cleared enough space in her mind to focus on the blue beliefs—the poisoned well from which all the other thoughts sprang. It upset Kennedy to know she was feeding herself such garbage. It felt like subconscious self-abuse. She would never treat anyone else this horribly. She sat down in her white recliner and drank them in. Thankfully, not all of them were bad...

I AM TALENTED.

I HAVE GIFTS.

I CARE ABOUT PEOPLE.

PEOPLE DON'T CARE ABOUT ME.

I CAN HELP PEOPLE.

I AM UNWORTHY.

I AM NOT GOOD ENOUGH.

SOMETHING IS WRONG WITH ME.

I AM A MISTAKE.

I AM SCARED.

I AM NOT SUPPOSED TO BE SCARED.

NO ONE ELSE IS SCARED.

I AM A HARD WORKER.

IT IS MY FAULT MY DAD DIDN'T WANT ME.

I AM A BURDEN.

I WILL LOVE MYSELF WHEN I AM PERFECT.

I AM A GOOD PERSON.

I DESERVE GOOD THINGS.

I AM BLESSED.

I AM GRATEFUL.

IT IS GOING TO BE OKAY.

She turned from the blue wall of beliefs to the green thoughts that were currently serving her.

I am happy.

I am healthy.

I am loved.

I am alive.

I am connected to infinite intelligence.

I am gifted.

I am blessed.

The serene thoughts made her feel much better. Focusing on them zapped more red thoughts out of the room. Zuele knocked on the door, and Kennedy quickly removed the Thought Projector from her ear. The thoughts disappeared back inside her mind. Zuele handed Kennedy a squishy Breathing Ball and asked her to breathe in sync with it. After ten minutes of this, Kennedy was once again calm.

Zuele rested her ankle on her knee. "Which limiting belief should we start with?"

"I am unworthy," Kennedy muttered.

"So, you would like to slay the biggest dragon first?" Zuele smiled.

But Kennedy did not.

Zuele sighed. "You have been telling yourself the wrong story, that's all. It is time to consciously tell yourself a new story."

"Can't you just fix my story with your alien magic, like you did for Molly that day in the desert?"

"You are an Evolver. You must learn how to do this in order to teach others."

Kennedy was grateful when they moved onto Dematerialization. Zuele and Kennedy accessed the Five Seasons Forest from the back of the Institute. "As Enforcer Tusk told you last night, the interiors of the Institute and Hover House are protected by a Dematerialization Web. If you so much as try to Dematerialize inside them, the web will catch you, and we will send you home with a modified memory."

Kennedy gulped.

"It is also forbidden to Materialize inside any of the living units or outside of campus until after you graduate. You are free to practice around the grounds, though."

Kennedy's Charge Ring began to glow a bright white color. "Why does it do that?"

"Because it is drawing in all the free energy surrounding us. A lot of things can go wrong while using this technology, which is why you will be studying it for years before you do it alone in the field. Dematerialization requires that your chips, clothing, and coordinates all sync up. If they do not sync, it could spell disaster. Several Evolvers lost their lives in the early days of this technology. Due to rigid safety protocols, we have now gone nearly a hundred years without losing one."

"What happened to them?"

"Remember the white light?"

Kennedy nodded.

"They never came back. All in all, it's not a bad way to go. It's instantaneous, and you kind of just reemerge into the Eternal Energy Field."

"What's the furthest anyone has Dematerialized before?"

"Not very far. In human distances? I'd say about fifty miles. Dematerialization is often used during combat. If someone is aiming a weapon at you, you could Dematerialize in and out of sight, so they would never be able to get a lock on you."

Today, Zuele expected Kennedy to Materialize two feet from where she was currently standing. Even though it was just a training exercise, Kennedy's mind grew busy with all the things that could go wrong. The extreme power of the energy terrified Kennedy, and, ultimately, she was unable to do it. They tried several more times, but Kennedy only seemed to be getting worse at it.

"Don't worry, you are going to get this," Zuele encouraged. "You are still using that linear human brain of yours. It is going to take some time. My advice? Release everything you *think* you know."

That part was easy, because right now, all Kennedy knew was absolutely nothing. By lunchtime, she was completely spiraling. She sat next to her roommates and picked at a grilled vegetable bowl, while her Sectnot urged her to take deep, cleansing breaths.

"Uh oh," Orien said, "you have first day face."

"What's first day face?" Kennedy asked.

"That face you make when you're in way over your head and know there's no way to get out of it. We all went through it, except for Geenen."

"That's not true," Geenen said through a mouthful of wax. "I came here to learn about advanced technology, but all my guardian wanted to talk about were my *feelings*. It's his favorite topic."

"Did he make you talk about your erroneous beliefs?" Kennedy asked her.

Geenen gave Kennedy an exasperated nod.

"What was one of yours?" Kennedy was hoping Geenen would say something about believing she was unworthy.

Orien answered for Geenen. "She thinks she knows everything. That is Geenen's erroneous belief."

Geenen elbowed Orien with her sharp, skinny elbow.

"Ahh," Orien yelled, "watch where you point those deadly weapons."

✦

"Focus is a superpower," Zuele said at the top of their next segment. All she wanted Kennedy to do was sit across from an object and focus on it until she was able to match its vibrational frequency. They started with a pen. Kennedy sat and stared at it for a few minutes before she was able to make it spin on the desk. Zuele clapped for her, and Kennedy took a bow. Then she tried to teach Kennedy how to write with it—without touching it. This was considerably harder, but by the end of the segment,

Kennedy was able to write "hi" from across the room.

In Planetary Studies, Zuele taught her about Symetra's five Continents: Parin, Boncreel, Adaviad, Sonluia, and Forritz. Today they focused mostly on Parin, the healing continent. Only Triphens lived there. They allowed other beings to visit for healing, but the intense energy prevented them from staying long. The training room was filled with a virtual tour of the frozen landscape—not just sights but smells and icy breezes against Kennedy's face. So far, Planetary Studies had been her favorite segment. Sitting next to Zuele and learning about Symetra was a thrill. She felt mildly disappointed when the lesson ended.

Kennedy put on a jacket and headed back outside with Zuele for Elemental Allies. There was now a chill in the air as the Five Seasons Forest transitioned into its daily autumn. Other recruits stood near Luminary Lake with their guardians, receiving lessons catered specifically to them. Zuele placed her hands behind her back. "Technology contains all the wisdom of fallible beings; nature contains the wisdom of the universe. Elemental Allies is about using this universal intelligence to assist you in all your endeavors. Since you were practicing some of these skills back in Tucson, Elemental Allies should be an easier segment for you, and it will also greatly assist you with Alignment Combat." Zuele motioned to a pile of rocks. "I want you to summon these rocks and aim them at the target." Zuele propped up a metal shield twenty feet ahead of them. "Here, I'll demonstrate." Zuele centered herself. The rocks lifted and fell in line beside her. She pushed her hands forward, and the rocks hit the center of the shield, one after another, like machine gun fire.

"That was incredible!" Kennedy now understood why Zuele was considered a legend.

Zuele waved her off. "You try."

The best Kennedy could do was hit the corner of the shield, and that only happened after several tries. *I suck*, Kennedy thought.

"*This thought will produce undesired outcomes*," her Sectnot warned.

Kennedy cleaned up her thoughts. *It's normal for me to suck right now, but one day, if I keep practicing, I'll get good at this.* These modified thoughts must have satisfied her Sectnot because it did not admonish her again.

Before their workday concluded, Zuele led Kennedy through a segment of gratitude, where Kennedy was to ruminate on all the things she was grateful for. Zuele smiled when Kennedy listed her as one of them. Zuele then asked Kennedy to set her intentions for the following day's segments and visualize them before bed.

After her segments, Kennedy decided to go and explore the autumn colored Five Seasons Forest. Kennedy beamed at a pile of red, orange, and gold leaves, as though they were dear friends of hers. She pointed her finger at them, and they rose to meet her. Her finger twirled them into a beautiful ribbon of color. Kennedy danced the thread of leaves around until a gust of wind came, sending her friends back to the forest floor. The leaves crunched beneath her boots and then disintegrated within minutes, making room for the following day's leaves. She pulled out her BELIEVE notebook and sketched the forest the way she saw it, like the inside of a champagne glass with the bubbles racing towards the top.

It did not take long for Kennedy's thoughts to turn to her father. If focus really was a superpower, then she would use it to bring her father into her life. She focused on him until it grew too cold for her to remain in the forest.

That night, after dinner, Kennedy's Sectnot informed her she could now contact home. She followed its instructions and walked to the far wall of her closet. She smiled when the wall slid open to reveal a small room that contained nothing but a pair of golden footprints.

Kennedy stepped onto the golden footprints, and the light swallowed her whole, just like it had in the Evolver house back in Tucson. The same shock passed through her cells. A voice filled her mind, informing her that she would only have fifteen minutes to spend with her family. Then she was standing in a place she had never been before. She assumed the technology had delivered her to the wrong address, but she had no idea how to return to her room. She knew she was in Tucson because she could see the Santa Catalina Mountains through a sliding glass door. The late afternoon sun sparkled off a swimming pool in the backyard. A chrome triangle shone from the nightstand, its faint golden aura matching Kennedy's.

Then Phantom jumped onto the bed. "Bubba!" Kennedy

screamed. Phantom sniffed her hand, observed her golden aura, and then ran back under the bed, instinctively knowing something was off with his owner. "Phantom, it's me," she said.

"Kennedy?" she heard her mother call from the hallway.

"Mom?"

"Kennedy!" Roberta ran inside the primary bedroom and wrapped her arms around her daughter. However, Kennedy could not get the full sensation of her; it felt like putting a shoe on a foot that was asleep. Roberta stepped back and cupped Kennedy's face between her hands. "You look beautiful." Then she hugged her again. "I'm so glad you're okay."

"Um, where are we?" Kennedy asked.

"Zuele didn't tell you?"

"Tell me what?"

Roberta smiled at her surroundings. "This is our new house, Kennedy."

Kennedy furrowed her brow. "What?"

"Zuele said it was your dream to buy me a house like this." Roberta grew emotional. "She said you would be able to focus better if you didn't have to worry about your family struggling back home. I thought she would have told you by now. She said she wanted to wait until after you left because she didn't want money to be the reason you decided to go. She said this house was just a drop in the bucket for you. You're a millionaire now, Nedy."

Kennedy needed to sit down. "What?" she said again.

"She really didn't tell you any of this?"

"I knew I'd be paid for my time here, but she didn't tell me—" Kennedy hyperventilated. "I asked her if I could send money home, but I didn't expect—" Grateful tears filled Kennedy's eyes. "A *millionaire*?"

"I had the exact same reaction... You told her you wanted to make something of yourself so I could quit working. Is that true?"

"Yeah."

Roberta wrapped an arm around Kennedy. "Well, I quit the restaurant, but I'm still selling real estate. In fact, I listed the house the Evolvers were living in by Sabino Canyon. Zuele received a cash offer for it, and she is letting me keep the commission. It will be enough for us to live off of for years."

Kennedy was still speechless. A king-size mattress with a tall, cream, button-tufted headboard replaced the queen-size bed they used to share. Kennedy could already see the places where Phantom had clawed it.

"Come on." Roberta picked up the chrome triangle Kennedy was emitting from and said, "I'll give you a grand tour."

The brand-new home was located inside a gated community called Sterling Canyon Estates. Moving boxes were still littered everywhere. Kennedy found her mother's vision board propped up against a wall in her office.

My mom has an office.

Roberta usually worked at the kitchen table, unable to concentrate because her children were watching TV only a few feet away. Roberta lightly kicked the vision board. "I guess I'm going to have to dream some bigger dreams now." Roberta turned serious. "Listen to me, Kennedy; we can give it back. If you decide you want to come home, if there ever comes a time when you don't want to be an Evolver, we can give it all back."

"Are you mental? We're not giving it back."

Roberta laughed. "Audrey loves it, too. She even saved you the better room."

Kennedy grinned. "She did?"

"Anyway, enough about us! What have you been up to?"

Kennedy told her mother about the two weeks since she had last seen her; she decided to omit the part where she had fallen out of an airplane. She tried to tell her a little bit about her roommates and the Five Seasons Forest, but the automated voice notified her she only had one minute left. Roberta cried on her shoulder. Kennedy pulled away as the voice counted down to thirty seconds. "I love you, Mom."

"I love you too, Nedy." They hugged until the transmission cut off. Once Kennedy was back inside the small, dark room, her Sectnot informed her she would be able to contact home again in ten moons.

Kennedy felt a strong sense of pride in herself as she prepared to go to bed. She didn't know what she would do with the extra brain space she would have now that finances were no longer an issue. She felt grateful that she could provide for her family. But most importantly, she felt a brand-new sense of purpose, a powerful new reason to be the best she could be. Her Sectnot notified her that her current line of thinking was achieving a very high level of vibration and that desired outcomes were extremely likely from that heightened state.

TWELVE

Kennedy was awake before the sun came up the next morning. She dressed in her athletic gear and made the trek down to Luminary Lake. Her Sectnot provided her with exercises she could do while she waited for Zuele. So Kennedy got to work. *"No one outworks us,"* her Nana had said. Kennedy could not guarantee she was going to be the best Evolver, but she could guarantee she was going to be the hardest working one.

Zuele arrived with the sun and seemed impressed to find Kennedy already working. "You're up early," she said.

"I talked to my mom last night," Kennedy said. "I want to thank you for what you did for my family... I don't know how to thank you."

"Don't thank me; it is your money, and you told me how you wanted to spend it. I aided your request. Plus, money isn't as difficult as you humans make it out to be."

"It doesn't feel that way when you grow up poor."

"Another limiting belief."

"It's the truth."

"It is also true that your beliefs shape your reality—this applies to all aspects of life. Money is a relationship you have to work on just like all other relationships; if there is no trust there, it is not going to be much of a relationship, is it?" Zuele removed a piece of lint from her white guardian uniform. "In any case, I'm delighted that your mother likes the home. She is an amazing woman who raised an amazing daughter. She deserves it, and so do you."

Kennedy fought the urge to violently hug her guardian.

Scrawl trudged towards Kennedy, stomping his large feet in the grass. "There they are! The softest hands in town."

Kennedy glared at him. "Shut it, you bucket of screws."

Scrawl laughed, then shoved Kennedy to the ground.

Kennedy looked at Zuele and cried foul, but Zuele put her hands up and said, "You've got to stay ready, especially when he's around."

✦

Kennedy's first few days were a blur of soreness and confusion. Every evening after her segments, she went to the Hover House and studied in the common room, which was filled with giant wooden tables, deep chairs, and a roaring fireplace. Then she would walk downstairs to the dining hall and meet her roommates for dinner. She was slowly beginning to adapt to life on a different planet, and with each new day, her nerves improved.

When her Planetary Studies assignment called for a report on the desert planet of Scotnath, Kennedy traveled to the third floor of the Hover House, known as the Information Level, and checked out a private research room. It was a narrow little room with nothing more than a glass desk and some chairs. After holding her Sectnot to the desk, a small avatar of Kennedy dressed in a Phase One uniform emerged and perched itself on the desk's corner, swinging its legs over the edge, waiting for Kennedy's search command. Kennedy couldn't believe how true-to-life her little avatar was. "Can I find something for you?" she asked, matching Kennedy's exact voice.

A thought hit Kennedy like a lightning bolt. "Find me the Submerged Station on Earth."

"Right away." Kennedy's avatar dove into the center of the desk, then disappeared. A hologram of the underwater station sprang from the glass top and filled the small room. Kennedy asked the avatar to show her the station's log from the year she had been born. A lengthy list of names scrolled in front of her. Kennedy beamed at the desk as gratitude, then doubt, washed over her. *Could it really be this easy?*

"I am looking for an Aaron," she said, knowing Aaron was not her father's real name. She wasn't surprised when the search came up empty; the name was obviously a fake, an attempt on her father's part to hide the fact he was an alien.

Kennedy asked the avatar to maximize the details of these records and cheered when they ballooned out to include an image of each passenger. It would take her days to go through the list of passengers who had traveled to and from Earth that year, but she couldn't wait to get started.

Kennedy scrolled excitedly through the register of alien faces. The Evolvers took before and after shots of the travelers, both with and without their earthly disguises. Kennedy could not believe how human some of them looked. She was not even a fraction of the way through the list when the lights flashed inside the room, indicating the Hover House was closing for the night. Kennedy hailed her ridership and went to her unit nearly blind from all the different species she had seen, but still she smiled as the hope of finding her father began to take root.

For every nine days they worked, the Evolver recruits received three days off. Kennedy had been eagerly anticipating her days off ever since she discovered the Submerged Station's register. She spent every second of her free time holed up at the Hover House, making her way through what seemed like an endless list of alien faces. But none of these aliens—who were required to provide a detailed itinerary to the Evolvers—had been anywhere near San Diego the weekend her parents met.

Kennedy was so frustrated that she threw her notebook against the wall, pulled her knees to her chest, and hung her head. Her Sectnot offered to guide her through some breathing exercises, but Kennedy silenced it. After a few minutes, she got up and retrieved the alien notebook her mother had bought her, which had fallen open to a page filled with doodles of Behemoth trees and her father's tattoo. Kennedy closed her notebook and ran her fingers across the letters on the front: BELIEVE.

Her avatar was once again sitting at the edge of the desk, waiting for Kennedy's next search command.

Kennedy flipped to the page of the notebook with her father's tattoo and held it up. "Do you know what this symbol means?"

The avatar squinted its eyes and nodded.

"You do?" Kennedy shouted. "Well? What is it?"

"That is the symbol for the Antastropolith Alliance," the avatar said. "They were a secret society, made of influential beings—from across the galaxy—who formed to remove Malant Tarish from power."

"Do you know who was in the Alliance?"

The avatar shook its head. "They wouldn't be much of a secret society if I did. Though the Alliance is believed to have been started by Xavian Seelos, who was Chief Minister of the Evolvers when Malant Tarish overthrew—killed—King Rimago."

Kennedy sat back down at the desk and began to furiously scribble down notes.

Her avatar came and stood at the edge of her notebook, as though she were checking Kennedy's work. "Chief Minister Seelos and King Rimago had been childhood friends, and they were working together to strengthen relations between Millintica and the Evolvers. When Xavian learned of Rimago's murder, he encouraged the Evolvers to get involved in the conflict, but the council refused. Instead, they voted Xavian out as Chief Minister and replaced him with Theein Brandth. That is supposedly when Xavian started the Alliance. The Evolver Council knew the sway Xavian still had over the Evolvers and threatened to excommunicate anyone who followed him—legend has it, that few obeyed."

"So, Evolvers joined the Alliance?"

"And so did beings from across the galaxy."

"Is the Alliance still operating?"

"Allegedly. Janekis Opris was believed to be one of them."

"What do they want? What is the Alliance's goal?"

"They want to remove Malant Tarish from power and liberate the galaxy from the threat of the Dark Panel."

The lights flickered in the room, and Kennedy knew the Hover House was closing.

"Wait," she told the avatar before it jumped back inside the glass desk. "Do you, by any chance, know who my father is?"

Her avatar blinked. "Yes."

Kennedy's breath caught in her throat. "Who is he?"

Kennedy leaned forward in anticipation, and then a hologram of a monkey scratching its armpits appeared. It banged its fists on the desk and flashed Kennedy its gums.

The avatar nearly fell over laughing.

"You're hilarious," Kennedy said, unamused. The only way to stop her avatar from laughing was to log out, so Kennedy did. But she could not stay mad at her avatar, not after the breakthrough information she had just gleaned from it. She updated her notes. *So,* she thought, *my father was in the Alliance.* She felt some relief that he had at least been on the right side of history, whoever he was.

Kennedy returned to her unit in a daze. Geenen sat in the living area, surrounded by holograms of alien actors performing an alien sitcom. A laugh track oozed from the floor and ceiling. Geenen was delighted by their hijinks, but not Kennedy, who had to walk through one of them doing a spit take to get to the kitchen. She poured herself a glass of water and then went to her room.

Orien emerged from her own bedroom when she heard Kennedy in the circular hallway. "Where have you been?" she asked.

Kennedy was still lost in thought. "I was doing some work at the Hover House. Good night." She walked inside her room, but Orien followed her.

Orien assumed Kennedy's preoccupation meant something was wrong, but instead of allowing Kennedy to talk about what was bothering her, she decided to get Kennedy off the subject altogether. Evolvers were big proponents of going to bed angry. They reasoned that trying to solve a problem with the same energy that created it only served to make the problem worse. It was law. And since Kennedy was not in an aligned enough state to solve any problems, Orien decided to distract her. She looked around the stark white room. "You haven't decorated yet?" Orien walked to a small panel on the wall and held her Sectnot to it. "You can program the walls; you can change them every day if you want. Let's see... Earth's categories... How about the northern lights? That sounds beautiful." Then the northern lights glimmered across Kennedy's ceiling. "Or the Eiffel Tower?" A beautiful Parisian skyline appeared on the wall behind her bed.

Kennedy had been so busy training and obsessing about her father that she hadn't even considered decorating her room. "Can I put a Beatles poster up?" she asked Orien.

Orien nodded, and Kennedy's walls were filled with crawling beetles.

"No, not actual beetles." Kennedy held her own Sectnot to the panel and searched through various images of the Beatles.

Orien pointed at George Harrison. "I like that one. What's his story?"

"He's dead."

"What a shame," she said, fluffing up her cotton candy pompadour.

Kennedy opted for an *Abbey Road* poster because it was her all-time favorite album. She dedicated one wall of her room to the fall foliage of the Five Seasons Forest. She changed her ceiling to make it look like there were fairy lights hanging from it, and then she put a few flickering jack o' lanterns on one wall, since Halloween was only days away back home. She told Orien about the human holiday, and Orien said, "Pengar's people have a holiday like that, too. It's called the Sacred Day of Resurfacing. Last year, Pengar carried around her great aunt's hip bone as an act of remembrance."

Orien offered to print some linens for Kennedy with her fabric printer, then pointed to a bare sliver of the wall. "You need some images of your family in here." Orien helped Kennedy pick out empty, sparkly frames and told her to fill them with her favorite memories. Kennedy remembered when her family went camping in the White Mountains last summer. She and Audrey had stayed up late talking about boys inside their tent, while Roberta sat around the campfire and drank wine with the adults. Audrey told Kennedy all about her new boyfriend, Cody Ramirez, and Kennedy told Audrey about the golf caddie who had asked if he could kiss her on the eighteenth hole, to which Kennedy replied, "I'd prefer on the lips."

Kennedy held out her Sectnot, and an image of Audrey laughing inside her sleeping bag appeared in one of the sparkly frames. Kennedy then thought of her mother and how many Saturday nights they had pathetically spent together watching predictable romantic comedies, and a memory of Roberta with a girly smile on her face appeared in a frame. She thought of her Nana's smile every time Kennedy spoke conversational Spanish with her. She remembered Grandpa Jim's smile when he would twirl her to one of his favorite songs. She thought of her Tías and cousins at the family Christmas party in their new clothes, her uncles cheering her on every time she played basketball with her boy cousins. Her sanctuary. Phantom sleeping with his furry belly up and his pink tongue peeking out over his white chin. All these memories were now on her wall.

Then there was only one frame left to fill. Kennedy thought of her father, the man she had spent most of her time thinking about since childhood yet had never even seen. It was odd because Kennedy had a distinct feeling of him yet no image. But now, because of her avatar, she felt she knew him a bit better. She held out her Sectnot and smiled as the Alliance symbol appeared inside the frame.

Orien tilted her head. "The Antastropolith Alliance?"

"How do you know what that is?" Kennedy asked.

"I'm from the Antastropolith Galaxy. How do *you* know what that is?"

Kennedy liked Orien but was not sure she was ready to share her life's quest with her.

Orien planted her feet. "I'm not leaving here until you tell me."

Kennedy tangled her fingers. "My dad has this symbol tattooed on his wrist. It's one of the only things my mom can remember about him." Kennedy told Orien all she knew about her father and everything she was desperate to find out.

Orien listened with rapt attention, then grabbed Kennedy by the arm and dragged her to their unit's center lift. "Pengar, we're having a meeting downstairs, now!" Orien yelled at Pengar's door.

Kennedy followed Orien into the study nook on the first floor. "Geenen, turn that off." When Geenen didn't listen to her, Orien went and turned off the alien sitcom herself.

"I was watching that!" Geenen protested. "You know I allow myself one segment of entertainment per progression."

"What? What happened?" Pengar ran towards the study nook and asked, "Is everyone okay?"

Orien projected the Antastropolith Alliance symbol from her Sectnot, and it now floated there between the four of them. "We have a new mission," she said.

"New mission? I didn't know we had an old one," Geenen said.

Orien ignored her. "We are going to help Kennedy find her father. We have a code in this unit."

"Since when?" Geenen asked.

"Yeah, I didn't know we had a code," Pengar chimed in.

"We stick together no matter what. That's our code," Orien said. "Now, Kennedy's father met her mother in a place named—"

"San Diego," Kennedy said.

"Right, all she knows about him is that he had the Antastropolith Alliance symbol tattooed on the inside of his wrist."

"A tattoo? That's it?" Geenen finally rose from her spot on the couch. "There are nearly a trillion beings in this universe, and those are just the ones we know about. How do you suggest we find your father, Kennedy? Go door to door?"

"No, but I figured that with all the advanced technology here, there's got to be a way. Now that I know he was most likely a member of the Alliance, maybe there's some DNA test I could take."

"Evolvers don't have a DNA sample of every sentient being in the universe," Geenen said. "However, we *could* run your DNA through the Evolver database. Of course, that would only work if your father was an Evolver, and clearly, he wasn't if he impregnated your mom and took off."

Orien backhanded Geenen.

"What? That's not very Evolver-like!" Geenen yelped.

Pengar shook her head. "You need a guardian to get into the DNA Lab. I know because Ethwin did research down there for a progression, but now he's been transferred to the Emerging Planets Lab," she said proudly. "He said the funniest thing today—"

Geenen cut her off. "Why don't you just ask your guardian for help?"

Kennedy *had* asked Zuele for help in finding her father. A few days earlier, she had brought it up casually during her Elemental Allies segment, but Zuele immediately shot it down. *"Kennedy, I need you to focus on your training, not your father."*

"She won't help me." Then Kennedy turned something over in her mind. "Geenen, what about that chip you used the other night? The one that turned you into that scary creature?"

"A Switchip."

"Yeah, can I use one of those to disguise me so I can get into the Lab? Do you have one that looks like a guardian?" Kennedy asked.

"No, I don't."

"Well, can you make one?"

"Sure, Kennedy, I'll just whip up a piece of leading-edge

technology in my room," Geenen said sarcastically. "Besides, it's illegal to make a Switchip based on a real being's identity without their consent. Plus, it's nearly impossible. It would take eons to make something like that—it would require skin grafts, bone density scans, vocal cord duplication—"

"Okay, it was just an idea. Forget I mentioned it," Kennedy said.

The four of them sat and racked their brains.

A few seconds later, Pengar perked up. "What about Marr Ameer?"

"Yeah, Marr Ameer! That's not a bad idea, Pengar," Orien said.

Geenen groaned and leaned towards Kennedy as though they were the only two intelligent beings in the room. "Pengar went to Marr Ameer when she wanted to know if Ethwin liked her."

"So, she's like a psychic?" Kennedy asked.

Geenen rolled her giant eyes. "No, she just tells you what you want to hear and then charges you for it."

"Hey, she used to be a Nextier—until they let her go for stealing—but she predicted a lot of stuff," Pengar said. "Like she knew before I did that Ethwin was going to become my intimate, and she knew our first date was going to be at Syncrocperience."

"Wow, what an uncanny prediction." Geenen rolled her eyes again. "There's no possible way she could know that *everyone* our age has their first date at Syncrocperience."

"Reddick once promised he'd take me to Syncrocperience," Kennedy said.

Her roommates stopped and scrutinized her.

"Not like on a date or anything; pretty sure he just meant as friends, but it's, like totally, whatever."

Orien gave her a dubious look.

Kennedy pretended not to notice. "So, we'll go in the morning?"

"I still think there are smarter ways to waste our allowances," Geenen muttered.

"Do you have a better idea?" Kennedy asked her.

Geenen shook her head.

Kennedy smiled. "Then it's settled."

The next morning, when the girls headed to the outskirts of Crystal City, it was pouring rain. Marr Ameer's Love Cottage was an unfortunate name for an unfortunate business frequented by unfortunate beings. Their ridership lowered in front of a lone cottage with a mirrored exterior perched atop a dreary volcanic cliff. Kennedy and her roommates ran down the ramp of their ridership and inside the front door of the cottage without knocking to escape the torrential downpour.

The inside of the cottage was lousy with silver—silver furniture, silver carpet, silver drapes—it looked like the inside of a mirror ball. A hologram of Marr Ameer in the lobby promised her customers everlasting love and happiness. Her shiny, silvery hair was styled into a large pile. Simulated fireworks went off and holograms of happy couples filled the room. Some shared their testimonies, while others stared adoringly at one another. The rain must have scared off the rest of the rapacious romantics because the place was completely empty, save for the holograms.

Marr Ameer's booming voice spoke in a throaty language to

them over the intercom, "You may enter one at a time. Please have your payment ready."

"There's just going to be one of us today," Orien said into the security camera. "Unless you have any pressing questions about your thrilling love life, Geenen?"

Geenen elbowed her, and Orien doubled over in pain.

Pengar offered to go in first, partly to make Kennedy more comfortable and partly to find out why Ethwin had yet to say he loved her.

Kennedy sat and tangled her fingers as she anxiously awaited her turn.

Geenen mimicked a beautiful couple who held hands and recanted the story of how Marr Ameer brought them true love. "Spare me," she said, scratching her scales. "No one's that happy except for Triphens, and that's only because they are incapable of lower vibrational frequencies."

Orien raised an eyebrow. "I don't know; that one on the left might be able to make me that happy."

Pengar walked out of the room a few minutes later with a smile stretched across her face.

"Next," Marr grumbled over the intercom.

Kennedy shot to her feet, while Pengar said, "Apparently Ethwin likes me so much he doesn't even know how to process it. Marr said we're going to end up together."

"Please," Geenen said, "no one who gets together at our age stays together."

Orien agreed. "I'm with Geenen on this one. Would you really want just one being for the rest of your life? Sounds awful. There's an entire universe out there to be explored and experienced."

Kennedy shuffled into the reading room and met a woman with a sagging, disinterested face. Thunder clapped, rattling the cottage. Kennedy sat on the silver throne opposite Marr's silver throne and watched her roommates in the lobby from a security monitor on the wall. Kennedy slid her hands beneath her knees and tapped her feet. A heavy, glittery love candle flickered on the table. The fierce wind was creating a whistling sound through a loose windowpane as Marr took her sweet time preparing for the reading.

Marr presented Kennedy with a computerized monocle. "That will be four hundred coyels." Kennedy held the monocle over her left eye. It scanned her retina, and the Symetran currency was immediately transferred from Kennedy's account to Marr Ameer's.

Marr held out her hand. "I'm going to need a piece of jewelry, something personal."

Kennedy forked over her St. Jude necklace.

Marr Ameer pancaked it between her rough hands, closed her eyes, and exhaled deeply. "Hmm, there is someone. You have a destined intimate... He is your helper, and you will be his." Marr was not exactly trying to sell this performance. In fact, she looked positively bored as she forecasted Kennedy's romantic future. "I see Fyorisc stones and a strange green plant with a red ribbon. Your souls have traveled through several lifetimes together. You will be very lucky in love; you don't have a lot of energetic debt to pay off from previous lifetimes."

Kennedy was suddenly worried that Geenen had been right about Marr being a fraud. Her jaw adjusted so her Lengualizer could respond in Marr's throaty language. "Um, excuse me? I'm sorry to interrupt, but—"

Marr Ameer opened one eye to glare at her.

"I was actually wondering if you could tell me about my father instead."

"What is his name?"

"I don't know."

Marr Ameer popped open her other eye. "I'm afraid it's going to cost quite a bit more. I naturally need compensation for the higher toll that family readings take on me. It is double the price." Marr knew Kennedy was good for it, but Kennedy—who had just recently come into money—felt like telling her to get bent.

Marr leaned back in her chair, as though it did not matter to her either way.

Kennedy turned her attention from the irksome feeling of being swindled to the reassuring energy of abundance. She reminded herself that she could afford this. Her Sectnot commended the shift in thought as Kennedy transferred more coyels to Marr Ameer.

"What do you want to know about him?"

"I want to know who he is," Kennedy said.

Marr peered at Kennedy, wondering whether she should charge her more. She closed her eyes and exhaled deeply again, then tilted her head as though she were suddenly interested in the images appearing inside her mind.

The silence was uncomfortable for Kennedy, who bit the inside of her cheek as hard as she could without making it bleed.

"Hmmm..." Marr Ameer held up a stumpy finger in the air.

"I see..." she said as though she were conferring with the spirits.

Kennedy gripped the edge of her seat.

"The Record Keepers are telling me... it's not safe." Marr's eyes were still closed.

"What's not safe?"

"For you, it's not safe for you... Go home."

"Go home?"

"Go home before..."

"Before?"

"Before..."

"Before *what*?"

"Before *he* finds you."

"*Who* finds me?"

In a fit, Marr threw Kennedy's necklace on the table and shot to her feet, nearly knocking over her silver throne in the process. She held her chest and panted. "I need you to leave."

"Why? What did you see?"

"Get out!"

THIRTEEN

Rain pelted the unit's windows, and wind whipped through the Behemoth tree as Kennedy sat on the couch and hugged her knees. She stared at the mirage of a firepit burning between her and her roommates. When Marr Ameer threw them out in the rain and bolted the door, they knew something was wrong, but they did not press Kennedy for information. Now Orien, Pengar, and Geenen sat patiently and waited for her to tell them what had happened.

Pengar made Kennedy a steaming cup of floral tea and wrapped a blanket around her shoulders. Kennedy took a sip of the tea and then repeated everything Marr had told her earlier.

"You have a destined intimate!" Pengar clapped.

Geenen leveled a glance at Pengar, and she stopped clapping.

"*It's not safe?*" Orien tapped a finger to her chin. "Symetra is one of the safest places in the universe."

"Before *he* finds out about you?" Geenen pondered. "Clearly, she was talking about your dad."

"What's wrong with your dad finding out about you?" Orien continued to tap her finger against her chin.

Geenen threw a dismissive hand in the air. "She probably just made it up to get more coyels out of you. Fear is a powerful sales tool."

Pengar agreed with Geenen. "It's possible. Marr once told Lib Alo she was shrouded in dark energy, and the only thing to clear it would be ten sessions, which she wanted Lib to pay for upfront."

Kennedy wished they were right, but Marr Ameer was either the greatest actor on Symetra or genuinely scared of what the Record Keepers had shown her.

Orien clapped her hands together. "So, what's next? We have to keep moving, momentum is everything in this universe."

Kennedy was devastated by Marr's reading. It seemed to confirm one of Kennedy's unspoken fears: that she did not belong here and was unworthy of such an opportunity. Her Sectnot encouraged her to fix her thinking, so Kennedy excused herself for a few minutes and headed to her room. She grabbed her Thought Projector from the triangular pack on her dresser, cuffed it over her ear, and then red thoughts stretched across her room like a tangled web of anxiety. Kennedy minimized the thoughts into piles, while her Sectnot applauded her efforts. Once she felt a little more space inside her mind, she returned to her concerned roommates.

Kennedy assumed the posture of a confident person. "We need to find out more about the Alliance. We need to figure out who was in it and where they are now."

Orien clapped. "Right."

Inside the study nook, Geenen read a floating screen. "I haven't found any concrete information about them, mostly just conspiracy theories. Some believe the Alliance is operating from the shadows, biding their time, waiting to defeat Malant once and for all, but that might just be wishful thinking."

"What about Xavian Seelos?" Kennedy asked. "My avatar said he was the one who formed the Alliance."

"Xavian was one of the most beloved Chief Ministers in Evolver history," Orien said. "I personally believe that he was the reason the Golden Phase was so great. Xavian handpicked and mentored them all himself, even though he had a million other things to do as Chief Minister. He made history when he recruited Zuele, Tusk, and Leandor into the program. Before them, Xavian was the only Millintican to ever serve as an Evolver. It was supposed to be a new era for Millintica. Xavian and King Rimago proudly built monuments to Cissoria Brandth on Millintica and began teaching about her in Millintican schools—you know she was originally from there, right?"

Kennedy shook her head.

"Malant Tarish, meanwhile, began spreading the rumor that King Rimago was nothing more than an Evolver puppet, which riled up the Possessors."

"Possessors?" Kennedy asked.

Geenen answered, "Millintica was the first planet in the galaxy to discover space travel, and the Possessors believe any planet they discovered—landed on—now rightfully belongs to Millintica, including Symetra." She huffed, "They even claim *my* planet belongs to them."

Orien jumped back in. "The Possessors *despise* the Evolvers, especially Cissoria Brandth, who they believe was a traitor. They desecrated all of the monuments King Rimago and Xavian created for her. Then they torched the schools that taught about her. I think Xavian assumed the decent beings of Millintica would rise up and stop the Possessors, but they never did. Not until Malant massacred the entire royal family and declared himself the new king, but by then it was too late."

Pengar was uncomfortable with the subject matter. She needed something to do, so she picked up Kennedy's teacup and took it to the kitchen.

Orien continued, "That was when Xavian formed the Alliance. Unfortunately, they weren't able to stop Malant, and he has been terrorizing the galaxy ever since."

Kennedy weighed all the information and then paced back and forth. "I don't understand why Janekis tried to break into the Deepest Layer. Why take a risk like that? Why now?"

Orien shrugged.

Kennedy mentally asked her Sectnot when Malant took power, it told her roughly twenty years ago. It was plausible that Xavian could have somehow escaped to Earth, which made it possible that he could be her father. "Where is Xavian now?"

Geenen read the floating screen, which produced blocks of information in her alien hieroglyphics. "Some say he's been operating the Alliance from the mountains of Adillon. Others say he's a recluse who has completely lost it."

Kennedy furrowed her brow, still wondering if he was her father.

Orien perceived Kennedy's thoughts. "I doubt it, Kennedy—

unless your mother described your father as ancient. He was an old man when he formed the Alliance. I can only imagine how old he is now."

Kennedy ruled out Xavian.

"There is a Syncrocperience that's just been rereleased about Leandor Everin," Geenen said. "Apparently, Janekis' death has renewed everyone's interest in the Alliance."

Kennedy remembered Orien mentioning Leandor the night she had arrived. "Wait, you said he was a veil—"

"A Veilless." Orien shook her head as though she were dealing with amateurs. "They are these powerful beings who can literally see beyond the veil and even jump dimensions. Their greatest power, however, is their ability to infuse technology with consciousness. They can give it a soul—or at least a piece of one. A Veilless named Omin Yarso *created* the Dark Panel. King Malant believed that if he found another Veilless, they could help him expand the Dark Panel, which is why he hunted Leandor for so long."

"This Syncrocperience is about how the Alliance tried to hide Leandor from Malant." Geenen scrolled her screen. "It received horrible reviews—still, maybe there's something there. We can go tomorrow."

"No, I want to go tonight." Kennedy got up and put on her shoes.

Pengar returned from the kitchen. "It's going to be packed. Tonight, everyone is experiencing *The Mangled Mutant*. In the experience, you get to be this pilot who makes a crash landing on the lava planet 31XNB. The pilot calls for help but quickly discovers she has bigger problems when a mangled mutant starts chasing her with a laser hatchet. I hear no one has made it past the first limb."

"First limb?" Kennedy asked.

"Well, yeah, the mutant lasers off your limbs."

"Why would anyone want to experience that?"

"Bragging rights," Pengar said.

Geenen sidled up to Pengar and brought her hand down into a chopping motion across Pengar's forearm.

Pengar screamed. "That's not funny!"

Kennedy and her roommates exited their ridership outside a large, domed arena in the heart of Crystal City. The rain had let up, and now a brilliant orange sunset outlined the city skyline. Pure selenite made up the arena's exterior, and its lighting changed every few seconds depending on which Syncrocperience it was currently featuring. Evolver recruits stood outside, waiting to get in. They gasped when the Mangled Mutant appeared on the selenite and flashed his laser hatchet at them. Pengar hid her face behind Kennedy's shoulder, while Orien flirted with a pretty ticket taker.

Inside the dome, projection lights illuminated the walls with popular Syncrocperience titles. Kennedy was thrilled by the vast array of alien experiences available to her but reminded herself that tonight was business.

Pengar stopped in front of a large screen and scrolled through some options. "Maybe we should experience something romantic instead."

"You guys can experience whatever you want, and I'll let you know if I find anything out in *The Anonymous Alliance*." Kennedy laughed at the ridiculous title.

"No, we all stick together," Orien said. "We have a code, remember? We have a mission."

Kennedy looked around the dome and found Reddick speaking with Xan Ilna. Reddick did not notice all of the other beings staring at him, but somehow, he caught Kennedy. Reddick walked towards her wearing his Evolver casuals—a royal blue zip-up jacket with matching pants and shoes. Kennedy wore the same thing in Phase One gray. She fidgeted as he approached—suddenly, she had no idea what to do with her hands or what hands were even for.

"Hey, buddy," he said.

She had been daydreaming about the next time they would speak. Of course, in all those scenarios, she was saying something brilliant and funny. In her daydreams, she was the most brilliant, funny girl in the entire universe—a stark contrast to what she was now, a mute who could not even string a sentence together.

The moment grew more awkward when Corijean arrived next to Reddick. "Come on," she told him, "I reserved us a room." Corijean finally acknowledged Kennedy with an up-and-down smirk.

"Kennedy, are you experiencing *The Mangled Mutant*, too?" Reddick asked.

"I doubt Phase Ones are even allowed to experience *The Mangled Mutant*," Corijean said.

"What is the hold up?" Xan approached Corijean and Reddick.

His neck tattoo was currently gray, showing that even Xan was nervous to experience *The Mangled Mutant*.

Reddick kept his attention on Kennedy. "Come and experience it with us. It's rated traumatic," he said, with a gleam in his eye.

"No thanks," Kennedy said. "I prefer to get my trauma the old-fashioned way."

Reddick laughed. "If you change your mind, we'll be on the third floor."

Kennedy watched as he walked away with Corijean and Xan.

Orien nudged Kennedy. "Are you crazy? You should have gone."

"What about the mission?"

"Screw the mission," Orien said.

Pengar clapped giddily. "Kennedy, maybe Reddick is the destined intimate Marr Ameer was referring to!"

Kennedy covered her face in humiliation. "Want to say it a little louder? I don't think they heard you outside."

Pengar, who did not fully understand sarcasm, was about to do just that, until Geenen impatiently elbowed her way between them and chose their experience. "The computer selected our characters at random. Let's get this over with," she said.

Kennedy, Orien, Pengar, and Geenen took an elevator to the thirteenth floor of Syncrocperience, which wasn't a good omen. Kennedy thought of telling her friends about Earth's thirteenth-floor superstition but did not want anyone to back out. They paired off into two dark rooms: Kennedy and Pengar in one, and Geenen and Orien in another. Kennedy stood on golden footprints next to Pengar, waiting for further instruction. A rosy-cheeked operator gave them a brief safety demonstration. He warned them that this Syncrocperience contained violence and that if it ever got too intense, they could pull the ripcord that would be hanging just above them. He belabored the point.

The golden light enveloped Kennedy and she became the passenger in the body of a one-handed woman named Bones. She looked over and saw Pengar in the body of a swarthy lieutenant named Meat. They took a moment to laugh at one another. Then Orien, embodying a character with alligator skin and a mohawk, approached them. Finally, Geenen's character waddled towards them. She had a ring of eyes around her head and a patch of yellow curls skimming the tops—she was hideous. "You got assigned all the good characters!" Geenen yelled at them.

Kennedy, Pengar, and Orien's characters laughed inside each other's minds, even though their characters remained stoic. They stood in a derelict building with the Antastropolith Alliance symbol spray-painted everywhere. The experience was surreal. Kennedy physically felt she was someone else and secretly wished she could keep Bones' comic book character body, bionic hand, and all. Orien's character motioned her friends over to a crate in the corner, which was filled with Energy Stealers. Kennedy's character strapped one on—a thick gold cuff that illuminated her entire right arm in golden light.

Then a silhouette appeared in the doorway and remained there for dramatic effect. "Soldiers," he said in a husky voice.

The characters stood at attention.

Xavian Seelos stepped into the light. This Xavian was a young male with hair dyed white and veiny muscular arms. "We, the Antastropolith Alliance, landed on the eastern hemisphere of Millintica three moons ago. We are wanted by the Evolvers and by the Millintican Guard. Malant has spies everywhere. We have one mission: to protect Leandor Everin at all costs."

A handsome man stepped out of the same doorway. There was something unnatural about him. "What's wrong with him?" Kennedy asked.

"They used Leandor's actual likeness," Orien replied.

"Is that legal?"

"He's not around to stop them."

Xavian paced in front of them. "Malant has been hunting Leandor ever since he found out he was a Veilless. If Malant captures Leandor, he will achieve his goal of expanding the Dark Panel. We cannot let that happen."

It did not take Kennedy long to figure out why the Syncrocperience had received such terrible reviews. Xavian seemed to be a caricature of himself. His clunky, exposition-heavy dialogue was so distracting that it kept her from fully disappearing inside the experience.

"I went from being Chief Minister to being your leader. They made me choose, and I chose you. I chose Millintica. I chose to fight." He clenched his veiny hand into a fist.

The actor playing Xavian stopped in front of Kennedy's character. "Bones, you haven't been the same since that Dark Panel Combatant took your hand, yet you remain one of my strongest soldiers." He addressed the others, similarly, making sure to recap each character's backstory as he did. "If the Evolver Council ever finds out you are aiding the Alliance, they will excommunicate you. I won't let that happen. No one will ever know rogue Evolvers are the backbone of this Alliance."

"Did you hear that?" Kennedy asked the girls. "That's probably why no one knows anything about them. Xavian is protecting them."

But Kennedy's character cut her off when she yelled, "We will follow you anywhere!" against Kennedy's will.

"Yeah!" cheered Geenen's clumsy character, Twenty, who somehow managed to knock over a table and tumble to the ground.

Geenen cursed inside her roommates' minds, "My character is going to die immediately."

Kennedy laughed, but the laugh did not extend to her one-dimensional character, Bones, whose face was only good for determined, sexy pouts.

Then something hit the building, and a loud explosion sent Kennedy's character to the ground. Bones choked on a cloud of debris. Kennedy choked along with her, feeling like there was actual dust inside her lungs. Her ears rang from the explosion, and flames surrounded her. The building groaned. More explosions followed.

Xavian strapped on an Energy Stealer, and his arm turned gold in response. "Move out!" Xavian shielded Leandor. Kennedy and the others followed Xavian out of the building. The Millintican Guard rushed out of the darkness with their beaked masks and animal pelts. They twirled scythes, with blue flames emerging from both sides, and charged at Xavian.

Xavian pointed his Energy Stealer at one of the guardsmen,

causing him to shrivel up like a dying plant. The stolen energy turned Xavian's arm a brighter shade of gold. "Stay down, Leandor!" Xavian yelled.

Kennedy activated her own Stealer; its kickback jerked her shoulder, but she still hit her target, a Guardsman charging towards her. His shriveled body collapsed at her feet. Orien's character took down two of them, while the Stealer's kickback sent Geenen's clumsy character into the mud. The only one unaccounted for was Pengar's character. Geenen and Kennedy dashed back into the collapsing building, searching for her, only to find her character, Meat, gone.

"Pengar!" Geenen screamed, searching around frantically, wiping mud from her eight-eyed character's face. Then she stopped, as a realization hit her. "Oh, no." Geenen said, and then her character dissolved from the Syncrocperience.

Orien's character ran into the building. "Where did Geenen and Pengar's characters go?"

Kennedy yelled over the explosions still happening inside the Syncrocperience. "We came in here looking for Pengar's character, but we couldn't find her, so Geenen pulled her ripcord."

"Oh, no." Orien repeated Geenen's words and pulled her ripcord, too.

Beams fell inside the burning building. Kennedy was now alone. She waited only a few seconds before she pulled her own ripcord and followed Orien out of the experience.

When Kennedy returned to the Syncrocperience room, she found Pengar lying in the fetal position, covering her ears. Kennedy fell to her knees beside her. "Pengar? What happened?

Are you okay?"

Outside in the hall, Kennedy could hear Geenen and Orien yelling for the operator to let them in. When he did, they rushed to Pengar. Geenen pulled Pengar into her arms. "You're fine," she told her. "You hear me? It wasn't real. You're fine. You're safe. It was a stupid Syncrocperience, that's all."

Kennedy remembered what Orien had told her about Pengar—how the Millintican Guard had bombed her town and killed her family members. Tears filled Kennedy's eyes as Pengar shuddered in terror. Geenen still held Pengar in her skinny arms. "Do you want me to contact Ethwin?"

Pengar clutched onto Geenen.

"We have to get her home." Geenen said. "Help me."

Pink flowers fell from Pengar's bun as they carried her out of the room.

FOURTEEN

Kennedy and Orien sat outside Pengar's room in their pajamas. Ethwin had been inside with her for hours. Technically, he was not supposed to be, but there were ways around the patrollers. Kennedy did not know what those ways were, but all the recruits in relationships did. Kennedy stared at Pengar's closed door. She felt awful. "Has this ever happened before?" she asked Orien.

"Nothing like this." Orien shook her head. "The Camavenians have the gift—or the curse—of long memory. Pengar has memories of the day she was born, and she vividly remembers the time she spent trapped beneath the rubble after the bombing." Orien swallowed hard. "Her dead brother was next to her the entire time."

Kennedy covered her face. "This is all my fault. I never should have made her enter that stupid Syncrocperience."

"I guess our Syncrocperience ended up being rated traumatic, too," Orien said, humorlessly.

Geenen walked out of her room and sat next to Kennedy. "Here." She handed Kennedy her formerly cracked cellphone. The damaged screen looked brand new yet still ancient when compared with the technology available on Symetra. "It was bothering me, so I fixed it for you."

"Wow." Kennedy ran her hand over the repaired screen. "Thank you, Geenen."

Geenen cracked her bony knuckles and glanced at Pengar's door.

"She'll be okay," Orien told her.

After sitting in silence for a few minutes, Kennedy asked, "Whatever happened to Leandor?"

"Leandor died at Mount Sleer—it's a volcanic lair where some of the Dark Panel were stationed," Orien said. "Malant tried to take Leandor, but rather than be captured and forced to help Malant expand his unnatural army, Leandor fell into the lava, sacrificing his own life to protect the universe from the threat of an expanded Dark Panel. It was a heroic act."

Kennedy looked Leandor up on her Sectnot, but he had died over two years before she was born, which meant he was not her father either. She hung her head. The day had been a total disaster: first Marr Ameer, and now this.

She tried to find more information about the Alliance, but her Sectnot was not forthcoming. In fact, most of the time, it pretended to not even know what she was talking about.

Geenen told her why: "The Evolvers have restricted a lot of information about the Alliance—they pretend it is for our protection, but it is really for theirs. They don't want any more of us joining Xavian's cause."

When Ethwin finally emerged from Pengar's room, he gave them a half-hearted smile. "She's asking for the three of you," he said, before he snuck back to his own unit.

Kennedy went and knocked on her door. "Pengar?" She let herself in. Orien and Geenen followed. Pengar hid her face beneath the covers. Her room looked like a honeymoon suite. The walls were filled with images of burning cream candles and decorated with fresh flowers growing in aerodynamic planters under artificial sunlamps.

"I just wanted to say I'm sorry," Kennedy said. "I'm so sorry. If there's anything I can do…"

Pengar pulled the covers from her face. "Will you sleep in here?"

Kennedy nodded and then got in bed beside Pengar, who immediately cuddled with her. Orien hopped in and wrapped an arm around Pengar, while Geenen tried to tip-toe out of the room.

"You too, Geenen!" Pengar said.

Geenen sighed and then piled in next to Kennedy.

Pengar smiled from ear-to-ear. "I can't believe we're having a slumber party!" She pretended to be okay, mostly for Kennedy's benefit. "It's so nice to have best friends!" Pengar seemed to be willing herself back towards the higher frequencies. She spent a few minutes harping on everything that was going right in her life, and soon she was bright-eyed Pengar again.

Kennedy told them she had not been to a slumber party since she had made Ellie Goldman float eight feet off the ground in seventh grade.

Pengar kicked off the covers and jumped from her bed. "Float me!"

"Are you sure?" Kennedy asked.

"Yes! It will be fun!"

"You have to lay down," Kennedy told her.

Pengar spread out on the floor, and Kennedy concentrated on her. She extended a hand, and Pengar hovered off the floor, squealing in delight the entire time.

Kennedy had finally begun to learn Scrawl's patterns, and one morning, she hit him so hard that he fell back. She felt great about herself until Zuele programmed him to a harder setting, resulting in a bruised rib for Kennedy and a trip to the Healing Center downtown. The next day, Symetra's advanced medicine had Kennedy back on her feet, just in time for Scrawl to knock her right back off them.

Kennedy enjoyed running through the Five Seasons Forest and around Luminary Lake. However, she did not enjoy hover holds, an exercise that required her to hover off the ground for seconds at a time. Zuele yelled for Kennedy to use her core, but Kennedy was pretty sure she had been born without one. Her Dematerialization skills had improved marginally, but they still were not great. She was a long way off from being able to try the real thing alone, like the rest of her friends.

In Elemental Allies, Zuele was teaching her how to create water vortices. Zuele pointed toward Luminary Lake, and with a twist of her finger, a water vortex rose from its center. When Kennedy tried to create one, the lake doused her with water. Unfortunately, it happened just as Corijean and her snooty Phase Three friends were walking by. Corijean laughed as though it was the funniest thing she had ever seen.

Kennedy's favorite subject was still Planetary Studies, where she was currently learning about the seven planets inside the Antastropolith Galaxy—Camaven, Madilieu, Adillon, Presrilen, Chandwist, Millintica, and, of course, Symetra. Her least favorite subject was still Empowering Beliefs. Whenever Kennedy complained about it, Zuele would place a blinding mimic stone inside her hand. With each complaint, the stone grew dimmer. "This is what complaining does to your vibration," Zuele said, making her point loud and clear.

Kennedy dwelled on the shame and hurts of her past during their micro therapy sessions, but Zuele never allowed her to stay there long. "Dwelling on the past is a lot like trying to vacuum a dirt road," Zuele said. "Both are exercises in futility. You have no power back there. Your power is in the eternal now." But Zuele did encourage Kennedy to look upon her former self with kind, forgiving eyes instead of harsh, judgmental ones. She was constantly reminding Kennedy that she could have any type of life she wanted, so long as she raised her vibration to the level of what she was desiring.

One afternoon, they were sitting by the lake when Kennedy mentioned she had recently been having dreams about her father. "In my dream, I know him. He's always been there, and this idea that he wasn't is just a huge misunderstanding. But he never looks the same in my dream. Sometimes he is someone I know; sometimes he is someone I've seen on TV; sometimes he is just a shadow. What do you think that means?" Kennedy asked, but Zuele did not respond, so Kennedy continued. "I wish my dream were true. I wish he had been here all along. My worst fear is that he knows about me and just doesn't want me." Then she told Zuele about her reading with Marr Ameer, and how scared Marr appeared before she threw Kennedy out.

Zuele took it all in and then laughed. "I wouldn't worry too much about her. My friends and I used to go see her when we were your age. She told us all kinds of tall tales."

"Did any of them come true?"

"One. She said I was going to be a guardian, and here I am."

Kennedy rubbed her hands together. "Sometimes it feels like I'm never going to find him."

"Then you won't."

Kennedy grew frustrated. "Look, I've tried positive thinking when it comes to him, and most of the time it feels like I am just lying to myself."

"You're not lying; you are assuming. You assume that he does not want you. You assume that he knows about you and doesn't care. Those are not facts; those are negative assumptions."

"Negative assumptions feel truer for some reason."

"Multiple truths can coexist." Zuele gestured towards the lake. "Let's use the lake as an example. You could think about someone drowning in that water, or you could think about how refreshing it would feel to swim inside it on a warm day. Which one feels best to think about? Which one raises your vibration? Raising your vibration is not about lying to yourself. It is about consciously choosing the best thought."

"You're never going to help me find my dad, are you?"

"I am not here to help you find your father. I am here to make you an Evolver. However, I will say this: right now, your father can be anyone or anything you choose. You can use the idea of him to propel you forward. Visualize who you want him to be. It doesn't matter. You don't have to honor who he really is because you don't know who he really is. Imagine his good qualities. Imagine that he is proud of you. Tell yourself that he wants to find you just as much as you want to find him."

"But what if he doesn't?"

"Then he doesn't. But in the meantime, you'll have given yourself everything you wanted from him. An Evolver uses her mind deliberately. An Evolver is a master of her thoughts." Zuele patted Kennedy's leg and headed back towards the Institute.

Kennedy stared across the lake and found Reddick sparring with his guardian, a gargantuan named Rantrin. Three perfect, pink claw marks scarred the right side of Rantrin's face. Rantrin reared back his massive fist, but Reddick Dematerialized out of sight before he could strike. Rantrin tried again, but Reddick was too fast. Reddick blinked in and out of sight as their sparring continued. His excellence was once again on full display as recruits gathered to watch.

Kennedy wondered what Marr Ameer would say to someone like him. Most likely, that his love life would be a revolving door of otherworldly beauties and his success as an Evolver was all but guaranteed.

Kennedy closed her eyes and started to imagine her father. He had been an Evolver for sure, descended from a long line of Evolvers. Currently, he was thwarting Malant's evil plans and bringing peace to the galaxy. He still loved Roberta, and he would tell anyone who would listen about how proud he was of his daughter. She wanted him to be wise, brave, and kind-hearted. Kennedy guessed some more details about her father, mentally stitching together a Frankenstein of virtues and strengths. Yet, imagining him this way only made her want to know him more...

There were certain benefits to being an Evolver recruit: the pay, the lodging, the access to life-changing technology, and then there was the swag. Kennedy and her roommates were constantly receiving free stuff from businesses all over Symetra—clothes, accessories, appliances—it was more than they knew what to do with, but they still enjoyed it.

That evening, the recruits were invited to an event sponsored by Aqua Haven, a Symetran water sports brand eager to get footage of future Evolvers using their equipment. When Kennedy arrived, the sun was setting beneath the turquoise waters of the Kathreeyan Ocean. She and her roommates kicked up white sand as they walked down a secluded, private beach protected by security. Dozens of Symetran teenagers fawned over the Evolver recruits, especially the Phase Threes, who sat in a VIP area just off the shore. Kennedy wore her official Evolver swimsuit beneath her athletics. Orien wore an expensive cover-up with actual gold sewn into the fabric and promised to kill anyone who got it *or* her hair wet. She fluttered from group to group, making sure everyone got a good look at it.

Kennedy, Geenen, and Pengar sat down near the bonfire with

Ethwin and his roommates. They watched as recruits played on their hover boards and did somersaults off them into the choppy water. Orien dropped a box into the sand near her friends and sat down in an uncomfortable way, trying not to wrinkle her outfit. When a rowdy Phase Two boy nearly spilled his drink on it, Orien held up her hand, and an anti-gravity sphere trapped the liquid before it fell. The liquid beads from his spilled drink now floated inside the sphere like a lava lamp.

"Watch it!" Orien told him. Then she swiped her hand to the left, and the liquid fell into the sand.

Ethwin's roommate, a green alien from a planet ruled by oppressive females, offered to get the girls something to drink or anything else they might need.

"You really want to help?" Orien handed him the box filled with promotional, oxygen-recycling masks. "Go pass these out."

"Thank you, thank you so much." He bowed his head and got to work.

Once he left, Orien said, "I thought one of the promoters was flirting with me. It turns out she was just looking for a volunteer; now she's got one." She fanned out the skirt of her cover-up so passersby could get a better look at it. "So, any leads?"

Kennedy shook her head dejectedly. She had created a makeshift investigation board inside their study nook and spent the last few evenings trying to connect her father to Xavian Seelos, whose image floated at the top of the chart like a mob boss.

"Do we have a next move yet?" Orien asked.

"Other than breaking into the DNA Lab? No." Kennedy threw a small piece of wood inside the fire.

"I can ask Ethwin," Pengar said.

Ethwin turned his attention away from the Phase Threes, who were performing tricks off their hoverboards. "Ask me what?"

Pengar wedged herself under Ethwin's lanky arm. "So, you know how you did research in the DNA Lab for a while?" She batted her eyes.

"How could I forget? It was the most boring progression of my life."

Pengar playfully shoved him. "Hey, we started dating that progression."

"No, I meant the Lab was boring, but come to think about it, it wasn't so bad. I got to sit there and ponder your beauty, my little nary flower." He kissed her.

Orien clapped her hands and ended their romantic moment. "Focus!"

Pengar reached into her triangular pack and reapplied her lip gloss. "Well, say we wanted to get into the DNA Lab. How would you recommend we go about doing that?"

Ethwin didn't take his eyes off Pengar's lips.

Pengar cuddled back into him. "We know we can't get in there without a guardian."

"You don't need a guardian," he said, "just a Rivil."

Kennedy thought of the small remote Zuele carried around her neck and frowned. "My guardian always wears hers."

"Mine too," Pengar and Geenen said in unison.

But Kennedy was not willing to give up that quickly. "Does the Hall of Labs have cameras?" she asked Ethwin.

"The patrollers are the cameras. They guard the Labs."

"Is there any way to avoid them?"

Ethwin thought about it. "If you stay out of their pink light and crawl beneath them very slowly, I suppose you might be able to avoid their sensors. Also, you cannot make *any* noise; their hearing is extremely sensitive. Me and my Lab partner used to get so bored we would release a Squeaker in the Lab just to watch the patrollers chase it for hours." Ethwin laughed, and so did Pengar, who thought everything he said was funny.

Kennedy did not get the joke. "What's a Squeaker?"

"It's this tiny device that can send high-pitched noises across the room. It drives the patrollers crazy. They won't give up until they find out where the squeaks are coming from. I think I still have one somewhere, I'll bring it to you."

Orien leaned in closer to Ethwin. "What if we *were* able to get a Rivil. What then?"

Ethwin thought about it. "I have never seen more than two guardians inside that Lab at one time, and they usually take their break together, that would probably be the best time for you to get in and out undetected."

"And once we're in?" Orien asked.

"The machine does all the work. Everything you need is in there. All you have to do is enter a cheek swab, and it will run your DNA through the Evolver database."

"Seems easy enough," Orien said.

"I'm going to go get in the water." Ethwin kissed Pengar. "You coming?"

"I'll be right behind you." Pengar watched him walk to the shore. "Isn't he the best?"

"I can get us a Rivil," Orien said.

"What? How?" Kennedy asked.

"I told you that my guardian is older than Symetra itself. She always loses her Rivil, leaving it in the bathroom or on her chair. Sometimes I hide it on purpose to get out of boring segments. The next time I see it, I'll take it. Then I'll hand it off to you at lunch. You can sneak in the Lab during break, run your DNA, find out who your father is, give it back to me, and I'll return the Rivil before my guardian even knows it's gone."

Geenen shook her head adamantly. "I think we should find a plan that won't get us kicked out of the Institute."

"I agree with Geenen," Kennedy forced herself to say, even though everything inside her wanted to enact the plan immediately.

A commotion near the beach interrupted their scheming.

Kennedy glanced in that direction and found Reddick a hundred feet in the air with no shirt on. His intricately toned arms, chest and stomach flexed as he balanced himself on a small hoverboard. Recruits from every phase cheered for him as he launched his body towards another hoverboard ten feet away. Then he launched himself for another, even further away, but missed it. He plummeted towards the shore, and Kennedy gasped. Luckily, Reddick was able to break out into a hover hold and slow himself at the very last moment. He landed on his feet, only waist-deep in the water. He walked out of the ocean toward his adoring fans. Xan and Reddick exchanged a secret handshake as everyone went wild—everyone except Kennedy, who could not understand how someone loved by an entire planet could possibly still need more attention. His recklessness infuriated her. The idea of him getting hurt, or worse, clenched her insides into a tight fist.

Corijean threw her arms around him and said, "My turn!"

Kennedy watched the two of them together. They were perfect.

Reddick caught Kennedy's gaze and grinned, but Kennedy turned away. She wasn't sure why she was so upset by the idea of losing him when he had never been hers to begin with.

"Reddick Brandth is staring at you," Pengar said without moving her mouth.

Kennedy did not respond. She was too busy trying to shove down her all-consuming feelings for a boy who was light years out of her league. Reddick rarely spoke to her anymore, and when he did, Corijean was always lurking closely behind. Kennedy got up and dusted the cold sand off her shorts. "I'm tired. I'm going back to the unit." She walked away before her friends could stop her. From her peripheral vision, she could still see Reddick watching her, but she would not look back. She did not want him to see how badly he had scared her. She knew he was scared too—that his stunts were a byproduct of fear, not courage. They were a chance for Reddick to look death square in the face and pretend he had some control over it, even though he knew at any moment death could take from him again without asking.

Kennedy was sitting with her friends at breakfast a few mornings later when the lights flashed on and off inside the dining hall. An odd chime echoed throughout the room, and everyone came to a standstill. Orien stood up to get a better look. "What is happening?" Kennedy asked her.

"It's a message from Chief Minister Brandth," she said.

A hologram of Theein Brandth appeared at the far end of the dining hall. Kennedy's Sectnot asked if she would like to switch to one-on-one mode, and she said yes, even though she had no idea what that was. A small hologram of Theein Brandth appeared in front of her. "Greetings, my fellow Evolver," he said, as though he were speaking directly to Kennedy. "I transmit myself to you with a heavy heart this morning. Earlier today, an Evolver ship was ambushed by the Millintican Guard as it traveled through the Hillian Galaxy."

Gasps and panicked whispers filled the room, but Kennedy kept her eyes on Theein Brandth. "The Evolver ship, piloted by seven-pointed star recipient Eka Mint, was forced to make an emergency landing on the planet Celail. Three Evolvers were killed in the attack—Eudence Fein of Adillon, Folis Ara of Presrilen, and Hoper Morrow of Chandwist."

Hoper Morrow? When Kennedy heard the name of the Demolition Dame's co-pilot, she covered her mouth. Hoper had taken the time to encourage her back on Earth. *"Bye, Missus,"* had been the last thing he said to her before she dropped to the

Submerged Station. It seemed impossible that someone so alive in her mind could be *dead*.

A stone-faced Theein continued, "Evolver Miles Pierce sustained life-threatening injuries and is being transported to Symetra along with other surviving passengers. I vow to keep you up to date with developments as they become available. Until then, I ask you to send the highest energy to the victims and their families." Theein made a visual prayer of alignment, and so did Kennedy. When the lights turned on inside the room, everyone began to panic.

Kennedy vacillated between thinking about Miles's injuries and Hoper's death.

Orien looked to her Sectnot. "King Malant has already claimed responsibility."

"Don't call him that," Pengar said.

"What?"

"King."

Orien corrected herself, "*Malant* released this statement a few seconds ago."

Kennedy and her friends were not the only ones watching the message. When they saw him, some recruits in the dining hall shuddered. "What happens next is up to the Evolvers," he said, in a deeply layered voice that sounded like five different voices shrieking in unison. "Chief Minister Brandth, I have one simple demand: turn over the Antastropolith Alliance."

Kennedy's mouth dropped open, and her friends turned to look at her.

Malant continued, "Turn them over, and all Evolver killings

will stop. If not, I will continue until every single Evolver is dead."

The panicked whispers became full-throated.

"Why doesn't Chief Minister Brandth do something?"

"He still thinks Malant will respond to diplomacy. I don't know how many more Evolvers have to die before he understands that some wars are necessary."

"Are we going to war?"

"Will they send us home?"

Reddick rose from his Phase Three table and stormed out of the dining hall with a clenched jaw.

"I wonder where he's going?"

"Probably to tell his father it's time to do something."

"Well, at least he didn't use the Dark Panel," Orien whispered to Kennedy.

"You don't have to whisper," Pengar said. "I can handle it."

Orien nodded at Pengar but still put a reassuring hand on top of hers.

"What is Malant up to?" Kennedy wondered aloud.

"I don't know, but Malant's patience and discipline are two of the most dangerous things about him," Geenen said. "Whatever he is up to, it must be big. Maybe this is all a way for him to start his war and blame the Evolvers for his assault on the universe."

"Or maybe the Alliance has him shook," Kennedy said, suggesting that they might be getting under his skin.

"The Alliance cannot defeat the Dark Panel. I don't even know if the Triphens can. If Malant ever decides to deploy them—" Geenen did not even want to finish her thought.

Orien forced her plate of food away, clearly having lost her appetite.

Kennedy looked down at her own plate, realizing she was no longer hungry either. "It just doesn't make sense. None of it makes sense. Why is he so obsessed with the Alliance? He has already won. He is the king of Millintica. He already has everything he needs to wage his war. What is he waiting for?"

Unfortunately, Kennedy's friends did not have any answers for her.

Then Orien gripped Kennedy's arm. "I'm going to get the Rivil today. It's the perfect time to break into the DNA Lab; everyone is distracted."

Geenen shook her head. "That is a terrible idea."

Orien ignored her. "We might not get another chance. Malant is hunting the Alliance, and we need to find out who your dad is before—" she stopped herself.

"Before what?" Kennedy asked.

Orien frowned. "Before it's too late."

Kennedy's shoulders sank at the thought of it. She turned to Orien and gave her a slight nod, then immediately felt horrible for capitalizing on the tragic moment.

Orien looked around the room, making sure no one was listening to their conversation. "When my guardian isn't looking, I'll grab the Rivil. At break, meet me by the statues, and we'll go together."

"I can create a diversion for the patrollers," Geenen offered.

"And I can distract Enforcer Tusk. I'll tell him Zuele asked about him or something," Pengar giggled.

"No. I'm going alone," Kennedy said.

Orien attempted to protest, but Kennedy would not let her.

"It's not a discussion. You're already risking enough." Kennedy placed her hand flat on the table. "Once I get it from you, I'll take the elevator to the Hall of Labs and run my sample while everyone's at lunch."

Orien relented. "Fine."

Meditation had been a waste of time that morning. Kennedy left before it was over and took the stairs to her training room, hoping to exercise some of her nerves, but it was no use. She was about to round the corner for her training room when she heard Zuele whispering in Spasoo, which was Chancellor Kirat's native language, "How did Malant even know where they were?"

"Someone obviously tipped them off," Chancellor Kirat replied in a hushed voice.

"Theein needs to call up the Evolver Legion. The Triphens can't be the only ones protecting us."

"Right now, the Chief Minister's only priority seems to be weeding out the Alliance. He may despise them even more than Malant. Theein still blames them for his wife's death."

Zuele scoffed. "If Vivith were still alive, she would be flying out to meet Malant herself, not feeding wayward Evolvers to him."

Some recruits arrived in the hallway and ruminated over worst-case scenarios as they walked to their respective training rooms. Zuele and Chancellor Kirat took their conversation inside the training room and sealed the door. Kennedy considered bilocating inside to eavesdrop, but ultimately thought better of it. She could not risk getting caught, not when she was only hours away from possibly knowing her father's identity.

Orien had been accurate in her assumption that everyone would be preoccupied. Zuele gave Kennedy reading assignments that morning and spent the rest of the time turning something over in her mind. Meanwhile, Kennedy tried to act as normal as possible, even though all she could think about were her lunchtime plans.

At break, she stood by Xavian's statue and waited for Orien. Kennedy drummed her fingers against her outer thigh and kept an eye out. She stared across the foyer at the lifelike statue of Vivith Brandth, wondering how different things might have been if she were still alive. Would Reddick still pull his dangerous stunts? Would Vivith encourage her husband to use the power of the Evolvers to ensure the galaxy's safety? This was a woman brave enough to sneak onto a Millintican lunar base and save hundreds of lives. If Vivith was brave enough to do that, then Kennedy was brave enough to break into the DNA Lab. After all, she wasn't hurting anyone; she was just using a machine. It was a victimless crime.

Orien approached Kennedy, placing the Rivil in her hand. "I'll be here," she said.

Kennedy slipped the Rivil under her sleeve and nodded. She waited for the foyer to clear out, then she took the stairs to the bowels of the Institute. She was grateful to find the Hall of Labs empty. The hum returned to her chest and rattled her already frayed nerves. She got down on all fours and crawled towards the DNA Lab, eager to stay out of the patrollers' line of sight.

Kennedy inched her way towards the door, hoping there was no one inside, hoping she was only minutes from learning her father's true identity. She was almost there when something slammed against the double doors at the opposite end of the hallway—the Adversary Lab. It startled Kennedy so badly that she nearly jumped out of her skin. Whatever it was, it sounded strong enough to break down those doors, and it sounded desperate to get out.

Three patrollers streamed towards the noise while Kennedy pressed her body flush against the cold tiles and remained perfectly still. She feared she had been caught, but their pink lights never touched her. Instead, they focused on the double doors of the Adversary Lab.

The pounding continued at the opposite end of the hallway; Kennedy used the distraction to quickly sneak inside the DNA Lab. She kneeled in front of the door and held the Rivil to it. When the door slid open, Kennedy crawled inside. The Lab was empty. Kennedy rolled onto her back as the door closed behind her, exhaling a breath of relief. Saved images of aliens danced around the dark, sterile room. Kennedy got up from the ground, sat at the first scanner, and took a swab from the kit. She swabbed her cheek and placed it inside the machine. A large screen lit up in front of her.

The scanner went through thousands of possible matches. This was the moment of truth. The moment she would know once and for all where she came from, who her father was, and hopefully where he was now. Then one of her deepest fears surfaced: what if he really didn't want her? What if he did not want to see her? What if he had carved out some nice, little, perfect life for himself and had no room for a half-human, illegitimate daughter? When the machine began to slow, Kennedy dropped the thought.

She tangled her fingers and awaited the results.

Then the screen read, NO MATCH FOUND.

Kennedy could not believe it, so she tried again. NO MATCH FOUND. She sat there for a moment, completely defeated, feeling like a fool for getting her hopes up again. *Why does it have to be so effing hard?* She silently screamed into the Eternal Energy Field. *Can't you just give me a break for once?* Then the Rivil that was sitting on her lap, fell to the floor. The noise of it landing echoed throughout the room.

Guess not.

Kennedy froze, hoping no one had heard it, but she was not that lucky. The door of the DNA Lab opened, and a patroller streamed inside. Kennedy was just able to clear her search when pink light filled the Lab. She immediately hid under a desk and held her breath.

The patroller made tiny, rhythmic beeps as it scanned the DNA Lab for illegal activity. Then, a small, squeaking noise caught its attention. Kennedy remained breathless under the desk as she controlled the Squeaker Ethwin had given her. She pointed it in the direction of the back corner of the Lab, and it squeaked again. The patroller chased the noise and tried to burrow itself into the wall like a cat looking for a mouse.

Kennedy rolled out from under the desk and crawled slowly out of the DNA Lab. However, just as she rounded the corner into the hall, three patrollers streamed out of the emergency exit.

Kennedy inched backwards, her movements so small and precise that the patrollers did not register them. After a few excruciating seconds of this, she was once again in the DNA lab.

Then she turned around and faced the initial patroller, whom she had managed to duck. It beeped a victory song and lit up with a blinding, pink light. Without thinking, Kennedy unleashed the girliest of slaps, the force of which thudded the patroller into the wall. The patroller hissed, and suddenly it was covered in poisonous spikes.

Kennedy bolted down the hallway, running as fast as she could.

The poisonous patroller was gaining on her.

Her Sectnot warned that she was in danger. "No shit," she spat. Kennedy held up the Rivil and was granted access to a research Lab filled with jars of alien specimens. Kennedy closed the door and hid behind a large table. The patroller unlocked the door and entered the Lab. It turned off its light and silently searched for her. Kennedy picked up a small, empty beaker and threw it towards the far side of the room. The patroller followed its shattering sound.

Kennedy ran back out into the hallway, only to find the other three patrollers blocking her path to the stairs. They unsheathed their poisonous spikes when they saw her. She would have to circle the entire floor to get back to the stairs. She ran in the opposite direction and nearly had a heart attack when something pounded against the Adversary Lab's doors once more, but she kept moving, too frantic to pay attention to the loud humming in her chest.

The patrollers followed closely behind, their venomous spikes only inches away from Kennedy's neck. She zigzagged and dove to avoid being latched onto. She had circled the entire floor. The stairs were coming into view. Then a looming figure emerged from the stairwell and blocked Kennedy's path to freedom. Kennedy came to a screeching halt, and the patrollers whizzed past her head. One of them tore her uniform, just to remind her that it could.

Enforcer Tusk now stood in front of her. The pink lights of the patrollers faded ever so slightly as they heeled beside their master.

Tusk steeled his ice green eyes. "What do we have here?"

FIFTEEN

Kennedy quickly tucked the Rivil back into the bottom of her sleeve.

"What do you think you are doing? Recruits aren't allowed on this floor without a guardian's approval," Enforcer Tusk said.

Kennedy knew better than to incriminate herself. Aside from panting, she remained silent.

Enforcer Tusk grabbed her arm with his cold hand and marched her up the stairs. Kennedy prayed she was not about to have her memory modified. Tusk's office was one of several offices located on the floor beneath the foyer. Two double doors at the end of a dark hallway were flanked by four patrollers. When they saw Tusk, they zoomed towards him affectionately, like dogs welcoming their master home. Tusk patted them on their metal heads and motioned for Kennedy to enter the office first.

Tusk's office functioned as a nerve center, with switches and screens covering nearly every inch of it. It looked as though he could control the entire Institute from there. Kennedy didn't know what the technology did, but she knew it was important. Tusk pointed to the screens that displayed footage from the patrollers' cameras—he had her dead to rights.

Enforcer Tusk pulled out a chair in front of his desk for Kennedy. Before she sat down, she moved the Rivil further up her sleeve.

Tusk sat in the high-backed chair behind his desk and watched her.

Kennedy could feel her chest growing red as she awaited her punishment.

Tusk smirked. "I remember being your age. This place seemed so huge. It seemed there were endless options, endless fascinations. The technology alone," he exhaled, "and that was eons ago. My friends and I used to get in trouble all the time."

"You were in the Golden Phase."

"Most seem to have forgotten that."

"My roommate is obsessed with the Golden Phase."

"I suppose my accomplishments fail in comparison to those of my distinguished phasemates." He rested his chin atop his steepled fingers and peered at her. "The Hall of Labs is no place for a Phase One. There is dangerous and sensitive technology down there."

Kennedy bowed her head.

"What were you doing down there?"

"Um, I think I pushed the wrong button on the elevator."

Tusk could tell she was lying. "And why were you in the DNA Lab?"

"I was in the DNA Lab?" She played dumb.

He pressed the pads of his fingers together as he considered how to punish her. "I should send you home."

"Please don't," Kennedy begged.

"Why shouldn't I? You have proven you do not respect the rules of the Institute."

"I'm sorry, really, I am."

Tusk spent a long time watching her. "Fortunately for you, I believe in allowing recruits to learn from their mistakes in the same way I learned from mine. So, I am going to give you another chance."

Kennedy looked up in shock. Maybe Enforcer Tusk really was a nice guy—a nice guy spending his days and nights in a thankless job.

"This will not go on your permanent record," he said. "Unfortunately, I am still going to have to contact your guardian."

There was the rub. Kennedy knew his leniency had more to do with his feelings for Zuele than his desire to let her learn from her mistakes. Still, whatever punishment Zuele had for her beat being sent home with a modified memory.

Zuele walked into his office moments later. "What is this all about?"

Tusk straightened himself out and went to stand in front of her. "I found your recruit wandering the Hall of Labs. She says she pushed the wrong button."

"She certainly did." Zuele gave Kennedy a stern look.

Kennedy continued to hide the Rivil up her sleeve, too terrified of her guardian to even make eye contact.

"Thankfully, the patrollers did not get a hold of her," Tusk said.

Zuele noticed the awkward way Kennedy was sitting.

"It is understandable that she would get confused. This day has been anything but normal." Tusk stepped closer to Zuele. "How are you doing?"

"I am fine."

He placed a hand on Zuele's arm, but she jerked away. "Xavian should just turn himself in so we can put this whole thing behind us."

Zuele cut him off the way she always did. "Thank you for alerting me to this situation, Elsid. I appreciate you giving me the opportunity to deal with my recruit in my own way."

He smiled, hopefully. "Hey, you called me Elsid. That's a step."

The first time Kennedy had seen Tusk, he had been in the palm of Zuele's hand, and judging by the current infatuated look on his face, he still was.

"We've got to be on our way. Kennedy just bought herself kitchen duty and thirty laps around the lake."

"Go easy on her. Remember what we were like at that age?"

Kennedy would gladly run thirty laps around the lake to escape the awkwardness between Enforcer Tusk and Zuele. Even with her emotion blocker on, Kennedy could feel how much Tusk loved her and how much Zuele despised him.

Zuele dragged Kennedy from the room and up the stairs to the foyer. Orien saw them coming and ducked behind Cissoria Brandth's statue.

Zuele headed straight for her.

Orien gulped. "Oh, hello, Guardian Zuniz. It is a pleasure to encounter your energy."

Zuele crossed her arms. "Kennedy, give Orien back the Rivil."

Kennedy pretended not to know what she was talking about.

Zuele reached into Kennedy's sleeve and grabbed it herself. "Here you are, Orien. Please return that to your guardian; I am sure she is looking for it."

"Are you going to tell her I took it?" Orien asked.

"No. You are," Zuele said. "Let's go, Kennedy."

Kennedy gave Orien an apologetic look and then sheepishly followed Zuele to her training room. When they arrived, Zuele pointed at a recliner and commanded Kennedy to sit.

Kennedy sat with her tail between her legs.

Zuele paced angrily in front of her. "Let me guess, you were trying to break into the DNA Lab so you could find your father?"

Kennedy did not answer.

"Am I warm?"

"You don't understand," Kennedy said.

"No, I really don't."

"I believe my father was in the Alliance," Kennedy explained urgently, "and now Malant is killing them, and I just wanted to—"

"What? Find your father before Malant does? And then what, Kennedy? What was your next plan? Were you just going to keep stealing and breaking rules until you figured it out?"

"We didn't steal it. We just borrowed it."

Zuele gave Kennedy a severe look. "This is not the time to poke around in the Alliance's affairs. Trust me, right now you want to be as far away from the Alliance as possible. If your father *is* in the Alliance and Malant ties you to him, he will kill you. You think he'll care that you don't know your father? Mass murderers don't care about insignificant details like that." Zuele shook her head. "Now, this has to stop. You hear me?"

Kennedy bit the inside of her cheek.

"Do you *hear* me?"

Kennedy glared at the ground. "What am I?"

Zuele snapped her head back. "Excuse me?"

Kennedy stood. "Why haven't you given me a DNA test? Why haven't you even tried to help me find him?"

"Because this obsession you have is unhealthy."

"So is having no idea who you are or where you came from." Kennedy's eyes filled with tears. "You have to at least know which planet he was from. Why won't you tell me? I have a right to know. I have a right to—"

Zuele interrupted her. "He is from Millintica."

Kennedy furrowed her brow.

"You are half human and half Millintican, Kennedy." She took a breath. "I did give you a DNA test, but all I could deduce from your sample was that you are fifty percent Millintican."

Kennedy sat back down, unsure of how to feel.

Zuele's expression softened. "I didn't tell you because, as you've probably noticed, Millintica doesn't currently have the greatest reputation. I wanted to spare you from the shame Malant has brought to *your* heritage." Zuele came and sat down next to her.

"Our heritage," Kennedy corrected her.

"*Our* heritage," Zuele nodded.

"Do you know anything about my lineage?"

"Malant now controls all that information."

For a while, neither one of them said anything.

Kennedy had been secretly hoping her father was from Symetra, not the wrong side of the galaxy. Knowing he was from Millintica had the strange effect of making everything feel more personal—Hoper's death, Malant, the Alliance. The dead end inside the DNA Lab confirmed Kennedy's father was not an Evolver, just one of the countless Millinticans who had joined the Alliance to fight for his home planet.

"It is nothing to be ashamed of, Kennedy," Zuele said.

"I'm not ashamed. I mean, I had been hoping for someplace less war-torn, but I'm not ashamed."

"Good." Zuele patted her knee. "Now, as for your punishment, you will be helping Chef Raka in the kitchen every night for the foreseeable future." She stood up and motioned to the door. "You'd better go get changed; you owe me some laps."

"Zuele?" Kennedy asked before she walked out.

"Yes?"

"Will you teach me about Millintica?"

Zuele smiled and said, "Of course."

Kennedy was in a foul mood for the next few days. Now, whenever Scrawl insulted her, she would punch him as hard as she could. "You're getting stronger," he said one morning. "You might even be strong enough now to fight your way out of a paper bag." Kennedy charged at him, then tackled him to the ground. Once she was on top of him, she punched him so hard that she nearly broke her hand. Zuele praised Kennedy for the hit, but not even Zuele's validation could put her in a good mood.

The entire Institute was still gripped by Malant's recent attack. Some believed that it was only a matter of time before Malant attacked Symetra. Some begged the Chief Minister to deploy the Evolver Legion, while others acknowledged the severity of the circumstances but still encouraged diplomacy. Kennedy did not have time for these debates, as all her time was usually spent training, running laps, or scrubbing pots in the kitchen.

The best part of kitchen duty was that Orien was right there with her, making all the cooks laugh with her unsolicited dating and fashion advice. The worst part of kitchen duty was Reddick seeing Kennedy in her uniform crusted with unpalatable alien cuisine. Corijean loved seeing Kennedy this way and would often intentionally spill things on the floor and say to her friends, "Oops, oh well, Kennedy will get it."

Kennedy still felt riled by Hoper's death and began having dreams about him. In the dreams, she was the one who remained inside the Demolition Dame, and he was the one who fell out. Her father was never far from her thoughts, though her search for him had come to a complete standstill.

Thankfully, her friends did not mind that Kennedy's father was from Millintica. Kennedy had been most concerned about Pengar's reaction, but Pengar's friendship remained steadfast. "My family took in some Millintican refugees after Malant took power," she told Kennedy. "They were kind and brave beings." She then picked a purple flower with sharp petals from the planter in her room. "This is a vanlyn flower. Vanlyn flowers are everywhere in the Crag Region of Millintica." She pinned it in Kennedy's ponytail. "There, now you'll fit right in."

✦

Zuele had made good on her promise to teach Kennedy about Millintica. So far, Kennedy had learned about the regions and the royal family, and now it was time for her to learn about the Dark Panel. Zuele pointed her Rivil at the windows, and the screens slid down to cover them, leaving the training room in near darkness. "The Dark Panel has been around even longer than the Evolvers," Zuele said. "Their story began with the discovery of Symetra. Cissoria Brandth, a prominent explorer, and Jasbir Tarish, the inventor of Millintican space travel, found it together. When they landed on the paradise planet of Symetra, Cissoria famously declared, 'I have found a place where I can keep one foot on the ground and the other beyond the veil.'"

A dated hologram of Cissoria meditating alongside the Triphens appeared in front of Kennedy. She was a middle-aged adventurer with long braided hair and sun-damaged skin.

"Cissoria encountered the indigenous Triphens and was taken with their peaceful culture," Zuele said. "She decided to leave her life on Millintica behind so she could stay on Symetra and learn about their evolved, energetic ways. Jasbir Tarish, however, did not support Cissoria's devotion to the Triphens." Jasbir's hologram showed a well-to-do being with a raised chin and thin mustache. "Jasbir encouraged King Amsden, the King of Millintica at the time, to immediately claim dominion over Symetra and enslave the Triphens. The King heeded Jasbir's advice and sent the Millintican Guard to Symetra, but the Triphens caused their ships to malfunction and fall from the skies." Zuele projected a video from the battle; it played against the wall. It showed the small Triphens standing with their arms interlocked and eyes closed, while massive Millintican spaceships crashed to the ground.

"After the humiliating defeat on Symetra, King Amsden made it his sole mission to create an army capable of destroying the Triphens with no expense spared. He built several prototypes, but they still were not powerful enough to defeat the Triphens." A hologram of King Amsden, replete with jewels and a metal crown, appeared in the room. He was in his fifties and looked as though he had never done a hard day's work in his life.

Zuele placed her hands behind her back. "That's when Omin Yarso entered the picture. Omin was the most famous Veilless in history." Omin's hologram was different than King Amsden's. Omin carried himself like *actual* royalty, whereas King Amsden just looked like he was playing dress-up. Omin had wiry eyebrows, a pointy beard, and a severe widow's peak. "Omin Yarso was born with rare energetic gifts, and he spent most of his time searching Millintica for others with similar powers. He fathered many children, but being a Veilless is rarely hereditary, and none of them inherited his gifts.

"When King Amsden learned about Omin's powers, he enlisted his assistance in the formation of his unnatural army. Omin told the king that if he wanted to defeat the Triphens, he would first have to match their vibrational frequency, which is something technology cannot do." Zuele turned to Kennedy. "Technology can think for itself, but it cannot feel, which means it can't enter the world of consciousness. Omin sought to change that. He understood that infusing this new army with consciousness would be essential if they were to ever defeat the Triphens."

Zuele clicked her Rivil. A hologram of Omin standing in front of thousands of Combatants filled the room and caused Kennedy to take several steps back. Zuele gazed at the impressive scene. "As a Veilless, Omin had the power to give fragments of his own consciousness to thousands of Combatants; it took him many progressions to complete the task.

"Meanwhile, the relationship between King Amsden and Omin Yarso grew to be quite acrimonious, with Omin making tweaks to the Combatants that Amsden did not approve of, like the ability to draw out another's shame and broadcast it for all to see."

"Why did Omin do that?" Kennedy asked.

"Because shame is a frequency killer." Zuele clicked her Rivil again. "When the army was almost ready, Amsden decided to eliminate Omin. You see, a Veilless is weakest right after they have shared their consciousness. It is crucial for a Veilless to surround themselves with protectors who can defend them until they can regain their strength. Knowing this, King Amsden ambushed Omin Yarso's protectors and killed Omin."

A hologram of a Combatant now stood in front of Kennedy. It was nearly as tall as the ceiling, and its face was nothing more than a blank screen. It had claw-like hands that emitted green lasers sharp enough to slice someone in half. "Omin Yarso had given all of himself to create the most powerful army the universe had ever seen," Zuele said. "No one really knows what the Dark Panel is capable of; all we can hope is that we never have to find out." Kennedy trembled, and Zuele brought the lights back up in the training room.

"What happened to King Amsden?" Kennedy asked.

"He slowly descended into madness. His unnatural army was the only thing he cared about. It was a poorly kept secret that his daughter, Anila, ruled the planet during the last years of his life. Anila understood what a threat the Dark Panel posed to the universe. So, after her father died, she moved the vast majority of them to the Deepest Layer of Millintica, where thousands of Combatants remain to this day.

"The royal family did their best to remove Omin Yarso from their history books. They created cautionary tales about the Veilless' and called them evil. They tortured and killed each one they found until the Veilless' learned to hide their powers at all costs, making it impossible to know if any still exist."

Chief Minister Brandth transmitted himself to the recruits nearly every night to champion his half-hearted efforts at diplomacy with the Millinticans. In the interest of peace, Theein demanded that the Alliance turn themselves over, then slandered them as though they were the true culprits of the attack.

"Who onboard that ship was a member of the Alliance?" A Phase Two shouted when Chief Minister Brandth opened the floor to questions.

"I cannot answer that question at this time." Theein Brandth had white hair and a muscular build. According to Orien and her encyclopedic knowledge of the Brandth dynasty, Theein had pursued Reddick's mother, Vivith, for years before she would accept him as her intimate. He was quite a few years older than her and already a high-ranking officer in the Evolver Legion when she was receiving her first assignments as an Evolver. Theein did not look anything like Reddick, yet they both had the same thinking face. Kennedy noticed this as Theein fielded questions from the recruits. His right eye would squint ever so slightly, and his head would tilt as he carefully considered his answer. It was one of the things Kennedy really liked about Reddick—the way he took a beat before he spoke, the way he assumed people would wait for his thoughtful response.

Kennedy and Orien had finally finished their tour of kitchen duty and were once again able to watch Theein address the student body from the center of the dining hall. Typically, Reddick held off on entering the dining hall until after his father's address, clearly not wanting to be held responsible for his father's actions, or lack thereof.

Kennedy was gazing at Reddick when Pengar sat down and sighed like a schoolgirl. "The most amazing thing has happened to me!" Pengar talked a mile a minute about her favorite subject, Ethwin, while Kennedy ate a meat substitute that tasted like buttery steak.

Earlier that afternoon, Ethwin had requested that Pengar meet him in the Five Seasons Forest for a special surprise. When she arrived, Pengar found some fake leaves that formed the words "I love you" in her native language. Yet, Ethwin's leaves remained while the real ones dissolved, because Ethwin said their love would last all seasons and that even though the leaves were fake, their love was as real as the Eternal Energy Field.

Kennedy, Geenen, and Orien listened breathlessly. Geenen's thin alien lips stretched into a reluctant smile, and Orien fanned away tears. Kennedy wanted to congratulate Pengar, but Ethwin sat down at the table before she had the chance. The three of them stared at Ethwin with newfound reverence while he handed Pengar a small plate of pink fruit. "The Madilieu line is serving your favorite today: temlo fruit."

Pengar smiled. "You stood in the Madilieu line just for me?"

"Of course." He looked up at her swooning roommates and said, "What?"

They looked down at their food and said, "Nothing."

Kennedy peeked over at the Phase Three table, where Corijean was sitting so close to Reddick that she was practically on his lap.

Orien followed the direction of Kennedy's gaze. "There's something we need to tell you, Kennedy."

Geenen elbowed Orien so hard that she nearly fell out of her chair.

"What is it?" Kennedy asked.

Geenen tugged at her emotion blocker—a neon orange bracelet that dangled from her skinny wrist.

Kennedy crossed her arms. "Geenen?"

Geenen gave Orien a reluctant go-ahead.

Orien reached for Kennedy's hand. "I just feel it's better for you to hear it from us."

Kennedy was losing her patience. "Hear *what* from you?"

"Corijean and Reddick are together—like, for sure, together. This morning, I overheard Corijean telling Thecla Atter. I guess they haven't told anyone because Reddick doesn't want it all over *Symetran Society*." Orien squeezed Kennedy's hand. "You *okay*?"

"I'm fine," Kennedy said, even though she felt like someone had just punched her in the stomach.

"I don't know what he sees in her. She's such a phony," Geenen griped. "She's probably lying."

Orien squeezed Kennedy's hand again. "This probably isn't the right thing to say right now, but I've never seen him look at her the way he looks at you."

Kennedy was in and out of listening. She was so mad at herself. Why did she have to like him? She hated that she liked him; she wished there were some way to turn it off. This was fine... She was going to be fine. She was already overwhelmed with everything that was in front of her. The last thing she needed was a boyfriend. This was a hidden blessing. She needed closure, and this was closure. Orien and Geenen stared at her, as though she had just received a terminal diagnosis. "I'm fine, guys, really. Obviously, they're dating. They can't keep their hands off each other." Orien and Geenen looked over to the Phase Three table, but Kennedy could not.

SIXTEEN

Later that night, Kennedy brooded in her room and scolded herself for thinking anything good was ever going to happen to her. Her Sectnot attempted to slow her downward spiral, but all she wanted to do was feel sorry for herself. She put on her Thought Projector and observed the thoughts festering inside her mind. It was an enormous responsibility, sometimes an unbearable one, to know she was the one creating her own reality. So many unevolved beings were ignorant of this crushing fact— she wished she could be one of them.

Kennedy could cry just *thinking* about Reddick and Corijean together. But it was something she had zero control over, so she tried to think of something else. Something simple, something easy. She thought of her cat, Phantom, and how they used to play fetch together. She often joked that Phantom was a dog stuck in a cat's body. She thought of him prancing towards her with a fuzzy ball clamped between his teeth, and she laughed. She thought of hummingbirds, butterflies, the meditation planetarium, falling leaves, the waves of the Kathreeyan Ocean, the Five Seasons Forest, and the saguaros inside her sanctuary. There were so many wonderful things to think about. Why would she settle for the things that made her feel terrible? She felt better after consciously directing her thoughts, but her hope was still in a precarious state, so she walked across the hall and visited the most blindly optimistic person she had ever known.

The inside of Pengar's room still looked like a honeymoon suite, filled with candles and fresh flowers. Pengar also had a small greenhouse on the roof, where she kept even more exotic plants. The girls had gone up there to watch the star harvest together a few moons earlier, and Pengar now had a memory of it on her wall. "Is everything okay?" Pengar asked Kennedy as she fed a small predator plant with razor-sharp teeth. The predator plant stretched out its stem of a neck and caught the dead insect Pengar lobbed above its mouth.

Kennedy shoved her hands inside the pockets of her red hoodie. "I just wanted to say that I'm really happy for you. Ethwin is a great guy, and you deserve everything," Kennedy shrugged. "I guess that's all I wanted to say." She didn't tell Pengar the true meaning of her visit, which was to leach off her surplus of positive energy.

Pengar patted a spot on her bed for Kennedy to take a seat. Then she turned and began to water her flowers. "When I was young, I had this dream about my brother, where he came to me and told me to be happy. He said that being happy was the best way I could honor him. So that's what I did." She picked a yellow flower with green speckles from her planter and handed it to

Kennedy. "Being happy is not always easy. It is so much easier to be miserable. Misery takes zero discipline, but being happy is an art form. That's why I love flowers because they remind me to be happy. They also remind me that everything is temporary. I still have my trauma flare-ups, and I probably always will, but that's okay; I just let them pass. Things usually go my way, Kennedy. At least that is the story I constantly tell myself, and most of the time, I am right."

In that moment, Kennedy went from thinking Pengar was a Pollyanna to thinking she was a spiritual master.

"Plus, when I'm happy, I can feel my brother near me, but when I'm sad, he feels far away. He can communicate with me in those high frequencies. I don't know if that's the way it is for everyone, but that's the way it is for me."

It did not take Pengar long to get back to her favorite subject, Ethwin. "I wish you could feel this way, Kennedy. I wish everyone could feel this way." She collapsed on her bed. "Being in love makes life worth living. Not even Malant himself could kill this feeling. Have you ever fallen in love before?"

"No, but I kind of think I know what it feels like."

Pengar raised an eyebrow when Kennedy asked her Sectnot to play 'I've Just Seen a Face' by the Beatles. The song blared out of speakers positioned all around the room. Pengar listened intently. She swooned and screamed over the lyrics, "Yes! This is exactly what it feels like." She pulled Kennedy up and twirled her. "It's the greatest feeling in the universe!" She removed her emotion blocker from her finger—a jade flower ring—and told Kennedy, "Here, feel."

Kennedy pressed her own emotion blocker against her chest. "No, thanks, I want to be surprised," Kennedy said, even though she had experienced the feeling of romantic love secondhand back on Earth.

Pengar asked her to start the song over, so Kennedy did. Grandpa Jim had once called the Beatles' music the language of the universe, and as Kennedy danced and sang with Pengar on Symetra, she knew he had been right.

✦

A dated hologram of a violet-colored forest filled Kennedy's training room. Glass buildings grew out of the forest and sparkled beneath the sun. Behind the buildings stood a majestic blue mountain with a domed castle built into the side of it. Zuele watched the beautiful landscape unfold with a homesick look on her face. "Sixty years ago, Malant Tarish was born in the Royal Region of Millintica," she said.

Malant's childhood hologram replaced the Royal Region. He was a thin boy with freckles and a cowlick; there was no visible indication this small boy would grow up to be the biggest monster the galaxy had ever known.

"Malant, was raised by his father, Tollirin Tarish, an unstable man who often lamented the steady deterioration of Millintican might. Tollirin was a strict Possessor and believed that all the planets that had been *discovered* by Millintica still rightfully belonged to Millintica." A hologram of Tollirin Tarish appeared before Kennedy, and just looking into his cold eyes made her stand up a little straighter.

Zuele continued, "As the greatest nephew of Jasbir Tarish, Malant was born into a world of extreme wealth and privilege, but money did not interest him... While the other children played schoolyard games, Malant played war. He kept to himself and quickly formed an obsession with the Dark Panel. He learned all there was to know about them, and when he came of age, he made the voyage to the Deepest Layer to see them for himself. His family connections provided him with the rare opportunity to witness this army he had been daydreaming about since childhood. Malant was cautioned by his handlers against getting too close, but he refused to listen. So, a Combatant showed Malant his greatest shame that day and then mutilated him beyond recognition.

"What was his greatest shame?" Kennedy asked.

"I do not know. Malant killed everyone who witnessed the attack."

"Because of that?"

"He has killed beings for far less." Zuele took a deep breath. "Anyway, Malant somehow survived the incident. Tollirin was embarrassed by his disfigured son, and he often said he wished the Combatant had finished the job and put Malant out of his misery.

"Malant decided he would show his father. He decided one day he would be commander of the most lethal army the universe had ever known. Malant leveraged his greatest uncle's name to gain access to influential circles. He commissioned an engineer and a weapons expert to make him a titanium suit, similar to the

Dark Panel Combatants he planned to command one day. Then he resurrected the Possessors and espoused their unevolved views to all who would listen."

The training room was now filled with a Possessor rally—their symbol, a strong hand squeezing the life out of Symetra. Zuele watched them screaming and chanting with Millintican might flags in their hands. They wore dark robes with hoods in the shape of an upside-down triangle. A black nylon fabric hung down from the hoods, concealing their identities.

Zuele continued the lesson. "Even though Malant had risen to prominence amongst his followers, Tollirin still could not accept his son. So Malant introduced his father at a Possessor rally as though he were an honored guest and saluted him with a toast, but when Tollirin drank from his glass, he collapsed to the ground."

Footage of the gruesome scene played out before Kennedy: Tollirin writhing on the floor as the Possessors looked on. Malant held up his gloved hand and refused to let anyone help his dying father, who was now foaming at the mouth. "Is this the Millintican might you always spoke of?" Malant asked as Tollirin drew his last breath.

"If the Possessors were ever going to have a moment of conscience, this was their chance, but it did not happen," Zuele said. "They cheered for Malant, and some even kicked Tollirin's dead body."

Kennedy was horror-struck. "Malant killed his own father?"

"That was never proven."

Kennedy motioned to the hologram of Tollirin lying lifeless on the ground.

"Tollirin died from ingesting poison, but no one could prove Malant gave it to him. Malant's followers blamed the Evolvers; they said the Evolvers were trying to frame Malant because Malant was the chosen one."

"You can't be serious," Kennedy said.

"Unfortunately, I am."

The image of Tollirin Tarish lying lifeless on the floor disappeared from the room.

Zuele continued the lesson. "By this point, Malant was so popular that King Rimago made him general of the Millintican Guard, even though Xavian and pretty much everyone else with a working brain advised against it. Rimago thought it better to keep Malant close; ultimately, he paid for that mistake with his life."

Zuele clicked her Rivil, and the famous class photo of the Golden Phase filled one side of the room. Zuele refused to look at it. Where Kennedy and her friends saw legends, Zuele only saw loss. "Everyone believed that Leandor, Tusk, and me joining the Institute would usher in a new era for Millintica, one in which the Millinticans and Evolvers could work side-by-side, but Malant ensured this never happened. The pendulum swung the other way, and whatever ground we thought we had gained was lost... and then some."

"How did the Evolvers allow this to happen?" Kennedy asked in anger.

"The Evolvers cannot override the free will of any planet or any being."

"That's a load of crap."

"Excuse me?"

"If you have the power to do something, you should do it. If the Evolvers had dealt with this when they had the chance, everything would have been different. Malant wouldn't be terrorizing the galaxy, and King Rimago, Leandor, Janekis, Hoper, Reddick's mom, and Pengar's brother would all be alive." Kennedy stewed. "What good is power if you can't help people with it?"

"I understand your frustration. Trust me." Zuele brought the lights back up in the training room. "Let's end there for today."

Kennedy lay in bed the morning of Thanksgiving, knowing that if she were home, she would be helping her mother bake pumpkin pies. She felt a sharp pang of homesickness and could not believe how much she missed Tucson. Thanksgiving was the holiday Audrey spent with her dad's side of the family, which meant Kennedy got to feel like an only child. Her tías would run their hands through her hair and call her pretty. Her cousins would speak to her as though she were a fully functioning, independent person, not just Audrey's little sister. Her uncles would encourage her to join the basketball team every time she beat the boy cousins at H.O.R.S.E. She *had* played basketball in middle school, but her mom made her quit after Kennedy mentally shattered a glass backboard because of a ref's bad call.

Her alarm buzzed inside her hand. Kennedy stood, stretched, and then changed into her athletics. She laced her sneakers and headed down to Luminary Lake. After sparring with Scrawl, she put in her earbuds and ran five miles. She went through her usual drills. Her Sectnot acted as her personal trainer, pushing her further than she would ever go on her own. When she was done with her work, she Dematerialized from the Five Seasons Forest to the base of the Behemoths and cheered when she arrived in one piece.

Kennedy gussied herself up that day, pretending she was getting ready to go to Nana and Grandpa Jim's house. During lunchbreak, she returned to her unit and transmitted herself home, able to get in an extra visit that week thanks to the American holiday. When she arrived, she was surprised to find Audrey in the kitchen, baking.

"Happy Thanksgiving," Audrey said cheerfully. She had a fall apron over her pajamas and a smear of flour on her cheek.

"Happy Thanksgiving, where's Mom?"

"She's getting dressed."

"I'm surprised you're not with your dad," Kennedy said.

Audrey cracked an egg into a large mixing bowl. "Yeah, well, he took his *real* family to Sedona, and there wasn't enough room for me."

"I'm sorry."

Audrey whisked cloves, cinnamon, ginger, salt, and sugar in a smaller bowl. "What about you? Did you ever find your dad?"

Kennedy sat on a kitchen barstool. "No, I've kind of quit looking for him."

"You don't know how to quit, Kennedy; it's why you're so annoying."

"Gee, thanks."

"I meant it as a compliment. Your determination got us all this." Audrey said, referring to their new home. "Sky's the limit for the shameless."

"Happy Thanksgiving, Nedy," Roberta said as she walked out and hugged Kennedy. Then she put on an apron and finished preparing the sweet potato casserole they would be taking to the family party that afternoon. The smell of butter and brown sugar melting on the stove was torturous for Kennedy, who could not physically consume any of it—even this technology had its limits.

"You look skinny. Are they feeding you there?" her mother asked.

"I'm not skinny. I'm buff, check it out." Kennedy flexed in her suit. "I can do five whole chin-ups now."

The flat screen against the living room wall played one of Miles Pierce's old movies. His human fans believed he was taking a hiatus between acting roles—they had no idea he was actually recovering from life-threatening injuries on the other side of the universe. Kennedy last heard he was on the Parin continent, healing with the Triphens.

Roberta snapped her fingers near Kennedy's ear. "What's going on with you? It's like you're not present. You seem to be a billion miles away." Roberta slapped her knee and laughed at her own joke.

Kennedy rolled a walnut back and forth on the counter, pressing her hand against it as hard as she could, attempting to imprint its wrinkles on the inside of her palm but failing. She wondered when and where Malant would attack next.

"Is this about Reddick?" Roberta asked.

The walnut went flying. "What? No!"

Audrey's ears perked up. "Reddick Vincent?"

"It's okay if you have a crush on him," Roberta said. "It's

understandable, he's a good-looking kid."

"Um, he's gorgeous," Audrey corrected her. "You and Reddick Vincent, huh? *Respect.*"

"We're just friends."

Roberta didn't buy it. "I can see you're putting some elbow grease into it now, with the makeup and the hair—I know it's been a couple of years since we had the talk, but I hope you still remember what I said."

Kennedy convulsed. "*Mom, please.*"

Audrey grimaced. "Yeah, Mom, not around the food."

Roberta would not relent. "I'm pretty sure you can still get pregnant in space, Kennedy."

"Mom!" Kennedy tried to tell her mom that, for once, she had *not* been thinking about Reddick, but Roberta didn't give her a chance.

"What have I always told you, girls?"

"*We're not the exception to any rule.*" Kennedy and Audrey mimicked their mother in unison. Technically, Kennedy was the exception to plenty of rules, just not the one about choices having consequences.

"That's right." Roberta pointed a sugar-coated spatula at her daughters. "If someone is going to get pregnant, it's you. If someone's going to get a DUI, it's you. If someone's going to get an STD—"

"Alright, we get it," Audrey said.

Kennedy cringed. "You're not going to pull out those pamphlets again, are you?"

"My point is that there is no mistake quota you get to meet before the hammer comes down." Roberta wiped her hands on her apron. Once she saw Kennedy was sufficiently scared, she asked, "So? What's your status?"

"I told you, we're just friends."

Roberta still wasn't buying it. "If you like him, you should tell him how you feel. What've you got to lose?"

Everything.

Roberta pointed the spatula at her again. "Be a lioness. Do your own damn hunting. If you're going to get anything done in this life—"

"—I'm going to have to do it myself, I know."

"Don't forget it."

Kennedy picked up another walnut. "He has a girlfriend."

Roberta frowned. "Ah, it's just as well. Boys *that* good-looking are never worth the trouble."

SEVENTEEN

Geenen's room was an absolute pigsty, overrun with different gears, wires, and chips from a wide array of alien technologies. Geenen's solution to the problem—which was starting to trickle out into the circular hallway—was to make a cleaning robot, something she was currently teaching herself to do. Kennedy offered Geenen moral support as she tinkered with the gnome-sized robot laid out on a makeshift operating table.

Kennedy picked up a sharp, bullet-shaped object off Geenen's cluttered desk. "What is this?"

Geenen beamed. They were finally going to talk about something *she* was interested in. "It's a Disintegrator well, a tiny one. This little pellet can destroy locks, burn through walls, and sabotage other weapons. I figure it doesn't hurt to have one."

"I thought we weren't supposed to get weapons until after we graduate."

"They never said we couldn't make them."

Kennedy laughed. "Remind me to stay on your good side."

Geenen kicked the makeshift operating table in frustration. "This stupid thing won't start! I've been working on it for an entire progression, and my room is getting messier every moon."

"Why don't you just clean it?"

"Because I am too busy working on my genius to clean my room."

"Then why don't you just *buy* a robot to clean it?"

"Where is the innovation in that?" Geenen began rummaging through a drawer overflowing with chips and gears. "There's one thing I haven't tried yet."

Kennedy looked at the wonky little robot on Geenen's table. "Have you named it?"

"No. It's a robot."

"I think we should call her Pile."

"Pile?"

"Yeah, she's a pile of used parts."

"Let's see if she starts first."

Geenen approached the robot with hope in her eyes, clamping a tiny wire between a pair of tweezers. She worked on wiring Pile, while Kennedy worked on willing Pile to life. *Come on, Pile. I know you're in there. You can do it. Come on...* Kennedy did the same thing she did with rocks and other inanimate objects: she focused on Pile until the robot felt like an extension of her.

"That should do the trick." Geenen wiped her long, scaly hands on her training suit.

Come on, Pile, you can do it.

Geenen stepped back. "Let's see if that works."

Then Pile turned her head and looked directly at Kennedy.

"Geenen!" Kennedy pointed at Pile, who got to her feet.

Geenen looked at Pile and gasped. "I did it!" Geenen picked up the robot and twirled it. "It worked!"

"Can you please put me down?" Pile asked Geenen. "This is demeaning."

"She's smart," Kennedy said.

Pile focused on Kennedy: "What can I do for you?"

"Nothing. You belong to Geenen."

"That is also demeaning," Pile said.

Geenen set Pile down and commanded, "Clean my room."

"Didn't anyone teach you manners?"

"You sure are opinionated," Geenen said.

"And you sure are a Rude." Pile looked around at the room and said, "Look at this mess! Haven't you ever heard of putting things away after you are done using them? What filth!"

"I'd prefer it if you cleaned quietly," Geenen told Pile.

"And I'd prefer it if you weren't such a slob! This really fries my wires." Pile begrudgingly got to work.

"I'm going to have to adjust her attitude a little," Geenen whispered to Kennedy.

Orien burst into the room and snapped her fingers. "Let's go, you marvelous beings! There is a huge party downtown that requires our attendance. Everyone is home right now because of Malant. This never happens. We have to go out." Orien looked at Pile, who was carrying a load of dirty training suits towards Geenen's closet. "*What* is that?"

"That's Pile," Kennedy said. "Geenen created her."

Geenen grinned proudly at her creation. "You better remember where you put everything, Pile."

"Only a Dumb would forget where they put something. Pile is not a Dumb."

Orien snapped her fingers again to get the attention back on her. "Get ready, we're going out."

Geenen and Kennedy both groaned at the idea. Kennedy felt exhausted and wanted nothing more than to curl up in bed and read or watch a movie. It was then that Orien reminded them both of the code. The guilt trip did not work on Geenen, but Kennedy couldn't deny Orien anything after all she had done for her.

Orien dragged Kennedy to her room, where she straightened Kennedy's hair and used makeup bugs to give Kennedy a dramatic, smoky eye. She dressed her in a burgundy sleeveless, belted jumpsuit with an asymmetrical neckline and handed her several pieces of jewelry to try before settling on some sparkly ear cuffs. Then Orien took a victory lap around her room, as though Kennedy were her finished masterpiece. "You are undeniable, Kennedy. Reddick's about to realize he made the wrong choice."

"Wait, Reddick's going to be there?"

"Probably. Everyone's going to be there."

Kennedy's heart stopped; she had not been expecting to see him that night. She had hoped to—she always hoped to—but she did not think it would actually happen. She took a long look at herself in the mirror. Her shoulders shimmered with a Symetran cream, which smelled better than any perfume she had ever smelled on Earth. Her dramatic makeup made her look years older than she was. Her chestnut hair, now straightened, extended to the middle of her back. "I look like I'm trying too hard."

Orien scoffed. "What is wrong with trying too hard? Why would anyone want to be around someone who *wasn't* trying hard?"

"Because it's supposed to come easy."

"If being your best self were easy, everyone would do it." Orien steered Kennedy towards the garage and up the ramp of their ridership.

Pengar and Ethwin were already inside the ridership, making out. When Pengar came up for air, she gushed over Kennedy's new look. "Wait until Reddick sees you!"

"He has an intimate." Kennedy reminded her.

"For now," Orien joked.

They made a pitstop at a shoe store downtown. Orien asked Kennedy for her size, and when Kennedy told her, Orien made a face as though she was surprised numbers went that high. A few minutes later, she returned with some stiletto boots.

Kennedy held one of them up. "I'm not wearing these death traps."

"You can't pair gray training boots with Lowin Pert couture. Do you want everyone to think humans are deranged? Put them on," Orien commanded.

Kennedy reluctantly obeyed. "Only because you asked so nicely."

The ridership traveled to a tall building at the edge of Crystal City and streamed inside a narrow entrance in the center of it. Kennedy followed Orien down the ridership ramp and wobbled in her high boots, like a newborn horse trying to find its legs. Then, flashing yellow lights blinded her. Kennedy shielded her eyes. "What the—"

A line of floating cameras recorded and photographed them—though they didn't look much like cameras. They reminded Kennedy of the beach binoculars set up on Earth's ocean piers—the kind she could stick a quarter in and search for dolphins—except that in this scenario, she was the dolphin.

"They're capturers, image-capturers," Orien said through the clenched teeth of a practiced and perfected smile. "I told you everyone was going to be here." Orien continued to pose, while Kennedy followed Pengar and Ethwin inside. They waited for Orien to finish posing, and then they took an elevator to the top floor. Boklin, an older boy with dark curly hair and dimples, greeted them at the party's entrance. "Orien, welcome! I am so glad you were able to make it," he schmoozed. Orien introduced him to Kennedy, Pengar, and Ethwin. He took Kennedy's hand by way of introduction and held it a little longer than she was comfortable with. "It is a pleasure to encounter your energy." Boklin ushered them inside the crowded high-rise and whispered in Orien's ear.

"He likes you," Orien told Kennedy when he turned to greet more guests.

"Me?" Kennedy was flattered that an actual Evolver liked her. "How do you know?"

"He just told me he thinks you're pretty. You should talk to him. His family is from Millintica; it'll be good for the mission."

"He lives *here*?" Kennedy looked around at the impressive unit.

"He shares it with some other low-level Evolvers."

Pengar and Ethwin quickly searched for a darkened corner to make out in. Orien, being the social butterfly she was, entered superficial conversations with complete strangers while Kennedy stared longingly at the exit. A live band was jamming in the middle of the party. Kennedy waved her hand through the band, only to discover it was a hologram. She smiled in amazement as the next song started, replacing the three-piece band with a lone girl playing a plucky-sounding, floating instrument. The mirage fascinated Kennedy so much that she failed to notice the group of beings threatening to approach her in the hopes of a dance.

Boklin got there first. "We have a beautiful view. Of course, it is nowhere near as beautiful as you are. Would you like to see it?"

Kennedy blushed. Then she looked over Boklin's shoulder and found Reddick sitting with some Phase Threes on the other side of the crowded room. Corijean's perfectly manicured hand rested on his leg. Reddick's gaze cut through the crowded room. He ran his eyes over the new, glamorized version of Kennedy. Reddick looked at her like he was trying to communicate a million things without saying a word. Kennedy tore her eyes from his and focused once again on Corijean's possessive hand. She reminded herself that Reddick no longer traveled in singular form; he was a '*we*', he was an '*us*.'" Kennedy quickly hooked her arm through Boklin's. "Sure, I'd love to see the view."

Boklin led her out onto the balcony. The snowy Five Seasons Forest sparkled in the distance. Kennedy was so cold that her teeth began to chatter. She had requested a jacket from Orien, but Orien said high fashion sometimes required sacrificing comfort.

Boklin removed his jacket and placed it around her shivering shoulders, making Kennedy feel like a proper lady. "Come and get warm by the fire." He motioned to a heated lounger in front of the firepit. "I'll get you some ial root tea. It will help."

Soon after, Boklin returned with a steaming mug of herbal tea and handed it to her.

Kennedy sipped the sweetened tea eagerly, while her Sectnot tried to share some nutritional information about ial root. Kennedy silenced it. "So, Orien tells me you're from Millintica."

"Well, technically yes, but my family managed to escape when Malant assassinated King Rimago. I haven't been there since I was young. I barely even remember it."

"My father is from Millintica."

"Which part?" he asked.

"I'm not sure."

"My family was from the Meadow Region."

Kennedy guzzled some more hot tea and felt slightly euphoric as she listened to him prattle on about her father's home planet. He was attractive—not really her type, not that she had one, but still cute. Then she grew lightheaded. She tried to focus on him—both of him. She blinked her eyes rapidly and counted again.

Yep, there's definitely two of him.

Her Sectnot broke through her muddled thoughts and told her to stop consuming the tea in order to prevent further intoxication. Kennedy spit out the sip she had been swallowing.

"Are you okay there?" Boklin asked.

She coughed. "What's in this?"

"It's ial root tea," he said, as though she should know exactly what that meant.

Kennedy searched for a solid place to stare. She did not like the feeling. She was used to being in control, and in this moment, she was anything but. Everything started to sway, including Kennedy. "I think I need to lie down." She fell back on the lounger.

He looked into her nearly empty mug. "You were supposed to sip it."

Orien walked out onto the patio. "How's it going out here?" she asked, then noticed Kennedy sprawled on the lounge chair. "Kennedy?" Orien took the mug from Boklin and sniffed it. "She's a human. She doesn't even know what ial root tea is!"

"She said she was from Millintica." Boklin apologized profusely and—after an earful from Orien—returned to the party.

"Just give it some time; it'll wear off." Orien reassured Kennedy after he left.

Kennedy focused on Orien: her cotton candy-colored hair styled into a pompadour, her shimmering olive skin, and her Cleopatra eyes. "You're so pretty, Orien..." Kennedy told her, "I wish I was as alive as you are. You're just... so... *free.*" Kennedy grabbed her arm urgently. "You're my bestiest bestie. I love you so much."

Orien pulled away. "Sorry, Kennedy, I don't like you like that."

Kennedy laughed so hard that she snorted. "You're hilarious! Have I ever told you that? You're like sooo funny."

Orien patted her on the head. "I'm going to go get you some water. I'll be right back. Don't move." She pointed a firm finger at her. "I mean it."

Kennedy saluted Orien like she was a drill sergeant.

Once she was alone, Kennedy flung off the uncomfortable boots and massaged her tortured feet, wishing she had worn thicker socks. Then came the star harvest. Kennedy could not believe no one else had come outside to see it. She slurred,

"Buncha losers." Her voice sounded weird, so she said it again to make sure the voice was actually coming from her. *Voices are weird*, she decided, and then she laughed at how weird they were and how weird it was that everyone had their own. "So random," she said, still laughing.

She watched in wonder as hundreds of stars fell from the sky. "Thank you," she said to the universe. "I can't believe this is my life." The gratitude was so overwhelming that she nearly wept. Then the door opened, and music and alien dialects filled the silence on the balcony.

"You almost missed it!" Kennedy turned around, expecting to find Orien, but found Reddick instead. She swayed in place and then laid back down, struggling to concentrate while tightening Boklin's jacket around her shoulders.

Reddick sat next to her and noticed her wearing Boklin's jacket—it was all he seemed to notice. "Did you lose your date?" he asked.

"Date?"

"Boklin. I saw you out here with him."

"I just met him. Did you know he's from Millintica?"

"Yeah, I did know that."

"He and I have a lot in common," Kennedy said. She was about to tell Reddick that her father was from Millintica. Now that he had a girlfriend, there was no longer a reason for her to keep something like that from him.

Orien returned and was surprised to find Reddick. She handed Kennedy a glass of water. "Here, drink this, all of it."

As Kennedy sat up and gulped the water, Boklin's jacket

slipped from her shoulders.

"Boklin gave her some ial root tea, and Kennedy mistook it for regular tea." Orien told Reddick.

Reddick clenched his jaw and peered over at Kennedy. "So you just drink anything a stranger gives you now?"

"He's not a stranger," Kennedy shot back.

"Oh, that's right." Reddick rolled his eyes. "*You have a lot in common.*"

Kennedy glared at him. "Why are you being such a dick right now?"

"Kennedy." Orien squeezed her arm, silently reminding her that she was speaking to Symetran royalty.

Kennedy ripped her arm from Orien's grasp. "Whatever, I'm going home."

"Yeah, that's a good idea. Let's go," Orien said.

"No, you stay." Kennedy held up her hand. "I know how to get there." Kennedy forced her way through the crowded party and got into the elevator, but before the doors closed, Reddick jumped inside with her. Kennedy crossed her arms and looked down at her feet, quickly realizing she had forgotten her new boots.

When they arrived on the ridership level, Kennedy bolted out of the elevator, but she did not have a plan beyond getting as far away from Reddick as possible.

Reddick hailed his own ridership for the two of them, then he removed his jacket and wrapped it around Kennedy's shivering shoulders.

Kennedy tried to hand it back, but he refused to accept it. "You're going to freeze to death."

"I don't need you to babysit me," she said.

"I'm not letting you walk around alone like this."

"I can handle it."

He looked at her socks. "Obviously."

Kennedy pressed the jacket against his chest. "You should go back to Corijean. She needs you a lot more than I do."

"Corijean knows how to take care of herself."

"I'm sure Corijean knows how to do *a lot* of things!" Kennedy whipped away from him, but the motion made her dizzy. She held out her arms in an effort to balance herself.

Reddick caught her and pulled her close to him. "I've got you."

She inhaled his clean scent. "I thought it was just tea, I swear."

"We've all been there."

Kennedy felt his warmth against her and looked up into his blue eyes.

A rushing sound approached, and he looked away.

"Come on, we'd better hurry," he said.

"What's that noise?" Kennedy asked.

"Capturers." Reddick pressed her into the side of his body and shielded her from them as they boarded his ridership. Once inside, Kennedy sat down, closed her eyes, and held her head, praying for the spinning to stop.

Reddick took the seat next to hers and slid it closer. Their knees were touching, but it was not enough for Kennedy, who leaned her head against his shoulder.

Reddick responded by wrapping his arm around her and pulling her to his chest. Kennedy rested there, feeling as though she had finally found her place in the universe. Her head rose and fell with each breath he took. She listened to his heartbeat and could not believe how human it sounded. She marveled at the miracle of him. In her opinion—her very buzzed opinion—he was the most beautiful miracle in the entire universe. Thankfully, she had just enough wherewithal not to say this out loud.

At first, liking Reddick only proved she had eyes. But now, it was different. His looks were no longer what drew her to him. It was something else, a kind of knowing, but she had no idea what she was supposed to know. Reddick was probably accustomed to girls throwing themselves at him; he was probably even bored of it.

"You smell good," he said.

Kennedy smiled against his chest. Then an image of him and Corijean filled her mind's eye. She pulled away. "Sorry to take you away from your girlfriend."

"Who's my girlfriend?"

"Corijean."

"I already told you she wasn't."

Kennedy was confused and then elated.

"We're just friends," he said.

"Orien overheard Corijean saying you were together."

"Maybe Orien overheard wrong."

"Or maybe Corijean is a liar."

"You don't like Corijean very much, do you?"

"She doesn't like me."

"It's only because she's threatened by you."

Kennedy laughed. "Why would someone like Corijean be threatened by *me*?"

Reddick looked from her eyes to her lips, then down to his

hands. "You have a light, Kennedy. You shine. I see it. And I know Corijean sees it, too. Instead of being inspired by it the way I am, she has decided she wants to dim it. Don't let her. Don't let anyone."

Kennedy was at a loss for words. How could she inspire someone as exceptional as Reddick?

His ridership pulled into the garage of Kennedy's unit. A patroller stopped next to the ramp, but once it realized the ridership belonged to Reddick Brandth, it streamed back out into the night. "They give us Phase Threes a longer leash," Reddick said. Yet Kennedy knew the patroller's deference had more to do with Reddick's last name than his phase.

"I'm sorry," she kept saying as he helped her inside her unit.

"It happens to the best of us." Reddick opened the door to her bedroom.

Kennedy went into her closet and discovered that Pile had organized her underwear drawer. "Pile, what are you doing in here?"

Pile held up Kennedy's large Live Aid t-shirt. "This has a hole in it."

"It's vintage."

"You like junk?" It was an ironic thing for a pile of junk to ask.

"It's not junk." Kennedy took it from her. "You are supposed to be cleaning Geenen's room."

"Please don't make me go back in there," said a traumatized Pile.

"You have to." Kennedy kicked Pile out of the closet. She removed her uncomfortable outfit, slipped the Live Aid t-shirt on, climbed into bed, and pulled the covers over her.

Reddick returned from the kitchen with a glass of water and handed it to her. "Feeling better?"

"Things are getting a little less spinny."

"That's good," he said as he sat down at the bottom of her bed.

She wrapped both hands around her water glass. "Sorry for calling you a dick earlier."

He smirked. "You can't spell Reddick without dick."

Kennedy held her stomach and laughed uncontrollably.

He observed her. "I like your laugh."

"What?" she asked, still giggling.

"You have a good laugh. It's infectious. It's like every funny thing you hear is somehow hurting you. Sometimes I can't tell if you're laughing or crying."

Kennedy covered her face with one hand until it returned to its normal shade. "Thank you."

"So, you're not mad at me anymore?"

"When was I mad at you?"

"That night at the beach, the way you looked at me..." he trailed off. "You looked like you were mad at me."

The memory of him hurdling toward the shallow end of the ocean wiped the smile from her face. "I don't like seeing you in danger."

"Why?"

"What do you mean, why? I just don't. You almost got yourself killed, and for what? A party trick? I don't know what you're trying to prove, but I wish you would stop it."

He smiled his wide, bashful smile at her. "I didn't know you cared so much."

She set down her waterglass, fell back into bed, and huffed at the ceiling.

"Okay, okay," he said, "no more party tricks."

She held out a pinky for him. "Promise?"

"Promise."

Kennedy grabbed his hand, wrapped her pinky around his, and then kissed her own hand. She pushed their hands back towards him so he could kiss his hand too, but instead he kissed hers. The feel of his soft, warm lips on her hand sent an involuntary shiver through her body. "You did it wrong," she said.

Reddick seemed to disagree. He slid the side of his hand down into her palm and left it there for a moment, his Charge Ring resting against hers. He caressed her thumb, and then he got up from the bed.

As he walked around her room, Kennedy tried to contain her smile.

He examined the frames on her wall. "How is your family?"

My mom thinks I should hunt you like a lioness, she wanted to say, but instead she said, "They're good."

He stopped at the frame of her father's tattoo and gasped. "Why do you have this framed?"

Kennedy propped up on her elbows. "What?"

"The Antastropolith Alliance," he said, as though he still could not believe what he was seeing. "Why do you have their symbol framed?"

Kennedy wasn't sure if she should answer the question.

Reddick waited.

"My father has that symbol tattooed on his wrist. It's one of the few things my mom remembers about him."

This piece of information seemed to blow Reddick away.

"Your father was in the Antastropolith Alliance?"

"I think so. Maybe. Why else would he have that symbol tattooed on his wrist?"

Reddick wore a stunned expression. "My mother was in the Alliance."

Kennedy sat all the way up. The idea of both their parents being members of the same secret alliance gave her goosebumps.

Reddick had some version of the same thing going on because he continued to stare at her in disbelief. "You still don't know who he is?"

"Zuele knows he was from Millintica, but that's it."

She expected Reddick to leave in a disgusted hurry once he discovered her unevolved heritage, but he didn't. "Makes sense; most in the Alliance were from Millintica. Plus, that would explain why he was on Earth. I hear a lot of them hid out there after Malant took power."

"You don't care that I am half-Millintican?"

"Why would I?"

"No reason," she frowned. "How do you know your mother was in the Alliance?"

"My father removed all my mother's belongings from our home when he remarried. He allowed my brother and I to keep what we wanted, and I was going through her things when I found this." Reddick turned the rubbery, charcoal band on his wrist inside out to reveal a large X with four other x's springing from the tips of it. "I think it was her emotion blocker at some point. I had to stretch it out so it would fit me."

Kennedy gaped at it.

"The symbol struck me for some reason. When I asked my father about it, he said that the symbol was the reason my mother was dead. He told me she cared more about her commitment to the Alliance than her commitment to her own family. He never mentioned the hundreds of lives she saved."

Kennedy felt she should say something, but she did not know what.

Reddick faced her. "After that, I became obsessed with the Alliance. I needed to know why my mom chose them over us."

"Did you ever find the answer?" she asked.

He shook his head. "On my best days, I believe she did what she did *because* of us. Because she loved her own family so much, she could not bear to watch other families suffer. On my worst days, well, we don't have to talk about those."

Kennedy felt a sudden urge to reach out to him.

Reddick changed the subject. "Do you have any leads?"

"No, just the tattoo." She told him everything she and her friends had done to find her father and how, so far, the search had come up empty.

"You've been busy," he said. "Maybe I can help. If you want, we can meet tomorrow out by the lake, and I can tell you everything I know."

"Really? That would be amazing!" She tried to get out of bed, but the spinning returned.

"Whoa, no sudden movements." He eased her back under the covers. "You need to sleep this off first." He sat beside her, his knee touching the side of her torso and searing her skin through the sheets. This was the second time he had been at her bedside, and it made Kennedy feel like he was there to take the night watch. He made Kennedy feel like it was safe for her to finally rest.

"You're really beautiful," he said, as though it were more of an observation than a compliment.

"*You're* really beautiful," Kennedy said, but Reddick just continued to stare. She wanted to hide her goofy grin beneath the covers but didn't. She did not know if it was physically healthy to like someone as much as she liked him. Her heart was skipping beats, her pulse was racing, her mind was malfunctioning.

He brushed a loose strand of hair from her forehead. "So, both of our parents were in the Alliance... That has to beat whatever it is you have in common with Boklin."

"It does," she said breathlessly.

He looked at her lips, then back into her eyes.

Kennedy could see his energy field growing brighter, and she could feel hers doing the same.

"Kennedy," he whispered.

Then the alert for curfew rang through their Sectnots.

The moment was over.

Reddick stood. "I'd better go... I'll contact you tomorrow about meeting up. Feel better."

But Kennedy did not think it was possible for her to feel any better than she did in that moment. It was all she could do not to scream giddily into her pillow.

EIGHTEEN

Somehow, during the night, Kennedy managed to kick all the covers off her bed. Most of her vivid dreams were about Reddick. In one of them, they were both standing on hoverboards over Luminary Lake, with Kennedy's hoverboard a few yards away from his. She tried to jump to get to him but didn't make it. Kennedy fell into the water and looked up, only to find Corijean standing on the board with him.

Kennedy rubbed out the crick in her neck and ran her hand over the spot where Reddick had sat the night before. His clean scent lingered in her room. The memory of his warm, soft lips on her hand resurfaced, and a blissful agony filled her entire being. Her Sectnot applauded the height of her current vibration, but Kennedy could not claim responsibility for it. It was all Reddick.

Kennedy hopped out of bed—thankfully, ial root tea did not come with any punishing aftereffects. She showered and then remembered her date with Reddick. Wait. Was it a date? Last night, it felt like it was, but in broad daylight, things felt different.

Kennedy had been out of it. Had she imagined it? Was he offering to help her as a friend? Or as something more? Either way, she couldn't wait to see him again. Once she was ready for the day, she flipped through the pages of her BELIEVE notebook, reviewing what she had already uncovered about the Alliance, which was not much. She only knew the names of a handful of its members: Xavian Seelos, Janekis Opris, Leandor Everin, and now, Vivith Brandth. Malant had killed everyone on that list, except Xavian himself. She was eager for any additional information Reddick could provide her.

Then her Sectnot vibrated inside her hand. She smiled when she saw that the communication was from Reddick. It was a moment before she could calm down enough to read it.

My guardian just told me we are leaving for the continent of Adaviad this morning. There is another Institute there for older recruits. Apparently, I am going to be training there this progression. I'm not going to be able to meet today. I am sorry. I will see you when I get back, Kennedy. Until then, don't take drinks from strangers.

The X on his XO was the Alliance symbol.

Kennedy's heart sank as she considered not seeing him for weeks. She was unsure of how to respond.

Okay, have fun. I'll see you when you get back. She signed off with the same XO, wondering how she was going to make it through an entire forty moons without seeing him.

Kennedy had been looking forward to spending time with him, not just because she was crazy about him but also because he knew things about the Alliance she did not. She went to the Hover House and checked out a research room for a Planetary

Studies assignment, but once she was in there, she went right back to thinking about Reddick. Her Sectnot kept interrupting her daydreams with information about him. It grew so distracting that Kennedy eventually had to turn it off. She did not want to learn Reddick's stories from her Sectnot; she wanted to hear them straight from his lips. Then she started thinking about his lips...

The entire morning went like this.

Once she finally finished her assignment, she sat and doodled the Alliance symbol inside her BELIEVE notebook. She began to wonder if there was a story behind it, so she asked her avatar. It dove inside the desk and returned with information about a Millintican fable called "No Way Out, Only In." The fable told the story of a child trapped inside a dark dungeon. The only light available inside the dungeon was an X capped by other x's shining through the bars. The child does everything he can to get out—he screams, he cries, and he beats his fists against the bars. Then one day, when he is exhausted and seemingly beaten, he is silent enough to hear a small, white ladybug say, *"There is no way out, only in."* So, the boy takes what little strength he has left and goes deeper inside his cell, to the darkest corner he had been avoiding at all costs. And it is there that he finds a secret door that leads to everything he has ever wanted.

Kennedy thought of her father hearing the fable as a child in early school. She listened to the fable three more times, pretending that he was the one telling it to her. Then she gathered her things and headed back to her unit.

It was a lovely autumn afternoon inside the Five Seasons Forest, and Kennedy was admiring the fall colors when she heard someone say her name. Two Phase Ones were whispering about her, and then some Phase Three boys struck up a flirtatious conversation with her out of the blue—something was not right.

Kennedy turned on her Sectnot and found she had thirteen missed communications from Orien. She immediately thought the worst and hustled back to her unit.

"There you are!" shouted Orien when Kennedy appeared inside the living area. "Why have you been ignoring me?"

"I was on the Information Level. I turned off my Sectnot," Kennedy panted. "What's going on?"

"You're on *Symetran Society*. That's what's going on!"

Orien drew a screen with her finger, and a toothy entertainment reporter named Hesta Muse appeared between them. Sparkling streaks of tinsel highlighted Hesta's dark bob.

Kennedy gasped as deceivingly intimate images of Reddick helping Kennedy inside his ridership appeared on the screen.

Hesta's eyes were vacant, but her frozen smile extended from ear to ear. "That is Reddick Brandth cozying up to the fashion-forward human, Kennedy Neff, who is seen here wearing a sleek Lowin Pert ensemble," she reported.

Orien backhanded Kennedy's arm. "You're welcome."

Hesta continued. "The Brandth House has yet to comment on the status of Reddick and the earthling's relationship, but my sources tell me this romance has been budding for quite some time."

Kennedy finally understood why everyone had been acting so strangely.

Orien waved her hand through the screen. "What happened last night?"

"Nothing." Kennedy plunked down on the couch. "He just brought me home."

"That did not look like nothing to me."

Kennedy was at a complete loss for words.

Orien squeezed Kennedy's shoulders and said, "You're famous now," as though it were a good thing.

⸻

The next morning, a swarm of capturers lurked at the edge of the property, waiting to get a shot of Kennedy entering the Hover House with her friends. Orien posed for them, while Geenen tried to hide Kennedy with her tall, skinny body. Luckily, some patrollers streamed out and chased the capturers away. Kennedy, who had spent most of her life in self-preserving obscurity, had no idea how to handle this extreme level of attention. Everyone whispered about her as she passed.

Zuele did not mention Kennedy's newfound fame until their Empowering Beliefs segment. She drew a screen with her finger and tuned into the ongoing coverage of her recruit on Symetran Society.

Kennedy couldn't bear to look at it. She considered contacting Reddick but did not know what to say; she wondered what he thought about all of this.

"Well, I can't say I am surprised," Zuele said. "Reddick was always asking me questions about you when we were in Tucson."

"Seriously?" It was the first time Kennedy had smiled all day.

Zuele exhaled. "He is a kind and decent being, but I cannot say

I approve of this relationship. Reddick is a Brandth. Wherever he goes, a circus of attention follows. It is not his fault, but I want more for you, Kennedy. You are too great a talent to wither in the shadows of his fame."

Kennedy tried to align her thinking with Zuele's but could not. She was tired of talking herself out of the things she wanted. What if she actually allowed herself to want Reddick? What if she allowed for the possibility that he might want her, too? She knew how the universe rearranged itself to accommodate a made decision. What if it could accommodate this decision? Kennedy felt vulnerable, thinking such hopeful thoughts, and soon she retreated back to her well-worn frequency. She tried to preemptively let herself down before anyone else could; at least that way she could say she was right even though, in this case, she would much rather be wrong. "It's not true. He was just giving me a ride," she told Zuele.

Zuele didn't believe her. "I hope you have prepared yourself."

"For what?"

"For fame, for constant attention, for living under a microscope."

"But we're not together."

"I remember how *Symetran Society* antagonized Reddick's mother when she began dating Theein, and Vivith was from a prominent Symetran family."

"We're not dating. I swear."

Zuele still would not hear her. "Theein Brandth will never approve of his son's relationship with a half-human, half-Millintican. Why do you think he sent Reddick away?"

"*That's* why Reddick is training on Adaviad? Because of me?"

Zuele nodded. "From this moment forward, Theein will be looking for any and every excuse to send you back to Earth, Kennedy. Don't give him one."

The speculation surrounding Kennedy and Reddick did not die down the way Orien promised it would. *Symetran Society* ran a new story about Symetra's son and the half-human every night. They accused Kennedy of seducing Reddick (like she even knew how to do such a thing) and questioned her motives. They also offered a handsome reward to anyone who knew her father's identity or whereabouts. "As evolved as we claim to be, we still can't get rid of this trash," Orien said, even though she never missed an episode.

Kennedy awoke the morning of December 2nd to her Sectnot playing 'Birthday' by the Beatles. *Symetran Society* made sure the galaxy knew it was Kennedy's birthday and wondered if Reddick would spend the special occasion with the earthling. Several of her phasemates wished her a happy birthday. Most were supportive of her rumored relationship with Reddick—everyone except for Corijean, who threw Kennedy a scowl every time she saw her. Corijean made it clear to anyone who would ask her—and even those who didn't—that there was no truth to the rumors.

At dinner, Chef Raka made Kennedy a strawberry cream birthday cake with the number 17 floating above it. The entire dining hall stopped what they were doing to sing out a jokey Symetran birthday song entitled 'Don't Waste This One,' as was custom when one of the recruits was celebrating a birthday.

Kennedy did not know what to wish for. She thought of making Reddick her birthday wish, but not even birthday magic could convince the most beautiful boy in the universe to love her—even though everyone else in the galaxy already thought he did.

In the end, she chose her usual wish—she wished that somehow, some way, she could know her father. The number 17 above Kennedy's cake burst into a dazzling display of fireworks. Kennedy's friends hugged her and slapped her on the back. Last year she didn't have a friend in the world, and now she had three of them, including Ethwin, who made four. They all enjoyed the cake, except for Geenen, whose body could not digest it.

Corijean and her clique of Phase Three friends sat down at the table nearest Kennedy's, which was unusual. They usually sat across the room in an elite corner, so everyone could admire their excellence from afar. Kennedy's ears perked up when Corijean's roommate, Thecla Atter, brought up her rumored relationship with Reddick.

Corijean picked at a purple lobster on her plate. "I have never seen anything sadder," she told Thecla. "Kennedy set the whole thing up just to get attention. She is infatuated with Reddick." Corijean spoke loud enough for Kennedy to hear. "Chief Minister Brandth despises her. Soon, he'll send her home with a modified memory. I only wish someone would modify *my* memory of her."

The Phase Threes laughed.

Geenen cursed in her choppy alien language and clenched her bony fists, preparing for a fight. She made to get up, but Kennedy stopped her.

"Just ignore her," Kennedy whispered.

Pengar shook her head, as though she were truly disappointed in Corijean. "How did someone so unkind get recruited into the Evolver Institute?" she asked in earnest.

"Because she's rich and has been training since birth." Orien crossed her arms. "Generational wealth can be a palace for the primitive, that's what my guardian said anyway."

Corijean continued to trash Kennedy. "You know she nearly killed a human right before she came here. He was in the desert just minding his own business, and Kennedy attacked him."

Kennedy glared at Corijean, and she laughed in response.

"I talked to Reddick yesterday—he contacts me all the time— and he said it's not true. I think he knows she is beneath him." Corijean made eye contact with Kennedy. "She is poor, and she is sad, and she is pathetic. Her mother does not even know who her father is. How many beings has that woman experienced?"

Kennedy slammed her hand down on the table. "Don't talk about my mom!" she screamed in Corijean's direction.

Corijean wore a satisfied smile. "Oh good. Perhaps you can settle this for us. Exactly how many interplanetary relationships has your mother had at this point, Kennedy? Or do you think she has lost count?"

Kennedy shook with rage. "Shut up!"

Corijean laughed. "That many, huh?"

Kennedy forced her hand forward, and the purple lobster flew up from Corijean's plate, stretched out its claw, and clamped Corijean's big mouth shut. Corijean let out a muffled scream as the lobster dangled from her lips. The dining hall broke out into laughter as Corijean's friends tried to remove it.

"Stop it!" one of them yelled at Kennedy.

"I can't. I'm too poor, pathetic and sad."

Kennedy's friends laughed hysterically.

When Kennedy felt like Corijean had finally learned her lesson, she dropped her hand, and the lobster fell back onto Corijean's plate.

Corijean's swollen pink lips formed into a hard line. Corijean focused her attention on Kennedy's birthday cake, and it exploded all over Kennedy and her friends. Geenen got the worst of it; her large eyes blinked away the frosting like vertical windshield wipers. Orien focused her attention on the food at Corijean's table, and it exploded too.

The skirmish quickly escalated into a full-blown food fight. Recruits at every table threw both delicious and disgusting food at each other. Kennedy was lucky enough to only be hit with palatable food. Unlike Pengar, who got hit with a face full of bloody innards, which were fed to the Polksequins—recruits that possessed both the skin and eating habits of alligators.

Enforcer Tusk rushed inside the dining hall. "Enough! Stop right this instant!" Everyone dropped the food in their hands.

"Who started this?" he asked.

One of the recruits pointed out Kennedy and Corijean.

"Everyone return to your units," Tusk said, glaring at Kennedy and Corijean, "except you two."

Everyone still stared.

"Now!" he screamed.

The dining hall cleared out.

Even though only he, Kennedy, and Corijean remained

inside the filthy dining hall, Tusk continued to scream. "On some planets, they scarcely have enough food to eat, and here you are throwing yours around! You ought to be ashamed of yourselves!"

Corijean tried to plead her case. "It is Kennedy's fault. I was just sitting at my table. You can ask anyone; they will all tell you. This is how humans resolve their issues: with violence. I do not feel safe around her."

"That's enough." Tusk held up his hand. "You two are not leaving here until this dining hall is spotless." He threw two aprons at them.

Kennedy put on the apron, retrieved a bus tub from one of the kitchen staff, and began tossing gobs of food into it.

"I can't," Corijean whined. "I'm leaving for Adaviad tomorrow. I haven't been able to travel because of the attacks. Malant is destroying my Phase Three experience," she said, as though she were the real victim of Malant's cruelty. "I have to go pack. I leave first thing in the morning."

"Then you'd better hurry and get this mess cleaned up." Tusk walked out of the dining hall.

The stench of the different food combinations made Kennedy want to vomit. She powered through it—the same way she used to at her job bussing tables back in Tucson. She made a game out of it and bet herself she could have it all done within two hours. Meanwhile, Corijean made prissy noises and moved slowly, bemoaning the injustice of it all. "I hope you're happy," she told Kennedy. "Now you are sabotaging my career, too."

Kennedy slammed her bus tub down, nearly shattering the plates inside it. "What's your damage, Corijean? I've never done anything to you."

Corijean slammed her own bus tub down. "You're trying to take what's mine."

"You don't *own* Reddick," Kennedy hissed. "That's the least evolved thing I've ever heard. It's like you haven't even learned anything during your time here."

"I've learned who my enemies are."

Kennedy shook her head in self-disappointment. She and Corijean had desecrated the entire dining hall over a boy, though they both knew he was much more than that. Kennedy looked down at the mess she made and realized she had no right to call Corijean unevolved. "This is stupid," she said, feeling like the worst feminist who ever lived. "There is no reason for us to hate each other. It's a waste of energy. I am not your enemy. We are on the same team." Kennedy wiped her hand on her apron, then extended it to Corijean. "Truce?"

Corijean recoiled. "Reddick and I are supposed to be together. We are excellent, we inspire, and we give others something to aspire to. It is expected. It is inevitable. It is destiny."

"Then what's stopping you?"

Corijean did not have an answer for Kennedy. In that moment, it was evident that the only thing they had in common was the shared agony of liking Reddick.

Kennedy sighed. "It's not like he can be with either of us anyway; neither of us are from Symetra."

"How dare you compare our situations?" Corijean struggled to regain the upper hand. "The Cabrin family and the Brandth family have been close for eons. When they visit Madilieu, they stay at our hotels."

"Good for you." Kennedy extended her hand again. "Come on, do we have a truce or what?"

Corijean took a step closer. "Fine, I'll make a truce with you. *If* you promise to stay away from him."

Kennedy unconsciously dropped her hand, and Corijean nodded as though she had known the truth all along. Corijean turned on her heel and left Kennedy to clean the rest of the dining hall alone. The next day, she left for the other side of Symetra as planned, proving that consequences did not apply to her kind.

NINETEEN

Kennedy had run out of ways to find her father. So, her new approach was to follow every lead, no matter how small. She sat inside her study nook and gazed at the famous class photo of the Golden Phase. Her fellow half-human, Miles Pierce, stared back at her from the old photo. Maybe *he* knew something about her father? Maybe he could help her connect the dots... She had to find a way to speak to him.

When Kennedy shared her thinking with the girls, they agreed that seeing Miles was a step in the right direction. "Miles was one of the most popular recruits in the Golden Phase," Orien said. "He was friends with everyone. I'm sure he knows something. He might even be a member of the Alliance himself."

"Didn't they just transfer him to the Healing Center from Parin?" Pengar asked.

Orien shrugged. "That's what I heard."

"I can't visit him at the Healing Center unless he specifically asks for me," Kennedy said. "When Scrawl bruised my rib, I had to name the beings I wanted on my list."

Geenen snapped her long, skinny fingers. "That's how we get in! You have to let Scrawl injure you again."

"Easy for you to say."

"Think about it," Geenen said. "If they take you to the Healing Center, you'll already be inside. Then, you can put us on your list, and we can create a diversion while you find Miles."

"It just might work," Orien nodded.

Kennedy put a hand over her ribs and swallowed hard.

The next morning, Kennedy sparred with Scrawl inside the Institute's largest gym. Oddly enough, her detachment from the outcome enabled her to fight better than she ever had before. She knew she was going to lose, so she tried to go down swinging, literally. He punched her in the ribs, but she got back up. She stayed in the fight until Scrawl delivered a fierce uppercut that made Kennedy fly through the air and land on her back. She could taste blood in her mouth but had no idea it was trickling down from a gash in her eyebrow.

"Never take your eyes off him!" Zuele yelled, but stopped herself when she realized the extent of Kennedy's injuries.

Scrawl laughed in Kennedy's face. "You're the worst fighter I have ever seen. Who allowed you into this program?"

Kennedy spat blood. "Shut your mouth."

"Maybe you're so awful because you don't have a father." Scrawl chortled. "You never had anyone teach you. Maybe he saw you fight, and that is why he decided to abandon you."

"That's enough," Zuele barked at Scrawl.

Kennedy was so enraged by his words that she tried to get back up, but Zuele held her in place while Scrawl continued laughing. "If you don't stop laughing," Kennedy warned him.

He laughed harder. "Like you could stop me."

Kennedy stayed focused on him until he felt like an extension of her. She wanted to break him but couldn't, so she spoke to him instead. *"From now on, you are going to respect me,"* Kennedy told him in her mind. *"You will never talk to me like that again. Do you understand me?"*

Scrawl's body suddenly locked up, and his eyes blinked rapidly.

"Do you understand me?" she asked him in her mind.

Scrawl began to nod his head, not just up and down but all around. Then he fell to his knees beside Kennedy, becoming an entirely different robot. "Are you okay?" he asked Kennedy. "I apologize. It will not happen again," he said, sincerely.

Zuele noticed the sudden, drastic change in Scrawl's demeanor. "Are you malfunctioning?"

It was then that the adrenaline wore off, and the pain finally caught up with Kennedy. It was a good thing that she was already on the floor because she felt faint. She held her ribs and attempted to wipe some of the blood from her face.

Scrawl scooped Kennedy up into his arms. "We have to get her to the Triphen Station," he told Zuele. "She's really hurt. I did this." Scrawl lowered his head in shame and apologized to Kennedy once more.

Zuele was speechless as Scrawl carried Kennedy from the room.

After examining Kennedy, two Triphens recommended her transfer to the Healing Center. This time, Scrawl had managed to break one rib and bruise two others. He also gave Kennedy her very first black eye, and her eyebrow required stitches. When Doreem Gem, the head healer, threatened to send Kennedy home with some firest weed, Kennedy pretended to not know what day it was, which bought her an overnight stay for observation.

Her friends arrived that evening, after Zuele finally left. Pengar placed some Get Well flowers in the corner, while Geenen looked over Kennedy's chart.

"Where is Orien?" Kennedy asked.

Pengar arranged the flowers. "She's flirting with a junior healer for information, trying to figure out which floor Miles is on."

"He really did a number on you," Geenen said, examining Kennedy's black eye.

Pengar handed Kennedy a single pink flower from the arrangement. "How do you feel?"

Kennedy held her ribs and winced. "Fantastic."

"They've got you on a lot of cell accelerator; you should be good as new in a few days," Geenen assured her.

Orien walked in holding a folded Healing Center uniform. She put the uniform on over her clothes and rolled out a floating chair from the closet, which was kind of like a wheelchair without wheels. "Miles is on the third floor. There's a guard posted in the hallway, so you're going to need to create a diversion, Pengar."

Pengar bit her lip. "How am I going to do that?"

Geenen chuckled. "You could always put them to sleep with one of your boring stories about the predator plants of Camaven."

"Boring? Predator plants are fascinating! I always keep some extra seeds on me for protection." Pengar patted her triangular pack. "I've got some nuclear ones that break the law of gestation. They can grow anywhere, at any time. Did you know the Camaven Army used predator plants during the first Intergalactic War to—"

Geenen pretended to fall asleep.

Pengar turned her nose up at her.

Geenen stuffed pillows underneath the sheets and sat next to Kennedy's bed. "I'll stay here in case the head healer returns."

Orien helped Kennedy onto the floating chair. "Let's go."

The halls of the Healing Center were filled with crystals from distant planets, and the walls were lined with trickling water fountains. Subliminal messages whispered throughout the center, affirming perfect health and alignment. The lights were dim; Kennedy just hoped they were dim enough to shield her from the eyes of curious healers.

They were almost at the elevator when someone called out. "Excuse me, Junior Healer?"

The girls froze.

"He's talking to you," Kennedy told Orien out of the side of her mouth.

Orien turned around. "Yes?" Her voice trembled.

The blue healer observed her closely. "I have never seen you before."

"Oh, that's because I don't usually work this floor."

"Which floor do you usually work on?"

"Um, the fifth."

"You look awfully young to work in Limb Regrowth."

"Good genes," Orien said. "You should meet my grandmother. She looks like she's still in early school."

He smirked. "My grandmother looks like she was left under the suns of Scotnath for too long."

Orien laughed hard at his joke—too hard. Kennedy cleared her throat, signaling for Orien to reel it in a bit.

The healer's hand vibrated. "Break's over," he said, holding it up. "It was an honor to encounter your energy."

"Yours too." Orien bowed.

Kennedy breathed a sigh of relief once he was gone.

Pengar called for an elevator, and Orien quickly floated Kennedy's chair inside it.

"Okay, when the doors open, you know what to do, Pengar." Kennedy whispered, even though it was only the three of them inside the elevator. Pengar nodded nervously. When they arrived at the third floor, they staked out Miles's room. A large Polksequin stood guard at the door. His alligator-skin and meaty limbs sucked all the soothing energy from the hallway. The three girls gulped when they saw him.

Pengar tiptoed towards him, while Orien floated Kennedy in the opposite direction. They circled the floor clockwise until they could see the guard's right profile.

Pengar came into view. "Excuse me. Is Miles Pierce really in there? I am crazy about the Golden Phase. I know everything about them. Did you know they were the first phase to have a recruit from every planet in the galaxy?"

The security guard did not respond.

"The Golden Phase is all I talk about, even though it drives my roommates insane. They were legendary! Zuele is my favorite. No, Leandor is. No, Miles is. Definitely Miles. Is he in there? What's he like? I already know what he's like, actually, because I know everything about the Golden Phase. Did you know Miles dated Vivith Brandth and Eka Mint?"

It was obvious that Pengar was imitating Orien.

"I don't sound like that," Orien whispered to Kennedy defensively. "Also, Miles didn't date Eka Mint; it was Janekis Opris. Does anyone even listen to me when I talk?"

"I wrote Miles a song. Do you want to hear it?" Pengar asked.

"No," the security guard grumbled. He did not look too concerned about the petite girl in front of him until Pengar started singing a nonsensical song about Miles Pierce's charms and the lengths she would go to for him. The situation escalated significantly when Pengar began to dance.

The guard shooshed her. "You need to keep it down. Beings are resting on this floor."

But Pengar just danced and sang harder.

The guard moved away from the door and guided Pengar back towards the elevator. "Alright, let's go."

Kennedy abandoned the floating chair and limped inside Miles' room, behind the security guard's back. The healing suite was much larger than hers. One of its walls opened to the elements and had a beautiful view of the Kathreeyan Ocean. Miles sat inside a floating contraption while robotic hands massaged and stretched his limbs. Gray streaked his new beard. Outwardly, he looked healthy, but his spirit seemed to be in a state of disrepair. "Kennedy Neff," he said.

"I'm sorry to barge in here like this, but I wanted to see you."

He removed himself from the contraption and gave her his full attention.

Kennedy felt guilty for intruding on his privacy. He was a movie star, and she felt like she was bothering him. Instead of inconveniencing him for a selfie, she was asking him to dredge up the painful past, and with that realization, she lost her nerve. "You know what? I'm sorry. I shouldn't have busted in here like this. I'll come back when you're feeling better."

"No, have a seat. I could use the company." He circled his eye, then pointed at Kennedy's. "What happened?"

"Training accident." Kennedy sat next to him in a deep, comfortable chair with a floating ottoman. "You should see the other guy."

"How have you been?"

"Chillin' in the high vibes," she said.

"Glad to hear it."

She lowered her voice. "I'm sorry about what happened."

"Let's not talk about that. I survived it once, and that was enough. What is going on with you? I saw you on *Symetran Society*. You're more famous than I am now."

"Not quite. You were famous even before you were a movie star. What was it like to be in the *Golden Phase*?" she asked.

He smiled wearily. "It felt a little like being in Motown. You know what Motown is, right?"

Kennedy was insulted. "Of course I know what Motown is."

"Had to ask. You never know with your generation. Being with that many talented beings at once was intimidating, but they were my friends—they were my family. They inspired me to work harder, especially Zuele."

"I heard she was the driving force."

"Zuele had one clear mission back then, one obsession—she wanted to evolve Millintica. And as hard as Zuele pushed the rest of us, she pushed Leandor and Tusk the hardest. She reminded them that, as Millinticans, they could not afford to slip up or become complacent; there was an entire planet watching them, depending on them. She was determined to liberate the Dark Panel, while the rest of us were just trying to pass our segments."

Miles closed the patio door, even though the chill down his spine had nothing to do with the room's temperature. "I think we all liked Zuele at some point, but she had no time for romantic entanglements—her words. Also, none of us were on her level yet. She didn't give Tusk a chance until *way* later."

"I can't believe they were ever together," Kennedy said.

"They were really happy together, but Tusk never could get out of his own way."

"What do you mean?"

"We all have moments that test our courage and show who we really are. Tusk has always failed those tests."

"I heard her and Leandor had something going on before he died."

"Nah, those two were like brother and sister."

There was a lull in the conversation, and Kennedy knew she did not have much time left. "Are you in the Alliance?" she blurted out. "Is that why Malant attacked your ship?"

Miles shook his head. "No, I am not in the Alliance. Are you?"

"No," Kennedy said, as though the question were ridiculous.

"I almost was," he said. "Xavian asked me to join, but I was already serving on Earth. I promised to do my best from there, but Xavian wasn't looking for half-commitments." Miles combed his long fingers through his beard. "I'll never forget the night I heard that Leandor died. I was on a movie set in London." He squeezed his eyes shut. "I should have been there, fighting alongside them, fighting alongside my friends... Then, a few years later, Vivith died. Then Janekis, and now my boy Hoper is gone... Kennedy, I don't know who is in the Alliance. All I know is that finally, after all these years, I am ready to be."

"I'm so sorry," Kennedy said, "for everything you've been through."

"Yeah, well, memory lane is closed for repairs."

"Why do you think they are back?" she asked Miles. "The Alliance. Why now?"

"I have a theory, but I can't prove it."

"What is it?"

"The Alliance ended when Leandor died. He was their secret weapon. As a Veilless, he was able to dismantle hundreds of Dark Panel Combatants before his death."

Kennedy furrowed her brow. "I thought Malant wanted Leandor to expand the Dark Panel. I didn't know—"

"Most don't know that Leandor was actively dismantling the Dark Panel."

"What do you mean *dismantling*?"

"Liberating the consciousness stored inside them," he explained. "It was a secret that both the Alliance and Malant kept for very different reasons. Leandor dismantled thousands of Combatants before Malant found him. Then, when Leandor sacrificed himself inside Mount Sleer, everything stopped. The Alliance went into hiding, and Malant closed the atmosphere." He lowered his voice to a conspiratorial whisper. "You want to know why I think the Alliance is operational again? I think they found another Veilless—I don't know who, how or where—but I believe that is what Janekis was doing inside the Deepest Layer. She was doing reconnaissance."

"Reconnaissance for what?"

"If my theory is correct, the Alliance would have to get the Veilless into the Deepest Layer of Millintica. That is where the vast majority of the Dark Panel is located. That is where this is all going to end."

Even though it was just a theory, it was the first thing Kennedy had heard that made sense. "But I thought the Veilless' were extinct. I thought the royal family killed them all."

Miles shook his head. "They tried, but the Veilless' occur randomly. No one knows where or why the next one will be born. Their parents are usually smart enough to keep them hidden. Many Veilless children have suffered terrible fates, thanks to the lies the royal family spread about them." Kennedy took out her BELIEVE notebook and wrote down some notes.

Miles observed her. "This is a pretty heavy subject matter for someone your age."

Kennedy closed the notebook. "I think my dad was in the Alliance."

"What makes you think so?"

She told him about the tattoo, and his expression softened. He turned his face away from Kennedy's.

"What? What is it?" she asked.

"Nothing."

"Do you know who he is?" Kennedy shot to her feet.

"No," Miles said without meeting her eye.

But Kennedy did not believe him. "If you know who he is—"

"I *don't* know who he is."

"But if you did, you would tell me, right?"

He finally turned to her. "Not if I thought it was dangerous for you to know. Now you need to keep your head down and leave well enough alone."

"You sound like Zuele."

"Good." He burned his eyes into hers.

"But what if something happens to him before I ever meet him?" Kennedy's voice caught in her throat. *Don't cry. Don't cry. Don't cry,* she commanded herself. She quickly wiped her tears and winced when she touched her black eye.

Miles looked at her with a face full of empathy, but before he could respond, someone rapped on the door. The Polksequin guard walked inside the room and bolted towards Kennedy. "How did you get in here?" Kennedy looked past him to Pengar, who held her arms up as though she had tried her hardest to stop him.

Miles stepped between Kennedy and the giant guard. "It's okay, Jayve."

"She is not on your approved list of visitors."

"That is my mistake," Miles said. "Anyway, she was just leaving."

Jayve still looked at Kennedy as though he didn't trust her. "Do you need me to help her along?"

"That won't be necessary."

Jayve walked out and left the door open.

"Thanks for covering for me," Kennedy whispered to Miles.

"Hey, us humans have to stick together." He patted her back. "You stay safe, okay?"

Kennedy forced a smile and walked outside. She lowered herself into the floating chair, while Orien gawked at Miles Pierce. Pengar snapped her fingers in front of Orien's face, and Jayve shooed them all towards the elevator.

When the doors closed, Pengar asked Kennedy, "What happened? What did he say?" But when a blonde healer boarded the elevator a few seconds later, they all went silent and remained that way until they arrived back inside Kennedy's room.

"Did you find anything out?" Geenen asked, pulling the sheets down for Kennedy.

"He knows something, but he's not going to tell me." Kennedy gingerly got into bed and told them about Miles's theory.

"Huh," Geenen said, lost in thought. "That's pretty genius."

"Of course he's a genius," Orien said. "He was in the Golden Phase."

They heard the chiming of Doreem Gem's skirt heading for them.

Orien began tearing off her junior healer uniform. "Distract her, Pengar!"

"Me? *Again?*" Pengar protested.

Orien flicked her hands, motioning for Pengar to move quickly.

"You're coming with me." Pengar grabbed Geenen by her skinny wrist and pulled her out into the hallway. "It's an honor to encounter your energy, Healer Gem," Pengar exclaimed.

"Yours, too, young creator." Doreem tried to get around her. "I am here to check on the progress of your friend."

"Oh, okay, but really quick. Um… Geenen, wasn't there something you wanted to ask Healer Gem?"

Geenen furrowed her brow in confusion.

"Yeah, you know, about that whole puss situation you have going on?"

Geenen glared at Pengar.

Doreem Gem turned to Geenen. "Puss situation?"

"Yeah," Pengar continued to vamp, while Orien removed the borrowed uniform. "It just oozes out sometimes. It's pretty concerning and, quite frankly, disgusting."

"We'd better take a look. Follow me," Doreem told Geenen.

Orien laughed once the coast was clear, but all Kennedy could think about was the look Miles had given her when she told him about the tattoo.

TWENTY

When Christmas Eve rolled around, Kennedy felt lower than low. She was painfully homesick and missed her family terribly. If she were in Tucson, she would be baking cookies and watching Christmas movies. Instead, she was on an alien planet facing an existential crisis and losing all hope that she would ever find her father.

Zuele must have sensed her distress because she called Kennedy to the training room, even though it was technically her day off. "This came for you earlier," she said, handing Kennedy a large parcel. "Lowin Pert sent you some clothing from his new line."

Kennedy took the parcel and set it on the ground beside her.

Zuele examined her face. "How's the eye?"

"Good as new."

"I think I fixed Scrawl," Zuele said. "I have no idea why he malfunctioned. Do you?"

"No idea." Kennedy shook her head, but Zuele did not seem to believe her.

"Well, he is back to his old happy self again."

"Great," Kennedy muttered.

"What are the girls doing today?"

"They went to Syncrocperience."

"And they didn't invite you?"

They had, but Kennedy's newfound fame made her afraid to go anywhere. The capturers had caught Kennedy leaving the Healing Center a few days before, and once again she wound up on *Symetran Society*. This time, they questioned whether or not she was competent enough to be an Evolver. Geenen offered to let Kennedy borrow her Switchip if she ever needed a disguise, but Kennedy knew that roaming the streets as a chalky, white alien with orange hair and green teeth would attract just as much attention.

Zuele gave her a concerned look. "Have you been using your Thought Projector?"

Kennedy did not look up from her hands. "Yes."

"Your Dematerialization skills have improved considerably."

Now that Kennedy knew how to Dematerialize, she wanted to Dematerialize everywhere. "I have been practicing a lot."

"It really shows." Zuele reached inside her desk. "Here, I have something that might cheer you up." She handed Kennedy a wrapped box with a candy cane taped to it. "Merry Christmas."

Kennedy beamed at her. "Merry Christmas, Zuele." She tore open the box and found a thick blue sweater inside, the kind the girls on Symetra wore, with real gold woven throughout. Kennedy held it to her chest. "I love it. Thank you!"

"Any big plans for Christmas?"

"No one here even knows what Christmas is."

"So, why don't you show them? We could go shopping this afternoon if you'd like."

There was an idea. Kennedy could throw her own Christmas party for her friends. She could buy them presents and decorate their unit! "Wait. What about the capturers?"

"We'll get you a disguise."

Zuele scrounged up a blonde wig and glasses for Kennedy, then they took Zuele's ridership to a kitschy district downtown that sold knickknacks from across the universe. The Earth section was filled with all kinds of useless stuff: Tupperware, TVs with rabbit ears, VHS tapes, cassette tapes, crystal dinnerware, mattresses, tires, and, of course, Christmas decorations.

"This place is incredible," Kennedy exclaimed.

"I used to shop here with my friends when I was your age." Zuele laughed. "We used to find the most useless things and gift them to each other. Vivith once gave me a steering wheel, and Miles gave me a Chia Pet." Zuele picked up a Chia Pet box. "He told me they were holy, sacred objects on Earth."

Kennedy laughed with her guardian. "And you believed him?"

"Yeah, until I bowed to a Chia Pet in front of a human who looked at me like I was crazy."

Kennedy bought a few strands of old-fashioned, multi-colored bulbs and a red-faced Santa cookie jar coated in what was probably lead-based paint. She bought plastic mistletoe, glass ornaments, garland, dusty wrapping paper, a pine-scented candle, and some presents for her friends. The only thing they did not have was a fake Christmas tree.

Zuele and Kennedy had Christmas Eve dinner at an earth food diner in Crystal City, which was literally called Earth Food. They both drank peppermint tea and laughed at the menu which was filled with ridiculous items like Elvis tacos and Shakespeare pizza, Kennedy ordered the Beatles pancakes. "What do the Beatles have to do with pancakes?" Zuele asked her.

"Absolutely nothing."

"I'm going to order Einstein's cheese-filled pasta."

Kennedy shook her head. "They should have named it Einstein's theory of ravioli—that's a missed opportunity."

After dinner, Zuele helped Kennedy unload all the bags into her bedroom closet. Kennedy invited her to attend the next day, but Zuele politely declined, saying, "Nothing kills a good time like a guardian lurking around. No, you have fun with your friends. You've earned it. You've been training hard."

Once Zuele left, Kennedy wrapped Christmas presents in her closet, while *Elf* played on a floating screen above her. When she was done, she decided to walk down to the Hover House. She locked her bedroom door—something she had been doing lately to keep Pile from cleaning her room and rearranging her stuff.

Kennedy listened to 'Christmas (Baby Please Come Home)' by Darlene Love on her earbuds as wayward snowflakes from the Five Seasons Forest flurried around her. Some capturers caught her outside of the Hover House but not even they could destroy her Christmas spirit. She went to the empty common room and thawed herself in front of the roaring fireplace. She thought about Miles Pierce, her father, and the Alliance. She imagined the Golden Phase as recruits sitting inside this very room, planning, and plotting, thinking they would be friends forever, not knowing their story would end in tragedy.

Kennedy took off her jacket, leaned back in a cozy chair, and decided to stay awhile. She unwrapped the candy cane Zuele had given her and sucked the bottom into a shiv. Her mind drifted to last Christmas, when Roberta had bought her a wallet—a pretty cruel gift to give to someone without any money. Kennedy thanked her mother and then searched for more presents under their tree, but there weren't any. The wallet was all Roberta could afford. Kennedy went into the bathroom and cried, not because she only received one present but because she knew she had unintentionally hurt her mother by searching for more. She found herself trying to vacuum that dirt road and then quickly brought herself back to the present moment, which, as corny as it sounded, truly did feel like a present. She thought of her mother in her new home; she thought of her friends; she thought of her unexpected good fortune; and as usual she thought of Reddick. She whispered, *"Thank you,"* into the Eternal Energy Field, hoping it would hear her and understand her appreciation.

Kennedy's eyes watered from the brightness and heat of the fire, and then she realized she was no longer alone. She hadn't heard him or seen him, but she *felt* him enter the room. Her eyes followed the direction of the feeling. Reddick stood a few feet away, the front of his hair swept to the side as though he had just run his hand through it.

Kennedy stood and faced him.

Reddick once again stared at her like he was trying to communicate a million things at once, as though all the languages in the universe could not describe what he wanted her to know.

Kennedy avoided his intense gaze. "When did you get in?" she asked, even though she already knew the answer.

"This morning."

"Candy cane?" she offered.

Reddick broke a small piece of the hook off. "I heard you were taken to the Healing Center. Are you okay?" he asked after he finished his candy cane.

"I'm fine."

"I'm glad to hear it..."

Reddick stood beside her and stared into the fire. He was so close to her.

Kennedy's body involuntarily leaned towards his, as if he were a magnet. She straightened herself out and tried to act normal, even though every cell inside her body was vibrating at a dizzying speed. Everything in her wanted to touch him.

Reddick ran his hand through the front of his hair again, Kennedy was not used to seeing him nervous. "Look, I don't mean to bother you, but Geenen said you might be here and—"

"You came here looking for *me*?"

He nodded. "I am so sorry, Kennedy, for all of this. I am sorry they have been hounding you. You don't deserve this. Any of it. It's my fault."

"It's not your fault, Reddick. It was a misunderstanding. They think we're something we're not, and I'll fix it if you want me to. I'll tell them the truth."

Reddick glared at her as though she had wounded him. "What's the truth?"

Kennedy did not know what to say. "I will tell them we are just friends."

His chest heaved. "I am not your *friend*, Kennedy. I am—well, I don't know what I am to you, but I know what you are to me, and what I feel for you is way stronger than friendship. And I've tried to make it go away, but it won't."

Now it was Kennedy's turn to glare at him. "Why does it have to go away? Because I am human? Because I am Millintican? Because I am not good enough for you?"

"What? No." He shook his head. "I tried to make it go away because I know you don't feel the same way."

Kennedy unclasped her St. Jude necklace. "You want to know how I feel about you?" She walked to him and removed the emotion blocker from his wrist. "*This* is how I feel about you—how I've always felt about you—and it's getting worse every single day."

Reddick gazed vulnerably at her, and in that moment, she realized Reddick's intense feelings mirrored her own. She felt there was no distinction between them. Reddick felt like an extension of her, and together they created a combined frequency exponentially stronger than any she had ever experienced alone.

Reddick occupied most of her waking thoughts. The thought of seeing him got her out of bed in the morning, and dreaming about him made her eager for sleep at night. The past month had been *excruciating* without him. She replayed that night in her bedroom more times than she was comfortable admitting. Now he was standing in front of her, saying everything she had dreamed of hearing from him. She felt that same urge to reach out for him, and this time she did. She took his hand and ran her fingers slowly over his knuckles, downloading the sensation of his warm skin on hers. Kennedy was brave enough to grab his hand but not brave enough to look him in the eye when she said, "I like you so much it terrifies me."

He searched her face, but she still would not meet his eye. "Is that why you stopped talking to me?"

"I stopped talking to you because I *can't* talk to you. Most of the time, I can't even breathe around you."

He smiled a wide, bashful smile. "How are you doing now?"

She smiled back at him. "About to keel over."

Reddick ran his fingers from her jawline to the base of her throat and slowly brought his lips to hers. He put his other hand on her lower back and pulled her into him until there was no space left between them. He kissed her deeply and held her tightly. The kiss was filled with peppermint, warmth, and a hunger that had not been present in her earlier kissing experiences.

He pulled away and pressed his forehead to hers. "I've missed you."

Kennedy kissed him in response, though she couldn't tell whose natural impulse it really was. They heard distant chatter in the hallway and knew they wouldn't be alone much longer. Reddick clasped her emotion blocker around her neck, and Kennedy slammed back inside her body.

The lights blinked inside the Hover House, signifying it was closing for the night. Reddick grabbed her hand, and they headed downstairs. Kennedy smiled as she followed the center of her galaxy through the entryway of blazing suns. Reddick's ridership was waiting for them when they got outside. The yellow flashes of the capturers flickered in the distance, but neither of them cared.

"Did your father really send you away because of me?" she asked after they boarded his ridership.

"He has bigger things to worry about than who I date." Reddick dodged her question. "What about Zuele? What does she think about us?"

"She doesn't like the attention that comes with you."

"Neither do I."

When his ridership pulled into the garage of her unit, he sent a file to her Sectnot. "Here, I made a list of everyone I think was in the Alliance."

Kennedy opened the list, which contained dozens of names. "How did you figure this out?"

"All these Evolvers have close ties to Xavian Seelos or Millintica."

Kennedy scanned the list. "Hoper Morrow?"

"His grandmother was Millintican. Malant killed her for being a King Rimago loyalist."

Kennedy and Reddick both formed a prayer of alignment in honor of Hoper.

Then Reddick walked Kennedy to the center lift, pressing his lips against hers once more. "Good night, Kennedy."

"Good night, Reddick." She watched him leave and then took the lift to the second floor of her unit. When she arrived in the living area, she collapsed on the couch like a love-struck schoolgirl.

Geenen had been eating a wax snack in the kitchen when she saw Kennedy crash onto the couch. She dropped her plate and rushed to her side. "Kennedy, are you okay? What happened? Are you sick? Do you need medical attention?" Geenen's enormous alien eyes blinked inches from Kennedy's face.

"He kissed me," Kennedy sighed.

"Who?"

"Reddick!"

Geenen's eye roll was so aggressive that it was nearly audible. "You scared me. I thought you were malfunctioning or something."

Pengar walked into the living area and saw Kennedy sprawled on the couch. "What's wrong with Kennedy?"

"Reddick kissed her," Geenen said.

"What?!?" Pengar screamed as she shook Kennedy's limp, love-struck body.

Geenen returned to her snack.

Orien appeared with a neon pink beauty mask on her face. "What's with all the screaming?"

"Reddick kissed Kennedy!" Pengar squealed.

"Finally!" Orien clapped and joined in the screaming. Kennedy, Orien, and Pengar jumped in a small, giddy circle, while Geenen plugged her tiny earholes.

✦

Kennedy had stayed up late with the girls, describing every detail of her encounter with Reddick. When she had rehashed the story enough times, she went to her room, programmed her bedroom walls with lit-up Christmas trees, and fell asleep thinking of him.

The next morning, she kicked her friends out of their unit and told them not to come back until the Five Seasons Forest reached its daily winter. "I'm throwing you guys a Christmas. It's a huge holiday on Earth. It won't be exactly the same because I couldn't find a tree, but you guys are going to love it!"

Once they were gone, Kennedy put an elf hat on Pile, and decorated the living area while Christmas classics blared in the background. Kennedy strung some lights around their largest houseplant, and Pile helped her set gifts beneath it. Kennedy transmitted herself home that morning and opened presents with her family. "This is from Santa," Roberta said, handing Kennedy a heavy box with her handwriting on the gift tag. Kennedy opened it to find a brand-new record player. She loved it. Then Audrey handed her a vinyl-shaped present that turned out to be *The White Album*. "I was going to get you an outfit," Audrey said, "but I figured it would be out of style by the time you made it back home."

Kennedy was able to stay long enough to watch them eat their traditional, fattening Christmas breakfast. She picked up a cinnamon roll and inhaled its sweet scent, wishing she could have it.

"What's with the perma-smile?" Roberta asked her.

"*What?* It's Christmas. I'm happy." Kennedy went and stood next to the tree to get away from her mother's knowing glances.

After her visit home, Kennedy did herself up. She put on the sweater Zuele had gifted her and thought only of Reddick while she got ready. She replayed their kiss over and over inside her mind, feeling her skin was not thick enough to contain such intense happiness.

At sunset, Orien contacted her. "We're here. Can we come up now?"

Kennedy turned up some Christmas music and then straightened herself out. The snow began to fall, as if on cue, over the Five Seasons Forest. She met them at the center lift of their unit and waved her arms above her head like a madwoman. "Merry Christmas!"

Geenen, Orien, and Pengar stared at her blankly.

"You're supposed to say it back," she said.

"Merry Christmas?" they replied in unison.

"Come on in, no wait, before you do." Kennedy pointed out a string of mistletoe hanging from the ceiling. "It's mistletoe. People back on Earth kiss under it."

"I've already told you, Kennedy, I don't like you like that," Orien said.

Kennedy kissed her cheek, then proceeded to kiss both Geenen and Pengar's cheeks, too.

Orien inspected the holiday haven that Kennedy had transformed their unit into. "What happened in here?"

Geenen observed some multi-colored bulbs hanging from the walls. "I don't know, but it looks like a fire hazard. Kennedy, you are aware that we live in a tree?"

"I think it looks magical," Pengar said.

Kennedy wrapped an arm around her. "Thank you, Pengar. Christmas is all about family and being with the ones you love, and since you guys are kind of like my family, I thought we could all celebrate together." Kennedy gave them some frosted Christmas cookies Chef Raka had made for her. She had also stacked a few wax balls together for Geenen and decorated them like a snowman. Kennedy told her friends all about Christmas and her family's Christmas traditions. They were about to open their gifts beneath the plant when an alert let them know someone was outside their garage.

"I wonder who that could be?" Orien asked like a bad actor.

"It's Santa!" Geenen yelled, making them all laugh. Santa Claus seemed to be Geenen's favorite part of the earthly holiday, not because he delivered presents but because he possessed the technology to physically visit billions of homes in one single night.

The center lift brought Reddick to the living area. Kennedy's heart skipped a beat, the way it always did whenever he was within a one-mile radius of her.

"Look who's here," Orien said. "I ran into him this morning and invited him to our Christmas. I hope that's okay."

"Uh, yeah, of course, definitely, come on in," Kennedy stammered.

"Aren't you forgetting something? Mistletoe. You have to kiss him." Orien pushed Kennedy towards the dangling plant. "You see, that's what they do under mistletoe on Earth, Reddick."

Reddick pulled Kennedy to him and kissed her as though they did not have an audience.

"Merry Christmas," he said.

"Merry Christmas," she responded.

Geenen made a kissy noise, and Kennedy launched a decorative pillow at her head.

"That's it! Naughty list for you, you violent human," Geenen laughed.

"We were just about to open presents," Kennedy told Reddick.

"Good, then I'm not too late." He took the lift back down to the garage and reappeared with a six-foot Christmas tree in a large planter. "Orien said you didn't have one, so I got this from the Five Seasons Forest. Technically, I'm just borrowing it. I have to take it back tomorrow."

Kennedy threw her arms around him. "It's a Christmas miracle!" She went to the plant and transferred its lights to the tree. Reddick and her roommates helped her collect the bulbs she had set up all over the room, and they hung them together. "Now we just need a star for the top of the tree," Kennedy said.

"On it." Geenen held up her Sectnot and projected a luminous, gaseous ball there.

Kennedy was about to correct it, but she loved that Geenen had unintentionally put her own touch on the human holiday. The five of them stood back and admired the tree.

Kennedy grabbed Reddick's hand and pulled him to sit on the couch next to her. They smiled at one another, and she caught her friends watching. "Open your presents, or I'm taking them back," she commanded.

Orien went first. She tore into a box and removed a frou-frou purple jumpsuit. She gasped and held the fabric to her cheek, as though it were a newborn baby or a miracle of life. "This is from Lowin Pert's new line!" Orien lunged at Kennedy and hugged her tight. "I love you, Kennedy! I don't care what people say about humans! They're alright with me!" Orien discovered more outfits in the box and nearly wept at their fabulousness.

Kennedy gifted Pengar with Symetran crystals and lotions, which were supposed to be lucky for love. She also gave her some packets of rose, lilac, and sunflower seeds. Pengar was overjoyed with the seeds. Then she lathered herself in the lotion. "Do you think this stuff works?" she asked Reddick.

"Definitely," he said.

Pengar lathered on more lotion for good measure.

Then it was Geenen's turn. Kennedy had managed to find some old computers from Earth. She knew Geenen would appreciate taking them apart and discovering their inner workings. Geenen rested her head on a twenty-year-old desktop computer, and for a moment Kennedy could not tell whether or not she actually liked it, until she got up and gave Kennedy an awkward hug. "Thank you," she said.

Pengar and Orien quickly dogpiled Geenen and Kennedy. "Merry Christmas!" they all told Geenen as she swatted them away.

Pengar ruined the special moment by saying, "This moment is so special!"

However, Orien did not miss the way Reddick stared at Kennedy. "Come on, girls, let's go up to my room and try out our gifts," she said.

"But your room doesn't have a tree. I like the tree," Pengar said.

"How about we drop you off in the middle of the Five Seasons Forest? There's plenty of trees out there." Orien grabbed Pengar's greasy, lotion-coated hand, and Geenen followed them, cradling two desktop computers inside her skinny arms.

Once they left, Reddick told Kennedy, "You made it beautiful in here."

"*You* made it beautiful in here," she responded.

"Here, I got you something." He pulled out a small jewelry box.

"I would have gotten you something, but I didn't know—"

He gave her a kiss mid-excuse, and suddenly she forgot what she was doing.

"Open it," he said.

Kennedy tore off the wrapping paper and found a beautiful pair of Fyorisc stone earrings. "Reddick, they're stunning."

"Which is why I thought they'd look perfect on you. They change colors depending on where the light hits them, just like your eyes."

Kennedy didn't know what to say. She almost asked him, "*Why me?*" but she spotted the self-defeating thought even before her Sectnot could point it out to her. "*Why not me?*" she corrected herself. Kennedy had liked Reddick from the moment she saw him, but she was not sure when she had started liking herself. Her militant Sectnot, with its constant corrections, had been successful in diminishing her negative self-talk, and now she actually felt *worthy* of an experience such as this.

Kennedy thanked him for the earrings, but really, she was thanking him for so much more. She put them on and remembered Marr Ameer's words when she said she saw Fyorisc stones and a strange green plant wrapped in red ribbon. Kennedy gaped at the mistletoe wrapped in a red ribbon.

"What is it?" he asked.

"Nothing." Kennedy wondered if Marr Ameer had been right about other things, too.

Reddick nodded, which reminded Kennedy of the way he used to look at her inside the halls of Desert Hills High School. She asked him if he had done it intentionally.

Reddick nodded again. "It was my way of talking to you before I was allowed to talk to you."

"I can't believe we've gone from that to this."

"I can," he said.

She raised an eyebrow at him.

"One of us had to believe."

"But what made you choose me?" She was genuinely curious. How does someone with an abundance of options choose *anything*?

"You don't get to choose something like this. It chooses you."

She nudged him. "Zuele told me you used to ask her about me."

"I thought I was being low-key," he laughed. "I remember the first time I saw you."

"In Principal Vasquez's office—my second home." Principal Vasquez cut the lecture he had been giving Kennedy short so he could give the new "transfer student" a tour of campus. Kennedy remembered thinking Reddick was the most beautiful boy she had ever seen.

"Zuele was adamant about me staying away from you. She didn't want me to sway your decision."

Kennedy squeezed his hand. "You definitely would have."

"It's one of my biggest regrets," he said sadly.

Kennedy furrowed her brow.

"I saw you struggling, and I did nothing. I obeyed the rules instead of being there when you needed someone. I should have told you the truth. I'm sorry."

"If it makes you feel any better, I wouldn't have believed you anyway."

Reddick's expression turned serious. "What you said last night— you terrify me, too, Kennedy. I have never felt—" He stopped him- self short and traced his finger inside her palm.

"Fear precedes all greatness," Kennedy reminded him of his

own words and then placed her hand on the side of his face. "You want to know what I like about you?"

"Sure," he smiled.

"That," she said, pointing to his wide, bashful smile. "And this," she said, placing her thumb inside the scar next to his eyebrow, which felt like some kind of watermark placed there by the Great Creator, proving Reddick was one of one. She told him she liked his hair and the way he ran his hand through it when he was nervous. Without thinking, Reddick ran his hand through the front of his hair, and she pointed it out. She told him she liked his character, his technicolor blue eyes, his deep voice, his hands, and his excellence. The way he was friends with everyone in Tucson, not just the popular seniors who followed him around.

He blushed. "Okay, you can stop."

She shook her head. "Usually, I use my words to try and hide how I feel about you. I don't want to use them that way anymore."

He leaned forward and kissed her. The kiss grew more fervent. They fell back on the couch and tangled themselves in each other's limbs. Reddick's warm hand gripped the curve of her waist beneath her sweater. Kennedy felt an urgent desire to do things with Reddick that she had no idea how to do. She could still hear her mother's advice on the subject when Roberta sat her down and said, *"Kennedy, teenage boys are more eager to start these types of relationships than girls are. They will rush you, and they will make you think you have a problem if you don't do what they want you to do. Many girls will fall for this— don't be one of them. Anyone worth losing it to will be patient with you."* Back then, Roberta paused to take a deep sip from her *wine glass. "Furthermore, boys your age are terrible at this sort of thing. You might as well hold out for someone who actually knows what he's doing."*

The talk worked. Then she looked at Reddick, who was the poster boy for competence in all things, and replayed the conversation with her mother all over again. Kennedy had spoken to Orien about sex once, but it quickly devolved into a bragging session. Orien talked about how many times she'd done it, how many ways she'd done it, and how many beings she'd done it with. Orien had zero sexual hang-ups. She clearly wasn't from Earth, where women were not allowed to be primal in the same way as men.

Kennedy wasn't a total prude; she obviously knew the mechanics of it. Everyone with internet access knew the mechanics of it. She also knew what felt good to her, but she wasn't sure how to make it a two-player game. What if she was lousy at it? What if Reddick had been with girls who *weren't* lousy at it? She began to wonder why she was pressuring herself so much. Reddick wasn't even pressuring her to do these things. Per usual, Kennedy was jumping miles ahead. She did not want to cross that bridge when she got there. She wanted to know every detail about that bridge, believing that if she did, it would somehow be less terrifying to her.

When the alert for curfew rang through each of their Sectnots, Reddick sat up and pried himself away from Kennedy's lips. "Goodnight," he said, after one more kiss.

But she would not say it back, because saying goodnight would mean that the night was over, and Kennedy never wanted it to end.

TWENTY-ONE

ennedy's feet did not touch the ground for several days after that. A coating of magical, tingly warmth rested permanently on the top layer of her skin; music sounded better, colors were brighter—life was the best it had ever been for Kennedy Ann Neff. She and Reddick were in their own little world. He sat with her at every meal and walked her to her training room every morning, not caring that capturers were documenting their every move. After their segments, they went for walks in the Five Seasons Forest and told each other stories about their childhoods. Reddick received special permission from Enforcer Tusk to study in Kennedy's unit, though very little studying actually occurred. They laughed and talked and kissed, and then they kissed some more, gradually getting worse at keeping their hands to themselves. At night, they would talk via their Sectnots until one, or both, of them fell asleep. Their favorite topic was the Antastropolith Alliance. Kennedy told him all about the month she had spent without him, how she had thrown the fight with Scrawl to win a free trip to the Healing Center, and about the look on Miles Pierce's face when she mentioned the tattoo.

"Do you think Miles knows who he is?" Reddick asked.

"I think he might have an idea."

"We're going to find him, Kennedy. Somehow, we're going to find him," he promised.

Zuele did not mention Kennedy's new relationship for many moons, until one day she saw the smile on Kennedy's face and said, "I am delighted to see you this happy. I just want to let you know that if you ever have any questions about *anything,* I am here. I am no expert, but I can try to give you advice if you need it." It was the first time Kennedy had ever seen Zuele act awkward.

"From what Orien tells me, you were an expert on dating back in the day. Did Gonzi Gretho really write the song 'Celestial Woman' about you? Orien wanted me to ask."

Zuele quickly switched topics, the way she always did when Kennedy brought up the past. "Be careful." Kennedy thought they were back to talking about the birds and the bees until Zuele said, "Theein demands the best of his children. No matter how evolved he pretends to be, he *will* try to end this between you two. You had better stay in line. As I already said, he will be looking for any and every excuse to get rid of you."

Theein Brandth was not the only one who disapproved of the relationship. Corijean made her feelings about Kennedy and Reddick clear. She insisted to Thecla Atter that Reddick was just going through his exploratory phase; "It was something all great beings went through." She predicted that ultimately it would be her and Reddick traveling the universe together; all she had to do was be patient. So, when Kennedy found Corijean whispering something seductively in Reddick's ear outside the Hover House, she took it as a credible threat. Xan noticed Kennedy watching them and cleared his throat loudly.

When Reddick saw Kennedy, he smiled. "There you are," he said, as though he had been waiting for her.

Kennedy felt a possessive rage that was anything but evolved. She Dematerialized and basked in the white light for half a second before she arrived in the Five Seasons Forest. Once she was inside her clearing, she kicked up a pile of leaves in frustration. Kennedy could not believe Reddick did not have feelings for someone as perfect-looking as Corijean; it was illogical. It brought up all of Kennedy's insecurities and suddenly she felt like that invisible girl standing next to her sister in Tucson again.

Kennedy sat with her back against a tree, summoning some autumn leaves toward her as they fell. Her summoning skills had come a long way since she arrived on Symetra, but summoning heavy objects remained a struggle. Reddick tried to contact her, but rather than communicate with him, she turned off her Sectnot.

A while later, Reddick found her there. Leaves crunched beneath his feet as he approached. "I've been looking for you everywhere. Why did you Dematerialize?"

"I didn't want to disturb you and your girlfriend."

"You're my girlfriend, genius."

Kennedy shot to her feet. "Corijean wants you, Reddick. Everyone can see that except you."

"But I don't want her." His gorgeous, sincere face immediately weakened Kennedy's resistance.

"She's the worst."

"She's not that bad."

"Now you're defending her?"

"No, I just know things about her that other people don't."

Kennedy held up her hand to stop him. "I don't need to hear all the gory details."

"No, it's not like that..."

"But you have *been* with her."

His expression gave him away. "It was before I even knew you."

"Gross," Kennedy said, mostly because she had no idea what else to say. "How many other beings have you been with?"

"How many other beings have *you* been with?"

"None." She thought that much had been obvious. It killed her to think Corijean knew him in a way she didn't. She turned her body away from his. "And I know I'm being an insecure human, but I don't care, that's what I am. And I understand if you still like her. She's beautiful—she's a total toolshed—but she's beautiful, and your family loves her."

"My family?"

"She said your dad stays at her hotel."

"Which means he loves her?"

"It means something! Your father wouldn't send you away for dating her! I'm sure he would much rather you be with a wealthy socialite than some cavewoman from Earth." Kennedy spat. "You two *should* be together; you're both perfect. So, if you want to go to her, that's fine. I don't need you."

"I know you don't..." He bowed his head. "That's what scares me the most about you."

Reddick walked away, and Kennedy immediately kicked herself. "Wait." She Materialized in front of him, surprised that she now had the skill to do so. "Don't go. I'm sorry. I *told* you I was an insecure human." She hugged him and was grateful that he let her. "I just don't understand why you would want to be friends with someone like her." Kennedy sat down and rested her back against a tree trunk. "She's so... mean."

"Before Corijean and I went to Earth, we trained for our Phase Three Assessments together." Reddick rubbed his jaw. "Our assignment was to fight a Dark Panel Combatant."

"A real one?"

"Yeah, there's one locked in the Adversary Lab. It has been in there for eons."

Kennedy wondered if that was the pounding she'd heard inside the Hall of Labs.

"Our guardians were there, preventing it from causing any serious damage to us, but Corijean was trying to show off and got a little too close to it. That's when it got a read on her. Trust me, Kennedy, you don't ever want one of those things to play your shame back to you."

"What was Corijean's shame?"

Reddick struggled. "I'm only telling you because I think it will help you have more empathy for her."

Kennedy doubted it, but she nodded anyway.

"Corijean comes from a rich family full of beautiful beings. There are even songs on Madilieu about the Cabrins beauty."

Kennedy crossed her arms, urging him to get to the point

quickly.

"When Corijean was a child, her mother decided she was not beautiful enough, so she made her daughter undergo dangerous, painful operations. They stretched her limbs, changed her face, her hair, everything. Once Corijean was "conventionally" beautiful, her mother decided she would only accept her if she became an Evolver recruit. Once Corijean became an Evolver recruit, her mother gave her another hoop to jump through: She wanted Corijean to marry a Brandth."

"A Dark Panel Combatant showed you all of this?"

He nodded. "If you would have seen the way Corijean tried to stop it, she attempted to attack this basically immortal creature with her bare hands. We had to hold her back. It was like she would rather die than show anyone the truth about her."

Kennedy uncrossed her arms.

Reddick continued, "After that, she avoided me for a long time. I wanted to show her that it didn't matter to me and that even though it hadn't worked out between us, I still considered us friends. I wanted her to see that she was enough. When we were on Earth, I brought it up, but she quickly turned it into a conversation about us getting back together. She doesn't want to be with me for me; she wants to be with me for her mother; she is driven by her mother's validation."

Kennedy realized she and Corijean had more in common than just their feelings for Reddick. They were both desperate for the love of a parent, which would probably never come. She hugged her knees as Reddick continued.

"That's why I'm so nice to her... I want her to know it's okay.

She's still worthy of love, no matter what. We all are. At least I hope so anyway."

Kennedy had never even considered having compassion for someone who looked like Corijean.

He came and sat down next to her. "So... are we okay?"

Kennedy leaned her head on his shoulder. "We're okay."

They sat in silence for a few seconds before Reddick's body began to shake with laughter. "*A cavewoman from Earth*?"

Kennedy worked hard to make sure her new relationship did not affect her training. She showed up early and stayed late to appease her guardian, though nothing seemed to appease Zuele these days. Lately, she had been on edge as Malant's forces patrolled the galaxy, testing every red line that the Evolvers had drawn for them. Anxiety was in the air for everyone except Kennedy, who was too in love to acknowledge the galaxy's problems.

When Pengar and Ethwin invited Kennedy and Reddick on a double date to Syncrocperience, Kennedy was excited. However, the capturers swarmed them the second they exited Reddick's ridership—their yellow lights blinded Kennedy, and one of them clipped her shoulder, leaving a nasty cut in its wake. Reddick reflexively shoved the capturer, and it crashed to the ground. That night, *Symetran Society* featured the chaotic scene and accused Kennedy of turning Reddick violent.

Zuele's response to the incident was, "It's only going to get worse." And it did get worse. Capturers hounded them everywhere they went, until eventually Kennedy and Reddick decided to avoid the circus altogether by not leaving the grounds. They would often take walks in the Five Seasons Forest or meet in Kennedy's unit, just so they could avoid the nosy stares of their fellow recruits.

One afternoon, while they were sitting on the couch, Orien walked into the living area and drew a screen with her finger. The *Symetran Society* theme song, which Kennedy had come to dread, played from all the hidden speakers in the room.

"I think you should see this," Orien said.

The floating screen showed Marr Ameer sitting on her silver throne, while Hesta Muse interviewed her. Marr Ameer was covered in silver makeup, as if she were the Tin Woman. "The young creator came here for a reading several progressions ago. As you know, Hesta, I have offered my services to many Evolver recruits, but Kennedy Neff stood out."

Kennedy's stomach dropped.

Hesta raised her chin in mock fascination. "In what way?"

"She is certainly a lovely young thing, but what really struck me was the way she carried herself, with an elegance and a confidence well beyond her years."

Kennedy remembered how she had actually carried herself that day—the way she had been hunched over, gripping her chair, and tapping her feet anxiously. It did not match the sophisticated version of herself that Marr Ameer was trying to sell.

"Can she do this?" Kennedy turned to Orien.

"It appears so."

"This is completely unethical," Kennedy complained.

Orien scoffed. "Whoever gave you the impression that Marr Ameer was ethical?"

"Did you see Reddick in your vision?" Hesta asked Marr.

Reddick leaned forward.

"Definitely. He and Kennedy seem to have known each other for many lifetimes, and their meeting in this one was inevitable. Kennedy is in love with Reddick," Marr said. "I fully expect them to have an ever-evolving, ever-loving relationship. They are destined intimates."

Kennedy wanted to crawl inside a hole and die.

Hesta attempted to frown, but her plastic face would not budge. "Well, Marr, there are many hearts breaking right now across the galaxy."

"I can only relay to your audience what the Record Keepers revealed to me."

"As you know, we have been searching for Kennedy's father and are still offering a reward to anyone who has any information to share." Hesta looked into the camera at her viewing audience and then back at Marr. "Did the Record Keepers reveal him to you?"

Marr played coy. "Hesta, I must protect Kennedy's privacy."

"You're doing a great effing job!" Kennedy got up and kicked the side table. "What a joke."

"Shh!" Orien scolded her.

Hesta pouted at Marr. "You won't even give us a hint?"

Marr grinned, and the silver makeup on her cheeks cracked to show her actual flesh beneath, but she still refused to answer.

"Marr Ameer, I must ask you again: *do* you know who Kennedy Neff's father is?" Suspenseful music played as the camera cut from Hesta to Marr.

Kennedy laughed, and Orien shooshed her again.

Marr delayed for an obnoxious amount of time. "All I can confirm is that his identity will be revealed very soon."

Kennedy ran a hand through Orien's screen until it evaporated. "She's so full of it. She doesn't know who my dad is. If she did, she would have collected that reward a long time ago."

Reddick stared at Kennedy with an imperceptible smile.

She put her hand on her hip. "What are *you* looking at?"

"My destined intimate, apparently."

Orien cracked up.

Kennedy glared at her. "It's not funny."

Reddick got up and wrapped his arms around Kennedy. "Aww, I didn't know you were *in love* with me."

"I'm not. Especially not right now."

"Why are you so flustered?" he asked.

Kennedy huffed. "Orien, tell him that Marr is lying."

Orien tapped a finger to her chin. "I do recall her saying you had a destined intimate."

"But she didn't say it was Reddick!"

"Unbelievable." Reddick pretended to be hurt. "After all the lifetimes we've been through, this is how you treat me?"

"A little help here, Orien?"

"I'd better let you two settle this." Orien took the center lift to her room, and left Kennedy hanging.

Reddick rubbed Kennedy's arms once they were alone. "But

seriously, what did you think about Marr saying she knows who your dad is?"

"I wish it were true." Kennedy didn't like to think about her reading with Marr—partly because it had been disappointing, and partly because it had scared her. "I'll never forget the look on her face; the way she told me to go home before *he* found out about me."

Reddick held her tightly.

Kennedy rested her head on his shoulder. "Anyway, sorry for all that crap she said about lifetimes. It's crazy."

"It's not that crazy." Reddick pulled away and looked at her hesitantly. "If I tell you something, you promise you won't laugh at me?"

"I promise."

"When I met you, I started hearing this voice," he said reluctantly. "It's like this peaceful, disembodied voice that I hear in my gut—it's kind of my voice but kind of not."

"Okay..."

"The first time I heard it was the first time I saw you."

"What did it say?"

"It said, '*There she is.*' It felt like part of me recognized you—like part of me already knew you and always had."

Kennedy thought of her own knowing when it came to Reddick, but she had no idea that he had the knowing, too.

"Then that night at the Submerged Station, after you fell asleep, the voice said, '*I just want Kennedy.*'" He ran a hand through his hair. "Then, when I kissed you that first time—it was like time stopped. And the voice said, '*You can stop kissing her now and everything will stay the same, or you can keep kiss-ing her and everything is going to change.'* I guess it's obvious which decision I made."

Kennedy was smiling so much that her face began to ache.

Reddick froze halfway through a shrug and kept his shoulders up. "I don't know anything about past lives. All I know is that this thing between us feels like it started before we even met."

"I know what you mean."

Reddick grabbed both of her hands. "Can I ask you something?"

"Anything."

"Why are you so obsessed with finding your father? I get why you'd be curious, but why do you *need* to know so badly?"

Kennedy let go of his hands and sat back down on the couch. "When I was growing up, I just wanted to be like everyone else. I wanted a dad, a house, and a backyard. I wanted to feel like I belonged, but I never did." Kennedy tangled her fingers. "I had this teacher in the seventh grade who laughed when she over-heard one of the other kids call me a freak, her name was Mrs. Henderson. So, when she went to sit down, I mentally moved her roller desk chair, and she fell back. Everyone in the class started cracking up, but I really hurt her. The paramedics came and everything. I didn't get in trouble because no one could prove it was me, but I still felt awful. Anyway, my mom asked me what would make me feel better, and I said finding my dad. And I guess for a while it just gave me something to do, but then... it felt like a purpose, a reason to keep going when all I wanted to do was quit. I assumed I inherited these abilities from him, so I just kept working at them, believing I could make him proud if I perfected them. It was the only thing that made me feel better." She smirked. "How's that for evolved?"

Reddick did not respond; in fact, he would not even look at her.

Kennedy laughed. "Do my dumpster fire daddy issues scare you?"

Reddick shoved his hands inside his pockets and said, "I've been thinking about my mom a lot lately. She would have liked you."

Kennedy was flattered. "Zuele said she would be flying out to meet Malant herself."

"Probably." Then Reddick disappeared inside a memory. "I used to run and jump in her bed when I was scared. I always had to have a foot or a hand touching her, just to make sure she was there. I don't know when I stopped reaching out; sometimes I think I still do."

Kennedy realized Reddick was suffering from a parent-sized wound, too—same disease, different symptoms.

"I want to be like her," he said.

"You already are."

"No." He clenched his jaw. "I want to be in the Antastropolith Alliance. I want to kill Malant Tarish. I want to make him suffer the way he has made the rest of us suffer. How is *that* for evolved?"

Kennedy looked into his eyes. There it was again: that recklessness, that need to face death head-on, to somehow be its master. It frightened her. She wanted to isolate their love from the fear and uncertainty in the air but knew she could not. This war, if there were one, would be the backdrop of their love story. And she knew there was a part of Reddick that would never be content until he avenged his mother's death, just like there was a part of her that would not be satisfied until she found her father. She doubted the Evolvers could train that out of either of them.

"You're right," she said after some thought. "My father—whoever he is—believed in the Alliance. He believed enough to get their symbol tattooed on him. Maybe they really did find a Veilless, or maybe it's on us to finish what they started. One thing's for sure: We have to stop Malant. I'm in, too."

After their dramatic declarations, they sat in silence again.

Kennedy rubbed her forehead with her palm's heel. "I just feel like I've stalled out. I've done everything I know to do, and I still haven't found him."

"I have an idea," Reddick said. "I don't know if it will help, but it might. Before she died, my mom donated an experience to the Institute. It's inside the Hall of Experiences; it's from the night Leandor died. She was there."

"She was?"

"It happened a few progressions before she became pregnant with me."

"Why do you think she donated it?"

"Because she believed in what Xavian was doing. She always reminded my father that he had Millintican blood, that my greatest grandmother Cissoria was from there, and that he should care just as much as Xavian did."

"You've experienced the memory?"

"Once, a long time ago. It's pretty hard to stomach, but it

might have some clues."

"Don't I need Zuele to enter the Hall of Experiences?" Kennedy asked.

"Technically, no. Chancellor Kirat made me your guide, remember? I can chaperone you in there for learning purposes."

"Can we go now?"

The Hall of Experiences was situated within the Institute's tallest tower. Two Triphens held its crystal doors open for Kennedy and Reddick as brilliant afternoon sunlight streamed through the skylights. Kennedy was mesmerized by the thousands of small crystal chips lining the shelves, each one containing a different Evolver's experience.

Corijean was speaking to Thecla Atter in front of the stained-glass wall when she spotted Kennedy and Reddick. She promptly dropped her conversation with Thecla and confronted them, "What's she doing in here, Reddick? Phase Ones are not permitted in here without the presence of their guardians."

Kennedy's newfound empathy for Corijean was the only reason she did not snap at her.

"She's with me. We are doing research." Reddick grabbed Kennedy's hand.

Corijean's smug expression vanished. "What are you going to experience?"

"That is none of your concern," Reddick said.

Corijean looked at Kennedy. "You do understand that once

you are inside the experience, you will not be able to escape until it is over? It's not like Syncrocperience."

Kennedy pretended to be unfazed. "Yes."

"If you'll excuse us, Corijean." Reddick put his hand on Kennedy's lower back and guided her towards a glass desk, where they checked out Vivith Brandth's experience. A floating screen warned Kennedy that this experience contained death, and just like Corijean said, she would not be able to escape once she was inside. Kennedy shifted nervously from foot-to-foot. It was terrifying to think of being stuck inside someone else's body, like a bad trip she couldn't get out of. Still, Kennedy signed the screen, hoping it would be worth the trauma inflicted.

"I'll be here the whole time," Reddick told her. "But I can't experience that again. Hearing her voice, feeling that she was once alive and isn't anymore—it's too much. It makes me feel like I can change what happened, and when I realize I can't, it makes me feel powerless all over again."

Kennedy held his face between her hands. "I understand."

A Triphen summoned a chip from a shelf that was easily five stories above the ground. He held out a silver tray, and the crystal chip landed in its center. Reddick and Kennedy followed the Triphen to a darkened room, where he handled the crystal chip with gloves and plugged it into a dock on the wall. Kennedy removed her emotion blocker and placed it on the tray. She stepped onto a pair of white footprints, which were a few sizes smaller than her feet. A white light engulfed her the same way the golden light did, but it felt somehow colder.

And then she was someplace else.

Vivith was shorter than Kennedy, and it was interesting for Kennedy to see things from the perspective of a petite being. Kennedy felt like a spectator inside Vivith's mind as she stood in a darkened tunnel. She felt an intense heat behind her and heard loud, animal-like screams coming from the darkness ahead.

"Keep them back!" a gravelly voice yelled beside her. Kennedy realized the voice belonged to Xavian Seelos, who was a tall, bearded man with scraggly white hair.

"On it!" responded Janekis Opris, who activated her Energy Stealer, illuminating the darkened tunnel with a golden light. When Vivith looked forward, she saw the Millintican Guard dressed in animal pelts and beaked masks. Vivith, Janekis and Xavian aimed their Stealers at them and watched as the first wave of the Millintican Guard shriveled to the ground. Vivith's golden arm shook with the massive amount of energy she had stolen. She relieved the pressure by aiming the energy at the next line of soldiers, who flew backwards, knocking the others down behind them like bowling pins.

"Eka!" Xavian shouted into his Sectnot, "Talk to me."

"Another ship just landed. You are severely outnumbered and about to be surrounded," Eka Mint's muffled voice played from Vivith's Sectnot as well. "Dematerialize now." Vivith looked down onto the screen of her palm, but Kennedy focused on a rubbery, charcoal bracelet on Vivith's left wrist, which was now Reddick's emotion blocker.

"No," Xavian told Eka, "it's not finished yet."

"I repeat, you are severely outnumbered. Get out now!" Eka screamed.

"How did they know we would be here?" Janekis asked.

"Someone must have tipped them off," Vivith said. An image of her toddler son, Harpier, flashed inside her mind. The guilt and the desperation to get back to him forced her to fight on as another wave of the Millintican Guard rushed towards her.

"Leandor, Zuele?" Xavian yelled down the tunnel behind them. "We're running out of time here!"

There was no reply, just a huge crash that caused the ground beneath them to rumble.

Xavian breathed a sigh of relief. "It is done," he told Vivith and Janekis. "Fall back!" They began moving backwards inside the tunnel, towards the heat, where the huge crash had occurred. The end of the tunnel opened to an enormous platform, which dangled high over a deep pit of lava. They appeared to be inside a volcano, but that was not what caught Vivith's attention. What caught her attention were the collapsed suits of dozens of Dark Panel Combatants surrounding Leandor and Zuele. Ethereal energies escaped from the suits and evaporated into the air. It was a sight Vivith would never forget.

Xavian ran towards Leandor and Zuele on the platform.

Zuele held onto the railing of the platform.

Xavian grabbed her elbow. "Are you okay?"

"I'm fine. I think it's just the heat." Zuele wiped her brow with the back of her hand.

Xavian turned his attention to Leandor. "How about you?"

"I'm okay," Leandor said.

Xavian placed a tender hand on the side of his face. His look conveyed how proud he was of Leandor. "We have to move, now."

Vivith and Janekis followed Xavian and Zuele across the platform, while Leandor stayed back and used his Energy Stealer to hold off the Millintican Guard.

"Forget about them!" Xavian yelled at Leandor when he reached the tunnel on the opposite side of the platform. Then he heard the sound of animal screams rushing towards them from that tunnel, too. "We have to Dematerialize, now!" he yelled.

Vivith waited for Leandor to catch up to them. That's when she saw Malant Tarish Materialize on the platform behind him. "Leandor, lookout!" she yelled, but it was too late. A large web sprung from Malant's titanium chest plate and trapped Leandor.

"No!" Vivith cried when she saw Leandor entangled in Malant's Dematerialization Web.

"Evolvers are not the only ones who know how to Materialize," Malant's layered voice reverberated across the platform, and he summoned Leandor's trapped body towards him.

"Don't stop," Leandor urged Xavian. "Go on without me."

Malant Tarish pointed at Leandor's throat, and a red laser claw emerged from his gloved hand.

"Go," Leandor mouthed to Xavian and the others, now surrounded by the Millintican Guard.

"Not without you," Zuele said.

Malant's dark screen of a face lit up with red eyes. "So, this is the Antastropolith Alliance. I wish I could say that I was impressed." He laughed a deeply layered laugh, and the Millintican Guard, who now clogged both tunnels, joined him. Malant looked around at the empty Combatant suits and pressed his laser claw even closer to Leandor's throat, burning the top layer of his skin. "Good thing you know how to fix this."

"Go!" Leandor yelled again.

Vivith tried to move forward to help Leandor, but Xavian held her back.

"Let me go," Vivith demanded. "He's my friend, I have to help him!" But Xavian would not let her. Zuele gazed at Vivith with a face full of sorrow as she struggled to free herself from Xavian's grasp. "This doesn't work without him! None of this works without him!"

"No, Vivith! It's me he wants. Just go!" Leandor pleaded, but the Alliance still stayed.

"He's right. The rest of you mean nothing to me, and we all know that you are nothing without him." Malant's screen lit up with a sinister smile.

Leandor tried to reason with Zuele. "Please," Leandor begged her. "Please, you have to go!" Zuele's eyes filled with tears, but she remained unmoving. So Leandor turned his attention to Xavian. "You have to get them out of here, now!" Leandor screamed and attempted to Dematerialize, but the Dematerialization Web only allowed him to blink out of sight for a second. He fell forward, and Malant instinctively ran his claws down Leandor's side.

Leandor created an energy sphere inside his hands and launched it at Malant, sending him back to the railing.

"Get him," Malant told his goons.

Leandor was bleeding profusely. He limped to the edge of the platform as they approached. He launched a few more energy spheres at them, and a wave of militants flew off the platform. Leandor watched them fall into the lava.

"Get him!" Malant yelled with more urgency.

Leandor locked eyes with Zuele and nodded.

"Don't," she said, shaking her head. "Please, don't."

Leandor gave her a meaningful look. Then he fell.

Vivith let out an agonized scream as she watched Leandor fall hundreds of feet into the lava.

"Dematerialize!" Xavian yelled.

Then the experience ended.

When she returned to the present, Kennedy had tears in her eyes. She did not realize in that moment she was shaking, but Reddick did, and he was there to hold her.

"Are you okay?" she asked him.

He placed his warm hand on the back of her neck. "Kennedy, you are the one who is shaking."

She searched his face. "They should have fought harder. Why didn't they fight harder?"

"I don't know."

The Triphen handed Kennedy back her emotion blocker and gave her his blessing, but not even that could improve her vibration. When she and Reddick stepped back out into the sun-drenched Hall of Experiences, Zuele was standing there waiting for them. Corijean stood behind her and wore a satisfied smirk.

"Training room," Zuele told Kennedy. "Now."

"I thought I told you to drop this," Zuele said once the doors of the training room closed behind them. "Which part of *this is dangerous,* do you not understand?"

Kennedy raised her chin. "I want to be in the Antastropolith Alliance."

Zuele laughed.

But Kennedy was undeterred. "I just watched Leandor die."

Zuele turned away from her. "You shouldn't have seen that."

"You are still in the Alliance, aren't you?"

Zuele would not look at her.

"The Alliance found another Veilless, didn't they?"

"Who told you that?"

"Miles Pierce."

"When did you speak to—" Zuele was able to come up with the answer before she even got the full question out; her face turned livid.

"The Alliance is somehow standing in Malant's way. That's why he has never waged his war. That's why he is hunting them."

"That's enough."

Kennedy did not give up. "Who betrayed you?"

"You are a Phase One, Kennedy. You are not privy to classified information."

Kennedy kept trying. "Who told Malant you were at Mount Sleer?"

"This conversation is over. Now if I were you, I would think long and hard about whether or not you would like to continue in this program."

"Marr Ameer said my dad knows about me, but you are keeping us apart." It was a lie, a big one, but Kennedy felt they were even since Zuele was clearly lying, too.

Zuele rolled her eyes. "Well, if Marr Ameer says so, then it must be true. It's not like she has never been wrong about anything before. Tell me, did she predict you would be sent home with a modified memory? Because if she predicted that, I just might believe her." Zuele snapped her fingers and motioned towards the door. "This is your final warning, Kennedy. Now get out."

TWENTY-TWO

"She's lying to me," Kennedy told Reddick when they sat down to dinner. "She knows who my father is. I know she does." Kennedy flipped open her BELIEVE notebook and wrote her memory of Vivith's experience inside. "Ugh!" she groaned in frustration.

Kennedy put her busy head down on the cool pages of her open notebook. She felt awful for fighting with Zuele. A few seconds later, Kennedy scooted over so Geenen could join them. Geenen slid Kennedy's notebook towards her and looked at the cover, examining it for the first time. She pointed her long, scaly finger at the green alien there and said, "That is offensive."

Kennedy looked up at Geenen's alien face and then at the little green alien on her notebook. Then she burst out into laughter. She couldn't stop. Tears of laughter rolled down her cheeks. She did not know why she was laughing so hard; it wasn't even that funny, yet the harder she tried to stop, the more she laughed.

Geenen opened the last page of Kennedy's notebook and drew

a crude picture of a dumb, hairy human walking on its knuckles. "That's what my kind thinks you look like." Now Geenen was laughing, too.

Kennedy held her side and begged Geenen to stop. It was a cleansing experience for Kennedy, who was chockful of trauma, confusion, and anger. Eventually, everyone at the table was laughing with them, even though no one was quite sure if it was appropriate.

Enforcer Tusk heard Kennedy laughing raucously and looked over at her table. She thought he was going to tell her to keep it down, but instead he stared at her as though she were someone else. The look on his face sent a chill down her spine, and she stopped laughing.

Reddick placed a hand on her leg. "Everything okay?"

"Yeah." Kennedy glanced back at Tusk, but he had vanished. The whole thing left her feeling unsettled. She was so unsettled that she forgot her notebook on the table. She was halfway to her unit when she realized her mistake. Reddick offered to get it for her, but Kennedy decided she could use the fresh air after the day she'd had.

The dining hall was cleared out by the time she got there. She looked towards her table and found Enforcer Tusk standing where she had been sitting. She hid next to the entrance, watching him. He appeared thunderstruck as he flipped through the pages of her notebook. Kennedy had no idea what could be producing such a reaction from him, considering that her notebook was filled with more questions than answers.

Tusk grabbed the notebook and stormed out of the dining hall. Without thinking, Kennedy followed him. When Tusk vanished inside the Ivy Tunnel, Kennedy crept distantly behind him. Inkblots of moonlight appeared through cracks in the ivy, lighting her path. Tusk nearly ran towards the Institute's entrance as Kennedy struggled to quietly keep up with him. Tusk pulled open the front door, and Kennedy managed to wedge herself inside before it shut. He turned around, and Kennedy hid beside the statue of Xavian Seelos.

Tusk hopped on an elevator, but Kennedy remained crouching until a patroller finished its sweep outside the Hall of Experiences. Once its pink light disappeared, Kennedy tiptoed down the stairwell off the foyer and turned down the hallway that led to Tusk's office, hoping he was there.

She inched towards his door, careful not to make a sound, only to find it closed. She tried to press her ear against it but could not hear anything.

She needed to get in that room.

Kennedy walked to the end of the hallway, sat down, and attempted to bilocate inside his office. She tried to remember every detail of Tusk's office—the screens and switches, his large desk, the map of the Institute. Then her consciousness was inside; it floated to a corner and hid behind a coat rack. Her notebook sat on his desk, while Tusk stood in the corner. He was not alone. Another voice sounded from the room—a deeply layered voice that sounded like five voices shrieking in unison.

Malant Tarish was being emitted from a Communicator sitting next to Kennedy's notebook. Tusk was elated to be in his presence. "This is what you have been looking for," Tusk said. "It's over. The galaxy will finally belong to you, to Millintica."

Malant paced Tusk's office as though it were his own, the transmission so real that the clank of his metal boots echoed throughout the room. "I require proof."

"How do you expect me to prove something like that?" Tusk asked. "If what I'm saying is true, any proof will have been destroyed."

"*If* what you're saying is true? I thought you said you were positive."

"I am. I know it is true, but I have no idea how to prove it."

"You are resourceful, you will find a way."

Tusk deliberated for a moment. "Fine, but if I find you proof, I will require safe passage to Millintica."

"You do not make demands of me, Elsid Tusk."

"I have been loyal to you. Everything you have asked for, I have done proudly. I have never failed you, my King, and I won't fail you now."

Tusk saw his own pitiful reflection on Malant's screen of a face. "If you can get yourself as far as Adillon, I will have someone there to bring you the rest of the way."

Tusk hit his knees and bowed before King Malant. "Thank you, my King, I will not let you down."

Malant ended the communication, leaving Tusk on his knees.

Kennedy could not risk letting Tusk sense her energy, so she quickly merged her consciousness with her physical body. She was still sitting in the dark hallway, but when she opened her eyes, three patrollers floated in front of her and blinded her with their pink lights. Their beeps were victorious. She had been caught.

Tusk opened the door and discovered them. He snapped his

fingers, and their lights dimmed. Tusk reflexively became the concerned enforcer he had been pretending to be for most of his life. "What are you doing here? Is everything okay, young creator?"

Kennedy looked inside his office and tried to summon her notebook, but he caught it as it floated past him.

He ran his hand across the cover. "Quite an intriguing read... I'm impressed. I expected it to be filled with gossip and teenage melodrama, but instead I found symbols of war. Dangerous symbols. Symbols that could get you killed." He perused its pages. "It seems you have all the pieces but no idea how they fit together." He handed it to her.

Kennedy glared at him. "You are a traitor."

He grabbed her arm and pulled her into his office. "Actually, quite the opposite. Everything I do is for my home planet. Evolvers don't appreciate Millinticans like us stinking up the place. I am sure Zuele tried to hide your Millintican heritage from you, too. She has been running from her heritage since King Malant took power." His eyes brightened. "But soon, the entire universe will be Millintican. Millintican might will dominate once and for all."

"The Evolvers will never allow that to happen."

He laughed at her.

"You're not an Evolver. You never were. You're a Possessor!" Kennedy looked at him in disgust. "Why aren't you on Millintica with your precious king then? Why are you here?" Yearning flashed across his face.

Kennedy answered her own question, "Because of Zuele." She tried to keep him talking while she schemed up a way to get out of there. The patrollers floated at eye level. If she could somehow find a way to duck and roll beneath them, she might have a chance to make a run for it. She took a deep breath and prepared to enact her plan, but Tusk grabbed her by the wrist before she could get away from him.

"Ah!" Kennedy exclaimed as he squeezed her wrist with all his strength.

"Where is that arrogant smile now?" he asked through clenched teeth.

Kennedy tried to wriggle out of his grasp but couldn't; her hand was turning purple from lack of circulation. She struggled to remove his cold fingers from her wrist. And it was there, in the middle of that struggle, that Kennedy looked down at Tusk's exposed wrist and found a tattoo of an X with four other x's springing from its tips.

All the fight left Kennedy when she realized she had finally found her father.

Tusk followed her gaze to his wrist. "I told you that symbol was dangerous."

Kennedy could not breathe. Her thoughts spiraled, and her body shook. Her Sectnot tried to find her an exit route, but there was no escaping this truth. She was the daughter of a traitor. He was the exact opposite of everything she had dreamt of him being.

"I know who you are, Kennedy," he said, squeezing her wrist even harder, "and I don't care if you live or die."

Painful tears filled her eyes. She had wasted so much time thinking about him, thinking that meeting him would somehow heal all her insecurities. Believing his love would give her the permission she needed to love herself. How could her mother have fallen for someone so callous and self-serving? Kennedy wished she had listened to Zuele, but all she thought about was herself, which made her more like her father than she was comfortable admitting. A voice cut through her thoughts.

"Let her go," Chancellor Kirat said from the doorway.

Tusk still gripped Kennedy's wrist. "The truth was always going to come out, Chancellor. It was a valiant effort, but you made a huge mistake bringing her here."

"I *said*, let her go."

"I need you to retrieve Zuele for me."

"I have already contacted Zuele. She is on her way." The Chancellor frowned. "Do you really think she will go with you? After all you have done?"

"I can keep her safe. We'll take Kennedy to Millintica. We'll start over. We can go home. Finally, we can go home. Malant will reward us. He'll protect us. We'll be safe." Tusk's grip on Kennedy's wrist was gradually lessening. "Zuele and I can be together again. We can go back to the way things were."

"How far do you plan on going back?" Chancellor Kirat asked. "How about that night when you sold out your friends and led Malant straight to Leandor? Who knows how much information you've shared with Malant since then? You will never change, Tusk, no matter how many chances you get."

"Chancellor, I live in reality. The Alliance was and is a fantasy. You cannot stop King Malant. He is too powerful. There is the way we want things to be, and then there is the way they are."

"And then there is sacrificing your friends for power."

"Enough!" he yelled. "I want you to bring Zuele to me now!"

"She will never love you," the Chancellor assured him. "Never."

Chancellor Kirat's words must have landed a punch because Tusk dropped Kennedy's wrist. Kennedy took advantage of his heartbreak and rolled beneath the patrollers. Poisonous spikes ejected from their floating, metal bodies. Their pink lights blinded her, but she kept moving, knowing she was not going to get another chance.

Chancellor Kirat created three energy spheres in her hands and launched them at the patrollers, who exploded immediately. Their debris hit Kennedy in the arms and legs, but it did not hurt anywhere as badly as their poisonous spikes would have. Kennedy didn't stop running until she was standing next to the Chancellor, who used her free arm to force Kennedy behind her.

"No!" Tusk screamed. "My babies! No!" He collapsed before their smoking remains and cradled them to his chest. He cared more about the lives of these robotic creatures than his own friends or his own daughter. It was a pathetic sight. With each passing moment, Kennedy lost more and more respect for him.

"The Triphens are on their way," Chancellor Kirat said. "It is over, Elsid."

Tusk rushed to the wall that controlled the entire Institute's security functions. He held his Sectnot up, and the lights flickered. A robotic voice filled the room: "Dematerialization Web deactivated." Tusk kept his eyes on Kennedy, and then he Dematerialized into a cloud of particles.

Chancellor Kirat examined Kennedy's anguished face and pulled her in for a hug. "You are going to be okay. You are very loved, young creator. Just take a few breaths for me."

"I am here." Zuele rushed inside the office a few moments later and peeled Kennedy away from the Chancellor. "It's okay. I am here." She cradled Kennedy's face and asked, "Are you hurt?"

Kennedy shook her head.

Chancellor Kirat placed a hand on Kennedy's arm. "I know this is difficult, but I need you to tell me exactly what happened."

Zuele wrapped a supportive arm around Kennedy as she cried her way through it.

A handful of Triphens and guardians, including Reddick's, congregated in the hallway. Zuele handed Kennedy off to the Triphens. "They will make sure you get back to your unit safely."

Kennedy held onto Zuele. "Where are you going?"

"I'm going after Tusk. We can't let him escape."

Kennedy shook her head adamantly, not wanting Zuele to leave. But Zuele, Chancellor Kirat, Rantrin, and the other guardians disappeared from the hallway before she could stop them. One of the Triphens reactivated the Dematerialization Web and then accompanied Kennedy safely to the garage of her unit. He gave her his blessing, which only made Kennedy cry harder. How could he love her so easily when her own father did not care whether she lived or died?

Kennedy took the center lift to the second floor of her unit, which was filled with alien actors pandering to Reddick and Geenen from an alien sitcom.

"There she is," Reddick said. "I was starting to get worried." When he saw Kennedy's red, puffy eyes, he rushed to her. "What happened?"

Geenen turned off the sitcom, and the alien actors

disappeared from the living area.

Reddick helped Kennedy take a seat, but it was a while before she could compose herself long enough to speak. "Elsid Tusk is my father," she finally said through residual sobs, "and he is a traitor. He sold out the Alliance. He's the reason Leandor is dead."

Reddick and Geenen looked at each other.

Kennedy held her sore wrist.

"Did he hurt you?" Reddick got to his feet. "Where is he?"

"He's gone," Kennedy said. "Zuele, Chancellor Kirat, Rantrin, they're all out looking for him."

Reddick clenched his jaw and paced in a small circle, willing himself to calm down as Kennedy told them the rest of the story.

Geenen grabbed some firest weed and rubbed it on Kennedy's wrist, which brought her instant relief—unfortunately, the relief did not extend to her emotional pain. "'This is what you have been looking for?' That's really what he said to Malant?" Geenen asked. "Maybe he was talking about the Alliance?"

"Didn't sound like it," Kennedy said. "He wanted safe passage to Millintica. He told the Chancellor he would take Zuele and me there, like we could be some happy family or something."

Geenen exhaled. "How can you be sure he is your father? Did he actually tell you he was?"

"He's from Millintica, and he has the tattoo—the same tattoo my mom saw on my father's wrist."

"But if Tusk was your father," Reddick interjected, "your DNA would have matched his in the Evolver database, and Zuele would know."

"Maybe she does. Maybe that's the information she has been

trying to keep from me."

"Why would Zuele recruit the daughter of a being she despises?" he asked.

"I don't know." Kennedy had not considered any of this. "I don't know anything."

He grabbed her BELIEVE notebook. "What could he possibly have found in here?" Reddick flipped through it and then stopped. "Kennedy..." He held up her sketch of the Five Seasons Forest, the one made of tiny, energetic bubbles. "What is this?"

"It's nothing," Kennedy said.

"It's not nothing..." He flipped to another page of Luminary Lake, sketched in the same manner. "Is this how you see the universe?"

"What do you mean?"

"You can *see* energy?"

"You *can't*?"

He shook his head. "I can sense it, but I can't see it."

"Let me see." Geenen grabbed the notebook from him and examined it.

Reddick gawked at Kennedy. "The Veilless... they can see energy; they can see beyond the veil, which separates the physical world from the world of consciousness."

Kennedy shook her head. "I think I would know if I were a Veilless."

Reddick continued. "You are unnaturally talented—you can bilocate. The only thing you haven't done is animate technology."

"Wait. Kennedy, you said you gave Scrawl an attitude adjustment that day." Geenen looked over at Pile, who was cleaning the kitchen. "And Pile! You are the one who brought Pile to life, not me. You were there that night. You are the reason she started working—the reason she's so opinionated and sensitive. You gave her a piece of your consciousness. Kennedy, you *are* a Veilless."

"That is why Zuele has been so protective of you," Reddick said. "That is why Tusk wants to take you to Millintica, because Malant needs a Veilless to expand the Dark Panel."

"Miles Pierce's theory was correct," Geenen said. "The Alliance *did* find a Veilless. They found you."

"I am not a Veilless," Kennedy repeated.

They stared at her in shock.

"Don't look at me like that!" Kennedy screamed.

"Like what?" Reddick asked.

"Like I'm a freak." No one had looked at Kennedy like that since she'd left Desert Hills High School. Reddick watched Kennedy with a pained look on his face, trying to find a way to fix the unfixable. Kennedy walked away from them and went to her room. She changed into her Evolver shorts and a tank top, then she washed her face and programmed her wall to look like her sanctuary back in Tucson—she needed to be someplace where the universe made sense again.

Someone knocked on her door, but she was too lost in thought to even hear it. She stared up at the fairy lights in her room.

Reddick let himself in and asked, "Do you want to be alone?"

Kennedy looked at his gorgeous, sincere face and shook her head. She lifted the covers and invited him to lie in bed beside her. He wrapped his arms around her, and she turned her back to him so they could fit together. "I don't want you to worry,

Kennedy. You are safe here."

Kennedy did not care if she was a Veilless; she did not care if Malant was hunting her; she did not care if her life was in danger. All she cared about—all she had ever cared about—was finding her father, and now she had.

"Why haven't I ever hated him?" she asked aloud. "I should have hated him for what he did to my mom and for what he did to me. Instead of hating him, I hated myself. Instead of blaming him, I blamed myself. I never thought he was a bad person; I never even made room for that possibility in my head."

Reddick ran his fingers through her hair. "He can't be all bad. He created you. He deserves credit for at least that much. Besides, Kennedy, we're not sure Tusk is your father."

She breathed a little easier when she considered that her real father might still be out there, might still be good, and might still care whether she lived or died. She thought of him hiding on Adillon with Xavian, preparing for the Alliance's next mission, yet that possibility somehow felt unlikely.

Kennedy turned and rested her head on Reddick's chest. He felt solid and warm, while she felt empty and cold. She listened to his heartbeat and breathed in his clean scent. Kennedy placed her thumb inside the scar next to his eyebrow, as though her thumbprint could somehow unlock him. Kennedy knew life was filled with paradoxes and gray areas, but her feelings for Reddick were certain; they were the only thing she was absolutely sure about.

He pulled away so he could look into her eyes. "If you are a Veilless, then I will be your Protector."

She smiled.

"I wouldn't trust anyone else with the job," he said.

"You would do that for me?"

"I would do anything for you. I love you, Kennedy."

Her heart swelled inside her chest. "I love you, too, Reddick." She reached up and kissed him.

His fingers traced the curve of her waist and then traveled lower.

Kennedy responded to his touch by arching her back. "You are trying to distract me again."

"Maybe," he said.

Kennedy held Reddick tighter, pressing her body against his. She could feel the effect it was having on him. Suddenly, she needed to be even closer to him. She ran her hands hungrily across his body, trying to find ways to make him as happy as he made her. His warm hand traveled up her tank top as she removed his Phase Three shirt. They explored one another, taking their time initially, before finally losing patience. Kennedy was safe here. Safe to express every version of herself. This realization made her kiss him with renewed intensity.

Kennedy had cried out most of her anxiety earlier in the night and now felt like a raw, exposed nerve, in a good way—a very good way. She wanted this, and only this. When the alert for curfew rang through their Sectnots, they stopped. Reddick made to get up, but she held onto him. Tusk was gone, and their guardians were preoccupied with their hunt for him. They would never know if Reddick stayed the night, and even if they did, who cared?

"Stay," she said.

"Are you sure?"

"It's the only thing I'm sure of." She opened her nightstand, where there was an assortment of protection. "Here, I don't know which one is right."

Reddick peeked inside the full drawer and laughed. "Are you expecting the Evolver Legion?"

Kennedy chuckled. "Orien gave them to me; she is very big on safety." Kennedy shyly pressed her cheek against his toned back and waited for him to pick one. She felt like the luckiest girl in the universe, but then quickly remembered that she was not his first. She tangled her fingers in her lap as her Sectnot listed all the consequences and benefits of the decision she was about to make. She turned it off and tangled her fingers again.

"We don't have to do this," he assured her.

"No, I want to... I really want to... I just..." She struggled to find the words, "Just don't..."

"Don't what?"

"Don't judge me."

"Why would I judge you?"

"Because I have no idea what I'm doing."

Reddick removed her emotion blocker, and then he removed his own.

"We'll guide each other," he said.

Kennedy's emotions immediately revealed how important this moment was to her, and she was relieved to feel that it was just as important to him.

TWENTY-THREE

Kennedy awoke the next morning with Reddick's muscular arm still draped around her. She swooned at how boyish he looked when he slept. When Reddick rolled over, Kennedy tiptoed to the bathroom and laughed when she caught sight of herself in the mirror. Her cheeks creased with lines from her pillow, her lips red from kissing, and her hair a proper bird's nest. "You are a woman now," she told herself, and then laughed hysterically, fearing she might be losing her mind due to the gamut of extreme emotions she had spanned the day before.

Kennedy stood under her showerhead and rehashed a day that contained both the best and worst experiences of her life. It made her feel safer knowing that Tusk was probably already on his way to Millintica. Both Geenen and Reddick made strong arguments for why Tusk might not be her father, but only her mother could confirm or deny it.

After Kennedy got ready, she went into the dark room off her closet, being careful not to wake Reddick as she did. She transmitted herself to her mother's bedroom, but unfortunately, she was the only one there. In Tucson, it was the middle of the night. Kennedy called out for her mother and sister, but no one responded. "Where are they?" she asked Phantom when he jumped onto the bed.

Kennedy waited until there were only three minutes left of her visit. She ended the transmission and decided she would try again later, praying that wherever they were, they were safe. She returned to her closet and attempted to reach Zuele, but her communication was unsuccessful. It frustrated her. She needed to know what was going on. She could not just sit here and do nothing.

Marr Ameer popped into her mind. During her *Symetran Society* interview, she implied she knew who Kennedy's father was. At the time, Kennedy assumed she was full of it, but what if she wasn't? What if she really did know? Marr had been right about the Fyorisc stone earrings and the mistletoe, which had to count for something. With that, Kennedy decided she would go see Marr Ameer, this time not to discover who her father was but to prove who he wasn't.

When she walked back into her room, Reddick was awake, with his head propped up on his hands. Kennedy tried not to stare at his impressive body, only half covered by her sheet. She blushed as flashes of their night together resurfaced inside her mind.

"There you are," he said. "I thought I got one-night stand-ed."

"I just tried to contact my mom. I was going to show her an image of Tusk and see if she recognized him, but she's not home."

Kennedy was too embarrassed to look him in the eye, but he seemed to have no problem looking at her. "How are you feeling today, otherwise?" he asked, referring to what they had done the night before.

"Like I got probed by an alien."

Reddick laughed and pulled her down next to him. The easiness between them returned immediately. "Going somewhere?"

"I'm going to see Marr Ameer. She said she knows who my dad is; she might be lying—I'm almost positive she is—but it's the only move I've got left."

"Alright." Reddick picked his Phase Three casuals up off the floor. "I mean, obviously I can think of better things we could do on our day off, but no one asked me." He zipped his pants. "Let me go to my unit and change. I'll go with you. Be back soon. Wait for me."

"My whole life," she said, like they were on a soap opera.

Orien caught Reddick on his way out and gave him a salacious smile. "Good morning, *Master* Brandth."

Once he left, Kennedy walked into the kitchen.

"I want to know everything," Orien demanded.

"What do you want to know?"

"Was it a *pleasure* to encounter his energy?" Orien stalked her around the kitchen.

Kennedy pulled out the ingredients for a smoothie.

"Come on, I need details—graphic ones!" Orien picked one of the strawberries out of the blender and ate it. "We have a code! I tell you *everything*."

"Yeah, I've been meaning to ask; can you please stop doing that?"

Geenen entered the kitchen and asked Kennedy, "Did you tell Orien?"

"She didn't need to tell me," Orien said. "I guessed."

"Can you believe it?"

"Well, it kind of seemed inevitable. It's natural." Orien patted Geenen's skinny shoulder. "You'll see one day when you find an intimate, although I am not entirely sure how your kind does it."

"What are you talking about?" Geenen asked.

"What are *you* talking about?" Orien asked.

"Enforcer Tusk attacked Kennedy last night."

Orien gasped. "He what?"

Kennedy told her the entire story, and when she was done, Orien asked the same question everyone else had. "What has Malant been looking for?"

"Show her the notebook, Kennedy."

Kennedy turned on the blender, pretending not to hear Geenen.

"Kennedy is a Veilless!" Geenen yelled over it.

Orien started laughing. Geenen retrieved the notebook from the couch and showed Orien Kennedy's sketches. The smile faded from Orien's face.

Kennedy poured her smoothie into a glass and tried not to look at them.

"Kennedy was the one who brought Pile to life. That's why Pile always cleans her room first."

"No, it's because I'm nicer to her than you are," Kennedy argued.

"Malant said he needs proof," Geenen said.

"Proof of what?" Orien asked.

"Proof that Kennedy's a Veilless!"

Orien glanced at Kennedy. "Why aren't you freaking out about this?"

"Because I really don't think I'm a Veilless. Are there some coincidences? Sure. But not enough to make me think I *am* one. Plus, right now, all I'm focused on is proving that Tusk is not my father. Reddick and I are going to see Marr Ameer this morning." Kennedy rose to her feet and gulped the rest of her smoothie. "If you guys want to come with us, you can."

Geenen groaned. "You're not going to become one of those beings who has to take their intimate everywhere, are you?"

Orien backhanded Geenen. "Leave her alone, she's obviously in love."

Geenen craned her long neck towards Kennedy. "Are you?"

Kennedy turned bright red. "Can we please go back to talking about the maniacal dictator who might be hunting me? Those conversations were way more fun."

Orien fretted. "Aren't you worried Marr's going to tell everyone your business again?"

"If she does, it'll probably be better than the lies they're spreading about us on *Symetran Society*. According to them, Reddick and I have already broken up two times."

"Three," Orien corrected her.

"You think Pengar wants to go with us?" Kennedy asked them.

"I'm sure," Geenen said, "she probably wants to know why Ethwin only gave her eleven flowers instead of the twelve she is accustomed to. *What could this mean?* She'll ask Marr Ameer. *Does this mean he has lost interest?*"

Kennedy took her BELIEVE notebook back from Geenen. "Be nice."

"She doesn't know how," Orien mumbled. The comment

landed her a predictable elbow jab from Geenen.

They knocked on Pengar's door, but there was no response, so Kennedy sent a message to Pengar's Sectnot and told her where they would be should she want to join. Kennedy threw her notebook in her bedroom before she, Orien and Geenen went down the center lift to the garage.

Reddick was already there, programming the trick tint of his ridership to make it look like he and Kennedy were inside. He then sent his ridership into Crystal City and smiled when the capturers waiting outside the Hover House chased it.

"No Pengar?" he asked once he boarded the ridership belonging to Kennedy and her roommates. "Doesn't she have her own parking spot at this place?"

Kennedy laughed. "I think she's off frolicking with Ethwin somewhere." Then she suddenly got a bad feeling in the pit of her stomach.

Reddick noticed her change in demeanor. "What is it?"

"Nothing. I hope."

The ridership dropped them on the volcanic cliff of Marr Ameer's Love Cottage. Kennedy looked both ways for capturers, but she could not see anything because of a cloud passing through the cliff. She knocked on the front door, but there was no response. "Maybe she's not open?"

Orien pushed the door open. "Now she is."

They entered but stopped in their tracks once they saw the state of the Love Cottage. Two chairs lay on the floor next to Marr Ameer's scattered love manuals, and the happy couples' holograms repeated a complicated code warning of an internal error. Kennedy and Reddick traded a concerned glance.

Geenen picked up a love manual and set it back on the table. "What happened in here?"

They waved their hands at the camera, waiting for Marr Ameer to acknowledge them, but the cottage remained silent. Kennedy entered the reading room which was in an even worse state than the lobby. The two silver thrones and the table where Marr conducted her readings had all been turned over. "Ms. Ameer?" Kennedy called out. The others followed her inside. "Hello?"

Orien gasped, then pointed to a pair of feet with silver slippers peeking out from behind one of the toppled thrones.

Kennedy's heart stopped. "Hello?" she called out again. Kennedy walked towards the slippers and found Marr Ameer's dead body attached to them. A streak of dried blood ran from her head to her open, lifeless eyes.

Orien covered her mouth in horror. The glittery love candle Marr lit during her readings now had a huge dent in it, as well as a blood stain. "Someone murdered her."

Kennedy saw something flashing from the corner of her eye.

"It's a Roterin Key," Geenen said, pointing to the triangular key that was flashing blue.

Kennedy had not seen one since Zuele modified the memories of Truck Nuts and Molly back in Tucson.

"Someone was trying to modify her memory." Geenen declared.

"Or break into it," Kennedy said.

Orien furrowed her brow. "Why would someone want to break into Marr Ameer's memory?"

"For proof." The answer left Kennedy's lips before it even

registered inside her brain.

Orien and Geenen both wore fearful expressions, but Kennedy kept her expression neutral. She pretended to have the situation under control even though, clearly, she did not. "I think you all should just stay away from me. Whatever this is—whatever I've gotten myself into—I don't want you guys anywhere near it."

"It's too late for that," Orien said. "We're in this whether you like it or not. We have a code."

Geenen stood over Marr's lifeless body. "It looks like she's been lying here for quite a while."

Reddick had yet to say a word. He focused his attention on the two security screens floating beside Marr's table and rewound the footage. Kennedy watched the four of them travel in reverse across the screen, back into the lobby, and then to the front entrance. Geenen was right; Marr Ameer had been lying there for quite some time. The footage went from the light of midday to the dark of the early morning hours. Then two people filled the screens, but Reddick kept rewinding and did not stop until both screens were empty again. He pressed play and watched Marr Ameer approach the front door. Her robe and slippers showed she clearly had not been expecting company. She peeked her head through a crack in the door, but Elsid Tusk forced it open with all his strength, launching Marr Ameer into her holograms and manuals. Marr got up and ran into the reading room, with Tusk stalking after her. She cowered behind her silver throne and shouted at him. Her posture and frantic expression made it evident she was begging him to spare her life. The triangular key floated out of Tusk's palm and shot a thin blue light into Marr's temple.

Kennedy and her friends couldn't see what Marr's memory contained from either angle, but it was clear Tusk had not found what he was looking for because he proceeded to tear the room apart in a rage. He knocked over both thrones, then the table. The Roterin Key dropped from Marr's temple, which brought her back to consciousness. Marr blinked her eyes in confusion, then Tusk grabbed the love candle rolling on the ground and bashed it into her skull. Marr fell back. Tusk dropped the candle and turned around to look directly into the camera. Then he left the Love Cottage and closed the front door as though nothing had happened.

Kennedy and her friends stood in stunned silence. They turned away from the sad footage of Marr's body lying alone on the screen, only to see the real thing on the other side of the room.

"I guess I should contact Evolver Law Enforcement," Geenen said.

Kennedy and Orien agreed, but Reddick still stared at the screen, lost in thought. They waited for him to say something, but instead he created a sphere of energy inside his hands. It percolated and spun, releasing little sparks of light.

Geenen was impressed. "You can create energy spheres?"

Reddick aimed the sphere at the security equipment.

Kennedy gasped as the equipment exploded into a hundred pieces. "What are you doing?" she asked him.

"Destroying evidence. No one can know you were here."

"But she didn't do anything," Orien said.

"It doesn't matter. If my father finds out she was anywhere near here, he will send her back to Earth."

"He can't do that." Orien protested.

Reddick gave her a look, as though they both knew he could and would. "I need the three of you to leave *now*. Once you're gone, I'll call this in. I'll tell them I wanted to see Marr Ameer because I've been anxious about my Phase Three assessments and needed guidance. I don't know. I'll come up with something. I just need you to go. I can get away with being in the wrong place at the wrong time. Unfortunately, Kennedy can't."

"I'm not leaving you alone."

"Kennedy, if you don't go, your memory will be modified of any time we ever spent together. This is me making sure that doesn't happen." He shook her lightly. "Now, please, go."

"He's right," Geenen said, "we have to get you out of here."

"I'll contact you when I have this under control," he promised.

Kennedy kept her eyes on him as Orien and Geenen dragged her from the room. When Geenen opened the cottage's front door, flashing yellow lights blinded them as the capturers fought to gain entry. Geenen shoved them back, but it was too late; they had already captured Kennedy. There was no point in running now.

TWENTY-FOUR

A half-knit sweater sat on a chair inside Marr Ameer's office. Kennedy ran her fingers over the fabric, realizing it would never be completed. Squat beings with Marr's same plump features filled the frames on the wall. Kennedy wondered if they knew yet. She wondered if Marr had prophesied her own impending doom, whether her psychic abilities extended to herself or only worked on others. The day before, Marr had been on *Symetran Society,* claiming to know the truth about Kennedy, and now she was dead. Kennedy's presumed father was no longer just a traitor; now he was a murderer, too.

Marr's office had been Kennedy's holding pen since Evolver Law Enforcement arrived at the scene. Reddick, Orien, and Geenen's guardians had picked them up long ago, but Kennedy was still waiting on hers. Zuele would not respond to Kennedy's communications, which had her fearing the worst. She didn't know what she would do if something happened to Zuele. Even though they fought, she knew Zuele had her best intentions at heart. Kennedy felt incredibly lucky to have such a brilliant guardian, she only wished she knew where she was.

When the door opened, Kennedy stood, expecting to find Zuele, but instead she met the disapproving eyes of Theein Brandth. "Please, have a seat," he said. Theein carried himself as someone who had been important his entire life. Kennedy knew she had blown her chance at making a good first impression, and it reminded her of a story her mother had once told her. When Roberta was younger, she dated a rich guy. When the rich guy brought her home to meet his parents, the first thing his father told Roberta was that her car was leaking oil on his driveway. This felt kind of like that, only worse, because that was just a guy, and this was Reddick.

"Where is Zuele?" she asked.

"I would like to know the same thing." Theein Brandth pulled up a chair and sat directly across from Kennedy.

She wanted to tangle her fingers, but she knew this was not the time to show how nervous she was. "Where did everyone go?" she asked, referring to her friends.

"They are in their training rooms, receiving trauma counseling. Dead bodies have a way of lingering in the mind."

Kennedy knew that much was true.

Theein picked up one of Marr's trinkets—a small elephant-like creature with a corkscrew trunk. "It is a dangerous thing to live alone. You could fall, hit your head, and no one would be there to help you." He put the trinket down and annunciated every word so Kennedy would understand his meaning. "That is what happened to Marr Ameer, isn't it?"

Kennedy crossed her arms and legs, hoping to create an energetic barrier between her and Theein Brandth.

He leaned toward her and spoke slowly. "Tusk was never here. Those image-capturers were never here. But most importantly, my son was never here."

Kennedy looked to Marr's family once again. They would never know the truth; they would never have to see the terrified look on Marr's face as Tusk backed her into a corner; they would never know that their loved one had been murdered.

"Also, you will no longer date my son," Theein said, as though this information were merely incidental.

Kennedy uncrossed her limbs. "*Excuse me?*"

"Reddick is destined for greatness. It's in his blood. Ever since you arrived, his focus has been lacking. And now this. You have opened old wounds—wounds he had previously healed from. Despite all his talent, he is still ruled by his emotions. His guardian will work hard to train that out of him. Naturally, your absence will make the process that much simpler. Now, name your price."

"You want to pay me off?" Kennedy nearly laughed at how cliche he was.

"I want you to leave here, but not empty-handed. I know Zuele bought you a home, so you obviously respond to money."

"She used my Evolver compensation to buy it."

"Zuele has no access to your compensation. That was Zuele's money."

Kennedy furrowed her brow again. *Why would Zuele do that? Why did Zuele do anything?* Kennedy was beginning to feel like she did not know her guardian at all.

"So, what will this cost?" he asked.

"I don't want your money."

"Then what do you want?"

That was a loaded question to which Kennedy had no clear answer. She wanted a lot of things. She wanted to know where her guardian was and why she had lied to her at every turn. She wanted to know who her father was. She wanted Malant gone. She wanted her family and friends to be safe. She wanted to be a normal teenager with normal teenage problems, but mostly she wanted Reddick, even though Theein was telling her, in no uncertain terms, that he was the one thing she could not have.

"I can help you find your father. That's what you are after, isn't it? I can help you find him today." Once he had Kennedy's attention, Theein leaned back in his chair. "Additionally, I will double your Evolver compensation. All of this in exchange for you leaving Symetra at once. I will send you to one of our satellite campuses to complete your training. You can keep Zuele as your guardian, of course, but you cannot keep my son. I'll do everything in my power to make sure you stay as far away from him as possible. This is a pretty good deal for someone in your position."

"What is my *position*?"

He smirked. "Well, that is the point; you do not have one."

Kennedy had never been more insulted. She sucked in her quivering lip and looked away.

Theein Brandth lowered his chin to reclaim her eye contact. "You know I don't have to do any of this. I am well within my rights to modify your memory and send you back to Earth."

Kennedy thought of Reddick's mother, the brave Evolver,

who fought alongside the Alliance and saved hundreds of lives while Theein sat on the sidelines. Kennedy rose from her chair and channeled every powerful woman she had ever known, including those she didn't. "The answer is no." It was evident that Theein did not respect her, but that was fine because Kennedy did not respect him either.

"I will give you some time."

"I don't need time. I love Reddick. The only thing you love is the status quo."

"If by status quo you mean peace, then guilty as charged." He stood and looked down his nose at her.

Kennedy was about to repeat her definite answer when one of Theein's security guards busted inside the room and whispered something in Theein's ear. Theein's smug face went slack. "What do you mean it *escaped*?" he shouted.

Kennedy and the security guard both jumped at his outburst.

Theein waved a dismissive hand in Kennedy's direction. "Take her back to her unit."

"What escaped?" Kennedy asked. The security guard dragged her towards the front door, past a team of beings tidying up the crime scene. He took her to a ridership waiting at the edge of the volcanic cliff and loaded Kennedy inside it.

Kennedy's head spun the entire way back to her unit. She tried again to reach Zuele, but she would not accept any of her communications. "Answer, damnit!" Kennedy slammed her hand down on the armrest and cried frustrated tears.

Her unit was eerily quiet. Kennedy rushed to her closet and contacted her mom. She was relieved when she found Roberta unpacking a small suitcase on her bed. "Where were you this morning?" Kennedy asked.

"Audrey and I went to the White Mountains with Nana and Grandpa for the weekend. Why? What happened? Kennedy, have you been crying?"

Kennedy did not answer her; instead, she drew a screen in the air with her finger and projected an image of Elsid Tusk on it. "Is this my father?"

Kennedy's ability to create a screen out of thin air astounded Roberta. "No," she said.

"You're sure?"

"Positive. I have never seen that man before. Why would you think he was your father?"

"He has the tattoo."

"Well, it's not him."

Kennedy was infinitely relieved by her mother's confirmation, but if Tusk wasn't her father, then who was? Kennedy was no longer sure that she wanted to know. *Maybe ignorance really is bliss*, she thought.

The voice warned Kennedy that her time would be up in forty-five seconds. She smiled at her mother, feeling incredibly homesick for Tucson and yearning for the time when her world felt small and safe. Roberta used to check for monsters under the bed, but Kennedy was beginning to realize monsters were too busy to hide under beds.

"You look different, Nedy."

"How?"

"I don't know. Older somehow."

Kennedy wrapped her arms around her mother, wishing they were able to have a different conversation right now. She held her mother tightly. "I love you, mom."

"What is going on? What's wrong? You're scaring me."

"I'm fine."

"Don't lie to me."

Kennedy was down to fifteen seconds. "Don't worry about me. I'll be okay."

When Kennedy reentered her room, it was nearly dark outside. She knew her roommates were still in their training rooms, processing what they had seen earlier in the day. Kennedy wished someone would help her process it, because every time she closed her eyes, she could see Marr Ameer's lifeless ones looking up at her.

Kennedy tried to steer her thoughts toward the positive things in life. She smiled as she reminisced about her night with Reddick, but broke down into tears when she thought about Theein sending her away from him. She hugged the pillow he had slept on, knowing Theein could easily get rid of her. Someday soon, she could wake up back in Tucson, having no idea how she had gotten there. If she was lucky, she might remember pieces of her time at the Institute in the same way her mother remembered pieces of her time with Kennedy's father.

Kennedy could not think anymore, so she pulled the covers over her, closed her eyes, and fell into a deep sleep. When she awoke, it was dark outside her window. She had no idea what time it was or how long she had been out. The unit was still quiet. Kennedy called out to her roommates, but no one responded.

She went to her bathroom and splashed some cold water on her face, and then her Sectnot vibrated. Kennedy quickly accepted the communication, hoping it was Zuele.

"Hello, Kennedy," Elsid Tusk said.

Kennedy froze.

He did not emerge from her hand; instead, a dark screen filled her palm. She could barely see him. "I have your friend here. I caught her this morning on her way to meet her intimate," he said. "Unfortunately, she had to cancel. Pengar, is there something you'd like to tell Kennedy?"

Kennedy's heart sank. There was a struggle, which told Kennedy that whatever he was doing to hold Pengar, she was fighting it. "Pengar, did he hurt you? Are you okay?" Kennedy yelled.

"She will be."

"What do you want?"

"Just you, Kennedy. You in exchange for Pengar. I need you to Materialize at these coordinates," he began reading them. Kennedy opened the BELIEVE notebook on her bed and wrote them down. "Come alone, or I'll kill her. If I even sense that you are not alone, I will kill her *and* anyone else you bring with you. I expect you promptly." He ended the communication.

Kennedy paced inside her room. She wished she had time to use her Thought Projector, to slow her racing mind and heartbeat, but she didn't. She tried to contact Zuele once more. *"I'm sorry, but the Sectnot you are trying to reach is no longer in working order,"* the female voice of her own Sectnot replied. It was one thing when Zuele was not responding; it was another to know she was no longer able to. Once again, Kennedy feared the worst. She did not know what other choice she had. If she didn't go, Tusk would kill Pengar, and she couldn't let that happen. She put on her Evolver jacket, entered the coordinates Tusk had sent, and took a deep breath. Then she Dematerialized from her unit.

She rested in the white light of Dematerialization, wishing she could stay in that tranquil place forever. The energy carried her to the edge of a clearing near the peak of Star Grave Mountain. She stood there alone beneath the three moons, one of which was full. Snow blanketed the pines and squeaked beneath her boots. The frosty air nipped at her ears and nose. Her breath escaped in clouds before her. In the distance, the Evolver Institute shone like buried treasure at the bottom of the mountain.

Her Sectnot warned she was in danger and urged her to extract herself from the situation immediately, but then it died mid-warning. Tusk stood a few feet in front of her, pointing his Rivil at her palm. "You will not be needing that." Two patrollers flanked each side of him.

"Where is Pengar?" Kennedy asked him.

Tusk showed Kennedy Pengar's white Charge Ring. "Don't worry, she's not going anywhere."

"Where is she?" Kennedy screamed.

A patroller shined its pink light on a large pine tree and illuminated a bound and gagged Pengar. Her eyes warned Kennedy to run.

"Let her go," Kennedy demanded. "I did as you asked. I'm here. I came alone."

Tusk searched the clearing. "Where is Zuele?"

"I haven't seen her all day."

Anxiety swept across his face as he looked over his shoulder at a dark ridership idling inside the forest. "We cannot leave without her."

Kennedy connected with the energy inside the clearing, trying to remember everything she had learned in her training. *"Your focus is your superpower,"* Zuele had once said.

The two patrollers blinded Kennedy with their pink lights and unsheathed their poisonous spikes. She avoided them by diving into the snow. Tusk whistled, and the patrollers returned to his side. "Do not be hasty, my darlings. I suppose I should bring out our surprise guest." He laughed. "It has been dying to meet you."

It?

Kennedy could hear Pengar telling her to run through the gag in her mouth, but Kennedy refused to leave without her. As heavy footsteps approached, the ground began to shake beneath her. The sound echoed throughout Star Grave Mountain, shaking clumps of snow from the trees. A massive figure stepped into the clearing. The patrollers shined their pink lights on it to reveal it was a Dark Panel Combatant. Its screen of a face flickered on and off, shining down onto its titanium suit. It was eight feet tall and wider than two doorways. Tusk stood behind it with an electrical prod and kicked it.

Kennedy shuddered, thinking of the consciousness that had been trapped inside it for centuries. The hum returned to her chest, and Kennedy held a hand over it as it vibrated. Adrenaline coursed through her veins. Everything became still. Pengar still urged her to run, but there was nowhere for Kennedy to go—she had no choice but to fight. This was proof that Kennedy was not a Veilless. A Veilless would know what to do in this situation, and Kennedy did not.

Tusk zapped it in the back, and the Combatant resumed its military march towards Kennedy. Its gloved fingers lit up with green lasers, so long that they nearly reached the forest floor.

Enforcer Tusk gleefully watched the unnatural creature approach Kennedy, who backed up until she was nearly out of the clearing. This would not be much of a fight, but she had to try. She closed her eyes and connected with the energy of the forest, specifically the trees. The tree tips responded by snapping back and blasting mounds of snow at the Combatant.

"What a delightful little trick." Tusk wiped the snow from his face, but he still shielded himself behind the Combatant.

The snow melted against the Combatant's hot suit. The smell of wet metal mixed with pine filled Kennedy's nostrils. She focused on the rocks hiding beneath the snow. The rocks broke free of the snow and levitated in the air, surrounding Kennedy like an asteroid field. She mentally organized them into a perfect line and motioned her arm forward. The rocks hit the Combatant's metal exterior like machine gun fire, but did not stop it from advancing.

Tusk kept kicking the Combatant, wanting it to move faster, but it would not. Then Kennedy saw something move in her peripheral vision. Reddick, Orien, and Geenen Materialized outside the clearing. When they saw the Dark Panel Combatant, their mouths dropped open.

"What are you doing here?" Kennedy asked them.

"We found the coordinates in your room," Orien said, assessing the situation. "And your Sectnot wasn't working."

"You guys shouldn't be here. You have to leave, please," Kennedy begged.

Reddick shook his head. "We are not going anywhere."

"Pengar!" Geenen cried when she saw her tied to the tree. She opened the triangular pack around her waist and removed the Disintegrator pellet she had created inside her bedroom. Geenen held it inside her small, scaly palm and whispered to it in her alien language, "Disintegrate rope," she commanded." The Disintegrator flew towards Pengar, turned red hot, and burned through the rope around her until fiery pieces of the rope were extinguished in the snowy forest floor. Once Pengar was free, she ran towards her friends.

All the activity seemed to be agitating the Combatant.

"They are all going to die," Tusk assured Kennedy.

The horror of that possibility prompted Kennedy to find another reserve of energy. She ripped her hands into the air, and the network of tree roots encircling the clearing emerged from the forest floor. The roots ensnared the Combatant's feet and brought it down with a ground-shaking thud. The Combatant landed on Tusk's leg, and he screamed out in pain.

Kennedy heaved in exhaustion. It had taken everything out of her. Orien, Pengar, and Geenen rushed to hold her up. Reddick stood resolutely in front of them. He forced his hand forward and launched the Combatant back down to the ground.

The Combatant slashed Reddick with its laser-green claws, and Reddick held his right arm in pain. "It's okay," Reddick shouted when he heard Kennedy scream out, "it's not that deep."

The Combatant's screen flickered on, and he prepared to play

Reddick's shame for everyone to see. Kennedy tried to pull Reddick back, but he stood firm. *The screen showed a young Reddick in his childhood bed. He slept while Vivith ran a hand through his hair. "One day you will understand why I must do this," she said. "I hope you can forgive me. I love you, my little Evolver." Young Reddick stopped pretending to sleep and watched his mother leave his room.*

Then the screen cut to Vivith's funeral. It showed young Reddick standing to say the Evolver pledge and using the wrong fingers to make the visual prayer of alignment. It showed Reddick confessing to his big brother, Harpier, that it was his fault, and that he could have stopped their mother from leaving but didn't. Harpier pushed him in a grief-fueled rage, and young Reddick cracked the side of his face against a nearby counter. He lay crying on the floor as blood gushed from the side of his left eyebrow.

Reddick unconsciously covered his scar.

"Stop!" Kennedy screamed, and the Combatant's screen went dark. She stood next to Reddick and held his hand. "It's okay," she said, trying to shake him out of it. "It's okay, Reddick. You were just a little boy. You didn't know."

Orien, Pengar, and Geenen stood ready to take the Combatant down with whatever strength they could muster, but it only seemed to be interested in Kennedy.

It was now so close that Kennedy could see herself in the reflection of its screen, along with Symetra's three moons. She waited for it to play her deepest shame—there was plenty to choose from. She took a deep breath, fully expecting it to be her last, and then the Combatant did something Kennedy could have never imagined...

It knelt in the snow and bowed down before her.

TWENTY-FIVE

Kennedy reached out her hand and set it on the Combatant's warm head. The second she touched it, a bone-rattling hum blighted all of her senses. She swirled inside a heavy, timeless presence. Kennedy had never believed in destiny, not until that very moment, when the details of her past and the hopes of her future all became irrelevant compared to what she had actually been put inside this body to do. The moment was profoundly silent. Kennedy unfocused her eyes and could see Omin Yarso's effervescent consciousness pulsating inside the Combatant like an unnatural heartbeat. It called to her, and Kennedy merged her consciousness with Omin's. *She* was the reason this Combatant had pounded against the Adversary Lab's doors—it had been trying to reach her, like a loyal dog scratching and barking for its owner. Kennedy removed her hand and took a step back, but the hum inside her body remained.

Reddick stared at Kennedy in amazement.

Orien blinked rapidly to make sure her eyes were not deceiving her. "It's true."

Pengar could not believe what she was seeing, either. "Why is it doing that?"

"Because Kennedy's a Veilless," Geenen whispered.

"Since when?" Pengar asked.

"I knew it!" Tusk exclaimed, using the electrical prod as a crutch, and dragging his damaged leg behind him. "I knew it!"

Kennedy still gaped at the kneeling Combatant. She had been born with otherworldly powers, but this was the first time in her life that she had ever felt *powerful*, and it scared her.

"Now that we have gotten that out of the way," Tusk whistled and a dozen patrollers zoomed into the clearing. They formed a grid of pink light and unsheathed their poisonous spikes. "Kill them all," Tusk commanded, "except for Kennedy. I'm taking her to the King."

The patrollers dispersed evenly among Kennedy's friends. The first three went for Reddick, who Dematerialized out of sight before they could catch him. Reddick created an energy sphere in his hands and launched it at a patroller, exploding it into a thousand pieces. When he created another one inside his hands, he was able to take out two more patrollers simultaneously.

Orien created an anti-gravity sphere around a patroller and watched it float into space, but when one of them scratched her fabulous coat, she went berserk and beat it to death with the smoking remains of a patroller that Reddick had destroyed.

Geenen summoned her Disintegrator back inside her palm and whispered, "Disintegrate patroller." The small pellet obeyed her command and burrowed itself inside one of the patrollers targeting her. The patroller melted from the inside out and made a warped beeping sound as it fell from the sky.

Pengar reached into her triangular pack and planted a seed in the snow beside her. Seconds later, a huge predator plant that resembled a purple Venus flytrap burst through the forest floor. It captured two patrollers inside its mouth and then swallowed them whole. Their pink lights traveled dimly down the plant's thick stem of a neck before the predator plant digested them several feet below ground. Pengar looked at Geenen and said, "I told you they were fascinating!"

Tusk held up the electric prod and approached Kennedy, but the Combatant would not let him anywhere near her. It grabbed Tusk's prod and snapped it in half—Tusk clearly had not thought this part through. The Combatant tore its claws through the air and eliminated the rest of the patrollers with a few easy swipes. The remains of the patrollers smoldered in the snow. Tusk hit his knees and held up his hands.

The humming in Kennedy's chest grew as the Combatant ripped the shame from Tusk's memory. The Combatant's screen flickered on:

Tusk's greatest shame occurred when he was in his early thirties. He donned his gray enforcer suit and walked towards Zuele with his arms wide open. "Zue, I am so glad you are back." He tried to pull her toward him, but she recoiled in disgust.

"Do not touch me," she threatened. "You betrayed us. You told Malant where we were—you were the only other one who knew."

Tusk tried to deny it.

Zuele crossed her arms. "Haven't you lied enough? I want nothing to do with you. You hear me? Stay away from me. Theein might be giving you another chance, but I never will, not ever."

Tusk's face contorted in pain.

The Combatant's screen went dark, and its hands lit up with laser claws once more.

"No, Kennedy. Tell it no. Please show mercy on me," Tusk pleaded.

"The way you showed mercy to Marr Ameer? You murdered her!" Kennedy spat.

"I had no other choice. I did what I had to. Don't you understand? It's a miracle. You're a miracle! You can help Millintica rule the galaxy. You can restore Millintican might."

The Combatant's green laser claws illuminated Tusk's desperate face.

"No, wait, I can explain," Tusk said. "I can explain everything, just please."

Kennedy held up a hand, and the Combatant retracted its claws.

Tusk hyperventilated. "I needed proof of your identity. I thought Marr could give it to me, but she made the whole thing up. The Record Keepers did not show her that you were a Veilless or who your father was. They showed her the hotel where your parents met, they showed her the day you were born, and they showed her King Malant, but they did not show her anything I could use. She was a liar. I did not want to use the Combatant, but it was the only way to prove what you are.

"Last night when I saw you smiling, Kennedy—I can't believe I never noticed it before... You look just like him, and then the notebook—I admit the timeline still does not make sense to me, but—"

"Wait. You know who my father is?"

"You still haven't figured it out?"

Kennedy's face gave her away.

Tusk lowered his hands. "If I tell you who he was, will you let me go free?"

"No. She won't," came a voice from behind them. Zuele had Materialized outside the clearing with Chancellor Kirat. Zuele ran to Kennedy to make sure she was okay.

The Combatant tilted its head at Zuele.

"Zue! You came. I'm so glad that you received my message." Tusk smiled. "My Zue."

"What is going on here?" Chancellor Kirat asked.

"Kennedy's a Veilless," Pengar said proudly. "My best friend is a Veilless!"

Kennedy peered at Zuele. "But you already knew that."

Zuele surveyed the destruction surrounding her. "It is a very dangerous thing to be."

Kennedy tried to make sure she had it straight. "And now Malant wants to use me to expand the Dark Panel."

"No." Chancellor Kirat corrected her. "Malant wants to use you to *access* the Dark Panel."

Kennedy furrowed her brow in confusion.

"Malant has never controlled the Dark Panel, and neither has any member of the Royal family," the Chancellor said. "When Omin Yarso created the Dark Panel, he infused them with consciousness, something only a Veilless can do. King Amsden, who commissioned Omin to create this unnatural army, wanted to make sure the Dark Panel would only serve his bloodline. He wanted to make sure his family would always rule Millintica, but Omin believed the Dark Panel should only serve those who were *truly* powerful." She placed her hands behind her back and stared down at Kennedy. "Only a Veilless possesses the power to command the Dark Panel. King Amsden did not find that out until after he killed Omin Yarso, but by then it was too late. This was why he went mad. Amsden had created the most powerful army the universe had ever known, but he lacked the power to command it. The Evolver Council has always praised the royal family for their restraint in using this unnatural army, but the only reason they didn't was because they couldn't. Twenty years ago, Malant killed King Rimago and the rest of the royal family, erroneously believing that if they were all gone, the Dark Panel would be his. But the Dark Panel served another."

Kennedy nodded. "Leandor Everin."

Geenen turned to her. "And now it serves you, Kennedy. You are the only Veilless left."

"She's not the only one." Zuele reached into the triangular pack around her waist, sanitized her left palm, dug a scalpel inside, and tweezed out a Switchip. The same kind Geenen had used to prank Kennedy her first night on Symetra—the kind she said were usually reserved for undercover missions.

Kennedy watched in astonishment as Zuele's hairpins fell to the forest floor beside the bloody Switchip. Zuele disappeared inside a cloud of effervescent particles that reorganized themselves into a larger pattern, which the adaptable guardian suit accommodated. Then the particles turned solid, and Leandor Everin was standing in Zuele's place. He was older, though still ruggedly handsome. He wrapped a bandage around his bloody palm once the transformation was complete.

Kennedy's breath caught in her throat. Her friends gasped beside her. She walked to Leandor and lifted the sleeve of his white guardian suit. There beneath the fabric was a large X with four other x's springing from the tips of it. He smiled, and it was then that Kennedy recognized the similarity between them. Everyone else noticed it, too.

"You're Leandor Everin," Orien exclaimed. "You were the most famous member of the Golden Phase. You're alive? You're alive!"

Geenen grabbed Orien's arm. "Read the room."

"Right. Sorry," Orien told Kennedy.

Tusk stared at Leandor in bewilderment, as though he were seeing a ghost.

"But you're dead," Kennedy murmured. "You died two years before my parents even met. I saw it in Vivith's experience." An image of him disappearing inside the lava resurfaced in her mind, and Kennedy shuddered.

Leandor shook his head. "You watched Zuele die. She was the bravest Evolver I ever met and the best friend anyone could ask for." Leandor picked up the bloody Switchip from the snow. "We spent the final years of her life creating *these*. I became her, and she became me. We were both willing to die for our home planet—Millintica. It was all her idea. She said that if Malant ever caught us, these Switchips would give us an extra life—an extra chance to get it right. She gave the Alliance even more chances when she fell into the lava and destroyed all evidence of the Switchip. Thanks to her sacrifice, Malant has believed me dead this entire time, as has everyone else—well, almost everyone. Chancellor Kirat here has always known, and so has Xavian."

"Zuele's *dead*?" Tusk wailed and then got to his feet. "She's dead because of you! I knew you weren't her. She loved me!"

"She did love you," Leandor said.

Tusk wiped his eyes, exposing the Alliance symbol tattooed on his wrist. "You killed her!"

Leandor glared at the tattoo. "No, *you* did when you sold us out. We trusted you."

"*You* are the one I gave up! Not her." Tusk sobbed. "You have taken everything from me!" Tusk hobbled towards him. "You were my best friend, and you tried to steal her. I knew something was going on between you!"

Leandor held up the bloody Switchip again. "This is what was going on between us. Zuele died so she could protect the universe from Malant's reign of terror. She switched places with me to keep Malant from the Dark Panel. Not only did you kill Zuele, but your treachery has killed her life's work, too."

Tusk screamed as he rushed towards Leandor.

The Combatant stood in front of Leandor and ran its green lasers through Elsid Tusk. Leandor attempted to shield Kennedy from the gory scene, but it was useless. Tusk collapsed lifelessly to the ground; his eyes open like Marr Ameer's had been. Blood slowly pooled out of him, turning the snow pink.

The Combatant turned around and bowed before Leandor the way it had bowed before Kennedy. Leandor placed his healthy hand on the Combatant's head. "On behalf of the Veilless, I liberate you. I thank you for your service to Millintica and I beg your forgiveness." An ethereal energy escaped from the kneeling creature, and its prison of a suit clanked heavily to the ground.

The hum inside Kennedy finally faded away.

Leandor swayed a bit, as though he were lightheaded.

Chancellor Kirat rushed to hold him up. "Are you alright?"

Leandor nodded. "It's just the cold."

Snow began to fall silently over the clearing, which was now a graveyard of both flesh and metal. Reddick reached out and touched Kennedy's arm. In all the commotion, he wanted to make sure she was alright. She nodded at him, and he nodded right back, letting her know he was there should she need him.

Leandor walked to Tusk's body and made the visual prayer of alignment. "No way out, only in," he whispered. As Leandor closed Tusk's open eyes, Kennedy recalled the Millintican fable of the small boy trapped in the dark dungeon. She took the moment to stare at her father, overwhelmed by all the emotions currently flooding through her. She looked at his bloodied, bandaged hand, knowing that the same blood flowed through her veins. He turned around and smiled at her. Then Kennedy watched in horror as ten more patrollers sped into the clearing behind him, their chrome bodies covered with poisonous spikes, their pink lights aimed right at her father. "*No!*" Kennedy screamed. The "no" was guttural. It came from a place deeper than Kennedy—deeper than the snow or the core of Symetra. The "no" came from the very fabric of the universe, and in that moment, Kennedy felt her energy attach itself to the patrollers.

"Kennedy!" She could hear Reddick's voice, but it was muffled and far away. Her consciousness exploded across the clearing, like paint splattered on a white canvas. Everything vibrated at an intolerable speed, and that was the last thing Kennedy remembered before everything went dark.

Kennedy heard her roommates speaking with Chancellor Kirat. She opened her eyes and realized she was lying on the couch inside her unit, covered by a blanket. Her father sat on the couch beside her, backlit by the fake firepit, while everyone else stood in the kitchen.

"You're okay," Leandor said.

Everyone stopped talking.

Kennedy caught eyes with Reddick, who gave her a relieved smile.

"What happened?" she asked her father.

"You gave a piece of your consciousness to those patrollers."

"Have I been giving away my consciousness my entire life?"

"No, only when you were truly determined to. When Scrawl insulted you that day, you were determined to shut him up." Leandor looked over his shoulder at Pile, who was yelling at everyone in the kitchen to remove their shoes because she had just cleaned the floors. "And you gave your consciousness to Pile because?"

"I wanted Geenen to get a win. She'd been working on her for so long."

"You were determined. And tonight, with the patrollers?"

Kennedy bit the inside of her cheek. "I thought they were going to kill you."

"You were determined to stop them." Leandor motioned outside the window, where a line of patrollers floated with their backs to Kennedy's unit. "You did more than just stop them. They have not left your side. They serve you now."

Kennedy looked out the window, and ten patrollers turned to face her. They bowed their dimmed pink lights before returning to their duty of guarding Kennedy's unit.

"Did I faint?" Kennedy asked.

"A Veilless is weakest right after they have shared their consciousness. Here, drink this." Leandor handed her a mug of bitter tonic.

Reddick stood a few feet away. He looked worried and still did not seem to know if he could trust Leandor.

"When did you find out you were a Veilless?" Kennedy questioned her father.

"It happened during my Phase Three Assessments. I was terrified when I found out I would be battling a Dark Panel Combatant and even more terrified when it bowed before me. Zuele, Xavian, and Chancellor Kirat were the only ones present when it happened. After that, Chancellor Kirat, my guardian at the time, tried to hide my truth at all costs, the same way I have tried to hide yours. It went on like that for years, with no one except the four of us knowing what I actually was, and then Malant killed King Rimago." Leandor took the tonic from Kennedy and sat it on the table.

"The galaxy prepared for war, confident that Malant would

launch an attack and use the Dark Panel. But Malant did not attack; instead, he offered an obscene reward to anyone who could deliver him a Veilless. Many assumed he wanted a Veilless to expand his army, but Chancellor Kirat didn't buy it."

Chancellor Kirat stepped out of the kitchen and sat on the couch across from them. "Malant already had the most powerful army in the universe. Why did he need to expand it? Then I remembered what happened in Leandor's Phase Three Assessments and surmised that Malant could not command them. It was just a theory at first. We needed to test it. So, the four of us traveled to a Millintican outpost and located a small regiment of the Dark Panel." Chancellor Kirat looked at Leandor and smiled.

"And they all bowed before *me*—a nobody from a Millintican farming village." Leandor shook his head as though he still couldn't believe it. "I remember the sound of their knees hitting the ground. I will never forget it." He shook his head again. "Anyway, I freed them. I liberated the consciousness trapped inside them, and if I thought the sound of them kneeling before me was impressive, it was nothing compared to the sound of their titanium suits crashing to the ground."

Kennedy was enthralled.

"After that, Zuele decided we had to switch identities. That was the day she became my protector."

"How did you end up on Earth?" Kennedy asked her father.

"After *Leandor* died," Leandor said, "Malant closed the atmosphere, partly to hide that he did not control the most powerful army in the universe, and partly to keep the Alliance out. I went into hiding while the Alliance tried to come up with a way to sneak onto Millintica and finish what we started. Every few progressions, Xavian moved me to a new planet. I felt like a coward, running. It is incredibly difficult to live inside another's body, especially the body of someone who died to protect you. When I arrived on Earth, I took the Switchip out. I could not handle looking at Zuele in the mirror anymore. Then I met your mother, and she gave me something to live for again. For whatever it is worth, I loved your mom. I meant what I said—she is an amazing woman who raised an amazing daughter. I wanted to bring her and your sister with me, but it was too dangerous. I knew my days as "Leandor" were numbered. Soon, I'd have to return to being Zuele. I modified your mother's memory, though not completely. I wanted her to remember me, to remember a bit of what we shared, even though it had lasted less than a week."

"So, you didn't know about me?"

Chancellor Kirat answered for him. "Not until your talent caught the attention of our recruiters. I took one look at you and knew you were Leandor's—that smile. Then a paternity test confirmed it. One could dismiss the smile as a mere coincidence, but not your DNA. No one could know Leandor had conceived a child almost two years after Malant watched him die. So, we falsified your medical records and removed Leandor's DNA from the Evolver database."

"When I came to Tucson, when I saw you," Leandor smiled. "Discovering I had a *daughter*..." Kennedy's heart swelled when the words caught in his throat. He had just called her his *daughter*. She was a father's daughter.

Leandor placed his healthy hand on her shoulder. "I am so

proud of the young woman you have become. I take zero credit for it, but you really are something, Kennedy. You are kind, and you are brave." Then he removed his hand. "I am sorry you had to grow up without a father. I am sorry your mother had to raise you alone. I've tried and will keep trying to make up for it in any way I can."

"Is that why you bought her a new house and gave her all that money?"

"It was the least I could do."

Geenen looked at Leandor's bloody, bandaged hand. "Ugh. Let me fix that before you bleed to death, and all of this will have been for nothing." She kneeled beside him, reached into her triangular pack, and got to work sanitizing his hand.

"Thank you, young creator," Leandor said when she applied a numbing agent.

"Hold still." Geenen yanked his hand back into place.

Leandor laughed and then returned his attention to Kennedy. "I realize now that I was selfish to bring you here and put you in this much danger just so I could get to know you. But I saw how you were struggling on Earth. I saw how difficult it was for you to be around humans who did not understand you. I knew immediately that you were a Veilless, too."

"But you said being a Veilless wasn't hereditary."

"I said it was *rarely* hereditary. There has only been one other documented case." He peered at her. "Do you have any idea how extraordinary it is to have one Veilless in a family, let alone two? When the Alliance found out about you, they resumed operations. Your very existence gave them hope. You gave us all hope that something bigger than ourselves *wants* us to win. Don't you understand what this means, Kennedy?" Leandor asked. "You're our failsafe. I can go to Millintica now and free the Dark Panel I am no longer the only hope. I can take more chances. All of us can."

"Wait, you are going to Millintica?" she cried.

"Once we find a way, yes."

Kennedy turned away from her father to hide the tears in her eyes.

"I would give anything for things to be different, but they're not." He frowned. "I should have told you the truth from the very beginning. I should never have brought you here. I made the wrong choice. Please forgive me, Kennedy."

Geenen finished her work stitching Leandor's hand, and he thanked her.

After a moment, Kennedy said, "You didn't make the wrong choice. I have found happiness here. I have found friends here." She looked at Reddick and said, "I have found love here. And now, I have finally found my father. This is everything I have ever wanted."

Reddick and her friends smiled at her, but her father did not. "Which is why I am so sorry to take you away from them," he said.

Kennedy's smile faded.

The center lift descended from the third floor, delivering Miles Pierce and Eka Mint to the living area.

Kennedy looked at Miles and rose to her feet. "I thought you said you weren't in the Alliance."

"I wasn't, not until today. Your father has given me the chance to make things right. By the way, I finally figured out who you remind me of."

Eka held up Kennedy's red suitcase. "She's packed."

Leandor stood. "Eka is going to take you someplace safe to hide."

"What about you?" Kennedy asked with a lump in her throat.

"You and I can no longer be anywhere near each other, not until this whole thing is over."

Kennedy's lip quivered.

Reddick rushed forward and grabbed Kennedy's hand. "You can both stay here. We can protect you."

"Yeah! We'll fight." Geenen said.

"Yeah!" Pengar repeated Geenen. "We'll fight!"

"We want to join the Alliance!" Orien chimed in.

Leandor smiled. "We would be lucky to have you."

Reddick continued. "Now that we know Malant doesn't have the Dark Panel, he is not as big a threat."

"As long as he lives, he is a threat," Leandor said.

Reddick pleaded with Leandor. "If you just let me speak to my father, I know I can talk some sense into him."

"Your father wants me gone," Kennedy said. "He tried to pay me off this afternoon."

"He *what*?" Reddick asked.

"I can't stay here, Reddick." Kennedy choked up. "I have no choice but to go."

Leandor looked at Orien, Pengar, and Geenen, whose eyes were all filled with tears. "You have been good friends to my daughter. I deliberately chose you three to be her roommates because of Pengar's ironclad optimism, Geenen's passion for innovation, and Orien's ability to bring beings together no matter their differences. Her exposure to such fine souls has given her skills as a leader that I could never have taught her alone.

"As for you, Reddick... Initially, I did not like the attention you brought to Kennedy, but I realize now that it is attention she was always going to have to face, with or without you," Leandor said with a sad smile. "You know, a few years before you were born, your mother dreamt she had a son named Reddick. When your older brother, Harpier, was born, I asked her, *'Is this him?'* And she said, 'No, Reddick is not here yet.' She knew you before you were born, and she continues to know you now that she is no longer with us. You have inherited her courage and her conviction. I know you do not want to let Kennedy go, but there is something bigger at play here. It is bigger than all of us. We have a chance—a real chance—to rid the universe of Malant once and for all."

"Does my father know what Kennedy really is?" Reddick asked.

"He will soon. Everyone will," Chancellor Kirat answered him.

"He doesn't get to do this." Reddick fumed.

Kennedy stepped close to Reddick, blocking his view of the others. "I have to go." She tried not to show her devastation, but it was too big to hide. "I don't want to, but I have to..." Then she focused on her roommates—the best friends she'd ever had. They all cried openly.

Leandor now stood next to Miles and Eka on the center lift. Kennedy turned to join them.

"Kennedy!" Geenen called out. Large alien tears were now dripping down Geenen's scaly cheeks as she removed her emotion blocker from her wrist. Kennedy removed her St. Jude necklace and felt the immense love coming from Geenen—it rivaled even that of the Triphens. Kennedy held her heart and trembled.

Pengar and Orien stepped forward and removed their emotion blockers, too. The four of them basked in their love for one another and sobbed. They hugged each other tightly and then dogpiled Geenen, who for once did not swat them away.

Leandor cleared his throat. "Kennedy, it's time to go."

Eka Mint stepped forward and unlocked the Dematerialization Cuff around her wrist, preparing to take Kennedy with her. "Are you ready?"

"Yes," Kennedy said, but remained unmoving.

Reddick couldn't even bear to look at her.

The tears spilled freely from Kennedy's eyes as she watched the pained expression on his face. Kennedy kissed his cheek.

Reddick clenched his jaw tight, unable to watch her go.

"I love you," she whispered, but he did not say it back. She began to walk away, fully prepared to accept her fate, when Reddick reached out and grabbed her hand.

"No," he said, and then met eyes with Leandor. "You are not taking her."

"This is not your choice," Leandor reminded him.

"And it is not yours either; it is Kennedy's. I love your daughter. She might just be a failsafe to you and the Alliance, but she is everything to me, and I'm not letting you take her, not without a fight."

Miles smiled his movie star smile. "Man, you are so much like Vivith."

Reddick ignored him. "The galaxy deserves to know the truth

about Malant. They deserve to know that Malant's power is a facade. They deserve to know that the Veilless' are back. They deserve hope. We all do." Reddick looked at Kennedy and said, "Now, what do *you* want to do, Kennedy?"

In that moment, Reddick awoke Kennedy from her trance. She couldn't believe how quickly she'd reverted to being the weird girl who needed to hide what she was at all costs. Reddick reminded Kennedy that she no longer had to be that girl. He reminded Kennedy that she had evolved beyond that girl. "I want to stay."

"Theein will not allow you to stay," Leandor said.

Chancellor Kirat stepped forward. "Let me deal with Theein. I know how to handle him."

"And who is going to train her?" Leandor asked Chancellor Kirat.

"I will, until we find her the right guardian," the Chancellor said. "I trained you, and you turned out pretty well."

Leandor's voice quaked. "But Malant knows she is here. He will find her."

"And we will protect her," Chancellor Kirat assured him. "Malant knows he can't take on the Triphens without the Dark Panel. Symetra is the safest place for her."

Leandor looked at Kennedy. "This is what you want?"

Kennedy nodded. "I want to help the Alliance, but Reddick's right—I don't want to hide anymore. I can't hide anymore."

Leandor searched his daughter's face. "Then I guess you are staying."

Orien, Pengar and Geenen cheered, but Kennedy ran to her father and squeezed him tight. "I don't want you to leave. I just found you," she said. It was impossible for her not to feel that this might be the last time she would ever see him.

Leandor kissed the top of her head. "I taught you a lot in the time we have spent together. Don't forget it, okay?"

"Okay," she said, but she still refused to let go, not until her mother flashed inside her mind. "What about my mom and Audrey?"

"They are protected. The Alliance has been watching them around the clock." He wiped her tears and smiled. "Speaking of, I guess your mom might be a little freaked out when she hears I'm back."

"I think she'll be more freaked out that you've been disguised as a dead woman for the past seventeen years." Kennedy joked, even though a large part of her was mourning Zuele.

Kennedy's father squeezed her shoulders. "We are going to finish this."

"I know."

Leandor gave Kennedy one more hug and then pulled away.

"Where are you going to go?" she asked him.

"It's safer if you do not know... Take care of yourself, daughter." Leandor kept his eyes on Kennedy until he, Miles, and Eka Dematerialized from the unit. Once they were gone, Kennedy's friends came and dogpiled her once more. "You're staying!" Pengar squealed in delight.

"Think of all the technology we can create now that you are a Veilless," Geenen said.

"I can't believe your dad is Leandor Everin!" Orien said.

Then Kennedy walked to Reddick. "Thank you."

"For what?"

"For reminding me not to hide what I am."

He pulled her to him. "That's what we do for one another. You remind me not to pull my dangerous party tricks, and I remind you to shine at all costs."

Kennedy kissed him.

"Alright, that's enough, you two," Chancellor Kirat stepped between them. "Kennedy, don't stay up too late. Our training begins tomorrow morning."

Kennedy looked up at her temporary guardian and said, "I can't wait."

www.ingramcontent.com/pod-product-compliance
Lightning Source LLC
Chambersburg PA
CBHW032111310726
48972CB00001B/180